promised
NIGHTS
A NOVEL

LOUISE BAY

ISBN - 978-1-910747-31-5

the nights
SERIES

Parisian Nights
Promised Nights
Indigo Nights

Each book in the series is stand alone,
following a different couple.

chapter
ONE

Luke

I wasn't a fan of weddings, especially when the only people I knew had their names on the invitation. I'd only met the bride and groom once, maybe twice. They were Emma's friends. Although Emma and I had been a couple for over three years, and even though we lived together, we still led quite separate social lives. I liked that independence from each other. I felt sorry for couples who couldn't do anything apart. If it had been up to me, I wouldn't have come to this wedding. Surely Emma wanted to spend the weekend catching up with old university friends. She didn't need me here. And while she was doing what made her happy, I could be hanging out with *my* friends and doing what made *me* happy.

"Aren't the flowers beautiful?" she whispered as the string quartet played a familiar tune to keep us occupied while the bride and groom disappeared to sign the register.

I glanced around the old stone church from our seats toward the back. Was anyone else cold? And what was that sweet, familiar scent lingering in the air? I hadn't noticed the flowers. I nodded as Emma glanced up at me. Weren't flowers always pretty? Did anyone go to a wedding and say the flowers were awful? I didn't share the thought with Emma. She was normally the more cynical of the two of us—part of the reason we worked so well, so maybe I was being unfair. The flowers *were* pretty.

The bride and groom beamed at each other as they reappeared and started the march back down the aisle. We all followed them back into the sun for the beginning of the endless photographs.

"They're using the same photographer as Julie and Tim," Emma said. "Their photos were fantastic, weren't they?"

I nodded and placed my hand on Emma's lower back, guiding her toward the tray of champagne. I took two glasses and handed one to her.

This was the third wedding we'd been to this year. Hopefully, this was the last of them. All my mates seemed to be getting married, and each time another engagement was announced, I did my best to offer my congratulations, but hell if I could understand why they felt the urge to tie the knot. Marriage was such an outdated institution, and it didn't seem to stop people splitting up. I really didn't see the point.

My parents had died when my sister and I were teenagers. Perhaps that was why all this pomp seemed so irrelevant. Life had proven to me that all good things came to an end and there were no happy endings. If there was any hope of me believing in the fairy tale, it died along with my parents. To me it was couples like them who deserved to have happily ever after. It was clear to everyone they'd been crazy about each other. We hated it as kids, of course, but looking back, their love for each other was what made our home so happy when we were young. If it hadn't worked out for them, what hope was there for the rest of us?

"To the last wedding of the season." I clicked my glass to Emma's.

"Try and be a bit more enthusiastic," she said with a frown.

"You can talk. You can't tell me you're enjoying this."

"Of course I am. Why wouldn't I be? Everyone's happy and in love. It's beautiful."

Emma handed me her champagne, opened her bag, pulled out a tissue and began to dab at the corners of her eyes. *Was she upset?* She was one of the toughest girls I knew. I'd seen her cry three times since I'd known her.

I bent my head to her ear. "Are you okay?"

She looked up at me. "It was just such a beautiful ceremony, and they seem so happy."

I rubbed her lower back, and she leaned her head on my arm. I'd never have described Emma as sentimental, but apparently she was at weddings. I slipped my hand around her waist. It wasn't a move I was particularly familiar with. We weren't the kind of couple who needed to be touching all the time. Surprisingly, her arm slid under my suit jacket, but her tears didn't stop.

"Hey, babe, what's the matter?" I guided us to the side of the throng of people that were gathered to listen to the instructions of the photographer. I was sure she wouldn't want anyone to see her upset. When my sister got like this, it was normally a hormonal thing. I decided not to bring that up. I wasn't sure Emma'd take the suggestion well.

"It's just such a nice wedding," she said as we wandered toward a tree at the far edge of the lawn. "And I was just thinking that when we get married, ours should be just like this one."

I had to work hard to keep my breathing even, my pace consistent, my hand on her back. *When we get married?* Where had that thought come from? That wasn't who we were, and it certainly wasn't anything I'd thought was meant for us. I'd always thought we were on the same page about this stuff. I had to fight off the feeling of my blood thickening in my veins and crawling through my body. I wanted to tense, to stop, but I kept breathing, kept walking. Luckily for me, we were interrupted by a squeal, and as I turned, I saw a tiny girl in a short red dress running toward us with her arms outstretched, clearly excited to see Emma.

I took the opportunity to excuse myself to the bathroom and made my way back to the church where I could consider the bomb that had just been dropped. I scrubbed my face with my hands. Had she made that comment because she was a glass of champagne in, or had she really been considering *our* wedding?

I had just turned thirty. The last thing I was thinking about was marriage. I wasn't ready for that step, not now and maybe not ever. I didn't believe in forever. My parent's accident had proven there was no such thing. I didn't want to think about until death do you part. It seemed so depressing.

Maybe I had conveniently assumed that because it had never come up between us, Emma and I were on the same page when it came to getting married. We'd never actually spoken about it, so I'd thought she was happy with how things were. She had been the one who suggested living together. Like she'd said, it made sense—we could save on bills and mortgage payments. It had been so logical. But marriage? That wasn't logical—there was no sense to it. I had never been moving toward things being any different between us. Had she? The thought was like a short, sharp shock to my brain. My head began to throb in response.

In the bathroom, I let the tap run cold before I poured myself a drink of water. I watched my reflection in the mirror as I drank, my throat bobbing up and down as the liquid passed through my body. I set aside the glass, grasped the counter and took another deep breath. I needed my body to return to normal, but I could still feel the thickness in my veins and the panic in my shortened breaths.

Ashleigh

"I'm so glad you could make it," Haven said as she opened the door to her and her husband's apartment. "I've missed you at Sunday night dinner."

Haven and I had been best friends since we were two, and Sunday night dinner was our thing. But I'd not been for a few weeks. I'd been dating and, well, that was complicated.

"Where's Jake?" I didn't hear the sound of her husband clattering about in the kitchen.

"Study. They've had a breakthrough, apparently." She shrugged.

"So, how was your date with Richard?" Haven asked, wandering down the hall to the large, open-plan living space that boasted cityscape views like a huge piece of art dominating the room.

I took a deep breath in, winded by the sight of London, the home I'd refused to leave when my parents left for Hong Kong when I was eighteen. "Good," I replied and took a seat at the breakfast bar while Haven busied herself preparing some wine.

"And? How was it?"

It was a loaded question. I'd been dating Richard a little less than three months, but last night was the first time I'd slept with him. Haven knew I'd planned to give it up last night.

"Yes, we had sex," I said, jumping right to the part she was really asking about.

She turned from the fridge, waiting for me to expand on my revelation. "And?" she asked when I stayed silent.

I shrugged. "It was fine. It was just sex."

"What was 'just sex'?" I spun on my stool as Jake entered the room. He pulled me in for a hug and then looked at me as if he was expecting an answer.

"We need you to solve the world's energy crisis for about twenty minutes longer and then you can come out and have wine," Haven said to Jake.

"But I want to hear about the 'just sex'," Jake said.

"I know, but so do I, and Ash will pretend to be coy until you leave." I laughed. "This is important girl stuff," Haven continued. "Give us twenty minutes and I'll make it up to you tonight." She winked at him and he grabbed her round the waist and kissed her neck. They were so happy together. Jake brought out the best in Haven and vice versa. They were what love was meant to be about—the real deal, not two people making do, no "there's nobody better so he'll do." I'd come to realize that love like theirs was more rare than the fairy tales had me believe.

"Enough," I said, covering my ears and closing my eyes.

"Okay, twenty minutes," Jake said, unwrapping himself from Haven and stalking back to the study.

Haven abandoned any pretense of dinner prep and brought over a bottle of wine and two glasses, placing them on the breakfast bar and then seating herself on the stool next to me.

Sunday night dinner was our family tradition. And family was what I considered Haven and her brother, Luke. Our close circle had expanded when Haven married Jake, bringing him and his sister, Beth, into the fold. Wine and gossip were essential components to the ritual.

"We have twenty minutes and we have a lot to talk about. So spill," Haven said.

"There's nothing much to say. I guess we've taken it to the next level." Unfortunately, the experience had been decidedly un-notable, but Richard was such a nice guy and he was so kind, it felt wrong to say that, to feel that. I wanted to like him. I wanted sleeping together to be explosive...but it hadn't been. It had been nice. But nice was good, right?

"But was it good? You said it was *just* sex. That doesn't sound like good sex." Haven's gaze skirted all over me as if I were going to start talking from somewhere other than my mouth.

"It was fine," I said, not quite knowing what to say. "I

mean, I think it has potential."

"Oh God, was it that bad?"

"I didn't say it was bad," I replied. It just hadn't been amazing. "He's a great guy. And he really cares about me. First time sex is never easy, especially if you're not hammered."

I envied Haven. She'd found *the one*. But most people didn't, did they? They certainly didn't find the love of their life twice—and I'd found mine a lifetime ago. Too bad the feeling had never been mutual. Still, I had no right to ask for *the one* twice. I needed to make peace with the fact that a nice guy was a good option—maybe the only option—for me.

The buzzer sounded and Haven slid off her chair to answer it. She answered the intercom and let Luke into the building then hovered at the entrance waiting for her brother to get to the door.

Luke.

I took a deep breath.

At any given moment, I could recall the exact second I fell in love with Luke. It was summer, and Haven, he and I were sitting under a magnolia tree in their parents' garden, joshing and giggling. He'd turned to me and grinned, his smile wide—his perfectly white teeth made brighter by his golden skin—his hair floppy and in need of a cut. He'd raised his eyebrows at me and tucked a strand of hair behind my ear. And that was it. A spell was cast. Even now, almost fifteen years later, my cheeks heated at the memory of that moment.

"Is Emma coming today?" I asked, changing the subject. I didn't know if it was just me, but things always seemed easier when Luke's girlfriend wasn't here.

"I don't think so," Haven said as she turned to answer the door. "I guess we'll find out."

I let out a sigh of relief when I only heard Luke in the hallway.

Even after all these years of knowing him, I had to consciously remember to breathe when he walked into a room. Like some fantasy Viking, he was tall, blond and underneath his tight, golden skin, his muscles looked hard as wood. His sheer physical presence almost overwhelmed me for the first seconds I was around him. It was always as if he took up all the air, all the space in the room—he was all I could see. I grinned as he walked in my direction.

"Hey, stranger, where have you been?" he asked as he pulled me out of my seat as if I were a doll and hugged me, his body cocooning mine, squeezing me tight. "You smell good," he said.

I ignored his question. If Richard and I were to have a fighting chance, I had to get some distance from Luke. I needed to see someone else in the room. I'd come to the conclusion that if I kept comparing every man I met to my long-time love, I'd die alone, surrounded by cats. So I'd stepped back from spending so much time with him, and hadn't been coming to Sunday dinner as regularly.

"You look well," he said. I smiled, giddy from his proximity, concentrating on not making my grin too wide.

"It's all the 'just sex'," Jake bellowed from behind us. We both spun around. "Now Luke's here, I can come out, right?" Jake asked.

Haven rolled her eyes as he grabbed two beers from the fridge and handed one to Luke.

"So what's this about sex?" Luke asked, before taking a swig from his bottle.

"It's Ash and Richard, I think," Jake said, knocking his beer against Haven's and my glasses.

"Right, that's about as much as I want to know." Luke grimaced and Haven looked at me and rolled her eyes. I had always been like a little sister as far as Luke was concerned. There had never been any ambiguity for *him*.

Richard had asked me out a few times before I said yes. He was a doctor at the hospital where I was a nurse. Wasn't that the stuff of romance novels?

It was just that when Richard was close by, I didn't get the thudding in my chest that I had at the moment because Luke was less than a meter away from me.

"Can't you two go and catch up on the rugby or something?" Haven suggested.

I watched Luke's neck as his beer slid down his throat, my eyes following the invisible liquid down to the triangle of bare skin exposed by the open collar of his shirt. I forced myself to look away. How did he still have this effect on me after all these years?

Jake clasped Haven's face between his hands and pulled her toward him, kissing her passionately, while she waved her arms about as if she was protesting. As if. He released her after a couple of seconds and wandered over to the other side of the room with Luke to watch the television, leaving Haven looking dazed and confused.

She grinned and rolled her eyes. "He's incorrigible."

I was delighted that she'd found such a great guy in Jake; she'd been unhappy for so long before him. I smiled and let out a steady breath as Luke's absence gave me more space for my mind and body.

"Anyway, back to sex with Richard. What's the deal?" she asked, turning to me and pulling me further away from my thoughts of Luke. Haven and I rarely talked about my feelings for Luke directly. As teenagers, we'd discussed it, but as adults, we skirted around it, aware of the volatility of the subject. I loved our world together—our bond, our shared experience—and I didn't want to destroy our family. I wanted to find someone special, someone who thought I was more than sister material. Haven had done it, and it had given me inspiration that I could, too.

There was no way Haven was going to give up on the subject of Richard. She wanted me to be happy even more than I did. "It was okay. It wasn't earth shattering. It wasn't awful." Richard was such a nice guy that I wanted it to be better, and with a little work, I was sure it could be.

She twisted her mouth as she considered my confession. "I think sex can improve as a couple gets to know each other, and you held off a long time. Maybe it was too much pressure."

I nodded enthusiastically. "Exactly. So, we'll see." I desperately wanted her to be right, but I was worried Richard was *too* nice a guy. I wanted to be fucked properly. I needed a guy who knew what he wanted—what I wanted—and made it all happen. Richard had been . . . careful.

"And he's so nice to you," Haven said.

"Exactly. He totally is." I was determined not to reject Richard just because he wasn't Luke. I'd been doing that for too many years.

I was ready for my happily ever after.

chapter TWO

Luke

I stayed at Haven's until she kicked me out at just gone midnight. Earlier in the evening, I'd offered to take Ash home, but she'd refused. I'd not seen much of her lately, and I could have done with a talk. I couldn't remember the last time it had just been her and me. We used to meet for lunch or after work sometimes, but it had been ages. When I'd hugged her hello earlier, I'd realized that it was her I could smell in the church the previous day. I'd never noticed the perfume that surrounded her, probably because she was just Ash scented to me.

I quietly opened the front door of the house Emma and I shared, trying to turn my key as slowly as possible in the lock, to avoid the overly loud clunk it made. It was late, and she had an early shift the next morning at the hospital.

I didn't switch on any lights and quietly got undressed to my boxers and slid under the blankets.

"Hey," she said.

I'd been sure she would be asleep.

"Having trouble sleeping?" I asked.

She turned over to her side, facing me. "Yeah, a little. How was Sunday dinner?"

"Good. Everyone asked after you." It wasn't entirely true, or even slightly true, but I was sure they had meant to ask after her.

"That's nice," she replied.

I sighed and slid my hand behind my head, my eyes drawn to the light of the streetlamps bleeding into the room from the edges of our window blind. The atmosphere was thick with the unspoken words of a conversation we were about to have.

"Did you enjoy the wedding?" she asked.

"Yeah, sure." I'd deliberately avoided the subject since her tears during the photographs on Saturday. "Haven cooked duck for dinner. We should try it sometime. It was good. She's turning into quite the chef."

"Sounds like marriage suits her. You ever think about whether it would suit you, too?" she asked.

My skin started to itch, and I needed some water. I pulled the bedcovers off me to go and get a drink. "Why would I? We're happy as we are," I said as I wandered into the bathroom, willing her to drop the subject.

"Marriage is the next step for two people who are happy and in love, isn't it?" she asked, raising her voice slightly so I could still hear her clearly, despite the rush of the faucet. I felt as if I'd just stepped in quicksand. There was pressure all over my body, as if I were being squeezed between two concrete walls—like the garbage compactor scene in Star Wars. I could do with a couple of Jedi mind tricks right at this moment.

"I don't see why." I hoped that would be the end of it, but knew it wouldn't be. This conversation felt as though it was taking us down a one-way street. I brushed my teeth again, wanting to give Emma time to fall asleep. Why had she brought this up? Things were just fine.

I stuck the toothbrush back in the jar, rinsed my mouth and went back into the bedroom. She was staring at me.

"You've never thought about us getting married?" she asked again, more directly this time.

"I said that I didn't. I don't lie to you, Emma." I slipped back under the blankets and lay on my back, staring at the ceiling, willing the conversation to be over.

"You don't want to be married before we have children?"

Jesus, now kids were part of the equation? "Now we're talking about children?"

"We need to talk about this stuff, Luke. I don't want to be just your roommate. Haven's married now. And she and Jake were together no time at all before he proposed."

"And it works for them."

"But you don't think it would work for us?" she asked.

I scrubbed my hands over my face. "It's late. I don't want to talk about this now. I need to get to sleep. And you have an early start. Let's discuss it another time, if you think it's important."

"If I *think* it's important? Of course it's important. We can't stay like we are," she said. "You can be a real prick at times."

"You're the one bringing this up out of nowhere in the middle of the night."

21

"Out of nowhere? Are you fucking kidding me? We've been living together for nearly three years. Look around, Luke. Everyone's getting married. People live together, they get married and then they have kids. Why do you think you're the exception?"

"So you want to get married because everyone else does? Sounds like excellent reasoning." The litigator in me instinctively wanted to win the argument, regardless of the merits and demerits of what was being said.

"I want to get married because I love you, you fucking idiot. I want to have kids with you because I want to have your children. Maybe not today, but one day. Jesus, Luke, why is this a shock?"

I couldn't argue with someone who was telling me they loved me, even if they spat the words out. I kept scanning through memories of conversations we'd had over the years, trying to find one where we'd talked about marriage. I couldn't think of a single one. I'd always assumed she was as unbothered by it as I was. Had I been wrong? Had I led her on? I lowered my voice and asked, "But why are you bringing this up now?"

She took a breath. "I want us to move on, take the next step of our lives together. I don't understand why you are so keen for everything to stay the same."

"I'm not sure what to say. This isn't something . . ." I didn't know how to end my sentence. *Something I ever want. Something I think I want. Something I have thought about?* I didn't want to hurt Emma, but I didn't see that in my future.

I needed to talk to someone other than her about this. I wanted to speak to Haven or Ash.

"Do you love me?" she asked when I didn't finish my sentence.

"Of course I do. I mean, we've been together for—"

"This is it, babe. This is what people do. They get married. I know that guys don't like to think they're getting older, but we are. All of us. We're not kids playing house anymore."

Had my parents thought like this? Had one of them wanted to get married and suggested it to the other and then they'd decided, rationally, that it was the right step? I just couldn't see it. I'd always felt that they were on a different path. I'd never seen my relationship with Emma as comparable with theirs. Something between them had meant they *had* to get married. If Emma and I didn't feel that we *had* to get married, then why should we? It didn't mean I didn't love her. Just that we were different from other couples.

"Think about it. This is what I want, Luke. A future together."

The next morning, I got up as soon as Emma left. I felt like a shit for pretending to be sleeping while she got ready so we didn't have another difficult conversation. By mid-morning, I was still jittery from lack of sleep and I couldn't concentrate on anything but trying to control the panic still flushing through my body. I headed toward the front staircase of our building and began to scroll through my contacts. I hit dial when I got to Ash. I needed something, someone that was mine, who knew me. Someone who wanted me to be happy, but would kick my ass if it needed kicking. Someone who would call me a douche if I deserved it, but ultimately wouldn't judge me.

Ash was that person. Haven and I were close, but she was my sister and didn't have the same perspective Ash did. Haven didn't have the sweetness about her that Ash did that made what came out of her mouth, however harsh, somehow more bearable.

"Fucking hell, I'm going to get into massive trouble, you phoning me on the ward. I hope your penis is falling off," Ash answered the phone in a loud whisper. Despite my mood, I couldn't help but chuckle. Maybe not everything she said was so sweet.

"How's the business of curing the sick and the dying?"

"I work in palliative care, you douche. No one gets cured, that's the point."

"Stop making excuses for being a shitty nurse."

I didn't know how Ash did her job and managed to stay so happy all the time. All I did was move money about between clients. She saw people at their most vulnerable, in their last few weeks and months in this world, and she seemed to take it all in her stride.

"I wanted to know if you could meet for lunch, or maybe for drinks after work?" I thought I had lost reception for a second, because she didn't answer straight away. "Ash?" I checked to see if she could hear me.

"Yeah . . . I don't know. I'm busy tonight, and I go on lunch in ten minutes—"

Fuck, I'd have to leg it up to Hackney if I wanted to see her. I started to speed up my descent of the stairs. "I'll come to you. I can be there in ten minutes—as long as we don't have to eat in the hospital cafeteria," I offered. I found a cab straight away. "Hommerton Hospital," I said to the cabbie, holding the phone away so Ash couldn't hear and change her mind. I really wanted to see her. I needed her consistency, her familiarity, her reason. She would know what I should do about Emma. There seemed to be more hesitation from her side. "Come on. We've not had lunch for a while."

"Okay, but I only have an hour." She hung up.

I grinned. My day was improving. Seeing Ash was what I needed.

Less than ten minutes later, I was still panting from running up the street where the cab had dropped me. When I looked up from my phone to find Ash standing right in front of me. I felt myself relax immediately and the corners of my mouth turned up. "Hey," I said.

"Hey yourself," Ash replied. She smiled at me and everything seemed better with the world. The panic that had threatened to engulf me earlier ebbed away.

Ashleigh

I shouldn't have agreed to meet Luke for lunch. We hadn't met on our own, just him and me, for months, not since I'd started dating Richard. There was a reason for that—I should have remembered that before I gave in and agreed to meet him.

My heart squeezed as soon as I caught sight of him. *Breathe, Ash.* He looked so big and handsome, so familiar. As if he belonged to me, because in my head he always had.

"What are you wearing?" he asked and raised his eyebrows at me. No wonder he never saw me as anything other than a friend. If I was dressed in a tablecloth, I would have been more attractive.

"I know, scrubs. I had an accident. Actually, someone else had an accident and my uniform got literally covered in shit." Luke grimaced. "Am I going to embarrass you dressed like this?"

"You look good in everything and you know it." He grinned at me as we made our way to the sandwich bar at the end of the street.

I rolled my eyes, trying to make out that I was annoyed with him giving me a compliment. "So, what brings you to Hackney, Mr. City Lawyer?" I asked. "Slumming it?"

"No. Can't a friend ask you to lunch without a reason other than wanting to see you?"

I wished he wouldn't be so nice to me, that he could just be a real asshole. Then I could hate him and have a chance of getting over him. But really, I had no desire to hate him. I wanted him in my life, even if it was as friends. I'd managed this far, and I'd just have to readjust and make sure our relationship worked, even when I was dating. "You saw me yesterday."

"Yeah, but you and I didn't get a chance to talk much. And I wanted to speak to you about something."

I led the way into the sandwich shop. Because we had known each other for as long as we had, we had shortcuts where he knew what I was thinking without any exchange of words. Did Richard and I need time to get to that point, or was it something more than just the number of years Luke and I had spent together that made us that way?

"Ham salad?" I asked him as he arrived at our table with a tray full of drinks and sandwiches wrapped in wax paper.

"Nope, try again." He grinned. It was a usual routine. I had to guess what he'd ordered me before I was allowed to see it.

"Roast beef and rocket?" I scrunched my face up exaggeratedly, waiting for the verdict.

"You hate beef," he said, his brows pulled together, looking at me as if I were nuts.

I laughed. "I know. I thought you might have forgotten. Ham and egg?"

"Nope," he said, unwrapping his sandwich then taking a bite. He was grinning at me as if he'd just won the lottery.

"Are you kidding? Coronation chicken?" It was my favorite and they only had it on special here every now and then. Our ritual distracted me from thinking about how I shouldn't be here with him and reminded me that when it came down to it, we were just Luke and Ash. Childhood friends.

He slid my sandwich across the table at me. I unwrapped it—I was right. "Thank you." I was glad to see him. Pleased to have him to myself, it had been a long time.

"So, what's going on? You've not woken up with a hangover in my spare room with my sister for ages now. Are you on the wagon?"

He'd not said anything before about the fact I'd not been around as much. I half wondered if Haven had mentioned something to him, even though she'd promised me she wouldn't. "Ha. Ha," I said. "Just busy, I guess. I've taken a few extra shifts, and Richard and I have been hanging out." That was all true but it wouldn't normally keep me away from him.

He watched me as if I were going to keep speaking. I had to look away. Those blue eyes of his could see right through me, and pull me under. I needed to keep my distance. "So it's serious with this guy?"

I shrugged and stared out the window, afraid of what my eyes would reveal. "It's too soon to tell. But he cares about me. And I want something serious." I wanted to be in love with someone who didn't see me as a sister, someone who loved me back; I just wasn't sure if I wanted Richard.

"So that's how it goes? You decide you want something serious, and you try and find the guy who fills the gap?"

My stomach lurched. I wasn't sure if he was judging me or interested, but I felt uncomfortable talking about it. Perhaps because I couldn't tell him the truth, which was that I couldn't have what I really wanted, so I was looking to see if there was something else out there. I continued to chew so I wouldn't have to answer him.

"It's just that I think Emma wants to get serious."

My chest contracted and I was sure I could feel my ribs against my heart. I swallowed. "Do you?" It was all I could manage.

He exhaled and his shoulders sagged. "I don't know. Emma says that I'm afraid of change, and I just want everything to stay the same." His voice was faint and I could barely hear him over the thudding in my ears. Fuck. This is what this felt like. I'd wondered for a while how I'd feel if and when Luke and Emma got married or had kids.

"Well that's true."

"I guess. But it's not just that . . . I don't think I'm that kind of guy."

"What kind of guy?" I was intrigued. How did he see himself and his relationship with Emma? I mean, I was totally biased of course, but I just didn't get them as a couple. They didn't seem to like spending time together.

"The marrying kind, I suppose." He looked at me and I raised my eyebrows. "Do I sound like a tit?"

I laughed, relieved to be normal for just a few seconds. "Maybe a little."

"I don't mean that I'm a player and I need my freedom. I've never cheated on Emma or anyone else. It's just, I don't see the point in marriage."

"But if it's important to her and you love her . . ." *Say no. Say you love me.*

"Right. Yes."

"Then . . . if you're not bothered but you just don't believe in the institution, I . . . You could do it—for her. Maybe you give her what she needs?" Was I really trying to talk Luke into marrying someone who wasn't me?

"Even though I don't think that's what I want? It's not that I don't believe in marriage. I do. I believed in it for my parents. But for me? I just don't think it fits."

I set my sandwich down in front of me. My appetite had officially died. This conversation was not how I imagined spending my lunch hour. "What are you going to do?"

He shrugged. "I don't know. She really wants this, and kids and everything." It wasn't a surprise, but hearing it made it real. A selfish part of me was relieved I was dating Richard. It was evidence that one part of my brain could use to show the other part that there wasn't a real reason to be devastated because, after all, I had a boyfriend.

"You don't want kids?"

"Not really. Certainly not yet. But it's clearly been on Emma's mind a while. God, I'm sorry to be bending your ear about this. It's a first world problem compared to the stuff you've got going on at work. You're right. I am a tit."

I rolled my eyes at him. "I didn't say that."

"Let's talk about you. If it's serious with Richard, how come we haven't met him yet?" he asked.

I couldn't picture that moment. Luke meeting Richard wasn't something I wanted to happen anytime soon. I didn't want to see them together. I knew I'd compare the two of them more than I did already, and Richard would likely come off the loser. He didn't deserve that. He was a good guy and a great catch. Everyone at the hospital continually told me how lucky I was, how perfect we were for each other.

"Just busy, I guess," I replied. "What else is going on with you? How's work?" I hoped he'd take the hint and change the subject.

"Busy. They confirmed they're putting me up for partnership this year."

"Wow, Luke, that's amazing." I grinned at him. He'd worked so hard for so long. I was happy that he was finally starting to see some rewards. He was one of life's good guys. He'd gained success through determination and hard work, not politicking and backstabbing. He deserved this.

He smiled back, a little embarrassed. "There are no guarantees. I'd be one of the youngest partners ever made up if I got it, so . . ."

For a second, I forgot about the distance I was supposed to be putting between us, and I grabbed his hand and squeezed. "I'm proud of you," I said. "Your parents would be so, so proud." The death of Luke's mum and dad just before he started college had been horrific, but he'd kept it together, scooped up Haven and given her everything she needed emotionally. His college work had never wavered; he'd always kept his grades up at the same time as making sure Haven was looked after. I'd always been amazed at how adult he'd become, overnight. He'd inherited the mantle of the head of his family, and it was a responsibility he took seriously. He wanted to live the legacy of his parents—that kind, honest, hardworking people would win out in the end.

He looked down at the table and nodded, twisting his wrist so we were holding hands across the table. "Promise me you won't change, that I won't lose you, Ash," he said, his voice serious as he glanced up at me from under his brows.

My breath hitched at his request and my forehead crinkled. What was he asking me?

"Here she is," Richard's familiar voice came from behind me. "I thought I might catch you in here." The room tilted slightly, and I wondered if it was the sensation people felt just before they fainted. I turned my head and tried to pull my hand from Luke's. He resisted at first, but as he took in what was happening, he released me. The cool Formica soothed my tingling palm.

If I closed my eyes, could I transport myself somewhere else, so the moment that was about to happen, wouldn't happen? It felt as though the room slowed down and I was watching two airplanes about to collide. This was not what I wanted. Luke was Luke. Richard was Richard. For me, they existed in parallel universes, and if they met, everything would explode or implode, or something equally terrible would happen.

Richard bent and kissed my forehead and quickly turned to Luke, holding out his right hand. "I'm Richard, Ash's boyfriend." His smile met his eyes and I could tell that there was no territory claiming. He wasn't trying to make a point. He asked often about my friends and I imagine he was pleased to finally meet one of them.

I continued to stare at the table as Luke stood and shook Richard's hand. "I'm Luke," he said. He gave no explanation as to his relationship with me. I wasn't sure if it was because he was confident that Richard would know who he was, or because Luke wanted to keep him guessing.

"Oh, right. Haven's brother," Richard said. Assisted by my description, he knew Luke as simply my best friend's sibling. And that was what I needed him to be. "Can I join you?"

My stomach flipped up in my chest. I stood abruptly, the legs of my chair tearing against the floor. "Actually, I need to get back," I said. I flicked a glance at Luke, urging him to back me up.

"Yeah, me too," Luke replied after a second's hesitation, and I dared to take a breath.

I pulled on my jacket and picked up my half-eaten sandwich, wrapping it back in its wax paper then slipping it into my bag. "I'll see you later," I said, glancing at Richard.

He raised his eyebrows and nodded, his face warm and open. "Nice to meet you, Luke." He wasn't jealous or judgmental. He was honest and kind, like Luke.

Except that he wasn't Luke.

"And you. I'm sure I'll see you again," Luke said as he smiled at Richard.

I shot out of the door, not waiting to see if Luke was following me. Out in the fresh spring air, I paused. How was I going to explain to him that I'd cut our lunch short as soon as Richard had arrived? I heard the café door open and Luke appeared at my side.

"You okay?" he asked.

"Sure," I said, trying to sound normal. I started to walk back toward the hospital. "So what are you working on at the moment?" I was desperate not to mention what had just happened, and hopeful that he'd not sensed any kind of atmosphere that I'd singlehandedly created.

Luke was happily diverted. "You know I can't tell you that because it's classified."

I laughed. He loved to pretend his job was slightly more interesting than it was. "You're such a dork. It doesn't make you sound like James Bond, you know."

"What does it make me sound like?"

"Like a frustrated lawyer who is trying to be wilder than he is," I said.

He grinned. "You're killing me. You know all my secrets."

My stomach lilted. It was true. I knew his and he knew mine.

As we arrived at the hospital entrance, he hugged me. "Don't let Richard change things between us," he said over my shoulder, his tone darker than before, like it had been when we were holding hands earlier. He pulled back. "Will I see you Sunday?"

33

His words, his nearness, his solemnity flustered me. "Yeah, I think."

"Promise me?" he asked, his eyes intently fixed on mine.

"Okay. I'll see you at Haven and Jake's."

The black cloud over him seemed to pass as quickly as it arrived. He grinned, ruffled my hair and stalked off down the street. I stood for a few seconds, more words in my mouth than I'd let escape. What had he meant about Richard changing things between us? I was desperate to know what he was thinking.

chapter THREE

Luke

It had been a while since Ash had had a boyfriend. Everything was moving too quickly. Emma wanted things to change between us; Haven was married; Ash was getting serious with someone. I longed for things to be how they were. I wanted Haven and Ash to wake up hungover in the guest room; I wanted the three of us to have dinner together, for the three of us to have the easy laughs that I'd grown up with. None of that had happened recently. I wanted to be able to hold Ash's hand because we had been friends for forever, not pull it away because her boyfriend arrived.

Because Emma would be home and I didn't want her to bring up getting married again, I'd worked late. I'd thought of little else but her recent declaration, but I didn't have any solution for her. All I could focus on was how marriage would take away things from my life, not add them. It was almost ten, and I was just heading home. Hopefully, she was asleep.

I let myself in and immediately heard the sounds of the television. My heart sank.

"Hey," Emma called.

"Hi," I said, wandering into the living room.

"There's leftover spaghetti in the refrigerator," she said.

"Thanks." I shrugged out of my jacket, pulled off my tie and headed to the kitchen.

Emma got up from the sofa and followed me. "Do you want me to heat it up for you?" She never got me dinner unless it was her day off. We both tended to fend for ourselves when we were working.

"I've got it, thanks."

She pulled open the fridge, grabbed a beer and handed it to me.

"Thanks," I said, forcing a smile.

"No problem. There's never going to be a good time to discuss this, you know." she said.

I took a deep breath, and I tipped my head back. I really didn't want to have this conversation. "Emma, I'm really tired."

"I know, but there's barely ever a time when one of us isn't shattered. If we wait until we're both full of energy, we're going to carry on like this for years." Her voice was softer than usual, but I could tell she wasn't about to let this go.

"We've done okay 'like this' so far. I like my life." I was happy with things how they were. I was about to make partner. Work would be crazy for the next few years. And her job was really demanding—where did she think we were going to fit in kids? No longer hungry, I took my beer and went to collapse on the sofa.

Emma followed. "It's time to move to the next stage in our lives. Don't you feel that?"

I couldn't look at her. I didn't know what she'd see in me. Fear, maybe.

"I'm happy as I am. I thought you were too." I'd never led her to believe I wanted anything more; at least, I didn't think I had.

"I want to get married and have children," she replied. She didn't say whether or not she was happy now, as if it didn't matter. "Don't you?" she asked.

I could do nothing but focus on what I wouldn't have if I married Emma. Particularly if we had kids. We would give up our freedom. What I loved about Emma was that she was independent and she didn't *need* anything from me. If I became her husband and then a father . . . Those were roles that provided and protected. I'd done that my whole life with Haven. At the time, I'd wanted to do it, though my parents' death had meant I'd had to. But there was nothing in me that wanted to take on that responsibility with Emma, or anyone else. It would change our entire relationship.

"This is important to me," Emma said, kneeling on the sofa, facing me. "I want a family. I want *us* to be a family."

I focused on my heartbeat banging against my chest. Was I too young to have a heart attack? Haven was my family. Haven and Ash. And now Jake and his sister, Beth, had widened that group, but Emma had never really become a part of that. I didn't want to create a family that would pull me away from the one I already had. The banging in my chest got louder. I threw back some more beer.

"I've given you time and space. I've not been demanding or high maintenance. And now I need you to realize what you have with me."

"But isn't that why we work? Because we're independent? I didn't know you were wanting us to be different, waiting for us to change." I didn't want or need anything else from her.

"I want us to be a unit. A family. Our children and us. At the moment, I'm constantly competing with Haven and Ash, and that's not fair."

She was right—I had a unit. Haven and Ash. I turned toward her. "So this isn't about getting married—this is about you not wanting me to spend time with my sister?"

"Jesus, that's not what I said. I just feel second place all the time. I don't want a roommate. I want someone who I can grow old with, someone to share a life with."

Whenever I imagined getting older, it was Haven, Ash and me I thought of. Had I led Emma on all these years? She looked at me expectantly, waiting for me to say something that would make her feel better, but I couldn't. I wouldn't lie to her, and I had nothing truthful that she wanted to hear.

My conversation with Ash had helped me realize that this was more than me not wanting things to change. It was about me not wanting to get married—not only because I didn't believe in marriage—but because marriage wasn't right for me, and definitely not for me and Emma. We didn't work in that way.

Haven, Ash and I were a team. *We* were a family. Jake had understood that from the beginning, and he'd become like a brother to me in a short space of time. Emma hadn't got it yet, and I wasn't sure she ever would.

"Are you ever going to grow up? You can't hang out with your sister your whole life. I thought things might change after she got married. She can move on. She can hold down a relationship. What are you so scared of?"

I hated arguing. Life was too short. I regretted every argument I'd ever had with my parents before they died. I wished I could take it all back. For years, words I'd said to them—just typical teenager stuff—had swirled around my head, haunting me. The fact that Haven felt similarly made it slightly more bearable. Our pain was shared.

I stood up, wanting to create space between us.

"Oh right, so now you're going to walk away. We need to talk about this stuff," she said, her voice getting higher and sharper. "Tell me what you want. Tell me if you want me."

"I don't know what to tell you. I don't want to get married. I'm not ready. And I didn't realize you'd started thinking about kids."

"You don't think that most people get married in their thirties? Everyone does it! How is this a shock to you? It's what people do."

"Luke!" she screamed when I didn't reply.

"What?" I shouted back and then instantly regretted it. "I don't know what you want me to say," I said, more softly.

"Fine," she said. "If you're going to be like that then you can sleep in the spare room tonight. You can't say that you don't know what I want. I think I've been very clear. I suggest you think about what it is you want. I'll give you a month."

"A month?" I asked.

She took a sip from her wine glass. "Yeah. You've got a month to work out what you want."

"What? I have a month to work out if I want to marry you?" I asked.

"Yes, we have to put a time frame on this or . . ."

"And if I decide I don't want to get married?"

"I don't know." She sounded tired. "I guess that's it. These things are important to me. It's what I want from my life, a family, and if you can't give that to me then . . ."

She didn't have to finish. I understood. I had a month until my life changed forever, whatever decision I made.

Ashleigh

Richard looked at me across the table, his eyes narrowing slightly. We were in his favorite French restaurant. It was a little masculine for my taste—dark, with oak paneling and almost black wood floors—but Richard was greeted like an old friend here, which he liked. The waiters fussed over us and nothing was too much trouble. Sometimes it felt as if we were dining with the staff as well as each other.

"It was nice to meet Luke," he finally said.

I'd been waiting for him to mention our run in. Had he seen us holding hands? I nodded and took another spoonful of my soup to avoid responding to him.

"I didn't realize you were meeting him for lunch."

I swallowed. Was he pissed off? "It was a last minute thing. Haven, Luke and I all grew up together. I told you that."

"Yeah. You're still very close," he said.

I wasn't sure if it was a question or an observation, so I kept silent, concentrating on my soup.

"It's nice," he added.

"It is. We're like a little family."

He nodded and smiled a wide, generous smile. He wasn't jealous, apparently. He seemed to like whatever made me happy. He wanted what was good for me and that felt nice, healthy.

"How was work?"

"Good. I'm getting used to things now." Richard hadn't been at the hospital I worked at long. "Megan's been showing me the ropes."

"Megan?" I asked.

"Yeah, Megan Fable." He rolled his eyes and grinned.

Yeah, I bet she was. Megan was a notorious flirt and desperate to land a doctor. She had no end of male attention, but somehow she'd never managed to get serious with anyone.

"That's good," I said. "I'm glad you're settling in."

"She's a bit of a flirt. I mean, wow."

I laughed. "A little bit."

"She's a pretty girl, but not my type."

I realized he was heading off any jealousy I might have if I found out they were working together. It was a kind thing to do. I smiled at him. "She's very pretty."

"Not as pretty as you."

"Richard." I wasn't used to all this flattery.

"What? It's true. You're gorgeous."

"You're not so bad yourself." I blushed. I was as terrible at giving compliments as I was at receiving them.

"Are you playing rugby tomorrow?" I asked, changing the subject. Richard played for the hospital team.

"Yeah and it's a big night. You can come along if you like."

I liked watching rugby. Luke used to make Haven and I watch when we were younger, and it wasn't a hardship seeing all the super-fit men in tight shorts get dirty and sweaty. "And be the only girl amongst you lot? I wouldn't get out alive."

"That's true. One of them would be bound to steal you away from me. I take it back. You can't come tomorrow."

I laughed. He was sweet.

"You have a beautiful smile," he said, grinning at me.

"Thank you," I replied, trying to be a bit more gracious about his compliment than before.

"Yeah, that dress suits you. But everything looks good on you." My cheeks started to heat. Partly from his words, and partly because I was embarrassed that I was thinking about Luke saying at lunch that I looked good in everything. Had he meant that? Did he think I was attractive? I hadn't had much time to change when I got home, so I'd just pulled on the nearest thing and put on some makeup. I never wore makeup to work.

"Are you going to Haven's on Sunday?" he asked.

"Yeah, it's my turn to cook. We used to alternate venues, but now it's mainly at Haven and Jake's because they have such an awesome kitchen. But we still take turns cooking." I was looking forward to it. I loved to cook desserts, and I had a blueberry cheesecake in mind for tomorrow. I wanted Beth to give me her seal of approval. She was the best baker this side of the Atlantic.

"So if you're cooking, does that mean you get to invite guests?" he asked.

My stomach lurched. I'd been insensitive to mention it and then not invite him. I just wasn't sure I was ready. Luke would probably want to talk about Emma, and I wasn't sure how that would affect me. If he announced that he was going to marry her, I was pretty sure I would want to excuse myself and take to my bed for a week. Having Richard there would . . . complicate things.

And anyway, it felt too early. Haven's husband, Jake, had started coming to Sunday night dinners very quickly, but normally, casual boyfriends and girlfriends didn't make an appearance. There wasn't any rule about it, but that's how it had always been. "I think Haven has some stuff going on that she wants to talk about, so I don't think it would be a good idea for you to come along tomorrow. Maybe another time?"

"I'd like to meet your friends," he said. "Perhaps we could have them over to your place one Sunday. I could help you cook."

I nodded and concentrated on pulling apart my bread.

"What about next weekend?" he asked.

"I don't think it's happening. Haven's away, I think." I was lying, and I wasn't quite sure why. All I knew was I wasn't ready to introduce him to my family yet.

"Okay, so we should go away for a weekend then. Maybe the Lake District?" he asked.

"That sounds really nice." I meant it. I did like Richard, and I enjoyed spending time with him. He was kind and attentive, and he liked me. Maybe a little distance from London and Luke would be what I needed.

chapter FOUR

Luke

"Did I interrupt anything?" I asked Haven as she opened the door to her flat. I'd arrived early for Sunday dinner. I wanted to speak to her about Emma.

"No, just honeymooners having wild sex on every surface. That's all."

"Lalalala," I sang as I covered my ears, following her down the hallway. "Stop it. Or I'm not going to be able to look at you, and we need to talk. Have you got a beer?" I asked as we stepped into the kitchen. I headed straight to the fridge. I rarely talked about relationship stuff with anyone. It had been more difficult to talk to Ash than I'd expected, though our brief discussion had helped. I now knew I couldn't marry Emma just to keep her happy, as Ash had suggested. I had to want it. Hopefully, alcohol would help my words come easier.

"There are a few different kinds in there. I think Jake got you the one you like," Haven said, stirring something in a bowl. Another good thing about my sister being married was that there was always beer at her place now. "I'm doing cheese straws."

I took the lid off my drink and slumped onto one of the stools at the breakfast bar. "Do you want a hand?" I asked.

"Ash is cooking. This is just for fun. You concentrate on telling me what's going on with you and Emma."

I drew my brows together. "How do you know I want to talk about me and Emma?"

"Because I'm psychic," she replied. "And I know you. I know how you get when you're unhappy."

I scowled but she wasn't looking, too focused on the pan in front of her. "You think I'm unhappy?"

"Are you telling me you're not?"

I thought about it. How long did she think I'd been unhappy for? This was news to me. Before Emma voiced her desire to move things on in our relationship, I'd never seen us as unhappy together; I'd not thought I was miserable.

"Emma wants to get married," I blurted out. Haven met my eyes. She rolled her lips together as if she were stopping words from tumbling out and slowly nodded.

"Don't you have anything to say about that?" I was expecting a bigger reaction from her. I wanted to know if she was as concerned about breaking up our routine as I was.

"Well, do you want to marry her?"

I shrugged, focusing on the outside of the pan that Haven was holding, as if staring hard enough would give me x-ray vision, and I would be able to see what she was making. Did I want to get married? Married. It was such a weird word. *Married, married, married, married.* I just wanted things to be how they'd always been. So, no, I didn't want to get married. My dilemma, as I saw it, was that either way, break up or get married, I ended up unhappy.

"You can't be surprised," Haven said, narrowing her eyes. That was the problem. I hadn't been expecting it at all.

"Surprised at what?" Jake boomed from behind me.

"Emma wants to get married," Haven said.

I rolled my eyes. There really were no secrets between these guys.

"She's given me a month to decide, or I guess we're over." Things had seemed almost back to normal this morning. I'd gone for a run. She'd gone to the gym. I suppose things had been a little strained, but she wasn't shouting, so I saw that as a move forward. But realistically Pandora's box was now firmly open, and things were never going to go back to how they were.

"Sounds like she's serious. And you don't want to marry her?" Jake asked.

"Well that's the question," Haven said.

"No, not really," I said. "I don't see the point. But we've been a couple a long time and I love her, and as much as I can't see us getting married, splitting up would be . . ." I'd not thought much of what my life would look like without her. I mean, we lived together. I'd have to move out for one thing, so that would be a huge change for me. And the mortgage was in both of our names, and we had a joint bank account. Our finances were intertwined.

"Sounds like you shouldn't marry her," Jake said simply, grabbing a beer from the fridge.

"How did you work that out?" I asked.

"I'd never really thought about marrying anyone before Haven. I didn't understand it, didn't see the point. Then I met her and boom—it was all I thought about. I wanted to do everything I could to tell the whole fucking world she was mine. I wanted to be able to call her my wife."

I glanced at Haven; she was trying to suppress a grin, but her dancing eyes told me how much she was enjoying what he was saying.

"If you don't feel like that, then you shouldn't marry her," Jake said, taking a seat on the barstool opposite Haven.

"But not everyone's like you, Jake. What happens if I never feel like that about anyone? I mean, it hasn't happened so far for me. And it only happened to you and Haven because you started working together. Emma would be a good choice, in a lot of ways. She's a good girl."

"I get it, but you have to figure out whether you're prepared to settle. From what you're saying, she's just not the right girl for you." Haven prodded Jake's shoulder in semi-chastisement. "I'm not saying she's not a great girl. I have no idea—I've only met her a few times. All I'm saying is if you're not wanting to frog march her down the aisle then she's not right for you."

I took another swig of beer. I couldn't believe I'd ever want to march down the aisle with anyone. "We get on. I've been with her a long time."

"Jesus, if you have to talk yourself into marrying her then something's not right." Jake said. "You'd be desperate to get married if she was the right one."

I wasn't sure it was as easy as Jake seemed to think. I got that he adored Haven, and I wouldn't have it any other way, but honestly, I didn't think it worked that way for most people.

The intercom buzzed and Haven went to answer it.

I picked at the label on my beer bottle.

"You don't need to be a shit to her about it," Jake said. "You know the answer, and if she isn't what you want, then you deserve to let her go and find someone else who wants her in the way she needs."

My heart was tight at Jake's words. His reaction hadn't been what I expected. I'd thought he'd tell me how great being married was and how I should do it. I guess I was hoping he'd help me see the upside, because on my own? I was struggling. It wasn't that he wasn't making sense—that was the problem, he made it all very clear. I didn't have the *urge* to marry Emma. And if marriage was what she wanted, maybe I should let her find it with someone else.

"Seriously, dude. If you have to think about it, it's not right," Jake said.

Ash greeted us and helped herself to a glass of wine. I watched her as she peered into the fridge. She looked good tonight. Well, she always looked good, but she'd looked better, or different, the last few times I'd seen her. She joined us, sitting between Jake and me on the bar stools, watching Haven doing something with pastry and egg. It seemed kinda unappetizing, but I wasn't about to tell her that.

"Are you sure you don't need a hand with anything?" Ash asked, grimacing while she knew Haven wasn't watching. I snorted, and Haven looked up.

"I'm sure. I'll be out of your hair in a minute and you can do your thing," Haven said. "How's Richard?"

"I met him," I interjected.

Haven stopped what she was doing, her eyes on mine. "You did?" Her gaze darted between Ash and me. "When? How come?" Haven hadn't met Richard yet, so she was bound to be wondering why I had.

"I went to see Ash for lunch this week and we bumped into him," I explained.

"You guys had lunch?" Haven asked. I'd expected her to focus on Richard rather than the fact that Ash and I'd had lunch. A look passed between Haven and Ash I couldn't decipher. Was Haven pissed I got to meet him first? It wasn't really her style.

"So, what was he like?" she finally asked.

"He didn't have two heads." I decided not to mention that as soon as he appeared, Ash had been out of her chair faster than a bat out of hell. I hadn't quite worked out what had happened there. Haven rolled her eyes at me. "Well, what do you want me to say?"

"Did you like him?" Haven asked me.

"I met him for five seconds. He could be Gandhi; he could be Charles Manson. But he seemed like a decent guy and Ash has good taste in everything so . . ."

"Is he the one?" Jake asked. "I'm a convert to the theory of there being such a thing as *the one.*"

"Obviously," Ash replied.

"Obviously he's the one?" I asked as my gut twisted. Had Ash found her future husband? It hadn't occurred to me that that's what she'd been looking for. If that was the case, I wanted to know more about him. Was he good enough for her? Did he deserve her?

Could he make her laugh the way I did?

She smiled. "I meant obviously Jake believes in all that. See the pair of them." She lifted her chin toward Haven and Jake, who were throwing each other little glances.

"And you *don't* believe in all that?" I was suddenly fascinated by what her response would be.

I willed her to look at me, but she stared into her glass. "Yeah, I believe in it."

Ashleigh

The boys had gone to watch sports, and I knew I was about to face an interrogation from Haven. "So you two had lunch?"

I tried to brush it off. It really was no big deal. "Yeah, Luke called and asked me at the last minute. We used to do it all the time. It's not like I crossed some morally reprehensible line for lunching with your brother."

Haven cocked her head. "I haven't said a word. Do you think you might be a tad defensive? I just thought you were making room in your life for Richard, that's all. I want you to be happy."

"I saw Richard last night. There is plenty of *room* for him."

Haven tapped the side of the pan with her wooden spoon. "And how's the sex? Has it improved?"

"I don't remember saying it needed improving on." I threw a glance over my shoulder to check the boys weren't listening.

Haven raised her eyebrows at me. I think I *had* said something like that, but hearing her say it sounded bad. Richard was a good guy.

"It's not bad. He's sweet and caring and very attentive," I said. The sex had been . . . nice. But it was true, my world had not been rocked.

"And you want him to shove you against the wall and fuck you properly," Haven replied. She'd hit the nail on the head, as always.

I sighed. "Maybe. I mean, he's great in so many ways. I really should like him more than I do. He's nice to me; he's good looking; he has a good job. It's just . . . there's something that's not quite right, like I'm not quite feeling it. But then maybe I won't feel it, right? Or maybe it will come with time." I wanted her reassurance that staying with Richard was what I should be doing, because I wasn't sure. Should I want fireworks? Is that what would make me happy? All these years of loving Luke hadn't done it. Wanting more than Richard seemed selfish and immature when everything about him was so great . . . at least on paper.

"But whatever *it* is, you feel that for Luke?" she asked. We rarely talked openly about how I seriously I felt about Luke. I joked around with him, told him we'd get married someday, called him handsome, that kind of thing. And sometimes he'd flirt back. It was our game, or it had been. I didn't do it so much anymore. The difference between Luke and I was that my mock flirting was covering real feelings. Feelings I'd had since that day under the magnolia tree. Along the way, I'd fallen in love with Luke. I'd given him my heart. Luke was the fireworks, but I couldn't will him to feel that way about me. And he was almost certainly about to get married.

I shrugged. "It doesn't matter what I feel for Luke. I know he sees me as his little sister. I've accepted that, which is why

I'm dating Richard." I wasn't sure I had managed to fully wrestle my heart away from Luke, but I was trying. Maybe I just needed to give Richard and me more time. Maybe I needed to know him better, know him the way I knew Luke.

"I think that's a great idea. He and Emma have been together a long time, and she's in her early thirties—her biological clock is bound to start ticking sooner rather than later."

My heart started thundering at Haven's words. Had he agreed to marry her? Did Haven know something? "He told me that he's feeling some pressure to move things on," I said.

She blushed and looked away. "He told you?"

"Yeah, it's what we talked about at lunch."

"Right. What do you think?"

My stomach flipped over, once then twice. Fuck, I hated thinking about it, but more than anything, I wanted him to be happy. "I think he needs to decide either way—shit or get off the pot. He must love her. They've been a couple for ages. Whatever makes him happy."

Haven pushed her lips together. "Yeah, you're right. I just don't think . . . Anyway. Back to you. Maybe Richard's just not the right guy for you. You need chemistry. It's not all about ticking things off a list. Just because he meets some arbitrary criteria doesn't mean you're destined for each other," she said.

"Destined?" Had she really just said that? She'd become such a sap since she'd married Jake.

"You know what I'm trying to say." She laughed. "It doesn't mean you have to spend the rest of your life with a man just because he fits the description."

"He wants us to go away next weekend. To the Lake District. So I guess it will be good to have that time together. Hopefully I'll figure out if there's a future for us."

"And if there isn't, maybe you'll meet someone if you do that course you were talking about."

I turned the base of my wineglass on the counter, watching as the alcohol crept up the edges of the glass with the movement. "Yeah, I need to work out whether or not I'm going to apply."

"Apply for what?" Luke asked, poking me in the waist as he walked toward the fridge.

"Did I tell you?" I asked him. "I'm thinking about doing an MBA."

"You are? Wow," he said as he turned his attention away from refrigerator. He rarely shaved on a Sunday, and the stubble on his jaw looked long enough to feel good against my skin. I needed to focus.

"You think I shouldn't?" I asked. I hadn't mentioned it to Richard because I hadn't decided whether or not I should apply yet.

"God, no. I think it would be awesome. You should definitely do it. Do you want to change jobs, or will it help you get promoted and stuff?" he asked, setting two cold beers on the counter and staring at me.

"If I really want to be a director of nursing in a hospital, then it's what they look for, and if I want to get out of nursing and do something wider in healthcare, I guess it will help too. We can't stay still, can we? I can't be wiping puke from my uniform for the rest of my career."

His eyes were bright and his whole body seemed focused on me. I loved it when I had his full attention. "How come you haven't told me about this? When do you start?"

Haven pretended not to watch us as she set about slicing the onions I'd asked her to deal with.

"I haven't decided whether or not I should do it."

"Why wouldn't you? I mean, I think you're totally awesome at wiping vomit and myriad of other bodily fluids from your uniform, and I'm sure your patients would miss you, but you're a smart girl. You can do anything you want to."

"You think? I mean, I know I'm a good nurse, but I worried that in a class with a bunch of crazy-clever people, I would . . ." *Look foolish? Be the class dunce?*

"*You're* crazy clever. You could have done anything you wanted in your career. You can hold your own against a room full of management consultants. The thing is your heart is even bigger than your brain. *That's* why you're a nurse."

I loved that that's how he saw me. Luke always knew the right thing to say, and when he put it like that, I didn't have a good reason not to apply, apart from the cost. I shrugged. "I have to sit a test and fill out an application form. The deadline is coming up."

"You'd start in January?"

I nodded.

"Isn't this great, Haven?" Luke asked.

"Yeah, she should totally do it."

I grinned at them both. If I told them I was going to fly to the moon, they'd think it was a wonderful idea.

As promised, Richard had arranged a weekend in the Lake District for us. He picked a beautiful country hotel that felt as if it was in the middle of nowhere. I couldn't have asked for a more romantic setting.

"Wow, what a view," I said, staring out of our bedroom window across the mountains and down to the lake. I loved the way the sun turned everything yellow before it hit the horizon.

"It's beautiful, isn't it?" Richard asked as he came up behind me and put his hands around my waist. It didn't feel entirely natural, but it wasn't unpleasant. Just unfamiliar.

"How did you find this place?"

"A guy at work had his honeymoon here."

I could see why. Our room was huge, but cozy with an open fire and a four-poster bed. It was something that would pop up if you typed *romantic country hotel* into Google. In the same way, if you typed *romantic, attentive, kind and generous man* into Google, Richard would pop up. He *was* all those things.

"I thought we could just hang out here for the night. The restaurant downstairs is meant to be good. I made reservations for eight if that works for you."

"Sure," I said as I laid my head back on his chest. He was so thoughtful and kind.

"Or we don't have to go anywhere. I'm sure they do room service." He swept my hair to one side and pressed his lips to my neck.

We were three months in and this was our first weekend away together. I should be desperate to keep room service busy, but I didn't feel like that. It wasn't that I couldn't bear for him to touch me. When he kissed me, it felt nice. I was just ambivalent about his touch. About him really. I didn't miss him when he wasn't there, and I didn't get excited to see him—though when I did, I had a nice time. Hopefully, now that things between us were getting more serious, my feelings would grow. But Haven's words echoed through my head— maybe he just wasn't the right man for me.

My phone rang and although I didn't move to answer it, Richard released his hold around my waist. "You get that and I'll grab a quick shower," he said, then planted a kiss on my cheek.

Luke's name was flashing on the screen. Talk about timing.

"Hey," I said. Why was he was calling me?

"Hi, I'm at the supermarket. What wine did Haven say I should bring on Sunday?" The noise of the shoppers echoed behind him.

"Why would I know?" The shower began running in the bathroom, and I relaxed a little. It felt weird to be speaking to Luke while I was away with Richard. I went back to the window, not wanting to waste the view.

"You were there, weren't you?"

"I don't remember. But buy the pinot noir. Even if it's not the right one, she'll still like it."

"Okay. And I need to ask you a favor."

My stomach clenched. Was he going to tell me he was engaged and wanted me to do a reading at his wedding?

"I have this work thing. Like an awards ceremony. Will you come with me? It's black tie and everything." Over the years, I'd got used to accompanying him to events like this. But I'd not done it for a while. Not since he moved in with Emma.

I shifted my weight from one foot to the other. I was pleased he was asking me, but I knew I shouldn't go. "Why can't Emma go with you?"

"She's working."

I rested my forehead on the cool glass in front of me. I wanted to go. And that was the difference. If Richard were asking, I'd say yes, but I wouldn't really want to. If I went with Luke, we'd laugh all night and have the best time. "When is it?" I asked. I should say no. I should come up with an excuse. Spending time with Luke wasn't going to make me like Richard more, and that's what I needed to do.

"It's four weeks from today. Please say you'll come. I can't bear these things, and you'll make it fun."

"Can't Haven go?"

"I'm not taking my sister. How pathetic do you want me to look?" he asked.

I smiled. "I thought I was meant to be like a sister to you." I was prodding him, verging on flirting. I shouldn't be.

"Well, you are like a sister, but in an 'it's legal' way. No one has to know I've seen you pee yourself. We could pass as a couple." I'd long passed the point where playing at being a couple was enough for me. I needed something real.

"Jesus, I was five. Are you ever going to let me forget it?" Luke had been peeing on my mother's roses, and I'd thought

I would join the fun but ended up with wet underwear and a scolding from my mother. Luke had laughed until his eyes almost popped out of his head.

"I wouldn't hold your breath."

"I'll check my schedule. I won't know if I'm working until next week." How did Emma have her schedule already? She worked at the same group of hospitals, and doctors and nurses got their schedules four weeks in advance. Surely she couldn't know yet.

"You're the best. I'll see you Sunday."

I shook my head at his assumption that I would end up going with him. "I won't be there on Sunday, but I'll let you know."

"You won't? What are you doing?" he asked.

I hesitated for a split second then decided to be honest. "I'm away for the weekend. With Richard."

"Oh, right. So . . . So it's serious then?"

I didn't want to get into this with him. "I told you, we've been going out three months. It's three-months serious. Not you-and-Emma serious."

He didn't say anything.

"I'll speak to you next week," I said.

"Yeah, okay." There was something in his voice that hadn't been there before. I couldn't quite identify it, but he sounded uncertain.

The shower turned off, and I shoved my phone back in my bag just before Richard came out in his robe.

"Nice threads," I said.

"Thanks. There are his and hers on the back of the door."

He straightened the front of the robe to show me the word "hers" embroidered on the breast pocket.

I wanted to ask him if he'd left his penis back in London. I smirked at my own joke, but I wasn't sure Richard would find it funny. "Did you get the wrong robe?" I asked.

He stood in front of me, pulling at my waistband. "No," he said, moving toward me. "I wore it because I'm hers. Yours." He pressed his lips against mine, and I put my arms around his neck and closed my eyes, allowing our tongues to meet. "I'm all yours."

And that was the problem. I wasn't all his, but I was *trying* to be.

chapter FIVE

Luke

"Why didn't you bring Emma?" Haven asked as she opened the door.

"It's so good to see you, my beloved brother. How are you?" I responded sarcastically. I bent and kissed her cheek, and then we went through to the open-plan living space.

"So?" she asked.

Jake was in the kitchen, and we exchanged raised eyebrows.

"She didn't want to come. I can't force her," I said. The truth was I hadn't pushed very hard. I preferred it when it was just the four of us. Or the five of us, when Beth joined. We fit together well.

"Did you suggest she come? What did she say?" she asked.

"That she always felt uncomfortable because we all had private jokes or something."

"Well how come Jake doesn't feel like that? He's come on the scene more recently than Emma." Haven waved around a vegetable knife for emphasis. "Were you uncomfortable coming to Sunday night dinner?" she asked Jake, who seemed to be shredding some kind of vegetable with an unusually complicated cheese grater.

He shook his head. "Nothing would have stopped me from spending time with you, and I wanted to know your family better. Anyway, I love Ash and Luke; why wouldn't I like hanging out with them?"

"Stop, you're going to have me crying into my beer," I said, and Jake grinned at me.

"So she wants to marry you, but doesn't like your family?" Jake asked. He switched from shredding to stirring something on the stove, his eyes fixed on the pot as if he were expecting gremlins to pop out of the pan at any moment.

"It's not quite that straightforward," I said. "I can see why it would be more difficult for her than it was for you. Haven and Ash are quite the force to be reckoned with."

"What does that mean?" Haven's eyes narrowed as she pointed what looked like a very sharp knife in my direction.

"It means that you are both very protective, and that's great and everything, but . . ." Ash made things complicated. She wasn't my sister but knew me as well, if not better, than Haven. And I enjoyed her company, but girlfriends hadn't historically understood our relationship. "Let's get off the subject please. I hear Ash is away this weekend?" Something was always off when she wasn't around on Sundays. It was unsettling.

"Yeah, Richard's taken her to the Lake District. He's really serious about her. You can tell he has a green, flashing light right over his head," Haven said.

I looked at Jake to see if he was wondering what the hell she meant. He seemed as confused as I was.

"What?" he asked. "A light on his head?"

"You know, when guys are ready to get married, all the lights turn to green. Richard is ready and he wants it. You can tell."

"Where did you come up with this crazy theory?" Jake asked, and he pulled her toward him and kissed her roughly.

She pushed him away. "Watch that sauce, or it will burn," she said. "Everyone knows that guys can just suddenly turn their green light on, and when they do, they're married within a year."

"You reckon?" I asked.

"That didn't happen with you and me," Jake said with a confused look on his face. "I mean I wasn't green light until you came along."

"Yeah, but I'm special—the exception that proves the rule. Or something. All I'm saying is that I think if Ash wants to marry Richard, they'll be engaged by the end of the year."

My gut twisted at the thought of more change being thrust upon me, of Ash being engaged. I'd been focused on how marrying Emma would shift things, but if Ash married Richard . . . What would that do to our routine, our Sunday night dinners? Would I still be able to hang out with her? Invite her to work events? My head started to spin.

I wasn't sure if Jake and Richard being ready to commit so quickly meant that I was just different, or if it meant I just wasn't with the right woman. Haven was, for sure, the right woman for Jake, and Ash? Was she the right woman for Richard? Was Richard the right guy for her?

"You never know. He might propose this weekend," Haven said.

"What? That will never happen. He's barely known her three months," I said.

Jake nodded. "She might be right. When you know, you know. Took me less time than that to know I was going to marry Haven."

"You've got to be kidding me. Does she like him enough to marry him? I didn't get that vibe from her."

Haven didn't respond and just shoved some apples and a vegetable peeler in front of me.

I picked up an apple and started peeling. "I'm not sure they fit together, you know?" In my head, I'd always seen Haven married someday, but I'd never thought that would be for Ash. I'd always seen her as . . . belonging to me, somehow. Like we were a pair. Not that there'd ever been anything romantic between us, it was just . . . I knew that she was special to me, and me to her. We had a bond.

"I don't want her to end up married to some loser. It's bad enough having to put up with this one." I cocked my head at Jake and he grinned.

I tried to remember what Richard was like, but it really had been a fleeting introduction. I hadn't seen any kind of massive spark between them, but maybe that was wishful thinking on my part. I suppose he could be seen as handsome, and he would be able to look after her financially. He *was* a doctor. "I guess on paper he's a catch—"

"You might be married to Emma by the end of the year," Haven said.

"No way," Jake said before I had a chance to respond. Haven playfully swiped him on the arm. "What?" he asked her, and she shot him a look.

"Have you decided what you're going to do?" she asked.

Although I'd tried to put Emma's ultimatum at the back of my brain, I'd thought about little else. At first I'd been convinced she was bluffing, and that she'd calm down in a couple of days and things would go back to normal. But I knew that wasn't going to happen. The problem was we wanted different things. The more time that went on, the clearer it was I didn't want to marry her.

"Nope." All I saw was a lose/lose situation ahead of me.

"Hey," I called as I let myself back into our flat after dinner.

"Hi," she replied. That was progress. At least she was speaking to me tonight.

"Haven and Jake asked after you," I said as I joined her in the living room.

"Right."

"Emma—"

"Don't 'Emma' me, like I'm being some unreasonable shrew. I've done nothing but love you. I just want you to decide whether you see a future with me."

I slumped onto the sofa. I loved this couch. I'd had it since university, bought it when I shared a house in my sophomore year. Emma had tried to convince me to throw it out when we moved in together, but I'd bargained with her and given in to her choice of location on the condition I got to keep it. I smoothed my hand down the soft brown leather of the arm and took the comfort it offered. There was no point in replying. I didn't have anything to say, it was clear there was no talking her round. Things weren't going to go back to how they were, so she was right. I needed to decide whether or not I wanted to get married, have a family, do all those things that normal people did.

"If we split up, I'm keeping this flat. I'll buy you out," she said.

She'd clearly been thinking about this. Making plans. Jesus, I couldn't keep up. "You agreed to give me some time to think it over. It's a big decision."

Emma sighed and got up off the chair opposite me, taking her book with her, and headed toward our bedroom. "The thing is it shouldn't be."

It was early, but bed seemed like a good place to be. I needed some space to think. Would Ash feel like this when Richard proposed? Would she have doubts? I knew Haven and Jake never questioned their future together. They knew that it was right, and Jake worshipped my sister. But not every couple was like that, were they? The fact that Richard hadn't been to Sunday night dinner suggested that Ash wasn't as serious about him as Haven had been about Jake. But maybe if he proposed, she'd get more serious? I closed my eyes. I should have been concentrating on Emma and me, not thinking about Ash and Richard.

Should I take Jake's advice and wait for the right girl? Was I the sort of man who found the right girl? I wasn't sure. Emma was right; we'd been together long enough to understand our feelings for each other. And although I loved her, when it came down to it, if I was being true to myself, I didn't want to marry her. As much as I tried to imagine being married to Emma, it was easier to imagine us not together anymore, not in each other's lives. That feeling wasn't as uncomfortable. My mind drifted back to Ash. The thought of her not in my world because she'd built a life with Richard was . . . Well, it was unthinkable. Just the possibility made my temperature rise and my palms sweat.

I'd missed Ash this evening. It was never the same without her. Surely she would be back this evening from her weekend away? I pulled out my phone to message her.

Luke: Hey. Missed you at dinner tonight.

I scrolled through a few work emails, wondering if she'd message me back.

Ash: Good to know I'm missed.

I grinned at the screen. Of course she was missed.

Luke: Did you check your schedule? Can you make the awards dinner?

I was looking forward to that evening now I'd invited her. I hoped she wasn't working.

Ash: Yeah, I can make it. Richard's out that night too.

When had Richard being out become a factor in Ash's decision making? Maybe Haven was right and they were serious. My fingers hovered over the dial button. I wanted to call and ask her what was going on, whether she was going to marry him. I mean, I was like a brother to her. I had a right to know, didn't I? But it wasn't just protectiveness I felt.

It was jealousy.

Of Richard.

Ashleigh

"It's been amazing, hasn't it?" Richard said as he kissed me softly on the lips. We were putting our bags in the car, ready for the journey home from the Lake District.

I nodded. The weekend had been lovely, but not amazing. Richard had been kind, thoughtful and attentive as always. I had *nothing* to complain about. But I hadn't laughed as much as I normally did, hadn't been silly or . . . I just hadn't felt quite like myself.

"I always forget how beautiful it is up here," I said as I turned away from the car, back toward the view of the lake below me. The mountains jaggedly cut through the blue sky, and I took a deep breath full of mountain air. Before my parents moved to Hong Kong, we used to visit the Lake District quite regularly. Haven and Luke joined us once, before their parents died. Even when it rained, which was most of the time, it was incredible, magical and such a contrast to London. "Thank you for bringing me back."

"We'll have to come again. Maybe we'll have our honeymoon here. You never know," Richard said, grinning at me.

My stomach lurched at his suggestion, but I managed a small smile. It wasn't excitement that coursed through me. It was anxiety at the thought of a honeymoon with Richard, a life with Richard. He was such a great guy, and I knew that I was crazy with a capital C for not swooning at his suggestion. But as much as I tried, I wasn't as serious about our relationship as he was. I was disappointed in myself for not being able to fall for him. Part of me wondered whether I was just destined to be unhappy, or if I would choose the most difficult route to happiness and be bound for failure.

Richard opened the passenger door for me, and I got in, getting comfortable for the long drive.

"Have you got a busy week?" he asked as he started the engine.

I nodded. "Yeah, quite busy. I've got to study for my entrance exam, so the next few weeks will be brutal."

He glanced at me. "Sorry. What are you talking about? What entrance exam?"

"I told you that I was thinking about applying for an MBA program."

"No you didn't. Why do you want to do that?"

"I think it will be good. It'll help me if I want to head up nursing in a big hospital, or . . . I don't know. I might want a career change, to move into a more general healthcare role." I liked the challenge that an MBA provided, and it was increasingly common for nurses to get them. As much as I enjoyed my job and the contact I had with patients, I felt there was more I could do for people if I had an opportunity to influence policy within a hospital.

Richard didn't respond. He just stared out of the window at the road in front of us.

"You don't think it's a good idea?" I asked.

"I didn't think you were a career girl, that's all."

What did that mean? "What's a career girl?"

He frowned and looked in my direction, then back at the

road. "Wouldn't you want to stay at home with your children?" he asked.

"Well, unless you know something I don't, I'm not pregnant. Anyway, I like working. I don't understand how a girl with a career is a bad thing."

"I'm not saying it's a bad thing. I think it's great that you've been to university, but motherhood is the most important job you can do."

"Like fatherhood?"

"Well, yes but it's different, isn't it?"

"Is it?"

"Well, apart from anything else, my earning potential is more than yours, so it makes more sense if either of us is to stay home that it would be you."

Were we really discussing what married life was going to be like for us? I wanted to undo the top button of my shirt to relieve the tightness around my throat, but I was wearing a V-neck and it wasn't the collar that was creating the restriction.

"Who knows, maybe I'll end up earning more than you if I get my MBA."

"And is that what you want?"

"What? To have a successful and rewarding career? Sure. Isn't it what you want?"

"I know, but do you want that more than you want to have kids and be a stay-at-home mother?"

How were we having this conversation at the beginning of a five-hour car ride?

"I want to have kids and a career. I guess like you do."

Richard nodded but didn't reply.

Haven had been right. Richard wasn't the man for me. If I hadn't known before, how he saw our future together had solidified my feelings. Ultimately, if we didn't want the same things from life, then whether or not there was passion between us didn't matter. It was a relief in a sense. It gave me a sensible reason for not wanting Richard. I didn't have to worry about whether or not I was prepared to give up passion for a good guy, or that wanting someone who was my best friend, who made me laugh but also knew how to make my toes curl, was naïve and ridiculous. These were concrete compatibility issues.

I would have to tell him. Sooner rather than later. It was clear that he was serious about us, and it wasn't fair to keep him thinking that I was too.

"Hey, you've ordered the wine, I see," I said to Haven as I reached the table. We were meeting at one of our favorite restaurants in London. It wasn't fancy, but the staff was friendly and the tapas amazing.

"You look really good," she replied.

"Thanks." I'd been home to change. I wanted to feel good tonight.

"The Lake District agreed with you then?"

I grinned. "Kind of. I always love going back, but Richard and I didn't work out."

"What do you mean?" She paused just before pouring my wine. I pointed at my glass. I needed a drink.

"I ended it with him last night. Things weren't right."

"Because of the sex?"

"Yes and no. I think the sex was just a metaphor for our lack of connection on a lot of levels. We wanted different things, and I couldn't be myself around him; he didn't make me laugh. I think I would have been less with him—certainly not been everything I could be."

"It sounds like you made the right decision. You need someone who will make you more, bring out all your colors."

I nodded.

"How did he take it?" she asked.

I wasn't sure how he'd taken it. One minute he'd been mentioning our honeymoon and being really attentive, but he'd barely reacted at all when we'd met the next day and I told him that I didn't think we were going to work out. "Okay, I think. Sometimes I thought he was really into me, and then other times I wasn't sure if it was me, or the idea of me he liked. I'm going to start Internet dating, I think," I said.

"So this isn't about Luke?" she asked.

"What do you mean?"

"Ending things with Richard isn't because you still have a crush on Luke?" I looked over my shoulder to check who was around. The last thing I needed was Luke to be behind us.

"Haven, I've loved your brother a long time. I'm not sure that will ever change, but he's going to go off and have his two kids and picket fence with Emma. I'm pleased for him if that will make him happy. I just need to concentrate on what's going to make *me* happy."

She looked surprised. "You think you love him?"

"I know I do," I replied.

"I'm sorry," Haven said as she reached for my hand. "I didn't realize that you felt that strongly."

"It's fine. I've had a lot of time to get used to the fact that he doesn't feel the same way. If it hasn't happened by now, I know it's never going to." I took a deep breath. "I'm not saying I'm over him, or that I ever will be. I just know I have to make my world about more than him." Haven's eyes were glassy with tears. "I'm sorry. I shouldn't have said anything," I said, squeezing her hand.

"No, I'm pleased you did. I'm sorry you haven't felt you can talk to me about this stuff."

I pulled my hand away. "He's your brother. I don't want to make it awkward for you. Anyway, now we don't need to talk about it again. I'm moving on. Dating Richard was good for me. I just need to find the right guy. Can we clone Jake? That would work for me."

"You know, with his science-y contacts and his money, that's a real possibility. I'll ask him. In the meantime, more wine?"

I nodded. "Oh yeah, and he has to adore me like Jake adores you."

"From what you were saying, Richard adored you."

"I think he liked me. I guess it's mutual adoration that I'm after."

"You know that Jake and I hated each other when we first met. It's not always love at first sight."

"I know, but I gave Richard three months. I mean, you know by then, don't you?"

The more distance I had from Luke, the better. I needed to stop comparing what I had with him, what I felt for him, to whomever I dated next. Maybe practice would make perfect.

chapter SIX

Luke

I wasn't going to leave it until Emma's deadline was up. Now I knew where we were going, it seemed unfair to string things out. Emma had the day off tomorrow, so I was going to tell her this evening. I'd texted her earlier in the day to suggest we talk when she got home from work, and she'd replied saying she'd be home at eight. I'd also called Haven and asked if I could spend a few days with them while I got myself sorted out.

My heart was thundering in my chest. All the pieces were in place—I just needed to pull the trigger. I wasn't sure if I'd be met with tears or anger. She'd been so unpredictable recently. Part of me thought that I was giving her the conclusion she was expecting, and that she would simply want me to leave. Then the other part of me feared for my man parts. I didn't want to be Bobbitted.

I'd packed a suitcase of things I'd need over the next few days, and I was just putting it behind the door in the spare room when I heard Emma's keys in the lock. This was it. I had to say it quickly, get it out and then see where we went from there.

I moved into the kitchen and pulled out two glasses from the cupboard. I'd bought a bottle of her favorite wine. Was that insensitive? Would she think I was going to propose? Shit, maybe I hadn't thought this through. I didn't know what the right thing was. I didn't want her to be upset. I didn't want her to hate me. I wanted her to see that although I loved her, I just didn't want to marry her.

"Hey," she said softly as she came into the kitchen, taking off her coat. Her eyes went to the wine and the corners of her mouth twitched. Shit, she thought it was good news. Her eyes flicked to mine and she stilled. I passed her a glass of wine.

"How was work?" I asked.

"Fine. Someone threw up on me. You?"

My stomach was churning and I was conscious of my bones, as if my nervousness had penetrated right to my skeleton. "Okay," I said. She took her glass and collapsed on my sofa. I sat opposite her on the coffee table. I had to do this now, or I would lose my nerve. "I've thought about what you said." Her eyes were a mixture of fear and excitement, her knuckles white with her grip on the glass. "I've thought of little else since you brought it up, and it's not going to work out for us." The churning in my stomach was near overwhelming as I searched her face for a reaction. She was very still. "I'm sorry," I whispered.

"Do you need more time?" she asked in a quiet voice. It wasn't what I'd expected her to say. "I mean, I shouldn't have given you that deadline. If you're not ready, I can give you more time." Her words came more quickly and tears were forming in her eyes.

I leaned forward and took her hand. "You were right to push me. I'd not thought about it, and I should have. I should have understood how you felt about our future together and I didn't. I'm sorry." I'd been selfish. I'd wanted to freeze time and live in that exact moment for the rest of my life, because if that were possible then I didn't have to lose anything or anyone.

After my parents died, for months, I'd kept imagining the last time I'd seen them, the last time I'd hugged them, the last time I'd told them I loved them. I wanted to remember those moments as perfect. I did it so often that the pictures in my head had become distorted, and I couldn't separate out what really happened from what I had invented. In my own life, I'd clung to everything around me, afraid to lose anything, not questioning whether or not I really wanted those things.

It was time to grow up and move on.

"And you don't want to marry me?" she asked, her voice wobbling on the word "me". Shit, how did I make this better?

I took her hand and squeezed it. "I love you. You are amazing. You're bright and kind and all the things any guy would be lucky to have in a wife." Her tears spilled over and down her cheeks.

"But not enough for you?"

"I just don't want to get married. Not yet, maybe not ever. I don't see myself with kids. You do and that's fine. I want that for you but—"

"I'll wait. I can give you a year and see if you feel differently." She sounded so sad, and I hated that I caused it.

I shook my head. It would be easy at this point to agree to an extra year. It would keep everything just the same. But I couldn't do that to her. I wanted her to have the future she imagined for herself, and I would never be able to give her that.

"I won't do that to you," I said as I squeezed her hand. "I can't."

"I don't mind. I'll wait. I shouldn't have pushed—I knew you weren't ready. Please Luke, don't leave me."

A month ago, I never would have thought that we'd have this conversation. I thought we were happy. We had a relationship I enjoyed because we gave each other so much freedom. And I loved her. I really did. But now she was offering me this extra time, which I knew I couldn't take because it wasn't fair on her. But ultimately, I didn't want it. I *wanted* to move on. The churning in my stomach was no longer about the impact this conversation was having on me but what it was doing to Emma. I was ready for a different future.

"I don't think that's a good idea. I don't think anything will change for me. I'm sorry," I said.

She took a sharp intake of breath and narrowed her eyes. "Is there someone else?"

"Of course not." How could she think that? "I've never cheated on you or anyone."

"Not with Ash?"

My stomach twisted. Did she think there was something between us? My feelings about Ash and Richard had confused me, but I hadn't reached a conclusion about why. "Not anyone."

She nodded. "So you're going to move out."

"I'm going to stay with Haven."

"Right," she said, her throat tight. "I'll speak to my dad about getting the money together to buy you out."

"You know where I am. I'll let you know if I find a place."

She started to cry again. I just wanted to take her in my arms and make everything better. I moved toward her and she pulled farther away.

"I'm sorry," I said, again. "Do you want me to stay tonight?" I asked.

She shook her head. "No, I'll call Kelly. You should go now. I really loved you, Luke."

I closed my eyes. "I know and I love you. I really want you to be happy."

I stood, headed to the guest bedroom and collected my case.

Thank God the following day was Friday. My brain was close to a meltdown with all the adjustments and contemplations it had been doing recently. I didn't often go drinking with colleagues, but tonight was an exception. I needed to block things out. Alcohol was the perfect treatment. I could dive into those relaxed soporific sensations and let myself drown for a bit. I could use it to block out the guilt and unease, the anxiety over what was next.

Emma's reaction to our breakup had been heartbreaking. Somehow I felt guilty that she wasn't angrier with me. She had every reason to be. Unwittingly, I'd led her to believe that we could be something more. I should have been more sensitive to her.

"Shots!" Mark, one of the other lawyers, shouted as he placed a tray of vodka in front of the group of us gathered in Chancery Bar. I couldn't remember if this would be my fourth or fifth shot, but things were becoming pleasantly hazy.

"Oh, just to warn you, Wendy found out you're single," Mark whispered.

I shuddered. Wendy, our office manager, flirted with most of the lawyers who were single and a number of them had "experienced" her. I wasn't about to be another one of those guys. She wasn't my type.

"You not interested?" Mark asked. "She's sexy."

I shook my head. "Never a good idea to shit on your own doorstep."

That seemed to make sense to Mark, and he didn't push it. I scanned the faces in the bar. What was my type? Emma and I had been introduced to each other at a party. She was pretty and funny and smart. I wasn't sure I had a physical type.

We'd been drinking for hours when our group started to thin out. I checked my watch. It wasn't even nine. Jesus, it felt like two in the morning. I didn't often drink shots on an empty stomach. Perhaps it was time for me to go. But the only thing waiting for me at home was a couple that made me want to vomit, they were so in love. I pulled out my phone. What was Ashleigh doing? I could go round. We could talk. I hadn't told her I was ending things with Emma. What would she think? I wanted to know more about how she was feeling about Richard. I wanted to know more about him, whether or not he was good enough for her. More than that, I wanted to understand why thinking about them together made me jealous.

Seeing her suddenly became urgent.

Ashleigh

"The building better be on fire," I shouted in response to the banging on my front door. Who the hell was making such noise at this time of night? It was just gone nine and I was in my PJ's, my makeup off, watching television. It had been a perfect evening of doing nothing, and now someone was spoiling it.

I checked the peephole and flung the door open. "What are you doing here?" I asked Luke. "Are you drunk?" He squinted as if he was finding it difficult to focus.

"Yup. I really need some water."

I rolled my eyes and stomped off to the kitchen. The door closed behind him as he trailed after me. "It's late, Luke. Why are you here?"

"Shit." He stood up really straight. "Sorry. Is Richard here?"

I ran the cold tap and filled a glass full of water. Haven obviously hadn't told him about our breakup. I shook my head. He smiled and headed over to my sofa where he collapsed. "Do you have snacks?" he asked. "Maybe something with cheese?"

"You realize there are plenty of fast food restaurants that you can go to when you're drunk that will feed you carbs and water. There's no need for you to come to me." How was I going to keep my distance from him if he kept following me?

Luke groaned. "Stop complaining, Ash. You love looking after people. That's why you do what you do."

"You should go home," I said. "Shall I call you a cab?"

"Urgh, no. I can't face listening to my sister have sex. Let me stay a bit longer. Hopefully they'll wear themselves out and then I can go home."

He wasn't making sense. "Why are you going to listen to Haven having sex at your house?"

"Could I stay with you?" he asked, and his face lit up and then fell. "No. I don't want to listen to you and Richard going at it either. Maybe I can move in with Kate Upton. I wouldn't mind listening to her having sex."

He was equal parts amusing and annoying when he drank like this. I threw a cushion at him. "You're hammered. Just go back to your place and you can have sex with your own girlfriend."

"I need to find my own place. Will you come flat hunting with me?"

I didn't even pretend to know what he was talking about. "I'll make you a sandwich, and then you're leaving."

I set about making him a cheese sandwich, which I knew was his favorite. I didn't often see Luke drunk since he'd left college. It wasn't like him. And why was he going on about Haven and Jake? He seemed really out of it.

"If you feel like you're going to throw up, then make sure you hit the bathroom," I called into the living room.

He appeared at the door to the kitchen. "That water was good." He refilled his glass. "You're making me a sandwich?" He sounded a little more normal.

"Apparently I'm a sucker," I said as I cut the bread in half, put it on a plate and handed it to him.

"I shouldn't drink on an empty stomach."

"You think?" I chuckled at him.

"Did I interrupt your evening?"

"Yes." But as ever, I was delighted to see him.

"Was it a popcorn and pajamas evening?" he asked, grinning at me in a way that felt more flirtatious than he meant it to. It was just tortuous.

I laughed. "It doesn't mean that you didn't disrupt things."

"I'm sorry. I just went for a few beers after work and . . . I'm trying to distract myself." He scrubbed his face with his hands.

"Are you okay? You and Emma?"

"Yeah and you know, I know it's the right thing, but breaking up is always difficult. We were together a long time."

My stomach flipped over. Breaking up? I didn't respond.

"Haven told you, right?"

"Told me what? I've not spoken to her for a few days."

"Emma and I split last night. I moved out. I'm staying with Haven and Jake." He took a bite of his sandwich while my stomach took a dive and my head started to spin. "This is really good," he said, pointing to his snack. "You are Ashleigh Franklin? I'm in the right house?"

I tried to act normally. I pushed his shoulder and headed back to the living room. "Don't act so surprised. I can make a sandwich. Tell me about Emma."

"Call me thoughtless and naïve, but I'd never realized that she wanted a husband and kids."

"You're thoughtless and naïve."

He grimaced.

"You told me to call you that," I said.

"I know." He sighed. "Do you believe it? I mean, I feel horrible."

"I think when one person feels more than another in a relationship it's hard to get it right on either side. It's like you're using the same map to get to different places. If she was honest with herself, Emma probably knew that you didn't want the same things she did, and that she should have walked away sooner. But you could have been more sensitive too." It was easy to empathize with Emma. We both had a level of feelings for Luke that weren't reciprocated.

"I feel horrible."

I felt happy, and maybe a little hopeful, which I knew was wrong. Luke and I weren't together because he didn't feel that way about me—it had nothing to do with Emma.

"So you've split?"

He nodded.

"Maybe you'll work it out." I was trying to see how resolved he was. Would being away from her allow him to see what he was missing?

"She's not what I want. It's over. So I need to find somewhere to live."

"I'm sorry."

"Don't be. It's the right thing, and now that it's done I'm relieved and a little guilty. But there's no sadness or longing."

I understood. It was how I felt about my breakup with Richard.

"I'm so pleased you were in and not out with your boyfriend." He sighed as his head sagged back onto the sofa. He closed his eyes. "What would I do without you?"

His words rang in my ears as I took his plate from his hand, just before he fell into an alcoholic sleep.

Didn't he realize he hadn't just been torturing Emma all these years, but me too?

chapter
SEVEN

Luke

I scanned the dimly lit hotel bar, but I couldn't see her. Fucking hell, I knew she'd be late. Irritation prickled at my collar. I'd started to type out a text when I glanced up to see her walking toward me. She smiled at me with that wide, infectious smile she had, and I could do nothing but grin back.

My eyes wandered down her body. "Ash," I said because I couldn't think of anything else. She looked . . . well, beautiful. Like, model beautiful. Words stuck in my throat. Jesus, had she always been this pretty? The lights flickered off her cheekbones and lit up her face as her hair tumbled across her exposed shoulders.

"You're looking very handsome," she said as she fingered my bow tie. I took in her familiar scent as she came closer. I filled my lungs, wanting to inhale the way she smelled. It always calmed me. She'd been wearing the same perfume since college—it mixed with her warmth to make a scent that was bespoke to her. I'd dated a girl who had worn the same perfume, but it was different on her. It didn't feel as if it suited her. On Ash it smelled like home. "I saw you come in. Did you think I was late?"

"You look incredible," I managed to say, unable to concentrate on her question. I was stuttering, ruffled by the sight of her, and she was as calm and serene as ever.

She wore a black dress with an indecently low neckline, and although it went down to the floor, every now and then I got a flash of thigh. The fabric skirted across every curve, showing off her small waist and hinting at what lay beneath. "How is that dress legal?"

"Don't start the big brother routine," she said and rolled her eyes at me.

Fraternal was the last thing I was feeling. It felt odd to notice Ash like that—wrong in so many ways, but I wanted to kiss her exposed shoulder. Her skin looked so soft and, well, kissable.

I was going to have to get myself together. I was clearly having a worse reaction to splitting with Emma than I'd expected. I placed my hand on the small of her back and led her out of the bar toward to ballroom.

"What is this thing anyway?" she asked, glancing up at me. "And why am I here?"

"A boring awards dinner. Our firm is up for law firm of the year. We're not going to win, but think of it as free wine and it might not seem so dull."

"Okay. And why am I here?"

"Do you not want to be?" The thought of her being with me as some kind of chore made me wince. I wanted her to look forward to the evening as much as I was. Any evening was improved by Ash being a part of it. She was funny and clever, and she knew me better than I knew myself. How could we not have a great time together? Maybe I'd have to convince her.

"I'll tell you at the end of the evening. I'll give you a score if you like. And then I can tell you if it scored higher than the alternatives for the evening." She grinned up at me.

"What alternatives?" I asked her. What would she be doing this Friday if she weren't with me? Be with Richard, I guessed. "Were you being whisked off to Paris?"

"All right, no need to be sarcastic. I like a night in with Chinese takeout and a Ryan movie."

"A Ryan movie?" I wasn't sure I should ask.

"Reynolds or Gosling. Either of them would do."

I grinned as it took me a second to tune into what she was talking about. "But not Seacrest?"

"Are you kidding? So not my type," she replied as if I'd lost my mind.

What was her type? Movie stars with eight packs? Richard the doctor?

"But as you've brought it up, is Mr. Seacrest *your* type?" she asked. "Is that the real reason you and Emma split?"

I rolled my eyes. She may look like some kind of fantasy goddess but she was still the same old Ash, which was just fine with me—perfect even.

We stopped at the entrance to the ballroom in front of the seating plan. "Come on, we're at table twenty-four."

We entered the vast, soulless room, which was full of chatter. To the side, a stage ran across almost the entire length of the room, and the rest of it was full of round tables of twelve seats each. I'd been to a million of these events, and they didn't get more interesting. At least Ash was here tonight, so I'd have more fun than usual. Somewhere along the road, lawyer Luke had become very serious. I guess the more people relied on you and looked up to you, the less fun you could have.

I made various introductions to Ash at our table. She sat to my right, and on the other side of her was a junior partner from our banking department, Isaac. I didn't know him very well. I hoped he didn't bore her. She thought my job was dull enough; I didn't need to give her more evidence.

We all got seated and I leaned toward her. "Are you okay?" I asked. She seemed jumpy, nervous almost.

"Sure," she said. She wasn't being very convincing.

"I appreciate you coming."

"It's fine. I'm sure I'll enjoy myself."

"I'll make sure you do," Isaac interrupted. "What's a beautiful girl out with this old bore for anyway?" he asked, pointing to me.

Ash laughed. "He's not so bad. He got me out of prison a couple of years back. I owe him."

"Somehow I find that very hard to believe," he said, smiling at her as though he was imagining her naked. "What do you do?"

"I'm a nurse."

"A girl in uniform? My night keeps getting better and better." He winked at her and my irritation rose.

While Isaac was distracted by the waiter, I placed my arm on the back of her chair and leaned in close to her ear. "Do you want to swap seats?" I asked. "You can sit here if you can't see the stage properly."

Ash put her hand on my thigh and goose bumps radiated across my skin. Her dress was having a very bad effect on me. "He's fine," she said, knowing the motive behind my offer only too well. "Fun. And anyway, I can handle myself. What do you think I do when you're not around?"

How could she think he was fine? The guy was a dick, and he wasn't even drunk yet. "If he tries anything, you let me know."

"Okay, dad." She grinned and turned away to answer a question Isaac was asking of her. He wasn't going to monopolize her all evening. I would make sure of that.

The guest to my left, a woman from finance, asked me something about the wine. I tried to be polite, but I was distracted. I wanted to talk to Ash, and I didn't want Isaac anywhere near her.

"You think we'll win?" the woman on my left asked.

"Not a chance. But, what is it they say? 'It's nice to be nominated.'"

"That's bullshit," she said.

I nodded.

I glanced across at Ash and Isaac. He held her hand, her palm facing up, as if he were Madam Zorba about to do a reading. She was laughing. What was he saying to her? Why was he touching her?

I was relieved when we were called to order and the evening began. At least it meant Ash's attention was on the stage and not Isaac. The host was well-known television comic David O'Connor. I watched Ash as she sat engaged by his introduction, laughing at his jokes about how boring lawyers were.

She leaned into me. "It's like he knows you," she said, giggling.

Was that what she thought of me? A boring old lawyer? We had fun together, didn't we? I knew I always had fun when I was with her, but maybe the feeling wasn't mutual.

"I'm not that dull, am I?" I asked. To be heard over the chatter and the comedy act, I shifted my chair closer to hers. I got a waft of her familiar perfume again as I dipped my head to her ear. I reached across and moved her hair from her neck, exposing her delicate skin. Her eyes flitted to mine, and I thought I could see a blush color her cheek. I shouldn't be touching her like that. It wasn't something we did. I mean, we hugged and comforted each other, but we'd never touched in a way that was undeniably . . . sexual.

It felt forbidden.

She leaned away from me, and my stomach flipped at the thought I'd stepped over some line that we'd created decades before.

Ashleigh

My skin burned beneath the skim of Luke's fingers across my neck. Had he meant to touch me like that?

It had been a bad idea, coming tonight. I needed space, but I couldn't ever say no to him. I didn't need to be reminded of how much he made me laugh, how I could just be me around him, and how he seemed to like it. I certainly didn't need to be reminded about how good he looked in a tux. Some guys could just pull that off, and he was one of them. His frame was tall and broad, like something out of a Tom Ford advert—it was built to wear a tux. It should be mandatory for men like him. When I'd first seen him tonight I couldn't help but straighten his already straight bow tie. However much I resisted, I was drawn to him.

The guy on the other side of me, Isaac, was being very attentive and I was trying to concentrate on what he was saying. He was attractive, though not as naturally handsome as Luke. I let myself enjoy his attention a little. I tried to focus on him rather than Luke, who was sitting so close to me, looking like he did, feeling like he did.

"How long have you been with Luke?" Isaac topped up my wine glass. I was already light-headed. I shouldn't drink anymore.

I smiled. "We're not together. We're old friends." *He sees me as a sister*, I almost said. But I didn't *feel* like his sister, and he hadn't touched me in a brotherly way.

"So you're doing him a favor by being here. That's nice of you. He's a lucky guy. And a stupid one, if you've only ever been friends."

"Luke isn't stupid, but we've only ever been friends. And hey, it's not such a big favor. I'm having a nice evening."

"Well, he's done me a huge favor, introducing me to you. I feel like the luckiest man here tonight, sitting next such a beautiful girl."

I smiled. Isaac had a few cheesy lines, but they very obviously covered up a sweet guy. I'd dated a lot worse.

"Are you seeing anyone?" Isaac asked. I felt Luke's hand on my thigh, as if he wanted to interrupt.

"I just broke up with my boyfriend a couple of weeks ago," I replied. "Excuse me," I said as I turned to Luke.

He was frowning at me as I looked at him. "You split with Richard?" he asked. "Why didn't you say anything?"

"Because last time I saw you, you told me you and Emma were finished, and my breakup didn't seem very significant. I forgot."

"Nothing that happens in your life is insignificant to me." My stomach tilted at his words. I wished he meant them differently. "Are you okay?"

"Yeah, I'm fine. We weren't right." I had barely thought about Richard since the last time I'd seen him.

"You ended it?" he asked.

"Yeah. I didn't see any point in staying together if I knew we weren't really suited."

"He wasn't the one?" His eyes fixed on mine.

I blinked then held his gaze. "No." It was almost a whisper.

Luke's brow creased and he looked away. "Do you think I should have ended things with Emma sooner?"

I shrugged. "Only you know that."

"But you know me better than almost anyone," he said, and for a moment I wished it weren't the case. It would be so much easier if he were just my best friend's brother.

"That may be true, but I don't know what you want in a woman. I don't know what holds your attention." I was playing with fire.

His gaze drifted to my lips and then back to my eyes. I could see words start to run through his head—they had almost left his mouth when our table erupted with applause. The people we were seated with, including Isaac, were hugging each other and clapping their hands together. I glanced back to Luke, who was being slapped on the back by a guy on the table next to ours. They must have won.

Champagne corks started popping and Isaac thrust a drink into my hand. He clinked my glass. "This turned out to be a great evening. Maybe you're my lucky charm." he said. "I shouldn't let you out of my sight."

I smiled at him. "So, what happens now? People just get drunk? Or should I say drunker?"

"That and some dancing. Tell me you'll dance with me when the band starts?" he asked.

"I'm not much of a dancer. We'll see."

"Sounds like a promise to me," he replied. "Excuse me for a moment, I've just seen someone I need to say hello to." Isaac left the table.

I felt a hand on my upper arm, and I turned toward Luke. "You seem to have made quite the impression on him," he said, his gaze sweeping between my eyes and my lips. I didn't know how to respond. "But don't dance with him," he said softly.

It felt heavy between us, as if there were words all around us that we weren't saying. I needed air. I needed *us* back. I raised my eyebrows. "You don't want me to dance? Afraid I'll embarrass you?" I asked, playfully elbowing him in the waist, trying to dispel the tension between us, surrounding us, encircling us.

The band started up with a slow, soulful song that seemed slightly at odds with the party atmosphere in the room.

"No, it's not that. I just . . . I just don't want you to. If you're going to dance with anyone, it should be me."

I tried to keep my smile even. "What do you mean 'should'?"

"I don't know." He held out his hand, and I took it tentatively. "Come on," he said as he led me across the room to the dance floor.

I'd never danced with Luke. Come to think of it, I couldn't remember the last time I'd slow danced with a guy. High school, probably. I wasn't sure I could remember how. Thankfully, the dance floor quickly became busy, and Luke guided us through the couples to the far end, away from the tables.

"So, how do we do this?" he asked as we stood facing each other.

I laughed, relaxing at the fact that his thoughts were so similar to my own. "I really have no idea. We can go and sit back down if you like."

He bent to hear me, and his hands circled my waist. Sparks went off across my body. I reached up, pushing my palms up his chest to his shoulders.

"No," he said. "I want to dance with you."

He watched my face for reaction but I looked away. I couldn't let him see that I wanted to dance with him too. His hands slid up my back and he pressed me against him. My heart was racing; I wasn't used to this amount of physical contact with him. My whole body was touching his as we swayed in time to the music.

Luke bent his head to my ear so our cheeks were touching. "Are we doing this right?" he asked.

I didn't know how to respond.

"It feels right," he said.

It felt too good. I shouldn't have let this situation get so out of hand. I had had far too much to drink and now I was here, in Luke's arms, tricking myself into thinking what I was feeling was mutual. I should stop, push him away. I should go home. At the end of this dance, that's what I would do. I had spent the last few months trying to close off my heart to Luke, and doing a pretty good job, and now here he was opening up old wounds.

"You look beautiful tonight. I mean, bombshell beautiful," he whispered.

I should make him stop saying these things. He was feeding my addiction to him.

"What are you thinking?" he asked when I didn't respond. His hands roamed down to my waist then slid up my back again.

"I think I like dancing with you more than I should," I replied. His lips brushed my neck, but in the mayhem of sensations assaulting me, maybe I imagined it.

The song ended, and I started to pull away. "Not yet," he said. "Can we stay here, like this, for a bit longer? I don't want to go back."

Those words had more meaning than he'd intended, didn't they? What did he mean *like this*? Like Ash and Luke—lifelong friends—but closer, touching, on the brink of something?

chapter
EIGHT

Luke

She felt so good. *This* felt so good, so right. Did she feel it too? I didn't want to be here anymore. I wanted it to be just Ash and me. I didn't want to talk to all these people who were part of my working life. Ash was my real life.

The music changed to something more up-tempo. She pulled back again, and this time I let her. "Wanna get out of here?" I asked.

"Are you sure you don't want to stay and celebrate your win?"

"Have you still got that tequila you brought back from Mexico at your place?" I asked.

"Yeah, I think so."

"Let's go and have a celebratory shot."

She grinned, and we headed out, my hand at the small of her back. I didn't want to lose contact with her, not for a second. We didn't stop to say we were leaving; we just headed to the exit, found a cab. I was nervous. I'd been to Ash's place a million times, but tonight was different. Tonight, she wasn't just Ash my best friend, she was Ash the bombshell. Ash who I had slow danced with. Ash who I'd almost kissed. Ash who I *wanted* to kiss.

"So, thanks for inviting me tonight," she said, almost as if she was trying to find something to say.

"I'm really pleased you came," I said. I meant it.

"I'll be your fill-in date anytime." She grinned at me. She was so beautiful. The light collected around her, making her glow.

I took a beat just to savor that incredible smile. "You'll never be that, Ash." Her eyes narrowed, just slightly. If I hadn't known her, I wouldn't have noticed. "You're no-one's understudy."

"I just meant—"

"I didn't invite you tonight because Emma and I'd split—I asked you before that happened. I asked you because there was no one I'd rather spend an evening with." I meant it.

She didn't respond, so I searched her face to see if she'd understood. I found a mixture of confusion and apprehension on her face. Was I coming on too strong? Did she not feel this?

The cab pulled up to her building before I got a chance to ask her. I followed her into the night air and into her building. We were silent in the lift. Every atom of my body wanted to pull her toward me, but I resisted. I didn't want to scare her. I'd hate to spoil our friendship if she didn't feel the same way. I couldn't live without her in my life in one way or another—but in that moment I wanted her to be my whole life.

"So, tequila," she said as she flung her bag on the hall table, kicked off her shoes and made her way to the kitchen.

I followed her, pulled out two shot glasses from the cupboard above the refrigerator and then grabbed limes, quickly cutting them into slices. I knew her kitchen almost better than I knew the one I'd shared with Emma. Ash produced the tequila and the salt, and we settled ourselves in the living room, sitting on the rug, our ingredients set out in front of us on the coffee table.

We exchanged glances, as if we knew we were at the starting line. I raised the tequila bottle as a question and she nodded.

"We should do a truth or a dare before every shot," she announced.

I grinned. Perfect.

"You start," she said.

I carefully poured out the shots, trying to formulate a question that would open the door without scaring her off. "Did you find Isaac attractive?" I asked. I wanted to know the answer. What was her type? Was it Richard? Isaac?

Me?

She frowned and regarded me carefully. "He's good looking," she said as my heart sped up. It wasn't the answer I'd wanted. "And funny, which is important. I guess a little." Jealousy gnawed at my gut and I tried to take a deep breath without her noticing.

"Do you have a type?" I asked. My attention was focused on her lithe legs as she shifted to sit cross-legged in front of me.

"Hey, you can't have two questions in a row. Do your shot."

I grinned, licked the back of my hand, poured on the salt and did my shot. I felt Ash's gaze on me. What was she thinking? I closed my eyes as the tequila burned a trail down my throat. What was she going to ask me?

I watched as she refilled my glass. "Your turn," I said.

She ran her index finger across her bottom lip as she considered her question. Blood sped to my cock at the thought of her mouth on me.

"What do you want me to ask you?"

I held her gaze. She was clever. She'd asked me a question without asking me a question. She was holding back, and I understood that. This was new, shaky territory that we were in. The corners of my mouth twitched.

"Ask me something . . . intimate."

Did her breath catch?

She searched for the salt, and I picked it up as she reached for it. Instead of giving it to her, I took her hand, turning it to expose her palm. I leaned forward and licked a line across her wrist. She tasted as sweet as she smelled, and I had to hold myself back from pinning her to the floor and devouring her whole. Her eyes were fixed to mine and her mouth was parted. I poured salt across the wet mark I'd made, but didn't let go of her hand.

Slowly she bent her head, her tongue echoing the path I'd just made, and reluctantly I let go of her hand. She threw back her shot.

Keeping her eyes on mine, she licked her fingers free of lime juice.

"Your turn," she said, shifting forward, her dress revealing the curve of her breast. I had to suppress a moan. She was so fucking beautiful.

"When you put on that dress tonight, did you want me to notice you?"

She looked away and whispered, "I always want you to notice me."

My stomach flipped. She was raising the stakes. Quickly, I did my shot. I wanted to know what was next.

"Why are you here?" she asked, looking directly at me.

It was a good question. The ultimate question. Why was I there? I was there to risk everything. I could fob her off. Tell her we were celebrating, rather than mention how I wanted to spend every last moment of this evening with her. It was as though this urge to be with her had broken free within me and now was overwhelming my every thought, my every action.

"Because I want to kiss you," I said. It had been true since I'd first seen her in that dress; it just wasn't the whole truth.

Her cheeks flushed, and she looked away. "All of a sudden?" she asked, suspicion in her voice.

"Hey, you can't have two questions in a row. Do your shot," I said, using her words against her. "Do you want me to help?"

"I think I can manage this time."

I needed her to digest what I'd said. I wanted to give her time to think about whether or not she wanted to kiss me. Would I have to convince her to kiss me back?

Without sparing me a single glance, she went through the tequila ritual, squeezing her eyes shut at the burn of the alcohol.

"My turn." My heart was beating through my chest. "So you have to tell me the truth, whatever it is," I said, reminding her that there would be no way out of this question. She nodded. "Do you want me to kiss you?"

She looked away as if I'd wounded her. "Luke," she said. "You can't ask me that." Her voice was soft, sad even.

"Why?" I was genuinely confused.

"Because you know the answer," she said.

"I do?" Maybe I did. Maybe there had always been something beneath the joking and the teasing that felt true.

"You know that I've wanted you to kiss me since forever. I might joke about us, but it doesn't mean that I'm not serious."

My heart clenched at her honesty. It was one of the many things I loved about her. We didn't need to play truth or dare. Every conversation with Ash was honest.

I took a deep breath. This was it. This was the point of no return. I downed my shot of tequila. No salt, no lime. "You're beautiful." I leaned forward, my hand on the back of her neck.

"Luke," she whispered. It was half warning me away, half calling me home.

I was close enough to feel her breath against my lips. I moved forward and pressed my mouth against hers. She was soft and open, and I pushed my tongue into her mouth, wanting to taste more of her, all of her.

Ashleigh

Luke was kissing me.

Luke was kissing me! I felt it in every inch of my body. I wasn't quite sure how we ended up that way. All I knew was how right it felt, how it was as I'd always imagined it would be—perfect. He was strong and firm and eager—so eager—as if he'd forgotten it was me. As though he'd forgotten our history and all the complications that this kiss brought. Everything disappeared with the press of his lips.

He let out a small, contented sigh and pulled away from me slightly. "You're so beautiful," he whispered. It was what I'd always wanted to hear from him, but now I had, it didn't seem real somehow.

"Is that the tequila talking?" I asked softly, confused by what seemed such a sudden change of heart. Luke pulled back even more and moved to sit on the sofa. I'd ruined the moment, broken the spell. But then he held out his hand to me. I took it, and he coaxed me onto his lap.

He stroked my back as he buried his head in my neck. "No . . . I don't know. I think it's been building for a while, and I've only now noticed. I was surprised that I didn't really like you dating Richard. I couldn't figure out why it bothered me, and then tonight, when I saw you, I realized."

"Realized?" I asked.

He brushed the hair from my neck and bent to kiss it. "Yeah, that I wanted to kiss you."

It wasn't much of an explanation, but my brain was foggy with confusion and lust and tequila. My body bowed toward his as if I were under his total control. He trailed kisses down my collarbone. Did I need to know everything, right at this second? As if answering my question, his mouth met mine again, his tongue running along the seam of my lips. Did he feel what I was feeling? I reached for him. Completed our connection. I never wanted to let him go.

My hands roamed across his chest. I'd always imagined what it would feel like, but he was harder than I had expected, more defined. He shifted underneath me and groaned. I stilled for a moment, wondering briefly if I shouldn't be touching him. "Don't stop," he whispered, and he moved me off his lap and pushed me down on the sofa, crawling over me.

He kneed my legs apart and looked at me before diving for my mouth again. I could feel him properly now. He was hard against my thigh. He wanted me. In a way I never thought he would, he wanted me. This had been building in me for fifteen years, but somehow it had all happened so fast. It was nothing I'd expected.

"Jesus, you taste so good, Ash. How did I not know you tasted like this?" he asked, pressing kisses between my breasts.

My skin heated everywhere he touched. His words, his fingers, his lips—they all conspired to pull me under. It felt so good—almost too good.

"Luke," I said softly. He didn't seem to hear me. "Luke," I repeated. I put my hands on either side of his face.

He looked at me, his eyes burning.

"What are we doing?" I asked.

He dropped a kiss on my lips then moved to my side. With his leg slung over mine, he propped his head up on his hand. "You don't want this?" he asked as he trailed his hand up and down my body.

"Yes, of course, but . . ."

"But you wonder what happens next: Will we still be friends? What will Haven say? Will it be good?"

I smiled at him. "Yeah. That's pretty much it."

He nodded. "That's all I've been thinking about all night. Well, in between wondering how you'd taste, what it would feel like to be buried in you and what you look like when you come."

"Luke," I said, embarrassed.

"I can't help it. It's like someone's opened a door, and I've stepped through to this different world. There's no going back."

I placed my hand on my chest to try to calm my heart. "Do you think we should slow down?" I asked. We were moving quickly, and soon we would be at a point where things would change forever.

"Whatever you want. I don't want to push you into anything. My heart and my groin are saying one thing, but maybe my brain is in synch with yours."

"I'm pretty sure our groins are in agreement, too," I said with a laugh.

Luke grinned at me. "You have the most fantastic smile. I've always thought so."

"Let's make a promise that whatever happens tonight, we make sure we're always family."

"That's non-negotiable as far as I'm concerned," he said with that sexy grin that had made my insides melt since forever.

"Then kiss me." I was giving him, and myself, permission to cross the line of no return.

I could tell by the way he looked at me that he knew what I was saying. He searched my face, maybe to find a trace of doubt, but I knew there wasn't any. He stood and held out his hand to me. The nerves in my stomach danced as I took it. He led me down the corridor to my bedroom.

What if it wasn't good? What if he had some weird kink I couldn't get into? What happened if my body didn't respond to him the way my mind did?

"Are you nervous?" he asked as we stepped inside my bedroom.

"A little," I replied, breathlessly.

He swept a hand down my back then pulled me toward him. "Me too," he said. I'd never known Luke to be nervous about anything. Could he be nervous about being with me?

Our bodies were pressed against each other. I reached for the buttons of his shirt, methodically undoing the first, the second. I steadied my breathing then tackled the third. I trailed my finger down his exposed skin, eliciting a sharp intake of breath. I loved that I could do that to him.

He trailed his fingers round my neck and pushed the shoulders of my dress off. The fabric was loose, and as I put my arms to my sides, it just slipped off my body and pooled at my feet. I watched Luke, his eyes growing wider as they flitted across my body. He looked away and took a breath.

"You're so beautiful. I don't know where to start." He brushed my cheek with his knuckle. I finished unbuttoning his shirt. He was straining through his pants. I was desperate to get to what was next. Before I started on his zipper, I palmed him through the tight fabric and he groaned, his hands going to my shoulders.

"Jesus, Ash. I . . ." He moved me toward the bed and pushed me gently back. "Lie down. I want to taste you while I get a grip on myself."

I lay back on the bed, lifting my bottom to allow him to remove my underwear. He knelt by the bed and held my thighs wide. There was no room for self-consciousness. He knew me better than anyone in my life other than Haven. Him seeing me like this felt totally right.

His tongue seemed to know my body even better than his mind did, and as it circled my clitoris, I was lost. I arched off the bed, and Luke slid his hands under my ass and pulled me toward him, intensifying the pressure, the pleasure. I cried out his name, a prayer; I had no idea. I had lost control over my mind, body and heart.

chapter
NINE

Luke

Watching her body shudder with the aftershocks of the orgasm I'd just given her made me feel like a fucking god. She was so perfect. Perfect for me. I'd been an idiot, not seeing it all these years. I think I'd always known, but there had been some kind of invisible barrier keeping me away.

I stood over her, as she recovered from her first orgasm of the evening. I couldn't wait to get her to the next one. I quickly undressed, my hard-on verging on painful, soothed only by the thought of being inside her.

"Fuck," I said, suddenly remembering I didn't have any condoms.

Ash snapped her head up to look at me.

"I didn't bring any condoms. Do you have any?" I asked.

She shook her head. I collapsed on my back on the bed. This couldn't be happening. It was a promise I'd made to myself when I was seventeen that I would never have sex without protection. It was one of the last pieces of advice my father had given me before he'd died. He'd told me that

I needed to do everything I could to prevent my girlfriend from getting pregnant—or worse. It was good advice that I'd followed with no exceptions. Not even with Emma.

We lay next to each other. Would not using anything with Ash be the wrong thing to do? If Ash got pregnant, how would I react? Panic didn't sweep over me like it did when Emma talked about marriage and children, but maybe it was lust keeping those feelings at bay.

"I've never . . ." she said. "I'm on the pill."

It was all the encouragement I needed. "I've never, not once. Not with anyone. I'm safe. Are you sure?"

She smiled and nodded. I moved my body over hers and bent to kiss her, slowly, patiently, my tongue exploring her mouth. Her hands gripped my ass and her nails sank into my flesh.

"Jesus, I need to be inside you."

She opened her legs in response, inviting me in. I positioned myself at her entrance, desperate to feel her around me, but at the same time I wanted this delicious torture to go on forever. She thrust her hips forward.

"Patience," I teased her.

"Oh, I think I've been patient long enough," she said.

I sank into her slowly, inch by inch, reveling in the sensation of heat between us. I had to still when I got as deep as I could go. I needed to empty my head of the reality of what was between us, what was happening. If I didn't, this would be over too quickly, and I *never* wanted this to be over.

I started to move out of her slowly, watching her, wanting to see what she was feeling by looking at her beautiful face.

Her mouth formed a perfect "O" as I dragged my flesh against hers.

"Ash," I whispered.

"You feel so good," she replied.

I responded by slamming back into her. I couldn't stop myself. My body had overtaken my head. I needed to fuck her.

Small noises I'd never heard her make before slipped from her lips. The Ash underneath me was someone I'd never known before. I pushed my face into her neck and licked, wanting to taste the sheen developing on her skin. It was like nectar, and I bit down wanting more of it. She clenched around me, and I groaned as I dragged myself out of her. I was so hard, so close, so ready, but I wanted her there again, with me this time. I didn't know how her body worked yet. I didn't know what her turn-ons were. I grinned at the thought that I would be learning all of them very soon.

Without breaking our contact, I leaned back on my knees, lifting her ass to rest on my thighs. I ran my hands down her body, pinching one nipple, then the other, interrupting the movement of her breasts as they shifted in time with my thrusts. I wouldn't be able to hold myself back for long. My palm smoothed across her taut stomach, then lower until my thumb found her clitoris. She moaned as she flung her hands over her head, grabbing at the pillows behind her.

"Is that what you like?" I asked. "You like me to rub you while I'm fucking you?"

Her breaths were short and tight, and our eyes locked together as her mouth opened a fraction wider, giving me my answer.

"More, please God, more," she said breathlessly.

"I want you to come for me," I said as I increased my pace.

"Please, more," she replied. She looked so fucking beautiful—undone, open, mine.

I thrust harder and faster, gritting my teeth, trying to stop myself from falling before her. Then she was there; her back arched and she shuddered. And all the while her eyes were fixed on mine. I emptied myself into her, coming so strongly I thought I might pass out—a combination of the exertion and the ecstasy.

I collapsed on top of her and then moved to the side, pulling her closer. She was precious, like an abandoned treasure I'd finally found. I never wanted to let her go. I was still panting as I pressed my lips to her temple. "You're amazing."

We lay there, our breathing returning to normal, until Ash tried to move out of my arms. I pulled her closer.

"I need to go to the bathroom," she said.

"Don't be long," I said, not wanting to lose contact with her for a second. I would have followed her if she wouldn't think I was a total lunatic. "Water?" I asked and she nodded.

I came back to the bedroom from the kitchen with two glasses of water at the same time Ash returned wearing a t-shirt.

"What are you wearing?" I asked.

"A Wonder Woman costume. What does it look like I'm wearing?" She sounded as if she thought I was crazy.

"We can try that tomorrow. In fact, I insist we try that tomorrow," I replied and she rolled her eyes. "I mean, why do you have clothes on? I want you naked in my arms."

She looked at me coyly, and I reached for the hem of her shirt. She didn't resist as she lifted her arms so I could strip it off. "And underwear?" I asked, incredulous. "Off," I said.

She giggled and kicked off her panties and crawled under the sheets, and I followed. I pulled her to me, and she lay in the crook of my arm, her head resting on my shoulder. She smoothed her hand down my chest, and I felt myself harden again. Jesus, I was like a teenager.

"Do you feel weird?" she asked. I felt anything but weird. "No."

"But it's *us*, Luke. We're friends."

"We're best friends, and no, I don't feel weird. I feel stupid for not making a move on you sooner. What about you?" I asked.

She trailed her fingers over my chest, then lower where she found me hard and ready for her again. She circled my cock with her fist, dragging it up with the perfect amount of pressure.

"I don't think you feel weird," I whispered. "Tell me what you're feeling. Tell me what you want me to do to you."

She looked up at me, heat simmering in her eyes. "I want you to fuck me from behind. Hard."

I groaned at her words and rolled her onto her back, dipping my lips to hers. "Such a dirty mouth," I whispered between kisses.

I held myself above her. "Turn over." She twisted so she was lying on her stomach. I put my knees on either side of her and swept her hair from her neck. "Put your arms out and don't move," I said. She did as I asked, surrendering to me. I wasn't done kissing her. My mouth found her neck and then wandered across her shoulder blades. I licked down her spine to the small of her back. Her skin was so smooth, so perfect. My tongue trailed lower to the dimples just above her ass, and I smoothed my hands over her buttocks. Her ass was rounded and soft. I pulled her cheeks apart, and she squirmed beneath me and tried to look back at what I was doing.

"What—"

"Shhh. Lay back down." I blew across the exposed skin and she groaned. "Has anyone had you here?" I asked.

"No," she whimpered.

I tightened at the thought of being the first to claim her ass. Not today, but soon. I needed to be inside her quickly. I pulled back. "Get on all fours," I said and she scrambled to her knees. Her nipples had beaded and her breathing was shallow and quick—she was ready for me.

Without warning, I plunged into her.

"Luke!" Her hands gripped the sheets as her head dropped, and I thrust in again.

"You like this? You like it hard, baby?" I reached for her shoulders and clamped my hands over them, ensuring that I went deep every time I pushed into her.

"Yes, just like that." Her voice was bumpy and weak, as though her energy was somewhere else.

She was so tight, and I got so deep it was perfect. I picked up the pace, trying not to concentrate on the noises she was making. The sounds coming from her made me feel as though there was no one who could do this to her. It made me feel powerful, as if I owned her.

She clenched hard, milking my cock. "Jesus. Fucking. Christ," I shouted as her arms collapsed from under her as she gave in to her climax. As soon as I knew she was there, I let go, losing all sense of what I was doing.

I collapsed on top of her, feeling as if I'd run a marathon. My hands found hers, and I interlaced our fingers, wanting to stay as connected to her as I could.

Ashleigh

Sleep must have claimed us at some point because I woke up in the crook of Luke's arm to his gentle snoring. I glanced at the clock. We'd been up most of the night. I snuck to the bathroom, and as I got back into bed, he reached for me in his sleep. Did he know who he was reaching for? Did he think I was Emma? My gut churned at the thought, and I avoided his arms.

He turned toward me and opened his eyes. "Ash, come here."

I smiled, both at him wanting me close and at my silly assumption. He knew it was me. I got back into bed and let myself be enveloped in his arms.

"I'm going to need to get in the shower in a minute," I said. Spooning, I couldn't see his face.

"Sounds like a great idea," he said. "And then we can come back to bed."

"No." I giggled. "I need to go and get Mrs. Malcolm her shopping." Mrs. Malcolm lived on the ground floor, and although she still managed to get around, she found it difficult to carry groceries.

"Are you still doing that?" he asked.

"Yeah, a few of us take it in turns."

"Why do you have to be such a good person? I want you to stay in bed with me all day."

I laughed. "You can help and then when we're done we can . . . do other stuff." Was he going to stay with me the whole day? Were we a thing now?

"Other stuff is my favorite kind of stuff."

I playfully kicked his shin behind me. "You sound dirty."

"I feel dirty. I'm naked—you're naked. I've got a hard-on the size of the Great Wall of China."

"You wish," I teased.

"I don't actually. I think a hard-on that size would be fucking inconvenient." Luke's tone was serious, as though he was properly considering the practicalities of having a dick that big.

"You're a total geek."

"Speaking of, we also need to find you a Wonder Woman costume."

"No, we really don't. And don't you have plans today?" I asked, surprised that he seemed to be planning to spend the day with me.

"Are you trying to get rid of me? Because if you are, it's not happening. I'm not leaving you on your own to freak out. Do you think I'm crazy? I'm going to be here when you have your meltdown. I'll pour you wine and feed you chocolate, and then we'll have sex and it will all be fine." He grinned at me as if he knew that I wanted to punch him.

"I'm sorry, what was all that? What meltdown?"

"The meltdown you're overdue to have about us and this," he said, his hands circling my body.

I pushed against his chest, trying to create some distance between us, irritated with how sure he was about himself—and how right he might be about me. He just pulled me closer and kissed the top of my head.

"You wanna talk about it?" he asked.

"No." *Yes.*

"You're a crappy liar."

I sighed. "It's all happened so fast," I said.

"Not really. I didn't properly realize until last night, but I think it's always been there between us."

"From my side," I corrected him.

"No, not from just your side. From mine too. Except you were young, and I knew that when it happened, it would really happen and I'd be done for. I wasn't ready."

"And that's another thing. You and Emma. I mean, you only just split. I don't want to be your rebound girl."

"Cue meltdown," he said, chuckling.

I kicked him in the shin and he just clamped my legs between his.

"Emma and I have been done a long time. I should have told her sooner. I'm just not good with change—you know that. And I loved her, I really did, in my way. But not enough. There was something missing between us."

"I'm sorry," I said. I hated him being upset. Whether or not it was with me, I wanted him to be happy.

"Don't be. Whatever happened led us here, and I can't think of anywhere I'd rather be."

"Luke," I said, moved by what he'd said.

"Do I need to be worried about being your rebound guy after Richard?" he asked.

"No, he was the guy I dated to get over you."

"Really?" he asked.

I realized what I'd said, and my cheeks flushed with embarrassment. "Maybe a little."

"Did it work?"

I raised an eyebrow at him. "Apparently not."

He squeezed me closer, and I relaxed into him.

"So, shower, Mrs. Malcolm's shopping, Wonder Woman costume, back here?" he asked. "Do you want to have dinner out, or shall we stay in?"

"Maybe I had plans tonight. It is Saturday night," I said.

"Do you? If you do, that's fine. I can go back to Haven's, but don't tell me you have plans if you don't. Now we're more than, whatever we were, don't be the one to start playing games. If we're going to make this work, we need to take the best of our history and make it better."

He was right. "I'm sorry."

"Don't be sorry. I want to know what you want. If you want me here, I'm here. If you don't, I'm gone."

I clutched at him. The idea of him being gone was awful. "I want you here. Always. I'm just—I thought I was allowed a meltdown?"

"You totally are, but that doesn't mean I'm not going to call you on it. So, we're going to try this? I want to explore this with you, Ashleigh. Do you feel the same?"

How could he think that I could possibly say no to him? I looked up at him and nodded. "Yes."

He trailed his tongue across the seam of my lips. "Good answer."

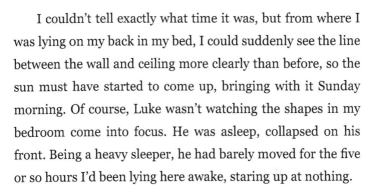

I couldn't tell exactly what time it was, but from where I was lying on my back in my bed, I could suddenly see the line between the wall and ceiling more clearly than before, so the sun must have started to come up, bringing with it Sunday morning. Of course, Luke wasn't watching the shapes in my bedroom come into focus. He was asleep, collapsed on his front. Being a heavy sleeper, he had barely moved for the five or so hours I'd been lying here awake, staring up at nothing.

There was a reason why people said that things always felt different in the morning. Most of the time, it was said to give comfort. For me, it felt anything but comfortable. My overdue meltdown had finally started to take hold.

It was Sunday and the bubble for two that we had occupied since Friday night was about to pop, and we were going to have to let the real world in. We were going to have to face Haven, and the reality of what we'd put at risk covered me like a cloud.

I felt stupid for thinking this could be easy. Luke had broken up with Emma a nanosecond ago. He wasn't in the right frame of mind to be making decisions about a potential new relationship. He didn't like change, and perhaps reaching for me had just been a way of giving himself comfort. He couldn't have been seeing things clearly.

I covered my face with my hands. What had I been thinking? Haven, if forced to choose, would always pick her brother, and then I would lose not just my love, but my family.

My stomach churned. How could I have been so reckless to put so much at risk?

This was going to be so hard; it was almost impossible that something between us could do anything but fail. But now that I'd tasted the promise of something, it was worse than if I'd never known what was possible. Luke's feelings for me weren't fifteen years old. This wouldn't break him as it could me.

I wasn't sure I could be with him.

But I wasn't sure I could ever get over him.

chapter TEN

Luke

Even though this was only the second morning of waking up with Ashleigh next to me, I knew it was something I could never tire of. Waking with that sweet, sexy smell of hers, the feel of her smooth, flawless skin heating mine supersized my hard-on. I groaned and moved to my side. Grabbing her, I pulled her toward me and buried my face in her hair.

"Morning, gorgeous." I shifted her hips so she faced away from me then skirted my hand over her flat stomach. She relaxed and melted into my body. God, we fit perfectly. I hooked her leg up over mine and cupped my fingers over her sex.

"Luke," she whispered, gently circling against my hand.

"Did I wake you?"

She shook her head, and I propped myself up so I could see her face. She didn't look sleepy; she looked incredible, her hair fussy and her skin already starting to flush. I began to move my thumb over her clit.

"That's not fair," she said.

"Making you feel good isn't fair? I know you like this. I'm coming to understand your body as well as I do the rest of you."

She closed her eyes and sighed as if she was giving in, and I started to rock my hips against the cleft of her buttocks. Jesus, she felt good any way I could get her.

"Luke," she whispered again.

"Ashleigh," I replied in the same wistful tone.

I dipped my fingers into her folds, coating them in her slick softness. Jesus, she was more than ready. She widened her legs. "Yes, please." She sighed.

"Yes?"

She reached behind and grabbed my hips, fingers digging into my ass.

"Tell me," I said. "Tell me what you want."

"I want you inside me, please."

"Tell me more." I loved her dirty words. They slipped from her as if they were just below the surface, ready to break free. They were a reminder of how the Ashleigh I'd known for so long wasn't the whole girl. That the one lying beside me, begging for sex, was the entire package—in more ways than one.

"I want you to fuck me and never stop. I want to feel your dick in me. Please. Now."

I slid inside her, right up to the hilt. That I'd managed to hold back so long was a miracle.

Her fingernails bit into my forearm, then receded as she got used to me. Blood rushed to my cock at the thought of being almost too big for her.

"Just like that," she said.

I started to move behind her, pulling out slowly and then thrusting in hard, the way I knew she liked it. My thumb changed direction, circling over her clit, and she clasped my wrist.

"No, it's too much; it's too good. I'm too close, too soon."

I groaned at the fact that I could make her body mine so quickly. I released my thumb. I needed a few more seconds like this, on the brink of climax. Feeling her come around me would send me over the edge.

She reached behind me, grasping at my ass, urging me deeper, harder. I pulled her leg open wider, wanting to get as far into her as I could. Fuck. This was the perfect way to wake up. Every day. Forever.

Her hand slid over her sex. I'd not seen her touch herself, and I closed my eyes, committing the image to memory. Her fingers, slick with lubrication, pulled at my balls, sending sparks of pleasure up my spine. Jesus, she was wicked. I began to thrust harder.

"I want to stay inside you forever." It was an effort to speak. My mind was so focused on how I felt, how I was making her feel, that my words were labored.

Her hand covered mine and brought my fingers back to her sex. She was ready. I dipped my thumb over the nub of nerves, and she rocked against the pressure.

"Yes, God yes." Her voice was husky, the way it got before she spiraled.

I picked up my rhythm, pushing into her, replacing my thumb with my fingers as she writhed beneath me. Sweat trickled down my back as I tried to pull out her orgasm before surrendering to mine. I wasn't going to be able to hold back much longer. I increased the pressure on her clit. She cried out and her body stiffened.

She reached for my head, and I bent and grazed my lips against hers in a sloppy half-kiss. I clasped her hips with my fingers and pushed into her again and again, allowing myself to drown in the remnants of her orgasm, stealing them, taking them as my pleasure. The feeling in my spine intensified, took me over, and I emptied into her.

I hadn't even stopped moving in and out of her before I began to harden again. Once wasn't enough with her.

"Again, baby?" she asked.

"Always. I never want to stop."

"How do you make it so good?"

"It's all about you. What your body does to me." It was such a turn on that every part of her responded to me as if she needed me.

She shifted beneath me, and although I couldn't bear the thought of not being inside her, the thought of her on all fours gave me the strength to move. She felt the urgency too as she flipped onto her stomach and drew herself up to her knees. Jesus, she was made to pose like that, as if she was just waiting for my dick.

"Put it back in, please," she begged, and then I was over her, my chest against her back, right up to the hilt again.

"Is that good?" I asked, teasing her. I knew by her bent head and the sheets fisted in her hands that it was good. I stilled, waiting on an answer.

"Don't stop," she whimpered. "Please, never, yes." I couldn't hold back. I stabbed my hips against her ass.

Having her felt urgent, desperate, primal. My fingers pulled at her hips, my thumbs pressing into the delicate flesh of her ass. I banged against her again and again, deeper and deeper.

Jesus, yes, I wanted to stay just like this forever.

"Look at me, Ashleigh." I needed to see her eyes, watch the effect of my cock on her face.

She turned her head slowly, as if it were made of lead. Her eyes were hooded and her mouth parted. She looked at me as her tongue circled her lips, leaving a glistening trail. I couldn't stop the groan that ripped from my chest.

"I need you to get there," I choked just as her back arched, and she screamed my name over and over.

My final thrusts pushed her over and into the mattress, and I collapsed on top of her, our breaths sharp and uneven.

Ashleigh had taken me over. She had given me a taste of something that I never knew existed.

Ashleigh

Luke and I managed to pull ourselves out of bed—a good thing, as I risked not being able to walk for a week if we didn't—and arrived for Sunday night dinner with Haven and Jake. I could still feel the after effects of Luke between my thighs, across my skin as we made our way to their apartment.

Arriving together was unusual but not unheard of, so I didn't expect Haven to be immediately suspicious. Still, I wanted to tell her what was going on. For one thing, I failed to keep anything a secret from her for long, and for another she'd be devastated if she put the pieces together herself and realized we'd kept it from her.

After a sleepless night of worry, and a morning of thought-erasing orgasms, I'd convinced Luke to let me tell her while he and Jake watched TV.

"Hey guys, good timing," Haven said as she answered the door. "How are you doing?" she asked Luke. "Did you work things out?" Luke had texted Haven to say he wouldn't be staying with them on Friday and Saturday night, but he hadn't told her where he was going to be. She'd obviously assumed that he'd gone back to Emma. My stomach churned. Why had she been so quick to think that's where he'd end up? Was that relationship as over as Luke seemed to think it was? Maybe Haven thought a reconciliation between Luke and Emma would be a good thing.

Luke deflected the question. "Where's Jake?"

"I love your little bromance. Go see your friend. He's in his study."

Luke leaned toward me as if to kiss me. My horror must have shown on my face as he stopped himself and started to chuckle.

"Be quick," he whispered.

"What?" Haven asked.

I shrugged.

I didn't see any wine on the counter. "Haven't you opened a bottle yet?" I asked as I looked inside the refrigerator.

"No, I was waiting for you. There should be a nice Oyster Bay in there."

Shit, I was going to have to do this while we were sober.

I poured us a drink and settled on the barstool. Haven was grating cheese. So, this was my moment—before she started anything with the knives.

"So, I went to that awards thing with Luke on Friday," I said.

"You shouldn't torture yourself like that, you know. Let him find his own date."

"I enjoyed myself, actually."

"You did? That's good. Sometimes those things can be okay. Depends who you sit next to and stuff." She fiddled with a couple of switches on the oven.

How was I going to do this? I wasn't sure what kind of reaction I was going to get from her. I wanted her to be thrilled, but a niggling feeling in the pit of my stomach told me that that wasn't going to be her response.

"Did I tell you I got that job for the Sunday Times?" she asked. Since Haven had gone freelance, her career had taken off. I was so proud of her.

"Holy hell, really? That's awesome." I stood up and gave her a hug. "I knew you could do it—that's amazing. What's that one about? The school thing?"

She nodded. "I can't believe it. I mean, I still want to do the independent, online stuff, but who's going to say no to the Sunday Times?"

"What's going on over there?" Luke shouted from the sofa. We were hugging and grinning. Maybe he thought I'd told her already.

"Haven got an article for the Sunday Times," I replied.

"Oh, yeah, I think she said." Luke nodded.

Haven rolled her eyes. "Brothers, hey?"

This was it. A natural break in the conversation. I needed to say it now.

"So, you know on Friday—" I began.

"I think these are done," she interrupted, glancing at the oven. "I've made cheese straws so the boys don't start whining about being hungry." She opened the oven door and took a baking tray out. "Guys, I've got snacks," she shouted across the room.

Luke bounded over, briefly rubbing my lower back as he passed me, then headed to the refrigerator. A shiver ran through my body. We should have just stayed home today. It would have been less complicated.

"What's going on over here?" he asked, fumbling for beers.

"We're cooking, and I'm telling Ash about the Sunday Times since you don't seem interested at all," Haven said.

Luke looked at me and grinned, knowing I'd chickened out so far. "So did Ash tell you we kissed on Friday night?"

"Luke!" I said. "I was meant to ease her into that. Not just blurt it out."

Haven looked at her brother, then at me and then back at her brother. "What do you mean?" she asked.

"I mean we kissed, and did other stuff. I have feelings. She has feelings." He shrugged. "We're, you know . . ."

"Very smooth, Luke," I said.

"What?" he asked. "At least I told her."

"I was going to tell her. I was picking my moment."

I looked at Haven as she stirred something in a pan as if her life depended on it.

"Haven?"

She took a deep breath. "I don't know what to say." To suggest she didn't look pleased was an understatement.

"Are you upset I've not told you until now?" I asked. She looked as if she were about to cry.

"Why now?" she asked. Luke tried to put an arm 'round her, but she shrugged it off. "You've had years to get it together. What's different?" It was a good question. What was different?

"Well, I was with Emma, and before that we were young—really young—and I didn't realize how I felt until recently," Luke said softly to his sister.

"Tell me what you're thinking, Haven," I said. "Please be honest." My stomach was churning. I hated to see her upset at the best of times, but this time I'd caused her unhappiness.

She turned off the stove and glanced between Luke and me. "I think we have a really good thing going here. We all love each other. We're family and now you guys get pissed together and put all that in jeopardy." She gave up stirring the pan and turned toward us. "Luke, you and Emma finished about five seconds ago and that was a serious, long-term thing. You can't just get over it in twenty-four hours," she said, pointing at Luke. "And you, you've loved this guy for forever, and I don't want him to break your heart." Her voice was getting higher and higher. "If you do, I'll be forced to make a choice between which one of you I spend holidays with and stuff. It will be horrible."

"Hey, what's going on here?" Jake asked, as he wandered over and pulled Haven close to him.

"These fuckers." She pointed at Luke and me.

"What's happened?" Jake was looking at Luke.

"Ash and I. We kinda, we . . ." Luke frowned, a look of confusion on his face.

I clutched my forehead. What had I expected? That we would just slip into being the happiest couple on earth? "We haven't even figured out what we're doing, Luke. Maybe she's right. You're on the rebound. I have no judgment around you. We acted rashly—"

"No!" Luke shouted, as he strode over to me. He put his hands on either side of my face. "No," he said, more softly. "We've known each other a lifetime. I would never treat your heart as anything other than the treasure it is. This is real. I'm not walking away, and I'm not letting you go anywhere." He dropped a small kiss on my lips and rested his forehead against mine. "Be sure of me."

I melted under his fingers. Had I always been so easily persuaded by him? Haven was right to be concerned. We should listen to her, but all I could see in Luke was the man I so desperately wanted him to be.

"Well, I think you're just adorable," Luke said. "Haven, this is good. This is two of your favorite people fornicating." Jake and Luke started laughing, and I took the opportunity to take a playful swipe at Luke.

"Oh my God, have you done it?" Haven lifted her hands to her ears. "Don't tell me. I don't want to know."

"I don't understand what's taken you so long. I thought your penis had shriveled up as you've been around this hottie your whole life and never made a move," Jake said to Luke.

"Jake!" Haven and I screamed in unison.

"Don't you want them to be happy?" Jake asked Haven.

"I do, but I don't want either of them to get hurt, and I definitely don't want to have to take sides if they break up."

Nausea washed over me at the thought of losing Haven or Luke from my life.

"We're not going to break up."

Even though my heart fluttered at Luke's words, Haven was right. It would be hard to ever go back to how things were. If Luke went back to Emma, or found someone else, it might just kill me. I wouldn't be able to go to Sunday night dinner and watch him with his new girlfriend. It would break up our routine, our family.

"You can't say we're never going to break up," I told Luke.

"Yes, I can. I've known you my whole life. This is it; I'm done." He tried to grab my hand, but I pulled away from him and shook my head. As much as I wanted it to be true, I knew it could never be that simple. Life never was.

chapter ELEVEN

Ashleigh

The dull light pushing through the curtains told me it was sometime around five. Five was an acceptable time to get up for some people. Runners, rowers, workaholics, new mothers—there was surely a world awake at this time of the morning. I reached across to the bed stand and found my phone. 5:12 AM.

My doubt about our immediate coupledom, about Luke's feelings for me and his motivations around what we were doing, had been circling me for the last twenty-four hours. Haven's words of caution at our Sunday night dinner last night had ignited a sense of fear. Luke's insistence that I was just "freaking out" as he described it and his assurances that everything would be okay had temporarily placated me. And with his hands on my face, the reassurance just free of his lips, I'd believed him.

So, we were good, right?

Having spent another sleepless night, his words dueling with my doubts, I knew we were not good. I was not good.

It was all too easy, too convenient, too sudden. I couldn't trust that he was ready. Only a few days ago, he and Emma had been talking about marriage. Whatever he felt now was almost certainly a reaction to suddenly finding himself single. Luke never dealt with change well, even in small ways, and in the last week his life had turned upside down. I couldn't help thinking that clinging to me—I was familiar, after all—was a consequence of that. And although I'd waited a lifetime for Luke and I to be an us, I wasn't ready to have my heart trampled on if he changed his mind again in few days.

Whatever there was between us felt thin and temporary and vulnerable. Risky. I couldn't handle that, not when I'd loved him for so long. This was not going to happen, not now. There was too much that could go wrong. Too much to lose.

If I ended things now, I might miss out on the love of my life, but there was still a chance that I wouldn't destroy my family, or my heart.

Perhaps when he was over Emma, and if he still felt the same way, maybe then I could let myself be with him, want him, love him. For now, we needed to end it for both our sakes. We needed time to make sure we were doing the right thing.

It would be better to be showered and dressed before I woke Luke to talk. I didn't want to capitulate under his touch again. If I was ready, I could leave for work while he left my flat. It would be easier, for me anyway, if I didn't have to be normal with him straight away.

On autopilot, I showered, dried my hair and dressed. Luke never moved an inch. Anyone else would have suspected he'd died in his sleep. Having known him for most of my life,

I knew this was just how he was. As teenagers, and even until recently, Haven and I'd had little consideration for those around us when we woke early, desperate to giggle about boys, parties and alcohol-induced shame from the night before. Until Haven married Jake, we'd regularly stayed over at each other's houses after nights out. Sometimes we'd even ended up in Luke's guest room. Unless you were an alarm clock, it was impossible to wake Luke. He insisted his body was tuned into some frequency that meant he never slept through alarms. Sounded like weird, boy logic to me. But whatever.

Ready to leave—and ready to talk—I programmed the clock next to him and sat at the end of the bed, close but not touching, and waited for him to wake. My heart was hammering through my chest. I knew ending this, or at least pressing pause on whatever there was between us, was the right thing to do. But I needed to get it over with before I had second thoughts. I was giving up the thing I had wanted desperately, longed for even. Luke. And even though it was the right thing to do, it wasn't going to be easy.

Luke's body immediately came awake as the alarm clock began to blare. It was almost cartoon-like, how quickly it happened. As if someone had plugged him in and suddenly, he was working.

"Hey," he said, turning as he caught sight of me from the corner of his eye. He started to grin and then, taking me in, the corners of his mouth settled back where they'd been. He knew me so well. Twisting, he sat upright, scrubbed his hands across his face and took a deep breath. He was so fucking beautiful, and right then it just didn't seem fair that he got to wake up, roll over and floor me with his bed hair, stubbly jaw and golden skin that I knew felt as smooth and warm as it looked.

Damn him.

"You want to talk." It wasn't a question. He knew me better than that.

My focus sharpened and I nodded.

"We got this, Ashleigh. Please trust me."

The sound of my full name curled around me. I didn't hear it often. And only twice from Luke before whatever was between us started. Once, when my parents moved to Hong Kong, and he and Haven came with me to the airport to see them off, and then again at the awards dinner a few evenings ago.

I blinked and filled my lungs. "I need you to listen. Not reassure me, not try to convince me I'm wrong, that I actually feel differently. I need you to hear what I'm going to say." I flicked my gaze toward him when he didn't answer. He was staring right at me, his eyes tight, his brows pulled together in anxiety. His face held all his effort to stay silent, to give me what I wanted.

"We've moved too fast, Luke. You are literally hours out of a long-term relationship that looked like it was heading toward forever. I have been in love with you my whole life—I want this too much. I want you so much that, for the past few days, I've been content to be carried away with this." I swirled my hand between us. The fear of what I was doing climbed up my spine and snatched my breath. I just had to get through the next few minutes and then it would be done.

"I need to be either nothing to you—"

"Ashleigh, you could never—"

I raised my hand at him, stopping him speaking.

"Nothing . . . or everything. And right now, I don't think you're in a position to be making decisions about what or who is everything to you. I need to know this isn't about you holding on to me because you need something to hold on to. That it isn't about you being uneasy about all the changes going on in your life right now." I sank my thumbnail into my finger in the hope that it would distract me from the pain in my heart. "I know you, Luke, and you like things to be ordered and predictable. And I don't want to be a security blanket for you. I want to be your lover, your partner, your best friend— the woman you can't live without. Not because it's easy, but because life would be less exciting without me, less joyous, less sweet. Not because you're used to me; not because you know me and it's comfortable."

I smoothed my palms over my skirt. I'd said what I needed to.

Silence pulsed through the space between us, and I tilted my chin up to look at him, anxious about what I would find on his face. It was as if he'd frozen to the spot, still holding himself back.

I rose from the bed and his hand shot out, grabbing mine. "Can we not talk about this?" His tone was pleading. "I understand what you're saying, but I don't know what it means." He linked his fingers through mine. "Are we done?"

"For now." I tried to keep the tightness in my chest from escaping into sobs.

"What does that mean, for now? Fuck." He pushed his hands through his hair, clearly frustrated.

"I just . . . I think you need some time—"

"I don't need time. I need you."

I took a deep breath. How long had I waited to hear that? Was I really going to walk away?

"Okay, I need time."

"How long do you need?"

I knew if I gave Luke boundaries, our relationship would simply become a task on his list. If I told him what I needed, how long I needed, he'd diligently work through the to-dos I created and wait. It would be all about me, when I needed it to be about him. My worry wouldn't dissolve in a set period of time. I needed him to experience life without me, work through the change, the uncomfortable feeling of uncertainty, get past it, enjoy it and then decide it was me that he wanted. Not as a cure, or a convenience, but because he was in love, with me.

"I need to know that you've sorted your life, and that you still pick me. That I'm not just convenient."

"Ashleigh, you would never—"

I couldn't listen to his counter arguments. "This is what I need. You asked me and I'm telling you. Make new friends, date. I don't know, get a dog, a new car. Get on with your life. See what it's like. Show me that I'm a conscious choice for you."

"Date?"

My stomach cramped at his question. What was I thinking? This was going to be horrific. The last thing I wanted was for him to find someone else, but if he did, then at least I knew we weren't meant to be. If I took what he was offering now, I would spend a lifetime wondering if he was ever really mine. I'd become insecure and needy—a shell of myself.

"Yeah, date." I looked out my bedroom window. I needed to leave or I was going to buckle, tell him it was all a big joke. I squeezed his hand, consciously trying to capture the feel of his skin against mine so I could replay it later when I was lonely and longing for him. I pulled my fingers from his and headed toward the door. "I know this is hard."

He jumped out of bed, pulling on his boxers. "Jesus, Ashleigh. Are you scared to be happy? Don't you feel this between us? Why are you walking away as if we're nothing?"

I couldn't turn and look at him. "Luke, you are everything to me. That's the point. We've so quickly slipped into this that it feels like it could be over tomorrow. And if I let myself fall any deeper, it might just kill me. This way it's only been a few days and we won't lose our friendship."

"We'll never lose that, Ashleigh. I promise you." His voice cracked and the sound tore right through me.

"Don't make promises you don't know you can keep. I need this, Luke. Please."

He sighed, and it took all my willpower not to turn and comfort him.

"If you need me to prove my feelings, then this is what I'll do. Because you are what I want, Ashleigh. What I need. My feelings won't change."

My heart ached. I wanted to say me too. But something kept me from forming the words.

Luke

"So you didn't go into the office?" Haven asked. She'd come home to find me staring into space. I'd left Ashleigh's flat and headed back to Haven's with the intention of jumping in the shower and heading to work. I hadn't been able to face the day surrounded by Ashleigh's scent, her words, her doubt. When I'd arrived, I'd sat on the bed, just for a second to gather my thoughts, and when I next looked at the clock half the day had gone.

I shook my head. "I called them. I've kept an eye on my emails. Things will wait." I would have been a mess at work. Better to feign illness than to turn up and give my clients reason to sue me for negligence. My head felt like a pinball machine as I jumped from being angry at Ashleigh for having so little faith in me, in us, to planning how I was going to win her back, then jumping again to an overwhelming feeling of loss. Perhaps Haven could help me make sense of it.

Haven looked at me, concern in her eyes. "I'm so sorry. I didn't mean to be so down on your relationship yesterday. I just got spooked. Do you want me to speak to her?" She watched me fill the washing machine with laundry. I'd been able to do nothing all day but think of Ashleigh. I hoped that if I could no longer smell her on my clothes, it would clear my mind, and I could figure out a way to get her back.

Haven looked at me, sheepish and guilty.

"It's not your fault. I knew she was likely to have a meltdown—I mean, come on, it's Ashleigh—but I thought I could talk her through it. I thought I knew her."

Haven narrowed her eyes. "Ashleigh?"

It took me a beat to realize what she was asking. "Yeah. That's who she is to me." Ashleigh had been right. My realization about her and my feelings for her had been sudden. In only a few days she had gone from being Ash—my sister's best friend, the person I asked to be my plus one if I didn't want to take my girlfriend, my family—to Ashleigh, someone who made me want to lobby Parliament to pass a law ensuring she had to be naked for the rest of her life. Someone who when she touched me, I felt the press of skin for hours afterward and yearned for it for hours beyond that. Someone I wanted to protect from the darkness, show the light. I wasn't sure whether it was because we'd known each other for so long, but even though Ashleigh and I had only been together a few days, it felt different, deeper—more profound than anything I'd experienced with anyone else.

I thought she'd felt the same.

"Did she say anything? Has she called you?" I asked, desperate to know how I could make it all better.

"No, I'm sorry." I could tell by how nice Haven was being that she was worried. Being with Jake had softened her edges, given her confidence, but it hadn't made her a pushover. She was still capable of giving me a good hard arse-kicking when she felt the need arise.

"She said that she wants to know that she's a conscious choice for me. But how can I do that if she's not with me? She's worried she's just . . . I don't know, available."

"Is she right to be concerned?"

I'd been trying to answer that question all day. "Yes and no."

"Fucking lawyers. Give me a straight answer."

I scrubbed my hands across my face and squeezed my eyes shut. I wished I were having this conversation with Ashleigh. I wished she'd given me more time this morning. "She knows me, right. So yes, I like constancy in my life. I cling on to things that maybe I shouldn't to create permanence. It was probably the reason I was with Emma for as long as I was." There was a dull thud where my heartbeat should be, as if it were cloaked in fog. "But no, that's not what my feelings, or should I say my change in feelings, toward Ashleigh are about. I don't know, Haven. I feel like someone took my blinders off and Ashleigh is a new person to me now. I mean she's still Ash, but she's mine now, too. Or she was."

"So tell her that. She's risking her family, being with you. You have to convince her you aren't going to break her heart. But she's right, you have to be sure she's who you want."

Ashleigh had been clear. She needed to see that she was my choice. "I've never been so sure. There's no going back for me. I just need to provide her with some evidence. But that's okay, because that's what I do, right? I build cases, uncover and present the facts. I just don't know how to do it yet. But I'll get there." I had to. Losing her forever wasn't an option. "How did Jake win you back?"

"By loving me. By giving me time and being there to catch me despite me pushing him away and losing faith in us both."

So that was it. I had to give her space, show her I'd had time and opportunity to think of every conceivable version of my life, and that I still wanted her at the center of it.

I'd prove to her that she was my choice.

My only choice.

I went to bed early, telling Jake and Haven I was tired. I wasn't. I had plans to make. A strategy to formulate. I glanced around, my overnight bag slung in the corner, clothes spilling out the top. A bunch of notebooks from work that I'd brought home on Friday were lying on the dressing table. This couldn't be my life. I pulled out my laptop and logged on. I grabbed a notebook.

Step one: Find a place to live.

The more I thought about it, the more I realized I was actually eager to move out of Haven's home. Perhaps it was partly because it was what Ashleigh needed from me, but all of a sudden, I relished the idea of moving on. As much as I loved my sister and Jake, I didn't want to be an appendage to their life. I wanted one of my own.

I fired up a real estate website and started to look at flats to rent near to where Emma and I had lived. As I clicked and scrolled, I realized the pictures were all from a place I'd left behind. There was no reason for me to live in that area. I was starting fresh with only myself to worry about. What did I actually want? Where did I want to be? I had no boundaries, no one to consider while making my choice. I could put a pin in the map and decide that would be the place. The possibilities were endless and in a sense daunting, but a decision had to be made if I was going to move on.

I did what I did best and buried myself in the details, working my way through different sites, firing off emails, setting up viewings for the coming days. I'd check a few places out and decide what felt right.

By the time I was finished, it was close to two, but the adrenaline pumping through my veins meant that sleep was a ways away. Was Ashleigh sleeping? Was she worried about if I would be able to do what she'd asked? I closed my eyes and imagined the contours of her body covered by her cream-colored sheets, her hair spread across her pillow, her lips parted. Over the years, we'd spent a lot of time with each other, but it was only in the past few days that I knew what she looked like while sleeping. Bold, funny, energetic Ash slept unguarded. She was soft, thoughtful—a Tennyson-imagined heroine. I logged on to my email.

Monday, September 12

Dear Ashleigh,

You've been in my every thought today. I miss you, but I want you to know that I'm beginning to understand what you've asked me to do and why.

I'm going to look at flats tomorrow. I wish you were coming with me. You could help me choose. But you'll see it soon enough, one way or another.

Believe in me. Believe in you.

All my love, Luke.

My mouse hovered over the send button. Was it too pushy? Did she even want to hear from me right now?

Eventually, I pressed delete and logged off.

Less than twelve hours after finding it on the internet, I stood in the middle of a furnished flat in the center of the city. It was the second one I'd seen. I'd skipped out of work early in order to progress step one on my plan.

Floor-to-ceiling windows spilled natural light into the flat—very different from the place I'd shared with Emma.

"You can see the river from outside," the agent said.

I slid open the balcony door and stepped out, peering over the wall. It was quiet and high and away from the hustle and bustle of London, despite being right in the middle of things. It was exactly the opposite of the flat I'd shared with Emma and the one I'd seen before this one. Our place had been a Victorian conversion in West London—and a forty-five minute journey into work. This was a ten-minute walk to the office. Emma had loved the original features and the garden at our place. To me a garden simply meant I had to cut the grass or pay someone else to do it. But I'd been happy to go along with whatever made her happy, grateful I didn't have to make the decision. Now I had to choose, and I found I preferred this sleek, modern, purposefully built flat in the center of town, with no commute and great views. It didn't require me to do anything. I could just move in and . . . live.

Would Ashleigh like it? I suppose I couldn't make this decision with anyone else but myself in mind. That was the point, wasn't it? This was what she wanted from me. To see the decisions in front of me, weigh each one carefully, then pick. Every hour I spent away from her, my focus was getting clearer.

Back inside, I ran my hand along the cool marble of the breakfast bar. Could I see myself reading the paper here?

"There are two bedrooms," the agent said as I followed her through the flat. She pointed out the master and then the guest bedroom. "There's a desk in there so you could use it as a study."

Perhaps it was difficult to picture myself living here because I'd never lived on my own. It struck me that I might get lonely. I could host a Sunday dinner. The dining table seated six, so we'd all fit. Seeing my family here would help me settle. "I can rent from month to month?" I asked. I guess I could try it and see how I liked it.

"Yes, you just need to give thirty days' notice after the first month, so a minimum two-month stay."

"I'll take it." There was no point in delaying. I needed to take the plunge and move forward.

The agent's eyes widened.

"And it's okay if I bring some additional furniture. A sofa . . ." My old brown leather sofa was the only thing I would take from the flat I'd shared with Emma. I loved that thing. It had been my first big, adult purchase, and it had seen a lot of beer, banter and girls. Where I went, the sofa came with me.

"I don't think that's a problem. When do you want to move in?"

"You can't make it happen quick enough."

The agent grinned. "Let's go back to the office and get you to sign the paperwork, and I can give you the keys."

I shoved my hands in my pockets and grinned.

Progress.

chapter TWELVE

Ashleigh

I stared out the window of the café where I'd lunched with Luke just a few weeks ago. It was raining and the windows had begun to fog up. I wiped the glass with the sleeve of my uniform so I could see the raindrops on the outside more clearly. It was like I was watching the inside of my heart. Damp, gray and miserable. Was Luke thinking the same thing? Was he hurting as I was? I wanted to call him, just to hear his voice. To let him tell me that everything was going to be okay. My brain knew that I had to give him space and time to figure out what he really wanted. My heart thought my brain was an idiot.

Adding to my pain was that I couldn't talk about it with Haven. I didn't want to create conflict when there was none, but I didn't want her to tell me I'd been a fool. Not for hoping that a relationship with Luke could work, or for pushing him away. My two best friends were suddenly people who I couldn't reach out to. The separation felt physical, slicing through me like a million tiny blades.

And then of course there was the guilt. I'd had two patients ask if I was okay. Jesus, that made my stomach tumble. I was distracted, feeling sorry for myself and surrounded by people in their last few weeks of life. How incredibly selfish was that?

"Hey, Ash." A voice from behind interrupted my self-pity. I was considering whether or not I had the energy to greet the person speaking to me when Richard came into view. "You okay?" he asked.

I nodded and forced the corners of my mouth up in an unconvincing smile. I'd not seen much of Richard since we'd broken up. That wasn't unusual, and it hadn't been long. He had probably been on nights. My shifts were more predictable, mainly eight to four with the odd Saturday thrown in. Who said there wasn't a bright side in palliative care?

"Can I join you?" he asked.

I wanted to say no. I wanted to be left alone with my head full of misery, but Richard was too nice to say no to.

"Sure." I sat back in my chair, my uneaten sandwich in front of me, as I watched Richard set down his tray, his eyes flickering between his food and my face.

"You seem upset."

I focused on his throat, not wanting to meet his eyes. How could I tell him that I was heartbroken, just not over him? "Tell me a joke," I said. "Distract me."

"A priest, a rabbi and a vicar walk into a bar. The barman says, 'Is this some kind of joke?'"

I rolled my eyes but managed a genuine smirk.

"Okay, we're going to need a bigger boat." He narrowed his eyes then said, "I cleaned the attic with the wife the other day. Now I can't get the cobwebs out of her hair."

Half-heartedly, I mimed a roll of the drums and the bash of a cymbal.

"It must be bad. That was funny. What's up?"

I shrugged and turned back to the rain. "This weather is shit."

"Yeah, but it's like this a lot and you're not normally miserable. How about I cheer you up?"

Richard was being nice, but I just wanted to disappear into myself. I didn't want to cheer up.

"I have tickets to see Bradley Cooper in The Elephant Man. Wanna come?"

I lifted my chin. What? Was he asking me out to improve my mood, or because he wanted another shot? Perhaps Luke would want another shot with Emma now I'd pushed him away. The thought made my stomach churn.

"Next Thursday, you're probably busy, but . . ."

"How come you have a spare ticket?" I sounded ungrateful, which wasn't my intention. I was just trying to establish on what terms he was asking me. "I mean, it's a popular show."

"I got them for my mum, but I got the date wrong and she's away on some yoga retreat. I hoped we were still friends, but if you feel uncomfortable . . ." This time it was Richard's turn to concentrate on the rain. God, I'd infected him with my bad mood.

"That's so sweet of you. I'd love to go to the theater." But how did I make it clear that I wasn't interested in trying again with him? "I mean, it's really very kind of you to invite me. Are you sure you wouldn't rather take someone else?" I didn't want him to waste a good date opportunity. But at the same time, I was curious how they were going to turn Bradley Cooper, of all people, into the Elephant Man. It was the first time I'd spent a full ten seconds not thinking about Luke. It was a relief to know it was possible.

"No, I'd like us to go together. As friends." He said the last words as if he were replying to his mother. Yes, I'll be back my dinner time. Yes, I've brushed my teeth. I'd never seen him look so young. He grinned, and I couldn't help but return his smile.

"I'd like that," I said. I knew I would. He was a good guy, and I needed to widen my social circle. Spending some time with people outside of Luke's world would be good for me.

"You never know, Ash, you might just fall in love with me once you see The Elephant Man."

I rolled my eyes. "Is that your plan?"

"I couldn't possibly tell you. All I know is the hottest woman at the hospital just agreed to go to the theater with me."

"Yeah, super-hot. Especially in my clogs." I pointed to my feet. I wanted to go, but I needed him to know we were in the friend zone.

"I know we're going as friends. But you can't rule anything out in this life." He grinned. "Remember that."

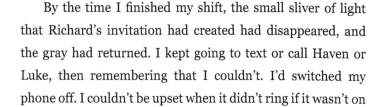

By the time I finished my shift, the small sliver of light that Richard's invitation had created had disappeared, and the gray had returned. I kept going to text or call Haven or Luke, then remembering that I couldn't. I'd switched my phone off. I couldn't be upset when it didn't ring if it wasn't on in the first place.

Girl logic.

I was staring into the fridge, trying to decide if I was hungry enough to make myself an omelet, when I jumped at the sound of the buzzer. Shit, I wasn't dressed for company. I wasn't mentally prepared to have to speak to people without coming off crazy. I'd managed it at work—at least I thought I had. No one else had asked if I was okay, so I felt like I'd pulled it off. But it had taken a tremendous effort. Now, all I wanted to do was sit and watch mindless television. My door vibrated under the force of someone's fist. Fucking hell.

My stomach flipped at the outside possibility that it might be Luke, here to tell me I'd been an idiot, to hold my head in his hands and give me a Hollywood-style kiss. It would be so much easier if that had been his reaction. I would have given in to him, and in the long run, it would have destroyed us. But at least I wouldn't be feeling as hopeless as I was, and right at that second, that sounded pretty good.

"Open the fucking door, Ash," Haven yelled. I sprinted to the spyhole to see if she was alone.

"I'm coming, you impatient shrew." Amongst the shouting, I forgot for a second that maybe it might be awkward, given that I'd had sex with her brother and then dumped him. Or sort of dumped him. Was she going to pick a side? Had she come here to give me a piece of her mind? Put her shoe up my ass?

I flung the door open, and before I got a chance to say anything, she pushed past me carrying supermarket bags.

Haven unpacked what looked like a year's worth of carbohydrates onto my kitchen counter. "So, I have all mandatory food groups. Wine, ice cream, chocolate, white bread and pizza. Oh yes, and of course, diet Coke." She began wrestling with the corkscrew. "What do you want to start with?"

I picked up a humongous bar of chocolate and pulled the corners apart.

"You look like you've showered," she said, clearly expecting me to be more of a mess.

"No one died," I replied.

"No, you just told the love of your life that you didn't want to be with him."

I let her words swirl around the kitchen as I tried to work out whether she sounded angry with me. Upset? Disappointed? But I couldn't hear any of that. Her tone was entirely neutral.

"You think I'm nuts?" I asked.

"I love my brother, right?" Haven glanced at me, and I had to look away. "And I love you. I want you to be happy. From what he's told me, I get it. I think. But I'm here for you. Until death do us part."

"You're a freak. I think those are the vows you exchanged with your husband," I said, shaking my head.

"The thing is you and I don't need vows. It's just how it is." She thrust a cold glass of wine into my hand and ushered us out of the kitchen, laden with alcohol and snacks.

"I was worried you'd tell me I was an idiot." I broke off a chunk of chocolate the size of my head.

"I can do, if you want," Haven replied.

"You know what I'm trying to say. I don't know if we should talk about this. I mean—"

"Of course we should talk about it." She took a swig of wine, placed it on the coffee table and sat forward expectantly.

"So, pretend he's not my brother, except I don't want to hear about his penis. Go."

I slumped back into the sofa, relieved she was here and wasn't mad. We were still us, despite what had happened with Luke. Now she was asking, there was no way I wasn't talking about it. I mean Haven would pin me down and experiment with five different kinds of Chinese water torture if she had to, the mood she was in, but I wanted to talk to her about it.

Tears formed immediately and my forehead became tight. I hadn't cried about this. I didn't want to cry because if I did, I was accepting the possibility that Luke and I were over. While I managed to hold back my tears, I was in the world where Luke and I were only temporarily apart. That he would pick me. That we would be together.

"There's nothing to cry about. You and Luke will happen," Haven said, vocalizing my thoughts. "This is just, I don't know, the prequel." Her weird analogy was oddly comforting.

"How is he?" I asked in a voice so small I wasn't convinced she'd hear me.

"Do you want to know?"

I slid my eyes across the room, away from Haven's stare. Did I want to hear about him? Would it make me feel better or worse? I nodded. "Yeah."

"He moved out."

"He did?"

"Yup." She reached for her glass and took another gulp of wine. That was it? Come the fuck on, I needed more details than that. I widened my eyes at her.

"Renting a swanky new pad in the City."

"Wow, really? That was fast." I wanted to hear all about it. I wanted to know why he'd chosen the city rather than West London. But I wanted to hear it from him. Still, it was good news, right?

"Yeah, I think he's surprised himself. He just needed a push. So thank you. Jake and I can go back to shagging like bunnies all over the flat."

"I'm so pleased I could help."

"He's trying to do what you want." My stomach flipped again. At least he wasn't angry with me. He hadn't given up. But I needed him not to be doing things so I would take him back. I wanted him to experience other things and still pick me.

"I just don't want to be the easy option."

"I totally get it. He's all for the status quo. I'm sorry if I put doubts in your head. Me and my big mouth."

"Come on, Haven. It wasn't you. Don't think that. This is about me feeling worthy. I need to know Luke loves me the way I love him. That we're not just together because it's the path of least resistance." I took a deep breath. "I always thought having him would be enough, but I need more."

"I think it's brave of you," she said.

"I might regret it. He might think I'm not worth it, or that there's someone else better."

"Then he's an idiot," Haven said. "And I can say that because we came out of the same womb. An alternative way of looking at it is that if the worst happens—and I don't think it will—then it wouldn't have worked in the long run anyway."

"And that is why we are friends," I said and pulled her into a hug.

chapter
THIRTEEN

Luke

Haven had asked me repeatedly why I wouldn't hire movers, and although I had insisted that real men didn't need to employ help in these situations—we hired a van, put on our oldest jeans and got the job done ourselves—I was beginning to think she might be right. I was knackered. And my lower back was starting to make its presence felt. Jesus, I felt fifty and I'd barely entered my thirties.

"God, it's so ugly," I said as Jake, my old uni mate Adam and I stood staring at my beloved brown leather couch, still trying to catch our breath from lugging the thing up four flights of stairs.

I'd arranged with Emma to collect my stuff from the flat. To be fair, the only big piece of furniture was the sofa, but there seemed to be endless boxes of I-didn't-know-what filling every inch of the hired van. Emma had packed everything then gone away for the weekend so we wouldn't run into each other. I felt bad she was still so upset that she was avoiding seeing me. Even though it had only been a few weeks, I'd truly moved on. Not just because I'd slept with Ash—it was more than that. I got to start life again. I'd never have left Emma if she'd not forced marriage, and I would have wasted my life. Since the split, somehow everything tasted slightly sweeter, smelled slightly sweeter. The sun shone slightly brighter. I had choices and opportunities that I could take and make happen . . . or not. It was entirely up to me. I felt invigorated.

"Yeah, it looks like one of the Rolling Stones. Like it's had a great life, had loads of fun and seen things that would make your toes curl—but it's old and exhausted and ready to die," Adam said thoughtfully.

"The Keith Richards of sofas," Jake chimed in. "And I don't give a shit about stuff like this, but it is very nineteen ninety-eight."

I chuckled. They were right. It was old-fashioned and falling apart. No wonder Emma let me have it. She'd kept every other bit of furniture in our flat, and I hadn't bothered to argue with her. I'd been more than happy to leave the evidence of our life together behind.

"It's time to let go, mate," Adam said. "You're going to be a partner. You've moved into this great new pad. Why the fuck do you want some disgusting student sofa in your shiny new life?"

Adam was right. In the last few days, I'd had a new world forced upon me, whether or not I wanted it. And far from finding it scary and unsettling, I was enjoying it. "I think you're right. I don't need it or want it. But you know what that means, don't you?" I asked. "We've got to take it back downstairs. We can leave it in that Dumpster on the curb."

"You're a fucking arsehole," Adam replied. "And you're paying for a curry and enough beer to knock me out after this."

"On my count," Jake said. "One, two, three." We heaved the sofa up and began to retrace our steps.

Despite the fact that I'd clung to this sofa for years, unwilling to give it up, letting it go felt like the right thing to do. We carried it down the stairs, almost beheading Adam on several occasions. It was ridiculous thinking it was so great for so long. I'd had my blinders firmly on around this sofa, around life in general. Jake was right—it was time to let go. This shift was exactly what Ashleigh had meant, and every moment I spent away from her, the more I understood. I was grateful—she'd forced me to take a wider, bigger look to the future.

Now that I was just around the corner, I got into the office earlier. The clock on my computer said it was just gone eight, and I'd been at my desk in our open-plan office for about twenty minutes, Googling triathlon training. Lugging that sofa up and down the stairs had left me half dead. I wasn't ready to descend into middle age quite yet. I needed some kind of goal to motivate me into getting back into regular gym sessions. Fuck me, the training looked tough. I liked to run, and I'd been on a few cycling holidays in my time, so a triathlon seemed like a good option. It would give me focus and something to do with my weekends when I wasn't working. Now that I wasn't part of a couple, I found I had a lot more time on my hands than I'd expected. Time I didn't want to just fritter away or give to my job. Completing a triathlon would be an achievement.

"Hey, Luke."

Fiona hovered at the side of my desk. An environmental lawyer, she was up for partnership this year too. Her brain was as big as a planet, but she had a quiet manner that meant unless you really listened, she came across like a bit of a flake. She was anything but.

"You a triathlete too?" she asked.

"Thinking about it. It looks fucking hard."

"It is." She raised her eyebrows and smiled.

I swiveled in my chair to face her. "Can you testify from experience?"

"I started training a few years ago after a bad breakup," she continued. "I hadn't been on a bike since I was a teen, and there were several times before and during the race I thought I might die. But the high after finishing is better than any drug. You should try it. I guarantee you'll be hooked after your first competition."

"You think it's realistic for someone to start at my age?"

"Oh my God, totally. You're young and you clearly work out." She glanced away and at the floor. "I mean, you'll love it."

I hadn't worked out much lately, but at least I looked as if I were in good shape, even if I didn't feel it.

I'd never had a conversation with Fiona other than about work. I'd not considered her existence outside of these four walls, but clearly she was passionate about what she was talking about.

"Any words of wisdom on where to start?"

She leaned across my keyboard and started tapping away. I sat back in my chair and moved slightly. "Here," she said.

"Try this website. If I were you, I'd start with a sprint, and see how you get on."

"Wow, fifteen miles is a sprint?" It sounded more and more brutal.

She clicked on several menus and scrolled through the site, pulling up a spreadsheet. "Start with a training plan, but don't be afraid to change the one you come up with. The first time you don't really know left from right. You're a big guy, and you look fit, but . . ." A blush bloomed across her cheeks, and she moved away from the keyboard, but continued to stare at the screen. "But you don't know how your body's going to react. I could take a look at your plan if you want me to. Perhaps give you some ideas of where to train."

"That would be great, thanks," I said through a grin. "It would be good to have someone to talk this shit through with. I have no idea what I'm doing."

"Okay, well, email me your plan when you have it, and I'll take a look. We could go for coffee sometime and look over it." She shrugged "But I'm sure you'll be—"

"Let's grab some time on Friday maybe?" Putting a triathlete in front of me was like the universe telling me I was on the right track. What had been a vague idea thirty minutes ago was firming up to be a realistic proposition. Having someone help me get started was just what I needed.

"After work?" I had back-to-back meetings on Friday.

"Yeah, sounds good." Fiona grinned and began to head off. Before she got to the door, she froze.

"You came to talk about the Nigelson, case, didn't you?" I laughed.

She slapped her forehead and spun to face me. "I did. I came to drop this off," she said, handing me the bunch of papers tucked under her arm. "It's the environmental report you asked for. I've emailed you my analysis, but thought you might want to see the original."

"Thanks, that's great. I thought it would take longer." She managed to get through work like a machine.

"Oh, I had some free time, so I got to it sooner than I expected." She smiled and turned to leave. "See you Friday."

Finally, things were coming together. The flat. The triathlon. Even catching up with Adam. I was getting on with my life, just as Ashleigh had wanted me to. But I couldn't help thinking everything would feel a little better if she were here to share it.

chapter
FOURTEEN

Ashleigh

Richard suggested a quick bite before the play, and I couldn't see a reason to say no. It would be good to have a distraction. At least I'd managed to get a seat on the bus. I had my book in my bag, but I couldn't bring myself to read at the moment. Everything on my e-reader was about couples bound to have a happily ever after. I was too concerned about whether or not I was going to get mine to read about anyone else's. As usual, I was lost in thoughts of Luke.

When would I see him again? Haven had cancelled Sunday night dinner, making up some crazy excuse about her hairdresser. I knew she'd intended to give Luke and me a little breathing space, and I was grateful, but I missed him so much.

Haven had mentioned he'd moved, and I wanted to hear every last detail. Hell, I wanted to see the place for myself. I didn't want to miss another Sunday dinner together. It wasn't that I'd changed my mind. More that I still wanted to be his friend, have a presence in his life while he decided what he wanted. Because, if he didn't want me, I needed to know we were still going to be friends, still be part of each other's worlds.

The bus stopped, and I watched as people filed off, creating room for those queuing at the front. I managed to scramble out just before the doors shut. I'd zoned out and not taken in that I'd reached my destination. I really shouldn't be responsible for people's healthcare needs at the moment—I could barely get off a bus at the right time. Thankfully, the restaurant was just a few yards away from the stop. I checked my watch. I was only ten minutes late.

I spotted Richard immediately, and relaxed as he smiled and waved. I handed my coat to the hostess.

"Hey, sorry I'm late," I said as I neared the table.

"No worries." He stood and kissed me on the cheek. "I ordered some wine. Is that okay?"

"There's never going to be a time in my life when I say no to wine, just for the record."

"Maybe when you get stuck in your MBA. You won't be able spend all your free time buzzed. How's the application going?"

It was a surprise that he asked me. He hadn't seemed very interested when we were dating. "Good. I sit the entrance exam in a month and start in January if I get in."

"I'm sure you will. You're clever. They'd be lucky to have you apply."

His response was far from what I'd expected. I raised my eyebrows.

"You are," he said. "All the doctors say so."

"They do? You talk about me? Us?"

"Of course we do. Are you telling me you don't talk about us?"

"Nurses are far too busy and professional. Doctors," I said, swirling my index finger in his direction, "are clearly a bunch of underemployed gossips."

Richard chuckled. "Well I don't know about the underemployed thing, but I'll cop to the gossip bit. And actually the blokes are much worse than the women."

I rolled my eyes.

"What?" He held his hands up.

"You say that like it's a total shock that men are just as gossipy as women. You're a nice guy, but sometimes I want to slap you about the head."

"Why? I was being nice and saying that women aren't the gossips you might expect."

I started to laugh. "Holy crap. I despair. And you don't see that by doing that you're reinforcing the stereotype? It's not a compliment."

He stopped suddenly, as if I'd pressed pause, his hand hovering over his wineglass. He blinked once, twice and pursed his lips. "Jesus, you're right. Fuck. You see. I said you were clever."

"I know I'm clever, but thank you." I grinned.

"Have I done that stuff before, you know, like when we were dating?" His eyes were the size of saucers, as if I were Galileo telling him the earth moved round the sun.

I shrugged. "Maybe. Once or twice."

"God, I'm sorry." I'd forgotten he could be funny. My life would be a lot easier if I'd have just been able to fall in love with him.

"It's fine, but now that we're friends, I'm calling you out on that shit."

"Excellent," he said, slapping his hand on the table. "Like my dating coach. Making me better for the next one, whoever that might be." He tried to hold my stare, but I looked away. It was my own fault if he made a pass at me. I'd agreed to go out with him again, after all. Even if we'd been clear we were just friends.

I laughed to break the tension. "Maybe. Now pour me some more wine."

"If you start snoring in the theater, I'm going to pretend I'm not with you."

"I can live with that. Besides, I'm not concerned. Bradley Cooper can normally hold my attention." I gave him a smile and picked up my menu.

Two weeks later, I shuffled back and forth on my barstool, then hopped off and started fiddling with it.

"You can't adjust the height. Here, drink this, you'll feel better," Haven said, setting a full glass in front of me on the breakfast bar.

I retook my seat and gulped down half my wine. My heart pulsed in my chest, and I kept rubbing my hands up and down my jeans to wipe the sheen of sweat from them. I'd never been nervous about seeing Luke before. What if he looked at me and anything he'd felt for me had fallen away? What if he saw me and realized he didn't find me attractive? I mean, he'd spent years not wanting me—it would be easy for him to shut those feelings off, wouldn't it?

Beth was peeling mushrooms, and Jake was carrying a decanter in one hand and seemed to be aimlessly wandering around with it. I couldn't concentrate on anything in the room right now.

A bang in the hallway sent my heart crashing out of my ribcage. It was him.

"Hey," he said, panting as he walked in. He bent forward, resting his hands on his knees, trying to catch his breath. He had a small backpack on and was dressed in running gear. The tips of his hair were damp with sweat, and his beautiful golden skin glowed. Had he run here?

"You look disgusting," Haven said.

He looked anything but. At that moment, I'd be quite happy to lick him clean.

"Cheers. I've been exercising. What's your excuse?" he asked as he stood up straight and grinned at his sister. I let myself giggle. I might want to trail my tongue over his entire body, but he was still the man I'd been friends with my whole life. Someone who could make me laugh within seconds of arrival.

I couldn't tear my eyes off him. Apparently, the après exercise look suited him. His shirt clung to him, the outline of his six-pack clearly visible as he began to stretch out his quads. Seriously? Snapshots of him naked and over me, his eyes closed as he pushed into me, filtered into my brain. I turned away from him and took another gulp of wine, concentrating on the stem of the glass as I put it down.

Out of the corner of my eye, Luke hovered in the doorway. "I'm going to take a shower, okay?" He slipped the backpack off and headed down the corridor.

"I should hope so, Sweaty Betty," Jake said, unscrewing a bottle of red wine.

Had he deliberately arrived, full of testosterone, looking invincible and physically perfect? Damn him. It was all I could do not to touch the back of my hand to my forehead and full-on swoon. If he'd been trying to show me what I'd been missing, he'd done an excellent job.

Luke

Pleased to have an excuse to leave the kitchen, I steadied myself on the bathroom sink. I should have prepared mentally for seeing Ashleigh. She'd looked so relaxed, perched on the barstool as if it were just another Sunday dinner. Maybe it was for her. But I felt an enormous pull toward her, a keen desire to touch her, kiss her, hold her. Even though I'd not stood close to her, I could see the flush of her first glass of wine across her cheeks. My dick stirred at the image scorched across my mind. She was wearing her favorite jeans and a top I hadn't seen before. Jesus, her ass. I turned the dial of the shower to cold—I needed to get my thoughts back into the box marked appropriate, but I wasn't sure there was a setting for arctic.

I showered quickly, pulled on some clothes, roughly towel-dried my hair, and went to join everyone back in the kitchen.

Beth stood with her back to me, and I placed a hand on her arm. She turned and I kissed her on the cheek. "Hi," I said as I accepted a beer from Jake. Ash was next. I had to greet her with a hug as I always did, but my limbs felt heavy, my joints sticky.

"Hey you," I said, moving toward her. She slipped off the stool and the thought of being about to touch her was almost too much. I had to suck in a breath.

"Hey," she replied as her hands smoothed over my shoulders and mine slid up her back. Her sweet, sexy scent surrounded me. It reminded me of home, of being happy, of summers spent beneath the magnolia trees in my parents' gardens. I pressed my hands against her back briefly and then released her. Our bodies parted, but I felt a pull toward her when I was close to her. I wanted to keep touching her.

Ignoring my instinct to pull her back into my arms, I strode across to Haven and placed a kiss on her cheek.

"Did you bring the wine?" she asked.

"Oh, yes. Here." I grabbed the wine off the console table in the hallway.

Get it together, Luke. You've know this girl your whole life. Act normal.

"So what's been going on?" I handed the bottle to Haven.

"You're the one that arrived in need of a shower. What's going on with you?" Beth asked.

I took a swig of my beer. "I'm training for a triathlon."

"What the fuck?" Jake's exclamation was loud and clear, but I was too busy not looking at Ashleigh to hear Beth and Haven. Ashleigh stayed quiet. Normally she'd be teasing me relentlessly about an early midlife crisis or something.

I sat on one of the barstools, leaving an empty seat between Ashleigh and me.

"So when's the competition?" Jake asked.

"Not sure yet. Fiona thinks that I shouldn't commit to a specific race until I'm a few weeks into training."

Haven held me with her stare. "Who's Fiona?" she asked.

"A girl at work who does triathlons. She's helping me with my training as she's really into this stuff. She's looking at my plan." Things had happened quickly now I had someone to give me an idea of what I should be doing. "We went running earlier in the week. She's fucking fast. Small but deadly." I grinned. "I need to get some new kit though. I'll obviously need one of those suits. Whatever Fiona recommends. She really knows her stuff."

"Good for you, dude. I'll come for the odd run if you like." Jake offered.

I nodded. "Sounds good. Fiona said that I needed to commit to training four times a week, but that's going to go up as my fitness improves." When I'd broken it down, I'd realized it was going to be quite a fair chunk of my free time, so I was going to have to fit it in where I could, which led to me running over to Sunday dinner.

"Sounds like Fiona is taking a keen interest in your well-being," Haven said.

I shrugged and glanced at Ashleigh, who was staring into her wineglass as if she weren't included in the conversation. Was she pleased that I was trying new things? Living my life? I wanted to interrogate her about her two weeks without me. Ask her if finding a place to live and starting to train for a triathlon was what she wanted. Was she happy? Had she been thinking about me?

"What about everyone else? Saved the world yet, Jake?" I asked.

Do you miss me like I miss you, Ashleigh?

"That's on the agenda for next week," Jake replied.

"Big news is we're planning a trip to Chicago," Haven said. "We're all going." She swept her arm around, indicating herself, Jake and Beth.

"Yeah, you might have to actually cook the Sunday we're away. Try not to give Ash food poisoning." Jake said.

"Can you believe it?" Ashleigh finally looked at me. "They're going on holiday without us." She tilted her head to one side and pushed out her bottom lip, as if she was almost flirting. She looked so goddamn cute. I wanted to bite that swollen bottom lip of hers.

"I've said you can come," Haven said.

"Nah. Chicago in October?" Ashleigh scrunched up her nose. "You've got to be kidding me. I thought you were a gazillionaire, Jake. Can't you take us all to Aruba?"

Jake grinned. "Next trip."

I relaxed as I settled into the banter between us. It was nice. Familiar. I was happy to let the sounds of my family's chatter surround me, rather than actively participate. I hopped off my stool and grabbed the wine from the fridge. First, I topped up Haven then rounded the counter, looking for permission to do the same for Ashleigh. She held the bottom of her glass with the flat of her hand and pushed it across the granite toward me. I tilted the bottle and placed my hand on the counter next to the glass, my fingers overlapping hers. I hadn't planned to touch her, but I couldn't be so close to her and not.

I needed to feel her heat.

Her mouth parted, and the redness in her cheeks deepened as her glance flickered from Haven to me. My chest tightened at the idea that the touch of my fingers could illicit such a reaction. I hadn't lost her, not yet. Her glass ended up fuller than it should have been, and I moved away. I turned from the fridge to find her watching me. She looked away sharply, nodding at whatever Haven was saying. I watched the floor on the way back to my seat in an effort to cover the grin spread across my face.

"I'm going to have to go." I looked at my watch. "I have an early morning run booked in tomorrow." It was almost ten and although that wasn't late, every moment I spent out of bed from here on out made it less and less likely that I'd keep to my training plan.

"Yeah, me too. Well, not the running thing, God forbid."

Ashleigh grinned at me. Over the course of the evening, we had somehow found a way to be around each other without it feeling anything but normal. I'd caught her looking at me a couple of times when she thought I wouldn't notice. I'd seen it because I was trying to steal my own private glances. She always averted her eyes quickly.

"Walk me to the tube?" she asked. It was our usual routine, but this time the question felt loaded. My pulse began to hammer in my neck. Time alone with her. I was desperate for it, but terrified she'd say something I didn't want to hear. The air was thick with what we weren't saying, and we avoided each other's gaze as Haven ushered us both out, barely allowing us to say our goodbyes.

"I'll call you about training," I called to Jake as Haven shut the door, leaving Ashleigh and I alone.

I stared at my shoes, my hands shoved in my pockets, as we waited for the elevator. I could barely stop from reaching for her.

"You seem good. About Emma and moving and . . ."

I watched her as she kept her eyes fixed on the chrome doors, as if she was trying to stay in control.

"I am good. About Emma and moving." I tried to be as specific as I could. I wasn't okay being without her, but I held myself back from telling her that. I didn't want to push.

The elevator door pinged open, and I reached inside, holding the doors for Ashleigh.

"Emma and I should have split a long time ago. It's not as difficult as maybe it should be. And it feels good to be moving on, trying new things." It was true. I liked being in the new place. I found living on my own wasn't so much of a shock as I'd thought. "The triathlon's a good focus."

"It sounds like it. I'm pleased you're . . . good," she replied and gave me a small smile.

I wouldn't be good until she was mine.

Ashleigh

I'd wanted to have him to myself all evening and now here we were, alone, and I had to work to contain my jealousy of Fiona, to not touch him, to keep from wanting him.

Even through my thick winter coat, I felt his hand at the small of my back as we exited the lift. I closed my eyes, trying to get a handle on myself.

"And your new flat? Being there, right in the city center. That's . . . different."

Luke nodded. "It is. But it's good. I think you'd like it. I have an almost zero commute to work, and after the place with Emma, this feels so easy. Like it's mine." He words tripped into each other. "You'll have to see it." He sounded excited.

"I'd like that." I hated that I'd not seen it already. I found it difficult to comprehend that there were parts of his life that I didn't know about. "Maybe you should have a housewarming party."

His shoulders dropped, and his lips pulled together tightly as if what I'd said upset him.

"And you should host Sunday night dinner one week."

"Next Sunday, while that lot is in Chicago?" he asked.

Were we going to have dinner together, alone, in his flat? Yes.

We'd stopped things at the right time. We were going to make it through as friends. Our family wasn't going to split because we'd had sex. The thought brought relief, and disappointment. Did that mean that friends were all we would ever be? I was always going to want more from him.

"Only if you promise to cook." I playfully poked him on the shoulder.

We headed left toward the tube. "Only if you promise to buy me a housewarming gift. A good one."

I grinned at his mischievous expression. "I miss you," I blurted out. Just as we had started to relax and tease each other, I had to add a layer of awkward. But I wanted to tell him. I wanted to know if he missed me.

Luke rubbed his face with his hands and stared straight ahead as we continued to the tube station in silence.

"I'm sorry. I shouldn't have said it." I wanted to rewind time.

"Not unless it means you're ready to give us a shot. Otherwise it feels like a head fuck."

I nodded. He was right. I'd asked him for this time and space, and I had to suffer the consequences.

"I'm sorry," I said softly.

He nodded as if he understood that I wasn't ready to trust his feelings just yet. I wanted to be ready. I wanted him to be ready—soon.

chapter
FIFTEEN

Ashleigh

For the first time in my life, I wished I had an office job. A job where I sat behind a desk and had access to the Internet. I'd been jumpy all morning—partly from all the coffee I'd been drinking, and partly because of my weird interaction with Luke. I'd told him I missed him and messed everything up. After he dropped me off at the tube station, I'd had almost no sleep. What I did have was a working knowledge of the four lawyers named Fiona at Luke's law firm. I was pretty sure our winner was Fiona Pritchard. Her Facebook picture showed her in running gear and a number strapped to her vest. I couldn't see any other photos of her because she'd selfishly set her privacy settings to anti-stalker, but she definitely seemed the most likely candidate.

Hearing Luke talk about another woman had properly shown me the consequences of the choice I'd made. I knew if he decided to be with someone else—Fiona or another girl—it meant that there had never really been a chance for us. Still, it didn't mean it didn't hurt. I'd wanted us to have some time apart for Luke to realize he couldn't live without me because he was in love with me. I hadn't counted on jealously obsessing over Fiona Pritchard.

She looked more serious in her official work photograph on the firm's website, but not unattractive. Not an obvious knockout, but then again, I wasn't going to start throwing stones. Her firm profile said she was in Planning and Environmental. I didn't know much about what Luke did, but I was pretty sure that meant they were in separate departments. I couldn't decide if that was a good thing or a bad thing. Good, because they wouldn't see much of each other, but bad because they'd be less concerned with getting involved.

Despite the fact I'd spent half the night stalking Fiona, I hadn't quite got my fill. I hadn't memorized every detail of her face. She looked about the same age as Luke, but I wanted to check again. I wanted to take another look. Was she the girl who would be the one to drive the nails into the coffin of Luke and me?

"You can take your break now if you like," the nurse in charge said. "You go off and get yourself something to eat. You're looking pale."

Food was the last thing on my mind, but I was grateful that she'd relieved me early. Just as I was leaving the hospital grounds, my phone vibrated. Haven.

"Hey, how're you doing?" I asked.

"On lunch. Thinking about you. How was last night?"

"Last night?"

"You know, between you and Luke after you left our

place? I mean, it seemed good between you guys when we were having dinner."

It had been good. I always enjoyed time with Luke.

"Yeah, that's the point though, isn't it? We stopped things before we couldn't go back to being friends. You said it yourself when you first found out about us—if it's not okay between us, then you'll be forced to choose and our family gets split up."

"I should have never said that. I was shocked and speaking before I'd thought about it. You know how I do that." Her voice was solemn. "I mean . . . I'd never choose one of you over the other. We'll always be family."

Haven shouldn't be feeling bad. She had made a really good point. "But you were right. It might not happen straight away, but if Luke and I can't get along then we'll drift apart. I can't lose either of you." I wished we were having this conversation face to face. I needed a hug.

"So you're giving up on something happening between you and Luke because you're afraid it won't work and you'll fall out and lose both of us?" That was exactly what I was afraid of, but I wasn't giving up on Luke.

"The way I see it is that he can't possibly have the feelings for me that I have for him. I mean, you know how I've felt about him my whole life. Now suddenly he's single for the first time in forever and he wants me? I just think if he can turn it on that quickly, he can turn it off just as fast." My stomach flipped at the thought that I may have lost him already. "It would kill me, properly break my heart, if I let myself think we could be something and then later down the line he decided he wanted someone else. And on top of a broken heart, I'd lose my family. I mean, what would I have left?" My stomach churned at the thought of losing Haven and Luke. I guessed I could start again in Hong Kong if that happened. I'd need to get away. "And if we stayed together, I couldn't go through my whole life knowing that I feel more for him than he does for me. That would turn me inside out eventually."

"I get it. I do. But, you know, sometimes it's worth the risk. Is it worth losing him to some girl at the office because you didn't want to take a chance?"

"I think if he can get serious about someone else then he and I were never going to work in the first place. I'd rather know that now." It would be painful, but less so. "Do you think I'm an idiot?"

"You're one of the smartest girls I know. I just worry that you and Luke could be good together. I don't want you to miss out on happiness. I want that for you. Is it just time you need?"

I didn't want to miss out either. And I wondered every second about whether I was doing the right thing. "I need time, but Luke does too. I need him to have space to think about his other options."

"Speaking of other options, is it weird that I've been researching this Fiona person?" she asked. "I mean, I understand you're not ready to be with him yet, but at some point I'm hoping you will be." Haven began to speak more quickly. "I'm rooting for you, and I don't want any triathlon queen fucking it up."

I couldn't have loved Haven more than I did in that moment.

"Now, I'm not technically getting involved, you

understand. I'm just acting like the BFF, which of course, I am."

"Of course," I confirmed.

"I've not asked Luke about her."

I had to swallow the disappointment that surfaced in my throat, although I understood she was trying to stay impartial. "But I have asked Jake. Because, you know, I'm married to him." I could hear the grin in her voice. "Apparently Luke's never mentioned her before."

"Right," I said, trying to keep my delight from seeping into my voice.

"But that's good. If he was into her, he'd have said something to Jake."

I wasn't convinced. There were a million reasons Luke wouldn't confess his urge to get naked with a coworker to Jake. One, Jake was married to his sister. Luke wasn't known for his fast decision-making in his personal life, which was a huge part of the reason I'd struggled with the way his feelings for me had switched so suddenly. He might not have decided if he liked Fiona yet.

"She's pretty."

"I knew you'd be stalking her. You think she's Fiona Pritchard? She's not that pretty." Haven knew exactly what to say.

"She is pretty. But I need to stop obsessing. Like I said, if he wants her then it was never going to work out between us. I asked him to live his life. This is what I wanted, and this is what he needs." My head and my heart were in a constant battle and my head was barely winning—staving off the short-term pain for what I hoped would be a long-lasting future together.

"Do you have a time period in mind for him to live his life? A week, a month, a year?" Haven seemed impatient.

I didn't have an answer for her. I needed to be able to trust Luke's feelings for me, and part of me wondered if that would ever be possible. I'd loved him my entire life. Perhaps I was asking something from him that he could never provide.

Maybe we were already over.

chapter
SIXTEEN

Ashleigh

It was starting to rain, but I still couldn't bring myself to hit the buzzer to get inside. Luke had dropped me a text during the week with his address, telling me to arrive at his new place for Sunday dinner at six. I was nervous to see him again, particularly as the last time we'd been alone, I'd told him I missed him and he'd rightly called me a head fuck.

The housewarming gift I'd decided on seemed to grow heavier with every second I carried it. Thinking of the right gift for Luke had kept me busy for the entire week. I wasn't sure if I should go practical or meaningful. I'd decided on the latter and purchased a magnolia tree for his balcony. I'd mentioned to Richard when I'd seen him on Friday that I was buying a tree and he, very graciously, had given me a ride and then hauled it up my three-story walk-up. I hadn't realized until now how heavy it was.

For me the present was symbolic, but I wasn't going to admit that to Luke. I wondered if he'd notice what it was, understand the symbolism. The tree itself was small, just a couple of feet high. The problem with my thoughtful gift was that it wasn't in bloom and wouldn't be until the spring. So I was basically turning up with a bunch of sticks poking out of some soil, and attached to them a label of how it would hopefully look. A promise of an almost impossible transformation, and a symbol of my favorite childhood memories. Memories of summers spent under a magnolia tree where I'd fallen in love with Luke.

As I was procrastinating, a young couple let themselves into the building and held the door for me.

I'm going in.

I declined their offer of help and they peeled off around the corner as I headed to the lifts. I quickly found the right flat number and dumped the pot where the welcome mat should be. I examined my hands—dirty and red from the indentation of the rim. I slid one palm over another, smoothing off the loose clumps of soil. The door opened. Luke stood over me, one eyebrow raised in a question.

"What are you doing here?" he asked.

"I . . ." I reached into my pocket and pulled out the phone. It was ten after six. I wasn't early. I mentally ran through the days of the week. It was definitely Sunday. I tucked my hair behind my ears, trying to displace the heat in my cheeks. Had I misunderstood? "You invited me."

"I mean, why are you standing outside my door? Why didn't you knock or buzz downstairs?"

I exhaled in relief. "Oh, I came in with some other people, and I was about to ring you." I gestured to the tree. "Your gift."

He grinned and stepped back to examine it. "Thanks."

"I thought it might brighten up your balcony."

"Great. Thanks." He bent and scooped up the pot as if it were groceries. I followed him as he turned and headed into the flat. His muscles tightened then loosened under his T-shirt. I stared at his back and tried to focus on something else, but kept ending up focused on his ass. Shit, I was five seconds into my visit and I'd lost control already.

Luke

I'd heard rustling at the front door and when I'd gone to investigate, I'd found Ashleigh bent over a plant pot. She seemed jumpy. I knew I was. Last week she'd told me she missed me. It had messed with my head and fucked me off. It felt like a game where she played Estella to my Pip. Training cleared my head. I'd run every day this week. The burning in my muscles helped dissipate my near-permanent hard-on I had when I thought of her. It dissolved the conspiracy theories I'd created about how Ashleigh had morphed from my best friend and lover into some sociopathic vixen. Her being so close soothed me—she was still my best friend and the woman I wanted to be here as my date.

I felt Ashleigh's eyes on me as I headed to the balcony door. I lifted my chin, indicating that she open it. She fumbled with the lock and pulled it aside.

I stepped outside and set the pot down. I crouched and grasped the label tied to one of the branches. When in bloom, the plant looked familiar. Pretty. Where had I seen that before? I turned, and Ashleigh joined me on the balcony.

"Thanks, Ashleigh. It will look lovely when the flowers come out."

She shrugged, pursing her lips. She shifted from foot to foot, giving away how uncomfortable she felt.

"If I don't kill it," I continued, trying to calm her.

"It's nice," she said, sweeping her hand toward the open-plan living, dining and kitchen space. "The light is . . . bright."

I chuckled. She was struggling and that helped me relax. We'd known each other our whole lives; it really shouldn't be this difficult. "Let me show you around. Can I get you some wine first?"

"Yeah, I think alcohol would be good."

"And I have snacks. I think. Assuming I've not burned them, I tried to do those cheese straws Haven makes." I'd been cooking most of the day. I was looking forward to seeing Ashleigh, and I wanted to make something nice.

"Do you want to do the wine while I deal with snacks?" I indicated to a cupboard where I kept the wineglasses and picked up an oven cloth. It was nice to have her here, near me, doing things we normally did, even if the venue was new.

I slid the hot tray onto the counter. The straws looked like they did when Haven made them. Awesome.

"The flat came furnished? You've not bought all this stuff?" Ashleigh set the wineglasses beside the cheese straws and headed back to the refrigerator.

"No, everything came with it. Except my sheets and things like that."

"And you've put the sofa in storage?"

I chuckled. My obsession with my old college sofa must have seemed ridiculous. It did to me now. "No, the sofa has gone to sofa heaven."

Ashleigh turned to me, her eyes narrowed.

"I threw it out. It was knackered."

"Wow, you loved that thing. I mean, it was ugly and thank God it's gone, but how come?"

I shrugged. "It just didn't seem important anymore. Time to let it go."

Ashleigh focused on unscrewing the wine. I could see her words bubbling beneath the surface. She never held back. What was she contemplating? I wanted to pull her into my arms and kiss her until she told me what she was thinking. The smooth, creamy skin of her neck seemed to be waiting for my lips. My fingers buzzed with frustration at not being able to touch her.

She poured the wine—it seemed to take more concentration from her than it should. Her unblinking eyes and her fixed frown suggested she was performing brain surgery for the first time, not pouring two old friends a drink.

"So, that's a big change," she finally said.

"What? The sofa? Not really. Or maybe it was, but now it's gone, I realize I should have thrown it out years ago. It doesn't feel like a big thing. It was time to move on."

I grinned, aware of what I was saying and the implications it had for us. She remained silent.

"Can you bring the wine through if I take this?" I pointed to the tray of snacks I'd prepared. "Shall we eat on the balcony?"

She nodded, her lack of words adding to the viscosity of the air between us.

I held the balcony door open and tilted my head, indicating she should go before me. As she stepped through, her hand brushed my torso and set the skin under my shirt alight. It was deliberate and flirtatious and the kind of thing I was used to from Ash, rather than Ashleigh. Was she trying to go back to before? Or was she deliberately making me want her? Instead of catching my eye, she took a seat and slid a glass of wine across the metal table to me.

"Wow, you can see the Shard. This place is great." Relieved she'd finally spoken, I relaxed back into my chair.

"God, I meant to show you around."

"It's fine. Later." She sank back into the chair, looking over the view, relaxed.

"I've cooked duck," I said, proudly.

"Double wow. Duck? Are you sure it's not from the Chinese place?" She raised her eyebrows at me.

"I'm sure." I rolled my eyes. "Heard from Haven?" She was more likely to have spoken to my sister than I was and talking about Haven felt neutral.

"Yeah. She's enjoying the city. Beth is dragging her around, showing her the sights. I think so Jake can spend time with his dad."

"Haven can fend for herself."

"I know, but you know how sweet Beth is. She's trying to keep her occupied, I think."

"Yeah." I knew everything there was to know about keeping occupied.

"How's the running?"

"The training's good. I went out this morning." Exercising in the morning created a calmness in me that stayed with me for the rest of the day, which helped my productivity at work and stopped me from calling Ashleigh every time I thought of her. "I'm trying to train six days a week."

"Wow, are you eating more?" She absentmindedly trailed her eyes down my torso. I knew it wasn't a muffin top that she looking at. The training had had an almost immediate effect on my body. I'd always been fit, but there was a definition under my skin that hadn't been as sharp before. My clothes fit slightly differently. I felt tighter, stronger, faster. It was a powerful feeling, but nothing compared to watching Ashleigh look over my body as if it were chocolate.

My dick stirred as she wet her lips. I reached for my glass of wine, trying to shake it off. My movement interrupted her perusal of my abdomen, and a blush spread across her cheeks.

It was different between us, not because we were in a new place, but because it felt like a date. This didn't feel like two old friends getting together for a dinner. She was watching me because she liked how I looked, and I couldn't stop myself from imagining how she felt.

Maybe Ashleigh had always felt this and had managed to navigate the just friends thing, but for me something had changed and I couldn't go back to how we were. I didn't want to. What I wanted was to spread her out in front of me and have her for dinner.

I considered her over my glass. If I pushed things, would she resist me? Could she? Should I tell her how I was feeling, or would that be too much?

"Can I top you up?" I took her drink from her hands, deliberately brushing my fingers over hers. She jumped as if I were conducting electricity. I did my best to bury a grin.

She was toast.

She was mine.

I continued to watch her as I poured more wine. She seemed determined to admire the London skyline.

"How about that tour?" I asked.

I stood and she followed me back into the living room.

I headed to the back wall, pushing back walnut concertina doors. "This is my study. I guess you could use it as a dining space if you wanted to."

"That's great. Big." She ran her fingers across my desk and along the back of my chair as she checked out the books on the bookshelf.

"Are these yours? I don't remember them at . . . Emma's."

"Yeah, they're mine. I never unpacked them."

"God, yes, I remember this one. Didn't you read this at school? You wrote an essay." She'd picked up a copy of Lord of the Flies and flicked to the back cover. "You were obsessed with it. You called me Piggy for the entire summer."

I frowned, but Ashleigh was turned toward the bookshelves so she couldn't see. "I don't remember that. I mean, I remember reading it and being obsessed, but I don't remember calling you Piggy."

"You don't? I didn't realize until years after that it wasn't because of my thighs—oh and this one. Do you remember? We used to take turns reading it to each other under the magnolia tree in your parents' garden."

I nodded as I remembered the summer we passed The Adventures of Huckleberry Finn around as if it were a secret treasure, which of course, it was. I think we spent the entire summer under that tree, reading, laughing, fighting. I moved toward Ashleigh, close enough to sweep her hair from her neck. I yearned to see more of that perfect skin.

She continued to talk about that summer, the blossom, the way that ever since antebellum had been one of her favorite words. She chattered as if my fingers weren't tangled in her hair, lingering over her neck, tracing her shoulder blades. God, she was mesmerizing. She smelled so sweet, so like summer. How had I resisted her allure for so long? Not seen how important she was to me? How precious, how sexy? My skin felt tight, as if I were going to burst if I didn't feel her lips on mine.

"Ashleigh," I whispered.

But instead of turning and reaching for me as I had expected, she stilled for a second before thrusting the book back on the shelf and hurrying out of the study.

What?

Had I done something wrong? Was I imagining the electricity between us?

I stalked after her to find her stuffing her phone back in her bag. Was she leaving? "Ashleigh."

"I can't. I mean, I melt when you're near me—"

My heart surged. I smiled and she looked away. "That's good, Ashleigh. Me too."

"But you don't get it. It's been happening to me for years. I mean, it can't feel the same for you. It's too soon. It's just been a few weeks since . . ."

"Since I woke up to what's been right in front of me? That makes me an idiot, not unsure of my feelings. If I could turn back time and do things differently, realize what I had with you before, I'd do it. But I can't, and I'm never going to be able to."

"I know." Her voice crackled as she spoke.

"It doesn't mean this can't work. Tell me what to do." I just wanted to get to the part where I could hold her. I was ready. Couldn't she see?

"I just need some time. You need some time."

"I really don't need more time." I exhaled. "Will you ever be ready to trust me?"

"I don't know, Luke. I'm scared. I'm sorry."

Ashleigh

I was fucking up everything. Having Luke so close was confusing. It was as if I were careening down a mountain in a car with no brakes. I didn't know what to do or how to stop it, but I knew how it was going to end.

Everything was so fucking perfect; it was maddening. He'd left Emma, rented his own place, taken up a hobby. Jesus, he'd even thrown out that bloody awful sofa he'd had since college. He was ticking every box that said he was ready. So why was I sitting with my head in my hands rather than lying naked beneath him?

The fact was, it was all too perfect, all too quick. I'd been worried Luke would see my concerns as a checklist for him to work though and conquer. I needed him to take the time to look at what he really wanted. Surely there was no way in the three weeks since we'd last kissed, last seen each other naked, that Luke could have worked through everything.

The problem was he looked ready; he seemed ready; he felt ready. His fingers on my neck lit me up. I was so tightly wound that maybe I was just seeing what I wanted to see. I needed to jolt some sense back into myself.

"Ashleigh." He said my name as if conjuring a spell. When had I become Ashleigh to him?

"I should go."

The sofa dipped as he sat beside me. "I'm sorry if I wasn't meant to touch you. I just . . . You look so touchable. I thought you wanted me to."

I exhaled. That was the problem. Luke touching me was all I wanted. I scrubbed my hands across my face. "I do," I said in a small voice. Instantly his hand went to my lower back, circling, soothing. He felt so easy, so right.

"Hey," he said, pulling my hands from my face, cupping my cheek and forcing my eyes to his.

This man I'd been in love with my whole life seemed like he wanted me. Why couldn't it be this easy? I tilted my head into his hand as he pulled me onto to his lap.

"I got it, Ashleigh. I understood why you put the brakes on at first. But now? I want this. I want you." His words had the opposite of their intended effect. He seemed so certain, and I knew he couldn't be. Not in such a short space of time.

I scrambled off his knee. "No."

"No, you don't believe me? No, you don't want me back?"

I did believe him, and of course I wanted him but it was too soon. "Not yet. You're not ready."

"Fucking hell, Ashleigh. How is it you get to decide when I'm ready? I'm telling you I am. And you know it. You're in my flat, flirting with me, teasing me. Is that what this is? Are you just trying to make me want something I can't have so I know how you've felt all these years?"

His voice became tighter, harder, louder with every word. He rose from the sofa, and I backed away from him. We'd had relatively few arguments over the years, but I remembered each one of them in their every detail. I regretted every cross word that had ever gone between us. "That's not fair, Luke. You think I'm trying to pay you back?"

"Well? Are you?"

My hand grasped my chest. How could he think I'd ever want to hurt him? All I was doing was trying to protect myself. I needed to get out. I didn't want him to see me cry, and I knew tears were next.

I grabbed my bag and headed toward the door. He followed me. "Are you just going to leave? That's it? No discussion? Fucking perfect."

"We're not having a discussion. You're shouting at me. I'm just trying—" I continued toward the door, stopping as I reached for the handle.

"To do what, exactly? Keep yourself and me miserable? Give yourself a reason not to be with me?"

The corridor was dark, but I could still see the shadow of Luke's enormous frame covering me. He stood so close that if I just moved back an inch, my body would be pressed against his.

"Please." I wasn't sure what I was asking for. For him to be patient with me, for him to let me leave.

"Tell me what you want." He spoke softly this time.

"I want to be sure of you and how you feel. If overnight you've decided you want me then just as quickly you can change your mind again. I want to be sure I'm not the easy option—"

"Believe me, I don't think you're the easy option. Especially not at the moment." He sighed, and I felt him move away from me. I turned to face him. He was leaning against the wall, his hands stuffed in his pockets, his head bowed.

"I'm sorry."

"Tell me how long I have to wait, what I have to do. I get that it was too soon after Emma when we first . . . But now—"

"There's so much at stake." My family, my security, my world were on the line.

"But so much to gain."

"It's still only a few weeks."

"But not in my head, Ashleigh. I don't think I was ever in deep with Emma. Not like I am with you. This is different. I can't go back. You mean too much to me for me to think that this can't work."

My pulse was jumping in my neck. He was saying everything I wanted to hear. "We just need time."

"I don't." He sounded so sure. "You might need time but I'm ready for the next stage of my life, and I don't want to miss a moment."

"Then will you give me time?" Maybe that was it. Maybe I needed time to adjust, to trust Luke's feelings for me.

"How long?"

"I don't know. Live your life, Luke. If we're meant to happen, we'll know when the time is right for both of us."

chapter
SEVENTEEN

Luke

"Wow, your pace has really come on." Fiona grabbed my wrist, pressing at buttons on my tracker. "Yeah. Your speed has gone up by twenty percent in just a few weeks. That's incredible."

I fell forward, grasping my knees and desperately pulling air into my lungs as I waited for the thudding in my chest to reduce so I could speak, think.

Fiona was breathless, but didn't seem close to passing out the way I was. How embarrassing. I knew she'd been training for far longer, but I hadn't started from nothing. I'd always been a runner.

"Jesus, you're fit," I said, glancing up at her, finally able to form words.

"Thanks," she said, coyly lifting one shoulder and giving me a small smile. "You've just started to train differently, but you're doing really well. You need to mix it up though. Maybe start some circuit training. Don't just concentrate on running, cycling and swimming. I know it sounds counterintuitive, but it will help." She tapped my upper arm. "Come on. Keep walking."

Fiona and I had been running a route around the city—it was so quiet at the weekends. All the commuters had dispersed, leaving behind empty office buildings and the few of us who lived within the square mile that made up London's financial district. It had been a peaceful run, a stark contrast to barely being able to squeeze onto the pavements when walking on weekdays. Fiona said the parks of West London, where I'd always run before, got too busy at the weekends, especially if the weather was decent. Hyde Park had always been a favorite, but then it hadn't mattered if people got in my way and slowed me down.

"Shall we grab a coffee?" I pointed to one of the few signs of life—a small cafe across the street. It gave me a reason to sit, which worked for me.

Fiona narrowed her eyes but nodded. "Sure."

We ordered coffees—or in my case a juice and water, I was laying off the caffeine—and found a table near the window. There was only one other couple in the place. No wonder nothing was open around here, there weren't any customers. I watched as they wordlessly swapped bits of the Sunday Times. I could have been watching Emma and me. Comfortable together. Unconsciously moving forward. Life didn't require you to evaluate your relationship constantly, so most people just floated along if there was no reason to split. In a way, I was lucky that Emma had brought up marriage because I'd been forced to make a conscious choice about my future. I guess that was exactly what Ashleigh was afraid of—that I was happy to drift into coupledom, when for her it was a positive action. I took a deep breath at the realization. Maybe these weeks since I'd last seen Ashleigh were a good thing for us both.

"Are you enjoying it?" Fiona asked.

I swallowed my grapefruit juice. "It's tangy."

She laughed, and I was drawn to the movement of her breasts. "I meant the training."

I rolled my eyes. "Oh, I see. Yes. It's brutal, and I'm not sure it's a healthy thing to like brutal, but yes."

I was enjoying the focus I was getting from it, the fact I didn't have too much time on my hands and that I was working toward something. I'd enjoyed the way Ashleigh had looked at my changing body the last time she'd seen me. The heat in her eyes had led me to believe she wanted me.

I'd not seen her since then. I'd made excuses to miss Sunday dinners in the few weeks following, and there had been no phone calls, no contact. I'd hated it, particularly at first, and checked my phone relentlessly, waiting for her to tell me she was ready. Now I was nearly resigned to just letting things settle between us.

Fiona laughed. "It is brutal, but I like the feeling now," she said, watching me twist the circular lid of my drink. "After running, the come down. The sweat beginning to dry, the awareness of the strengthened muscles under my skin, the adrenaline seeping away." She stretched her arms, lifting tall in her chair, the hem of her shirt riding up and revealing a band of soft white skin.

She relaxed and I glanced back up at her face. She'd caught me checking her out. She smiled and I looked away.

"Yeah. I guess this bit's good." I stared out the window at nothing, not quite knowing what I meant. She was good company. And attractive.

"So what made you want to start to train? Bad breakup?" she asked.

Ashleigh and I hadn't broken up; we hadn't had a chance to break up. It struck me that I was post breakup, just with Emma.

"I don't know about bad . . ." I shifted in my seat, more comfortable now that the focus was away from her body, and back onto safer territory . . . kinda.

"How long were you a couple?"

"Three years. We were living together. I moved out." A dull sensation radiated from my gut. It wasn't sorrow—it was irritation, regret maybe, that I'd stayed as long as I had. I should have been braver, moved on sooner. The problem was, each day in itself wasn't an issue. Emma and I didn't hate each other, or continually fight. There'd been nothing pushing me away as such. It was just when I added up those days, they didn't amount to much. All together we'd not mattered much to each other, there'd been nothing drawing us together, making us better as a couple. God, it felt like a lifetime ago. It had all happened before Ashleigh, and anyone before her seemed long ago. She was different. Every day with her mattered.

She nodded. "For me, it helped me clear my mind as well as kept me busy. I reckon I was over him the moment I passed the finish line of my first race."

"Yours was a bad breakup?" I asked.

"At the time, I remember it being so. I was so sad, so angry. I wanted to kill him. Now, I look back and it's difficult to recall why. I mean, he was an arsehole at times, but I blamed him for things I had no right to. I learned a huge lesson that we alone are responsible for our happiness. No one else can create that for us if we're not ready for it."

"But being with him didn't make you happy?"

"Exactly. So I should have left. Not stayed and blamed him."

I took a moment to absorb what she was saying. Was I looking for someone to make me happy? Was I afraid of being on my own? Maybe Ashleigh thought so, but that wasn't it for me. I thought if anything the reason Emma and I had split was because I didn't want to be responsible for her happiness, and I knew she couldn't be responsible for mine. With Ashleigh, it was different. I wanted to make her happy.

"And you're with someone now?" She'd never mentioned a boyfriend. What type of guy was she into?

A blush spread across her cheeks. "Not yet. But I've not lost hope that I'll find the right one." She focused on her coffee cup, swirling her spoon in what was left of the black Americano she'd ordered.

"Great job, Luke. A tremendous result for the client and the firm." Derek Mills, our senior partner, rarely stepped off the fifth floor. He certainly hadn't known my name until the Nigelson case. Although no one had said it to me directly, whether or not I made partner depended on this case. And today it had settled. Settled good and settled big.

"Thanks, Derek. We got the right result," I replied.

"Don't be modest. You got the right result." I grinned and took Derek's hand. "The Daniels surname will fit nicely on the letterhead," he said, and with that, he winked and walked away. Perhaps that's what they meant when they said that you "got the nod." I'd have to wait for the official decision on partnership, but it was looking pretty good.

I focused on getting back to my desk without breaking into a sidesplitting grin. I dropped Haven an email telling her we'd settled. My hand hovered over my phone. I was desperate to call Ashleigh; I wanted to share my good news, all my news, my whole life with her. I just wished she was ready to see that. Perhaps I should take the situation into my own hands and force her to see that I wanted her?

"Congratulations, Luke!" Fiona walked up to my desk. "It was that environmental report that swung it, though, wasn't it?"

I grinned at her. "Yup, you totally nailed it."

She clasped her hands together. "Thank fuck that's over."

I tipped my head back and laughed. "Shall we knock off early and go and get some beers in?"

"I'm not sure that's on your training plan. But yes, I'm up for that." She winked and turned to leave. Over her shoulder, she said, "I'll meet you downstairs in ten minutes."

"Champagne?" Fiona asked as she leaned over the bar, trying to get the attention of the barman.

I would have preferred beer, but champagne was sort of mandatory in this situation.

"You are totally going to get partnership now." She grinned at me. I was relieved that there wasn't a hint of jealousy or resentfulness about her. She really was a great girl.

"I can only hope." I shrugged.

"You know you're going to get it. Apparently the vote is next week. This settlement couldn't have been timed more perfectly. You deserve it."

I grinned and grabbed the champagne-filled ice bucket. Fiona took the glasses, and we made our way to a spot toward the front of the bar. Despite it being the middle of the afternoon, there were plenty of people filling the tables.

"We shouldn't be drinking when everyone else is back at their desks. It feels naughty," Fiona said in a half whisper.

My stomach churned. It did feel wrong in some ways, uncomfortable. The person I wanted to celebrate with was Ashleigh. I felt as though I should be with her, not Fiona. I needed to stop pining, to do what she said and live my life. "Day drinking always feels illicit, right?"

"I can't stop for long. I have a thing tonight." She tilted her head.

I raised my eyebrows in response. Did she have a date? Fiona, at least, was living her life.

"In fact, I shouldn't be drinking. I'm babysitting. Well, my nephew's twelve, so hardly a baby."

"So no hot date for you, then?"

"Not tonight," she replied.

I wondered why she was single. She was pretty, smart and had abs of steel. The kind of girl they called marriage material. Ashleigh had told me to date, right? "Would you like to go to dinner sometime?" It wasn't what I'd been planning to say, but now that I had, I hoped she'd say yes.

She narrowed her eyes at me.

I'd not asked a woman out for years. In fact, I didn't think I'd ever asked Emma out. We just found ourselves in the same circle of friends a few times, and we kind of evolved from a drunken kiss. It felt like a lifetime ago. I'd been a kid. I'd thought for a few weeks that Fiona might like me, but her reaction to my invitation wasn't overwhelming. "I mean, no big deal if you don't want to. I just thought—"

"No. That sounds good. Like on a date?"

Was I about to make a giant twat of myself? I shrugged. "Yeah."

Her cheeks flushed and she nodded. "Okay. Dinner."

If only everything in my life could be as easy.

chapter
EIGHTEEN

Ashleigh

"I'm sick of feeling so fucking miserable. I've totally lost my funny." I took a seat at Beth's kitchen counter and collapsed forward dramatically. Beth had asked for some help with a project, and I was happy to have the company.

"You've not lost your funny. You're hilarious," Beth responded.

"I used to be funny. I used to be able to make people laugh. Now, I'm a harbinger of doom. Wherever I go, I bring misery."

"Now, you're being funny, even if it is unintentional."

I grinned. It was entirely intentional. I was ready to be me again. I'd had enough of moping around the house and avoiding Luke. Well, avoiding Luke had been made easy. He hadn't been in touch. Not since the Sunday Haven and Jake had been in Chicago. That was over a month ago. I'd gone to Sunday night dinner the following weekend, but according to Haven, Luke was working. I'd not seen him since I'd run out on him.

"So you want to watch me get drunk?" I asked Beth.

"How can I resist an offer like that? But first can you help me with this?" Beth asked, gesturing behind me with the wooden spoon she was holding.

I glanced over my shoulder and saw a camera set up on a tripod facing our direction. What the what? I turned back to watch Beth pour honey into a mixing bowl. "Errr, excuse me, however much you're offering? I'm not filming us naked with honey doing . . . God knows what."

"Oh, I'm not going to pay you."

"Well, I'm certainly not doing it for free." I laughed. "What I mean to say is, not in front of a camera. And not with you. No offense, you're gorgeous and you have a banging bod, but no. I like dick. I mean, I've never . . . not on camera, and not with honey—"

"Really?" Beth was looking at me as if I were totally crazy.

"I've lost control of my mouth."

"You really have. Calm down. No one is getting naked."

"Okay, so what's going on?"

"I don't want you to tell Jake, but I need you to set up the camera for me. I thought I might film myself bake and then put it on the Internet. I'll film it tomorrow, but I thought you could set up the camera for me and I could leave it there until I'm ready."

"Oh, that's easy. I have to say I'm slightly disappointed. I thought my horizons were about to be broadened."

"By my banging bod? Thanks for that, by the way." She lifted her shoulder, playfully flirting.

"You're welcome." I grinned. There was a knock at the door and Beth went to answer it. I heard Haven chattering away in the hall. She and Beth lived in the same building. I probably should have told Haven when I arrived. I hoped she wasn't mad I hadn't.

"Hello, gorgeous. Room for a third?" she asked when she saw me.

I pulled her into a hug. "I've missed you."

"I feel like you've divorced me. I've not seen you in weeks."

"I'm sorry. I wanted Luke to have a chance to come to Sunday dinner, and that didn't seem likely if I was going, so . . ."

"Well, he's divorced me too. I've not seen him for weeks, either. How come when you two try and avoid each other, I end up missing you both? I wish you'd sort it out. He's running today, apparently. A fun run."

"Sounds like an oxymoron. Is he with Fiona?"

"I think so. It's her running club or something."

My stomach pinched. It had been raining all day. It was too easy to imagine him soaked to the skin and miserable, then peeling off his wet clothes, revealing his harder than hard body, his toned abs, his thick arms as he pulled me into the shower . . . My thoughts of him were endless, but somehow against all odds, I'd resisted the temptation to call him. He needed time to work out what he wanted. Maybe that was Fiona.

"Anyway," I said, elongating the word like a six-year-old. "I'm trying to get my funny back."

"You need wine for that," Haven said, rummaging in her bright pink Longchamp Le Pliage. "Sorry, Beth. Sober works for you, but not for this one." She lifted her chin and pulled out a bottle of wine. "It's already chilled."

I looked between Beth and Haven. I'd drunk in front of Beth before, but never in her house. "Is this okay with you? I was joking when I asked you about watching me get drunk."

"Of course. It's totally fine, although, if you catch me taking a swig, then we've got problems." She winked.

I shook my head. "Haven, no, put it away."

"She's joking. Aren't you?"

"Of course I am." Beth grinned. "Other people drinking isn't a problem. It's my drinking that's the problem."

Beth always seemed so wise beyond her years. She'd been through a lot and it showed—not because she looked tired or bitter but because she radiated a confidence that's only gained through experience.

"Actually, can you just position that camera while you're still sober?" Beth asked me as Haven found some wineglasses.

I hopped off my stool and went over to the camera.

"Should I ask about the camera?" Haven was frowning. "I mean, whatever you're into, there's no judgment here. In fact, I'm planning on filming myself for Jake while he's in—"

"There are some things you don't need to share," Beth said, covering her ears.

"Hmmm, not true," I replied. "Tell me more."

"Jake's going to Chicago in a month. I was thinking of sending him with a gift. I'll tell you the rest another time."

Beth rolled her eyes.

This was nice. I'd not felt this comfortable, this at home, for ages.

"Have you spoken to him?" Haven asked. Instantly my comfort shattered.

I shook my head.

"Ash, you know I love you . . ." My heart sank. I was about to get a verbal spanking. "But it's been weeks, in fact, it's been months since he split with Emma. When has enough time gone by?"

It was a question I'd asked myself a million times. But it wasn't about time. It was about experience. If Luke was staying at home, just waiting for me to come round, then there would never be enough time gone. "I don't know." I sighed. "I think we'll both know if it's right."

"That's bullshit," Beth said.

Haven started to chew the inside of her cheek and fixated on her wine.

"What's bullshit?" I asked.

"What happens if you just never see him again? The way you're going, you might just end up avoiding each other until you're both old and gray. He doesn't know what you want, and to be honest, neither do I."

My pulse was hammering in my chest. Had I been an enormous idiot?

"Sorry, I'm a compulsive truth teller. I sometimes forget we're not related and it's less acceptable," Beth said.

"Don't be sorry for telling me what you think." I welcomed her opinion. "It boils down to trust. At first, I thought it was all about me not trusting his change of heart. I didn't want to be the second prize—he couldn't be bothered to go out and find what he really wanted, so I got him by default. And that's only half of it. I need to trust myself as well. I need to be willing to risk it all—my family, my friends, my future—everything that's important to me to give it a shot with Luke."

Beth took a deep breath. "You need to understand how we'll support you and love you no matter what. You're not risking your family or friends. But, if you never take that next step with him, you might be risking your future."

Her words hit right to my core. Maybe she was right, that I was risking more by not giving us a chance.

Luke

"Would you like white or red?" I asked as our sommelier approached the table.

Fiona shrugged. "I don't mind. You choose."

This was new territory for me. Dating, and then having to think about what would make someone I didn't know very well happy. Emma always drank Shiraz no matter where we were or what we were eating. Haven and Ashleigh would drink pretty much anything, but sauvignon blanc was their favorite white and pinot noir their favorite red. Now I was learning another woman's preferences. It felt weird.

"We'll take a bottle of the champagne," I said to the waiter. I knew she liked fizzy stuff because we'd had it at the bar. "Goes with anything, right?" I asked Fiona as the waiter turned away.

"Sounds good."

She was smiling so that had to be good.

"You look beautiful," I said. She'd clearly put some effort into looking good and it suited her. She never wore much makeup to work, and none when we went running, but tonight she looked glamorous, sexy even, but not in a showy way. I'd never seen her brown hair down. It suited her, made her more feminine, as did her pink dress. She looked more like a woman than I'd ever seen before. This really was a date, which was . . . confusing.

"So do you. Handsome, I mean." Her cheeks flushed. It was sweet.

I smiled. I was aware of every part of my body. It was as if I had to consciously remember to put one foot in front of the other, lift my arm, breathe in and out. I filled my lungs and fisted my hands at my sides. I could do this. There was nothing to be nervous about. Fiona and I spent loads of time together. I liked her; we got on. I'd known her for a long time, but only for a couple of months as anything except colleagues. But tonight shouldn't be difficult. We had plenty in common and we liked each other.

"So, did you train today?" she asked.

I was grateful that she took hold of the conversation. I had migrated into idiot land and forgotten how to do small talk.

"Yeah, in the gym. I did a session with that trainer I told you I was thinking about getting. We did some weights then I went on the treadmill."

"It's good that you've got someone helping you with that stuff. I did the same thing at first. It's too easy to injure yourself, but I guess you've used them before." She brushed her hands up and down in the air, indicating the length of my body.

I shrugged. "Not for a goal like this race. What about you? Did you go for a run?"

"Yeah. Saturday mornings are my favorite. But I went early. At six. Then I got waxed and I had coffee with a girlfriend."

"You got waxed?" As I was finishing my question, I realized what she was saying and quickly broke eye contact. Shit, why did I have to ask her about the waxing? She'd been to the beauty parlor. She'd been preparing . . . for tonight. My palms started to sweat. Was she expecting to show me the waxed areas? I hadn't even begun to contemplate sleeping with her.

"It was a regular appointment. Not for tonight. I mean, if you're a girl and you're running, it's important to keep . . . Oh Jesus. Please kill me now." Her head rolled back.

I started to laugh. The mention of waxing had broken the ice. "Let's do a U-turn, shall we? How was coffee?"

She shook her head. "I shouldn't be allowed out. Yes. Thank you. Coffee was good. It was a friend I've known since I was five. We grew up together; she's getting married, and she asked me to be bridesmaid. So, yes, it was good to see her."

"Oh, that's really nice. When's the wedding?"

"Next summer. To be honest, I hate the idea. Can't bear the whole big show and ridiculous dress, but it's important to her so it's an honor really."

I smiled. It seemed we had more in common than just triathlons.

"Do you have brothers and sisters?" I asked. Our conversations up until now had been mainly about work or training, so although in some ways I knew her quite well, in reality my knowledge of her private life was limited.

"Two sisters. Both older. I'm the baby. The ugly duckling."

"The what?"

"My sisters are supremely glamorous. I mean knockouts. I was always the tomboy."

"Well you don't look like a tomboy tonight."

"God, did that sound as if I was fishing for compliments? I'm sorry, I really wasn't. I love having gorgeous sisters now, well, most of the time. But, you know, in those awkward teen years it was tough. What am I saying? I bet you didn't have those years."

I thought back. I didn't remember any. "I think that's more of a girl thing." I didn't really remember Haven or Ashleigh being awkward.

"Maybe. Anyway, they're happy; I'm happy. One lives in LA with her producer husband. The other lives in Barnes. She's a lawyer too."

I liked hearing her talk about her family. "Are you close?"

She seemed to think about that for a couple of seconds. "We don't fight. But no, we're not super close. I babysit and stuff, but we all have very different lives. What about you? You're close to Haven."

I realized she already knew I had a sister. I must talk about her without even realizing it. "Yeah, we're close. I get on well with her husband too." I didn't mention Ashleigh. Was I still close to her? Would we find a way back to each other, even if not as lovers? The thought turned my stomach. I hated not having her in my life.

"You okay?" Fiona asked.

"Yeah, fine. I remembered that I said I would call Haven today and I forgot." The lie was easier than the truth.

I shook my head and took a breath. I couldn't be thinking about Ashleigh.

After that, I relaxed and it became more natural to share

details of my life with her and her with me. It was comfortable and nice. I liked her. She was sweet and caring.

"Can you just wait here a minute?" I asked the cab driver as Fiona climbed out, and I followed her onto the pavement. "Thanks for a lovely evening," I said as we walked toward her building.

"Thank you. I had a really good time, Luke." She smiled a half smile at me as we came to her front door.

"So, I'll see you at work on Monday?"

She nodded. This was when I was meant to kiss her goodbye. She definitely gave the impression that it wouldn't be unwelcome, but it had been so long since I'd been in this position. I got that same consciousness in my limbs that I'd had at the beginning of the evening. I liked her, and it was just a kiss. Glancing at the ground, I took a half step toward her, put my fingers under her chin and tilted her head. My gaze flicked between her mouth and her eyes once, then twice and then I bent, pressing my lips to hers. Her body swayed toward me, and I caught the scent of her for the first time that evening. It was unfamiliar. She ran her hands down my arms, but before it could turn into anything more, I pulled away and whispered, "Good night."

I tried to remember the first time I'd kissed Emma. It had been similar. Nice. There'd been an awareness that we didn't quite fit yet, but that we might. With Fiona it was the same. She was a nice girl, easy to be around and we had a lot in common—more than Emma and I ever had.

But she wasn't Ashleigh.

chapter
NINETEEN

Ashleigh

"This one is super comfortable," I said to Richard as I rearranged myself on the sofa. Richard had moved into a new apartment and had asked me to help him find some new furniture.

"You don't like the brown leather?"

My stomach churned. Brown leather sofas always reminded me of Luke, even if he had finally thrown his away.

I shook my head. "Leather is cold in the winter and sticks to you in the summer. I've never understood its appeal. And it squeaks."

"Squeaks? Like talks to you? Have you seen a doctor for that?" Richard's eyes were wide.

"They do. You know—when you move around on them." I blushed and looked away. I had totally imagined having sex with Luke every which way on his battered old sofa, and every time I had, the squeaks had been off-putting, even in a fantasy.

Richard collapsed next to me. "Yeah, this one is comfortable. And it's nice and deep. Do you think two people could lay on it together? I think we should spoon. Just to be sure."

I elbowed him in the ribs. "Stop it." Richard had been flirting with me all morning, teasing me by saying we were going straight to the bed department to test out mattresses.

"You're meant to be here to help." He slipped his hand around my shoulders and stuck his feet on the low table in front of him. "This works. But if you've vetoed leather, can I at least get a corner one?"

What was it about boys and corner sofas? "If you have the space."

"Yeah, you've not seen it, have you? You should come round. I can cook. What about tonight?"

My heart sped as I remembered the evening at Luke's new place. I'd never gotten to taste the duck he said he'd cooked.

"It's no big deal. We can go straight to mine when we've finished here." He clapped his hands and rubbed them together.

We'd been firmly in the friend zone for weeks now, so I'd expected the flirting to stop. But it hadn't, and I was beginning to enjoy it. It was attention that felt safe.

"Maybe. Let's see how we get on." I appreciated his company, but the last thing I wanted to do was be a prick tease. I pointed across the showroom. "Let's try that gray one. I like it because it's a corner but not a corner with the bit that sticks out on one end for your feet."

"Very eloquent, Ash. Really." He squeezed my shoulder and stood, then offered to pull me up.

"I'm not an old lady. I can manage standing up just fine."

"Okay, Miss Grumpy Knickers. I was trying to be a gentleman." He turned and headed to the other sofa.

God, I was a witch sometimes. I was clearly channeling Haven. "Sorry. And you don't need to try. It comes naturally to you," I said as I caught up with him.

"That's better." He nudged my shoulder. "You see? You can be charming when you put your mind to it. Now, this I like." He flung himself full length across the cushions of the sofa. "I'm going to ask some random stranger to lie with me and test out the spooning capabilities of this sofa if you're still refusing to cooperate."

"Yeah? Good luck with that. You wouldn't dare."

He rested his head on his elbow and raised an eyebrow. "You're daring me? You're actually daring me?"

Richard seemed to have loosened up in the last couple of weeks. I suppose without the pressure of a relationship, I had too, and we were getting on better than ever. I'd started to see his fun side. My feelings for Luke had led to me label Richard as not being the one. I'd thought Luke was . . . but I hadn't made that work either.

Perhaps I'd been wrong to write off Richard too soon.

"Excuse me, Miss." Richard leapt to his feet and caught the attention of a woman with a pushchair. I watched, open-mouthed.

"My wife," he said, pointing to me, "doesn't like public displays of affection. She won't spoon with me on this sofa to see if we fit. Would you mind standing in for her?"

The woman turned her head toward me, and I could do nothing but shrug. She looked as if she were in pain, but replied, "I'm sorry. I'm running late." She scurried to the opposite end of the show room, toward the lifts.

Grinning, Richard turned to me. I rolled my eyes. "For the record," he said, "it's not a good idea to dare me to do anything. I find it impossible to pass up a challenge."

He winked at me as if I were next.

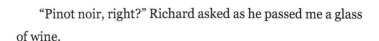

"Pinot noir, right?" Richard asked as he passed me a glass of wine.

"Perfect, thanks." How had he known which wine I liked? I'd had a really good time shopping with him. He'd bought the gray corner-not-a-corner, sofa, despite him being unable to spoon before he purchased. He'd been funny and laid back and all the things I'd wanted him to be when we'd dated. I genuinely didn't want our time together to be over, so when he asked me again to go back to his flat for dinner, I'd gone along with it.

"How come you moved?"

He joined me on his old sofa and rested his sock-covered feet on the table in front of him. "I think I was holding off until I found someone to share a place with. And then, after we . . ." He paused, and I took a sip of my wine, trying to ignore the discomfort that pushed between us. "I just thought I needed to get on and live in the place I wanted to."

I nodded, struck that he hadn't simply moved on to the next girl when I'd ended things. He'd got on with his life, but kept the door between us open. He'd basically done what I'd asked Luke to.

He turned toward me, rearranging his body so he was

sitting with one leg hitched on the cushion, his arm resting on the back of the sofa and his hand just behind my head.

"It's a nice place." I glanced around the room. Everything was neat and matching in various tones of gray. I turned to look at him.

He was watching me. "It's not very family friendly, but I reckon I can move again when the time comes."

"You feel ready for a family?"

"Yeah, I want to find that special someone and have a bunch of rowdy kids. Don't you?"

I thought about Luke, Haven and I sitting under the magnolia tree, reading, fighting, laughing. "At some point."

"I thought that maybe you and I were right. I think that's why I was so tense when we were dating."

"You were tense?" Had I not seen the real him?

"Yeah, I was crazy for you, and wanted to make it all just so." He shrugged. He seemed to find it easy to be open with me about how he'd felt, and I really liked that he did.

"Crazy?" I asked. Had we been dating long enough for him to be crazy for me?

"You know how I felt—how I feel. I could see how we could have been so perfect together. I was impatient and pushed when I shouldn't have."

"Richard . . ." I suppose we were bound to have this conversation at some point. We'd been spending time together, and we'd never discussed what had happened between us. Still, it felt uncomfortable.

"I just wanted you to know that I get it. I understand that I got it wrong. I don't want you to think that I'm a total idiot."

I shifted slightly so I was facing him, mirroring the position of his legs with mine. "I don't think you're an idiot. Not at all. But we learn from each relationship, don't we? And we take that into our next one."

"Maybe . . . it's just . . . I think when it's like this between us, I wonder if there's a second chance in there somewhere . . . for you and me." His dark brown eyes were staring at me intently.

I took a deep breath. If I hadn't been lost in the fog of Luke and I, I probably would have seen this coming more clearly. Maybe I'd even want that second chance.

"I don't think I properly gave you a first chance, Richard. And that wasn't your fault—it was entirely mine. I was unfair to you." I needed to be honest with him. "It's just, I've had feelings about someone else for a very long time." I stared into my wine, embarrassed that I'd perhaps led him on, even though I'd truly been trying to get over Luke when we dated.

"Luke," he said and I cringed. Was it that obvious? I nodded.

"But you're not together?"

My heart ached at his words. "No, we're not together."

"Have you ever been? I mean, is it unrequited?"

My cheeks heated. It felt wrong talking to him about this, especially as Richard had just declared he'd been crazy for me. "There was a brief . . . I really have no idea." Luke had told me that he had feelings for me—romantic feelings—and the sex had been incredible, but I didn't know what future there might be for us. All I knew was that I wasn't ready to move on from him. Not yet.

Richard's fingers crept along my arm. "He's a fool if he doesn't love you."

"Richard . . ."

"I mean it. I get that you're caught up with him, but if he doesn't get what an amazing, sexy, funny person you are, then he's a giant idiot."

I closed my eyes, willing myself not to cry. He was being so kind and understanding. A huge part of me just wanted to be taken in his arms and comforted.

"If and when you're ready to start dating again, I'd try not to mess it up," he continued.

"Richard—" He was being so nice, and I didn't know how to react.

"Don't say anything. Just think about it. No pressure."

I opened my eyes and stared at my lap.

"Hey, don't be sad. I wasn't trying to induce depression." He stroked my jaw. "Come on," he said, jumping off the sofa. "You can help me with dinner. Maybe I can win you over with my mad chef skills. Let's press pause on this conversation for tonight, and just have a nice evening. Agreed?"

I smiled. It was just what he needed to say. I wanted time to process what he'd suggested. He was a good guy who wanted a second chance. I couldn't just dismiss that, could I? But at the same time, I wasn't ready to give up on my fairy tale.

A pause button was exactly what the doctor called for.

Luke

"You look like my brother, but you can't be him. He doesn't come around here anymore," Haven said, clearly looking through the peephole.

"Ha bloody ha, Haven. Let me in."

I'd promised Haven I'd turn up to Sunday dinner this week. She'd been harassing me for days, but she'd been right. Ashleigh and I had to get through this—at least as friends—so I couldn't avoid her anymore.

The door swung open, but she was already halfway back down the corridor, and heading for the kitchen. "Way to make me feel welcome."

Jake stood at the counter, bent over what looked like a recipe book. "Hey, mate," I said.

He gave me a hug, his eyes bright. "It's so good to see you. Thanks for coming. Haven's been a wreck with all this shit going on with you and Ash."

My stomach dropped. I'd not thought about the impact on Haven. "I'm sorry. I just needed a bit of space."

"You don't need space from me, you dickhead," she said.

"Not you, from Ashleigh. I didn't want it be difficult between you two, so I thought . . . I don't know."

"He's here now, Haven. That's the main thing," Jake said. "It'll be a great night."

"Is Ashleigh coming?" I asked. Haven had been pretty fierce when she'd told me to get over it and turn up for dinner. She'd said she was making Sunday night dinner mandatory and would tell Ashleigh the same thing.

"Of course she is. I've told you, there's no choice. You two need to find a way because I'm not having my family breaking apart." Haven's voice quivered and Jake reached out to smooth circles on her back. "Not now." She moved away from him and scurried past me into the bathroom at the same time the door buzzer went. Jesus, I'd had no idea she was so upset.

"Can you get that?" Jake asked. "I'll go and check on Haven."

"Yeah, of course. God, I'm sorry. I—" I hated to see Haven sad. It was my job to protect her. The last thing I wanted was to be the cause of her sorrow.

"Listen, don't worry about it. I'll explain in a bit . . . You see in Ash." Jake hurried after Haven, and I went to answer the door.

Her smile faltered, just a tiny bit, when she saw me. "Hey." Her voice was quiet and unsure, and I had to muster up a burst of energy when all I wanted to do was stand and stare at her. To remind myself of her every soft curve.

I bent and kissed her on her cheek. "It's good to see you, Ashleigh. It really is." I inhaled her scent. It was a call home, a call to where I belonged. Every time I saw her I was more and more certain that we were meant to be together, that I needed her, wanted her . . . loved her. I'd been giving her some space by not coming to Sunday dinner, but I'd also been giving myself some space. It was too painful to be constantly reminded of what I desperately wanted but couldn't have. Of where I should be, who I should be with.

"Where's Haven and Jake?" She looked round the living room as we entered.

I frowned. "The bathroom, I think. Haven got a bit upset. I think because the whole Sunday dinner thing. I mean, I've not been coming. I don't know about you."

She shook her head. "No, me neither. I thought—"

She thought she'd give me room to keep on with our ritual, and I'd tried to do the same. "We should make more of an effort."

She nodded, the light catching on her hair, highlighting her beautiful face. I had to look away. How had I gone so many years without being totally mesmerized by her?

"God, that's not like her to be upset about stuff like this." She shuffled from one foot to the other. All I wanted to do was pull her close.

I held my breath as Haven's and Jake's voices became louder and doors opened and closed.

"So, it's this guy's fault," Haven announced, pointing her thumb toward Jake.

"What is?" I asked as Haven hugged Ashleigh. Why was Jake getting the blame?

"Me getting emotional." She pulled away from Ashleigh and put her arm around Jake's waist. "He knocked me up."

"What?" Ashleigh squealed. "You're pregnant? That's amazing."

"We wanted you both here, so we could tell you at the same time," Jake said.

"Beth, too, but she's in Chicago, and I wasn't drinking when she popped in earlier in the week. And well, she guessed . . ."

"Wow, congratulations," I said, shocked as I shook Jake's hand and pulled him into a hug. I looked Haven up and down, trying to spot evidence of a bump. She grasped at her stomach. My sister was pregnant. I was going to be an uncle. Fucking hell. I'd thought life was moving quickly before. "You're a braver man that I."

"Don't look at me like that." I pulled her toward me, and she wrapped her arms around my waist. Pride knotted in my stomach. A huge wave of relief passed through me that I'd never had an accident with Emma. I would have married her, of course, and it would never have been enough for me.

"I'm so proud of you," I said, my cheek resting on her head. "You're going to be an amazing mother."

"Turns out it's not that difficult to get pregnant," Haven replied. "It wasn't planned." My stomach churned. I hoped she was ready. I wasn't sure I'd ever be. A kid was going to change things in our family forever.

"That's because we're so good at baby making." Jake grinned proudly.

"Okay, enough already." Ashleigh covered her ears. I reached out to pull her into a weird double hug behind Haven. The three of us stood together like the unit we'd been for so long.

It felt good.

"Come on, guys, break it up. I'm starting to feel left out," Jake said.

The three of us dispersed and gathered round the kitchen island.

"So we need to celebrate. I should have brought champagne." Ashleigh clasped her hands together. She was excited, her eyes sparkling. Our earlier awkwardness had dissipated.

"I've got some. We've got lots to celebrate. Ash sat her

entrance exam to business school. And you won your whats-a-mathing case," Haven said. "I've not seen you properly since."

"You won the Nigelson case?" Ashleigh asked, her eyes wide.

I nodded and stuffed my hands in my pockets. "Well, it settled, in our favor."

"Oh my God, Luke, this is huge. Congratulations." She wrapped her arms around my neck. Shocked, I slid my hands around her waist, leaned down and pulled her close. "You should have told me," she mumbled against my skin. Her familiar scent wound itself around me, all sweetness and summer. I had to work hard not to smooth my hands over that perfect ass of hers. She moved her body against mine. Like flint on stone, sparks went off across my skin. Jesus, it was torture holding her like this, but being unable to peel off her clothes, lay her down, spread her out and enjoy her. My dick began to harden. I tensed and pulled back.

"I know." I would have normally told her, but I'd forgotten how to be normal with her. "How was the exam?"

"Good, I think. I won't know for a few weeks whether I got in." She wouldn't meet my eyes as we parted. She headed toward the refrigerator as if we'd just had a friendly hug. "Rule number one of your pregnancy is that you can't judge me for drinking. It's going to be bad enough knowing that I'm the only one out of you, Beth and me that's still on the booze, I don't need to feel your judgment."

"Deal. And shoot me if I become one of those women who start telling you that I didn't know what love meant until I had a baby. I mean, I might think it, but if I let those words out, feel free to stuff them back in. I also promise to put the kid up for adoption if all I start to talk about is nappies and breastfeeding."

"No one is being put up for adoption. Jesus." Jake looked ashen. I couldn't help but chuckle.

"I told you I'm going to be a terrible mother," Haven said, shrugging as if he should know better than to expect anything else from her.

Jake grabbed her by the waist and held her against him. I looked away, their moment too private. I caught Ashleigh's eye. She gave me a small smile. I missed her so much.

Things settled between us after that and entire minutes went by where I forgot the awkwardness between Ashleigh and me. It descended again when I had to resist smoothing my hand over her back as we sat at the table, and again when I was tempted to press my lips to her cheek as I passed her. I was forced to remember that we weren't together.

"So seriously, we should celebrate, properly," Jake said as he handed me a dish of vegetables. "Let's go out. Next weekend, maybe."

"I really want to go to Chiltern Firehouse," Ashleigh said.

"It's good." I said at the same time Jake did.

The girls snapped their heads toward us. Jake and I exchanged a glance.

"Have you two been dating each other when we weren't looking?" Haven asked.

"I went there ages ago, before us," Jake said pointedly to Haven.

Haven transferred her glare from her husband to me.

"I went last weekend. It was nice," I said.

I shouldn't have said anything. The implication hung in the air like a dreary fog. No question, Chiltern Firehouse was a date restaurant. Ashleigh focused on her glass. I wanted to shout, "But you told me to date." I didn't. If she still had feelings for me, it would smart that I was taking someone out. If she was dating, I was pretty sure I'd go down for murder. Somehow we were going to have to get through this.

Together.

chapter
TWENTY

Ashleigh

I was staring at the crack in my ceiling. It was late—or early, depending on how you looked at it—but I couldn't be bothered to turn my head to see exactly what time it was.

He'd been to Chiltern Firehouse last weekend. The weekend. So, not for work. I had willed Haven to ask him what he was doing there, but she'd busied herself with the plates and dishes in front of her.

Was it the kind of place Luke went on a first date, or was it more of a second date type of place? Luke would have definitely said if it hadn't been a date, wouldn't he? Otherwise, why hadn't he said why he went? He must have taken a woman. A girlfriend? Frantically, I ran through the time that had passed. Could he already have a girlfriend? Perhaps. Especially if he'd known her before they'd started dating. Someone like Fiona.

The thought made me feel physically sick. Both because he hadn't chosen me and I was never going to get my fairy tale, and because maybe I could have been okay loving him more than he loved me. I shouldn't have pushed him away and insisted on this time apart. Maybe Luke was only ever going to go along with whatever was easy, and I'm sure Fiona was making things way easier than I was.

My phone vibrated on the cabinet next to me. In a burst of energy, I twisted to grab it. I flicked my fingers across the screen to discover a text from Richard. I let out a sigh. Five in the morning. I'd not slept a wink.

Richard was suggesting dinner tonight. I took a breath. It would be a good way to try to get Luke and Fiona out of my head. Last night had been a reminder to me that Luke was doing everything I'd wanted. He'd been getting on with his life.

I agreed to dinner, and I pulled myself out of bed. There was no point lying there thinking about what Luke may or may not have done. I needed to get on with my life too.

I'd changed in the locker room so we could go to dinner straight from work as Richard and my shifts coincided.

Richard came up behind me, slid his hand across my back and he kissed my cheek. "You ready?"

"Yeah. I thought maybe we could go to that pizza place—"

"Pizza?" He grimaced.

"In Shoreditch. It's good. Iconic, or something. And I'm paying, so I get to choose." I started to walk toward the bus stop.

"You're not paying. And you're going to make me go on the bus?"

"Don't be a whiney baby." I elbowed him in the ribs. "Come out of your ivory tower and live like the rest of us." I grinned at him.

"Someone literally shit on me today. I'm not sure my ivory tower is as nice as you think it is."

I giggled. "Well no one is going to shit on you on the bus . . . I think. So, you're safe."

After we got on the bus, we had to stand as all the seats were taken, upstairs and down. I clung on to the pole as the movement jostled us backward and forward, occasionally pushing me toward Richard. Each time he steadied me, his fingers lingered longer than they needed to, his palm pressing unnecessarily—warm and possessive. It felt protective, comfortable.

"You've never been to Pizza East?" I asked.

"No. You see? You're constantly expanding my horizons." He reached for my face and tucked a strand of hair behind my ear.

My mouth went dry. He really wanted this. I mean, I knew he did, he'd told me as much, but it hadn't hit me until now how different our expectations were. My being here was all about hiding from my feelings for Luke, distracting myself from thoughts of him and Fiona. But Richard was all about me. I was being so unfair.

I looked away from him, watching the East End of London slip past. My stomach clenched at the prospect of our evening together.

"You know what you were saying the other night?" I looked out the window as I spoke.

"The other night? You mean about a second chance?"

A tightness formed across my forehead.

"I'm not pushing you," he said.

Our feelings were clearly uneven, and I really didn't want to lead him on. "I know. I just think . . . we make more sense as friends. I like hanging out with you, but not as anything more."

"I said I'm not pushing you." He moved to let someone pass and placed his hand on my waist as he stepped closer to me. Anyone watching us would assume we were a couple.

"I know. I just want to be clear. I don't want to lead you on or—"

"You're not leading me on. We're hanging out. Seeing how things go." This wasn't a conversation to have on a bus, but he obviously hoped our relationship would progress, and it wasn't fair to him letting him think so.

"Richard, I can't—"

"Shhh." He placed a finger on my lips as his eyes fixed on mine. "Let's just have a nice evening. Yes?"

I nodded. What else could I do?

"So when do you hear about business school?" Clearly the subject about our friendship was off the table. For now.

"Next week, I expect."

"You'll get in, no problem." He smiled.

"You think? I thought you wouldn't approve."

"What made you think that?"

I shrugged. I couldn't remember if Richard had actually said something about the MBA being a bad idea, or whether it was just the stuff he'd said about me being a stay-at-home mom.

"It's a lot of work. I had a mate who did it."

"It is. I don't think I'll have much of a chance for a personal life if I get accepted, what with working and everything."

When Richard didn't respond straight away, I looked up to find him staring at me intently.

"You could go part-time. Just while you're on the course."

"Are you crazy? I can't afford to go part-time."

His chest rose and he spoke just louder than a whisper. "Well, you never know how things will go in the next couple of months. By the time you start, we may be . . . even better friends . . . and you could move in with me and save on rent. I'm not rushing you, but think about it. It might make it easier for you."

Several times, I opened my mouth to speak but nothing came out. I was literally speechless.

It was if the sky cracked open at that moment, and his invitation suddenly brought me totally clarity. Richard was sweet, kind and generous, and if I couldn't fall for him, I'd rather be on my own than be with anyone other than Luke.

Anyone was a compromise I wasn't prepared to make.

Luke

The restaurant was quieter than I'd expected for a Saturday. Probably because it was in the city. Somehow, the lack of noise put more pressure on me to speak.

"You look lovely," I said to Fiona. She wore pink, which made her eyes look bluer than I'd noticed before.

"Thanks. You look nice too. Your face seems more . . . tan, if that's possible in this weather."

"Oh, it must be the fake stuff I'm using." I grinned at her.

"Really?" She looked shocked.

I smiled. "No, I'm not really a fake tan kind of guy."

She laughed. "Thank God."

Though we'd been hanging out a lot in between times, running and grabbing lunch at work on some days, tonight was my fourth official date with Fiona. Up until this evening, we'd not really done anything other than kiss. I was happy with that, but when I dropped her off last weekend, she'd invited me in. I'd panicked and made up an excuse. I needed to be more prepared this time.

"Do you want to get another bottle of red?" I asked. We were at a casual Italian place near my flat, and we'd already drunk one bottle. Was she as nervous as I was? Presumably she had also considered sleeping together tonight.

"Sure. I guess we don't have to drink it all."

"They have the most incredible desserts here." We'd finished our main courses, and I wasn't exactly putting off the short walk back to either hers or mine—we lived just a few blocks from each other—but a little more time before we went anywhere wouldn't be the worst thing. I was nervous. I wasn't sure I wanted to sleep with her. I liked her, and she was attractive. Before Ashleigh, I would have been thinking about how to get her into bed, because I hadn't known better. Now I did. I didn't long to touch Fiona, be close to her.

As if on cue, the waiter arrived with the dessert menus, and we ordered wine and pudding. Coffee could come after that.

"This is my last drink until the race," Fiona said.

"Really? You totally give it up." Having work and triathlons in common meant that although I felt pressured to speak, there was never a lack of interesting conversation. Emma and

I hadn't often gone out one on one, but when we had, we'd ended up talking about her friends and what they were doing. It had filled the silence, but I wasn't really interested. Fiona and I were a good fit in many ways, and much less complicated than Ashleigh and I.

"Yup, for a month before. It's like total rehab really. But then I go crazy after the race and live on chocolate and alcohol so it undoes all the good I've done."

"I thought that was a normal diet for girls."

Fiona rolled her eyes at the same time the waiter placed our enormous chocolate desserts in front of us and topped off our wine. I couldn't help but chuckle.

"Point made, Mr. Daniels."

"I'm not saying anything. But you are going to love this." I pointed at my plate with my fork. "I can't believe you've never tried this place. It's so close to you."

"I guess I don't normally hang out around here. But it's fun. Maybe we'll come again."

I smiled at her. It was fun.

As we left the restaurant, we headed in the direction of Fiona's flat without any discussion.

I dug my hands into my pockets, and Fiona linked her arm through mine and leaned into me. I liked that she felt comfortable enough to do that. "Do you have a busy day tomorrow?" I asked. It was an inane question, but I didn't like awkward silences.

"Hmmm, not really. I'll do some training but nothing other than that. Do you have dinner with your sister?"

"Yeah. She's pregnant, did I say?"

"You told me. You looking forward to being an uncle?"

I grinned. Better that than becoming a father. "I'm going to spoil the kid rotten." My stomach rolled over as we began the walk down her street. Sex with someone new was always nerve-racking. Except it hadn't been with Ashleigh, perhaps because we'd known each other for so long. That, and we'd been drunk the first time.

She released my arm and dug about in her bag to retrieve her keys. "You want to come in?"

"Sure." I swallowed. This was it. I was going in. I followed her straight into the living room.

"Can I get you a coffee? Or more wine?" She smoothed her hand over my chest.

"Wine would be good, actually, if you have anything open." I looked around and took in her apartment. "How long have you been here?" It looked like it was a rented place. The furniture and decoration didn't reflect who she was, and there didn't seem to be the details I was used to seeing in Haven's and Ash's apartments.

"Nearly two years. It's rented. I wasn't sure where I wanted to be when I split from James. I've been so busy; I've just stayed." She came back into the living room with two glasses of wine. We hovered in front of the sofa before taking a seat next to each other.

"You okay?" she asked. Perhaps I looked pale.

"Yeah, good, you?" My heart was thudding against my breastbone and the weight of expectation lingered between us. She handed me a glass, linked our free hands together and smiled at me. I squeezed her hand and rubbed my thumb over her knuckles. I needed to stop being a pussy and kiss her. "You look really pretty." I meant it. She was a gorgeous girl, and her kindness made it all the more true.

I took her glass and placed our wine on the table. I cupped her face and leaned into her, pressing my lips against hers. Immediately she moaned, opening her mouth, leading me forward. I slid my tongue across her bottom lip. She was warm and open and really wanted this. Her hands pushed up my chest and fiddled with the top button of my shirt. An image of Ashleigh flashed into my mind. She'd done the same thing the night of the awards ceremony. I squeezed my eyes shut, trying to get rid of the thought of her.

I rose up on my knees and gently moved Fiona to her back, and crawled over her. Her legs parted as I fit myself between her thighs. I held her waist with one hand. I tried to remember whether or not Ashleigh had felt like this under me, then realized that was the last thing I should be thinking about.

Fiona's fingers were at my shirt again, and she started to undo the buttons, stroking the exposed skin as she went. I delved deeper into her mouth, pushing my tongue against hers, my hand still at her waist, wondering if I should be moving higher or lower.

With my shirt undone, Fiona's attention turned to my belt buckle, and the reality of the situation crashed around me. When she sensed the tension in my body, her fingers stilled. I pushed up on my knees, then turned and sat down. "I'm sorry," I said.

She sat up on her elbows. "God, no. I'm sorry. Was I moving too fast?"

I scrubbed my hands down my face and stood. "No, this is . . . It's me. I'm . . ."

She swung her legs round. I could feel her looking at me.

"I thought . . ." she started.

"Yeah, I did and then . . . Crap. I'm so sorry; I can't do this." She was a lovely girl. Pretty, funny, good company.

She just wasn't Ashleigh.

Ashleigh was the only person I wanted touching me. Ashleigh was the only person I wanted underneath me. I wasn't ready to be moving on to anything else, wasn't ready to settle for someone who wasn't her. I wasn't sure I ever would be.

"This?" she asked me. "Is it too fast?"

"God, Fiona, I'm really, really sorry." I turned to face her. "You're a lovely girl. Really. I like you. I just don't think this," I said, indicating between us, "is right, for me. I think I'm not over things with . . ."

"Emma."

I didn't correct her, but she couldn't have been more wrong. I hadn't been in love with Emma all these years. "I don't know what to say. I shouldn't have . . . I thought—"

"Don't. Maybe I pushed. I liked you and I wanted you to like me as much."

The last thing I wanted was for her to blame herself. "I do like you; you're great. Really, you are. This is just me. I think I need to work out what I want." I wasn't being truthful. Being with Fiona, who was so right for me in so many ways, just showed me how Ashleigh was perfect for me. It was more complicated and we had way more to lose, but Ashleigh was worth it.

"Is it too soon? Do we just need to slow down?" she asked.

It would be easier if I said yes. But I couldn't lie to her.

"I'm sorry. I just don't think this is going to work. But I don't want you to think it's anything to do with you."

She stood and forced a smile. "It's not you, it's me?" She lifted an eyebrow. I shook my head. It sounded like an excuse, but it was true.

"I'm sorry." I couldn't say it often enough, and I meant it every time. "I wanted this to work. I mean it should work. I like you; I really do. I'm just in love with someone else, and I'm not ready to give up on that. I'm really sorry."

"Don't be." Her gaze was fixed to the floor, more disappointed than angry. I wished I'd got to where I was earlier, without hurting her.

"Can we still be friends?" I really enjoyed her company, and I'd liked getting to know someone new. As I got older, I'd retreated into old habits and friendships. I hadn't realized how much until I'd started hanging out with Fiona and training for the triathlon. "I really like you. Honestly. And I've really enjoyed the time we've spent together. You've helped me see more of the world. I don't want to lose that."

"You're going to have to give me a bit of time on that." She folded her arms, creating a barrier between us. "I know you're not a bad person, and you can't help who you love. I just need to regroup."

I nodded, kissed her on the head and left.

I knew where I needed to be.

chapter
TWENTY-ONE

Luke

Nerves jangled with determination in my stomach, threatening to spill the coffees that I was carrying. It was early on a Sunday morning. The combination of the two meant I was very likely about to have my bollocks chopped off and handed back to me by a sleepy Ashleigh, but at least I'd have had coffee. I couldn't and wouldn't spend another second without her. I'd wasted enough years failing to see what was right in front of me. I wasn't waiting any longer.

The night before with Fiona had brought things into focus. Even nice, comfortable, pretty Fiona wasn't enough. She simply wasn't Ashleigh.

Ashleigh was the one, and I was done waiting. I'd been prepared to be patient, for her to be convinced of my feelings for her, but as time went on, I couldn't help but think maybe she didn't trust her own feelings. Maybe I had to hold her hand so we could take a leap of faith together.

I took a deep breath and pressed the buzzer to Ashleigh's flat.

I waited. No answer. She was probably still in bed.

I pressed again. Still no answer. What if she was in bed with someone else? It hadn't occurred to me, but she might have gotten back together with Richard, or met someone else she liked better. Someone she wanted to get married to and have kids with. Panic started to crawl over me, leaving goose bumps in its wake. I pressed the buzzer again. I'd just have to convince her that they weren't right for her. That I was.

I pressed again, and this time I didn't let go.

"What the fuck?" came a voice through the intercom. I grinned. At least she was answering.

"Let me up, Ashleigh."

"Luke? Jesus. This better be good."

I heard the clink of the door and pushed the entrance open.

I found myself jogging to the stairwell. A cup in each hand, I tried to keep my arms steady as I took the stairs two at a time to the third floor.

As soon as I reached her corridor, I strained my neck to see her head pop out to welcome me, desperate for my first glimpse of her, but it wasn't until I stood on her doormat that locks started to clink behind the door.

"Coffee?" I asked, and thrust one of the cups forward.

She narrowed her eyes, but took the drink, heading back up the corridor. Was she mad I was here? Had I interrupted something, someone?

"You're up," I said.

"Why would you be surprised about that? Oh, yes, because it's seven on a Sunday morning. What are you doing here?"

"You're on your own?" I asked. "I mean, if there's someone here, that's fine. I'm gonna punch his lights out, but it's okay." I suppressed the urge to run from room to room, checking for hiding suitors.

"Who would be here? Of course I'm alone. I'm studying."

Good. That was the first step. At least I didn't have to throw a guy out before I explained why I was here, and why I was never leaving. "You got into business school? Is that why you're studying?" I asked, looking at the books and papers laid out on the coffee table.

"I'm not sure, but if I did I want to get a head start." Her forehead furrowed. She looked adorable.

"You are such a geek." A loveable, perfect geek.

She shrugged. I loved how she didn't give a shit about that badge. She was who she was, and she was okay with all of it. My heart grew bigger every moment I was near her.

"So?" she asked, taking a sip of coffee and bouncing slightly as she hit the cushions on the sofa. I took a seat beside her.

"Oh, what am I doing here?"

"Uh, yes."

"I'm here to stay. I'm here to hang out. To spend time with you, to convince you that I'm the only man you'll ever need or want. That kind of thing. No big deal." If I was just very matter-of-fact about the whole thing, but completely determined, perhaps she'd understand the inevitability of our future together. Just like I did.

She didn't move, didn't blink, didn't breathe. If I hadn't caught the flit of her gaze from my eyes to my mouth, I would have reached out to check her pulse.

"Well, I have to study," she said finally.

"That's okay. I can just sit here. I'm not going anywhere." If she tried to kick me out, tell me that she was over what was between us, I'd do whatever it took to convince her she was wrong.

"You're going to sit here, on your own, while I study?"

"If that's what it takes. I'm here to show you I'm serious. I'm not getting fobbed off anymore, Ashleigh. I'm not having you tell me that I'm not ready, that I need to choose you and not just end up with you.

"Here. I. Am. I pick you. I've had my whole life to decide, to know you, and I'm never going to be more certain about anything in my life as I am about you. I want you. And if I need to sit here all day, all week, all year, that's what I'll do." It felt good to say it. She needed to hear it.

She pursed her lips. "So, this is like some kind of sit-in? A demonstration of sorts." She was trying to suppress it, but I could see her smile in her eyes.

"If you like. Except I'm going to shower regularly, and if you leave, I'm coming with you."

"Like a stalker?"

She started to giggle but turned it into a cough. I couldn't stop my grin. I brushed my thumb over her cheek. Her eyes sparkled when she smiled. She couldn't hide it.

"Call it what you want. I know that I want you. And if you're not ready, that's fine. I'll wait for as long as it takes for you to be ready. But I am, and you can't possibly understand that or see that for yourself unless I'm here, with you. So here is where I'm going to be. I'm not going anywhere."

"Luke, this isn't about me . . ." She placed her coffee on the table beside her and waved her hands, as if they were trying to help her find the words. I caught them midair and interlaced her fingers with mine, desperate for a physical connection to her.

"Sure about that?" Ashleigh was scared and although she had made good points about my choosing her, that wasn't the whole problem, not now. "Perhaps part of you doesn't trust yourself. And that's okay because there's a lot at stake and neither of us have got it right when it comes to relationships so far. But this is different. We're different, and if you don't trust yourself then you've known me long enough to trust me."

She tried to pull her fingers away, but I wouldn't let her. I wasn't letting her go. "This was about you making a choice, Luke, not me."

"And I'm telling you that you're the choice I'm making. The most important choice I'll ever make." I slid toward her, our thighs touching, her warmth seeping through to me.

"But—" I pulled her onto my lap, finally having her in my arms, able to breathe in the scent of her, of forever, of home.

"You don't think I have other options. Maybe you were right. Maybe it seemed all too easy that when Emma and I split, I finally woke up. Perhaps it was. But that doesn't mean it wasn't the right choice." Ashleigh would always be the right choice. "And now? You think I don't have the opportunity to fuck other women? I've always known there are other options."

She winced.

"You're right; you've been right in front of me all these years, and for whatever reason we haven't happened until now, but I'm not thinking, Ashleigh's around and available, that would be easy. I'm thinking, what a fucking waste, I'm an idiot. We could have been happy all this time, together." I scanned her face, trying to read her reaction. Did she understand? "There will never be anyone else for me but you."

Ashleigh

My head was spinning and my heart was pumping. I'd woken from a dream of Luke to find him at my door less than an hour later. Every sign said it was time. Time to trust him. Time to take a chance. And I'd made that decision before he'd arrived on my doorstep.

Now, sitting so close to him, everything he was saying seemed utterly compelling. He was considered and passionate in equal measures. Part of me wanted simply to fall into his arms, but I was scared. Not because I didn't believe that he meant what he said, but because I did believe him. This was all I could have wished for from him. Now I was as capable of fucking this up as he was. The thought that I had equal responsibility for this relationship was terrifying. I'd dreamt about this for years. What happened if I messed it up? I had no excuses to turn him away, no more reasons to say no. He was ready. Things felt level between us, which was what I'd wanted.

It was scary as hell.

Luke tucked some hair behind my ear. "Tell me what you're thinking."

"I . . ." His hand lowered from my face and I caught it in mine, and his eyes filled with questions. "I'm glad you're here." It was time.

Staring at our linked hands, I took in the sounds of our breath synchronizing. Was the impossible actually happening?

"You are?" Luke asked as his fingertips tilted my jaw, forcing my eyes to his. I kept my gaze lowered. "Look at me, Ashleigh."

Slowly, I did as he asked.

"You're so beautiful," he whispered. He moved toward me, running his hands down my neck. "I'm going to kiss you now. Are you ready?"

I was, finally, and I believed he was too.

"Yes, I'm ready." My breath hitched. This wasn't to be a drunken kiss at an awards ceremony, or two friends forgetting boundaries for a moment. This was going to mean something.

His lips smoothed across mine, dropping a tiny kiss at the corner of my mouth. I closed my eyes, trying to take it in, but Luke was moving me off him. I blinked and he was standing.

"Here," he said, holding out his hand. "I'm going to show you how much I missed you."

My cheeks heated. As soon as I was next to him, his fingers slid around my waist and he buried his head in my neck. "You smell so good. You always do."

I smiled at his comment. The perfume I wore reminded me of Luke because it smelled of magnolias. I liked that he seemed to drink it in when he was near me. It was as if it bound us together.

He pulled me closer. He was hard against my stomach, and I was relieved not just to hear his words, but to see the evidence of his desire for me. His arms clamped around me, and he began to walk me backward toward my bedroom, bending and kissing my neck at regular intervals on our journey.

We stood beside the bed as he lifted the hem of my T-shirt, skimming my skin with his fingers. Goose bumps covered me as I brought up my arms and he pulled off my top, discarding it behind me. I rested my hands on his chest, feeling the hard shape of him underneath the fabric of his clothes. I looked up to find him smiling. I followed his lead, peeling off his shirt. He gently laid me down, his body over mine.

"Luke?"

As if sensing what I needed from him, he moved to my side, skimming his hand up and down my stomach. "We don't have to. Not yet if you're not ready. I just want to be close to you."

I smiled at him and pushed my hand through his hair. It was floppy, like it had been when he was young. "I'm ready, for you and me, for all of it, I just . . ."

"Ask me anything, I'll always tell you the truth," he said, knowing me too well.

"All these women you've had the opportunity to fuck . . ." Was it wrong to feel jealous, even though he'd only been doing as I asked?

"I've been close, but I've not slept with anyone since you." He dropped a kiss on my chest and then pulled back, giving me time to think.

"Close?"

His eyes closed and he took in a deep breath. "I had a few dates. I mean, you said—"

"I know, and it's fine. You don't have to tell me." I wanted to know.

"I know, but I want you to know everything you need."

I found his hand and linked my fingers through his, trying to tell him I was okay with whatever he was going to say.

"Fiona and I went out a few times."

Fiona from work. Fiona the triathlete. I held my breath, waiting for him to fill in the details. "You like her?"

"She's a great girl, but she's not you. I don't feel this," he said, squeezing my hand, "with her."

"And she was the one you almost—"

"I realized I couldn't, didn't want to. She helped me decide to see you today. To stay until I'd won you over."

I reached for his jaw, tracing the angles of his face with my fingers.

"What about you?" he asked.

It took me a second to realize what he was getting at. "Umm . . ." I was still distracted by his beautiful face.

"Wow," he said and fell onto his back.

I leaned across and dropped a kiss on his chest through my smile. "There's nothing to wow about. Richard and I spent some time together as friends. I think he wanted more, but I was clear that I didn't."

Luke sighed as if he were considering whether he could accept what I was saying as the truth.

"There will never be anyone else for me but you." I repeated his words back to him.

He grabbed my face and crashed his lips against mine. Heat crawled up my skin. He was my best friend but I wanted him. My brain, my heart and my body were all competing for his attention.

My body was winning.

He groaned into my mouth and pushed me back, bringing himself on top of me. Showing me what he was feeling, he ground his hips against mine, giving me a promise of what was to come.

"I need to taste you," he said. I lifted my head to capture his lips again. "No, not there. I want my tongue here," he said, circling his hips against me again.

He knelt between my legs and looked over my body.

"Luke," I whispered. What was he doing?

"You're so beautiful. I've been waiting so long for you. I need to savor it, but I can't wait." He reached for the button on my jeans and quickly stripped my legs bare, leaving me in just my underwear. "So beautiful. So, so beautiful." He shook his head as he kicked his trousers and boxers off and crawled over me. Reaching underneath me, he unclasped my bra and pulled it off, then cupped my breasts with both hands. Using the perfect combination of rough and smooth, he alternated palming and pushing each breast, brushing my nipples with his thumbs.

The slickness between my thighs intensified and I brought my knees up, skirting his waist. He fit me so perfectly in every way.

He bent into my neck, the sound of him sucking against my skin sending me wild and making me wriggle underneath him.

I pushed my hands into his hair.

Luke

The feel of her skin under my fingers was close to overwhelming. She felt so good—smelled so good—and now I wanted to see how she tasted. Every inch of her was tempting, trying to divert my attention, but I moved down her body studiously. I wanted to see, smell and taste that she wanted me.

I dropped soft kisses along the top of her underwear, enjoying her gasps as every now and then my tongue dipped below the elastic. When I got to her hipbone, I dragged her panties down, closing my eyes until they were completely free of her legs, so I couldn't see until I had an entirely unobstructed view.

And there she was. Glistening at her edges.

Waiting, wanting.

It was such a sight, my cock twitched in celebration so hard it was close to painful. It would be some time before I came. I needed to show her what I could do, and why she could never give me up again.

"Spread your legs for me." The voice echoing in my head was deeper than normal, thick with desire and anticipation. Her eyes darted from my mouth to my dick.

"Spread. Your. Legs."

Tentatively she parted her knees, and I slid my palms down her thighs, pressing her wider. I had to consciously slow my breathing so I didn't come right there. She was slick, soaked. I groaned and kissed the top of her slit. My tongue pressed against the nub of nerves. I had to hold her down as her hips pushed against my mouth.

She cried out, my name amongst words that didn't seem to fit together. The power of being able to make her lose her mind was what I needed. I had to know I could do these things to her.

My tongue trailed lower, between her folds. She was soft and hot and oh-so-wet. Jesus, I couldn't wait to feel her clenched around my cock. It wouldn't be long. Her hands pushed violently through my hair and her feet rested on my hips as if she were climbing my body. I started a rhythm, sliding up and down her slit, rounding her clit each time I reached the top. Her breath got shorter and shorter, her sounds louder and louder until her body went rigid and her back arched. The power I felt at being able to do that to her was unlike anything I'd ever experienced before. I reduced the pressure of my tongue, but kept up my rhythm until her body went limp, her knees closing around my shoulders.

"I'm going to give up my job and make you come for a living," I said as I crawled up her body, my cock making her shiver as it trailed up her legs. "It's the most satisfying thing I could ever do." I licked my lips, tasting her on me. She grasped my neck and pulled me toward her, unashamedly licking herself off my mouth. Fuck, she was the hottest thing I'd ever known.

"I want you inside me, Luke."

She didn't have to ask me twice. I positioned myself at her entrance, checking her reaction. Her lips were open, her eyes wide as she twisted beneath me, trying to get closer, trying to draw me in. I loved seeing the desperation in her eyes, the desire, the need. For me. My heart clenched with the knowledge that I hadn't lost her. That she was mine.

"You feel this?" I pressed forward. "This is what you're going to feel for the rest of your life." I pushed into her in one swift movement, and she let out a deafening cry.

It was as though she was made for me. Her muscles gripped me as if they didn't want to let go. I dropped my head to her shoulder, growling against her skin. She felt so good. The smell of summer, sex and softness that was unmistakably Ashleigh hit me.

I started to thrust, knowing I was going to have to concentrate if I was going to last longer than fifteen seconds.

"Oh God," she whispered. I tried to block out the perfect pressure on my cock, her arms gripping my shoulders, her skin beneath my lips, and focus on her words. This. Yes. There. Oh. God. Yes. Oh. Oh. Oh. All that mattered was that she felt good. That I made her feel good. Her nails dug into my flesh, and she thrust her pelvis toward me, calling my name over and over before going limp. I was done for. I picked up my pace, chasing the white light in front of me. How had I waited as long as I had to feel this again? I lifted my head, my eyes meeting hers. In an instant, my orgasm barreled up my spine and split me in half.

I collapsed on top of her, my head in her neck, my body pressing against her. I wanted to feel as much of my skin against hers as was possible. My heart pounded against my chest. I was sure she could feel it. I reached out and laced my fingers through hers, our arms outstretched.

I brushed my lips against her shoulder and was once again intoxicated by her scent. I worked my way to her mouth. "Am I crushing you?" I asked between kisses.

"I don't know where I end and you begin," she said.

The idea warmed me. We were inextricably linked.

Worried about my weight, I rolled us over so I was on my back but still inside her. I wasn't sure if it was conscious, but her muscles continued to pulse around my cock. I started to stiffen.

"You feel so good," I said, running my fingers up and down her back. "You're going to have me hard again if you're not careful."

She pushed herself up, her hands pressing into my chest, her arms squeezing her tits together. Jesus, all these years and I'd never realized how incredible her tits were. There was so much about her I was still to learn. I shoved one hand behind my head, content just to watch her for the rest of the day, as she lay naked on top of me. She smiled at me and started to tilt her hips, rocking back and forth in tiny movements, maybe thinking I wouldn't notice. I raised my eyebrows, silently asking what she was doing as her muscles gripped my dick, pulling it deeper into her.

"I need to come again, baby, are you with me? I need you to come again." She seemed insatiable, and I was happy to spend however long it took quenching her thirst.

I grabbed hold of her hips, and pulled her roughly onto my hardened dick. "I want to know what you like. I want to give you everything you need."

"I need you," she said. "Just you."

Words in bed had never been a particular turn on to me. Like most men, I concentrated on the visual stuff—a nice ass, a good mouth. Everything about Ashleigh was a turn on. But her words, that she needed me, and the way she said them, as if my body were pulling them from her—it was the most powerful aphrodisiac I'd ever experienced.

She continued to look at me as she rocked back and slowly heated the blood in my veins. I'd never felt so relaxed and at the same time so ready to explode.

My eyes kept dropping to her tits bouncing with her movements. "You're a boob man," she said as if she were taking note for later. I reached for them, grazing my thumbs over her hard nipples. Her head dropped back as she groaned.

"There's nothing about your body I don't worship." I'd never felt so sure about anything. I'd missed just watching her, seeing every part of her.

She took one of my hands and moved it to where our bodies joined. I loved how she asked for what she wanted. I pressed lightly on her clit and her words got more fervent. I savored every yes, every more, every oh, every there, every please. I wanted every one of her words. I knew what it was not to have them—I'd never take them for granted.

A sheen of sweat coated her as my fingers became wetter and wetter, and her movements became faster and sharper.

"Luke," she cried. I pulled her down, claiming her mouth and pushing my tongue against hers as I held her hips and thrust up into her. I took over, unable to hold back any longer. She whimpered into my mouth for just a few seconds before I felt her spasm around me, and I poured myself into her.

She lay in my arms, panting and relaxed. I couldn't imagine being any happier than I was at that exact moment.

chapter
TWENTY-TWO

Ashleigh

I woke so hot I thought I had a fever. As I opened my eyes, the brightness surprised me. I lay facing the window—my curtains were open. Realization crept up on me. Luke. I must have fallen asleep after . . . Oh, yes, the sex. I could still feel the shadows of him between my legs and over my skin. Right now his arm was across my shoulder, his leg over mine as if he were trying to climb me, capture me. I grinned and cupped my hand over my mouth. No, no grinning. I had to figure out what this meant. It had all been so sudden. Well, maybe not sudden, but the timing was unexpected. He'd been resolute, decisive. His words replayed in my head.

There will never be anyone else for me but you.

I knew that was how I felt about him. But could it really be how he felt about me? I grinned to myself again. Maybe it could. He and Emma had been apart for months now, and as he'd told me, he had an opportunity to choose someone else and hadn't. Time had helped me as well. Luke was laid back enough that he wanted an easy life, but not so much so that he'd risk the bond Haven, he and I shared if he wasn't serious about me, about us. I was able to see that more clearly now.

I shifted under his limbs, needing to think when he wasn't touching me, when I couldn't smell him, us. Carefully, I slid out from his grasp and padded into the bathroom.

My hair stuck up as though it had regressed to the eighties. I took out a brush from the cabinet and began to take out the tangles.

There will never be anyone else for me but you.

My stomach flipped over. Was this it? Was this the beginning of Luke and me? It felt like it. I knew that if I ever lost him, it might just kill me. I had to get this right. Being apart from him had been so painful, I'd felt the loss of him so viscerally—I couldn't let it happen again. We needed to be cautious, not run before we could walk.

There was no way I was going to Haven's smelling of sex. And anyway, he and I needed to talk before we went anywhere. It was almost midday and we were both expected for Sunday dinner, so I texted Haven and showered quickly, drying myself off and pulling on the jeans and shirt I'd had on before Luke had arrived.

Sleeping Luke was one of my favorite sights in the world. I had no idea how a body that big could look so completely relaxed and vulnerable. I sat next to him on the bed, close so I could feel his warmth against me, and began to turn on the alarm on my phone to wake him. He opened his eyes before I'd finished.

"Hey," I said.

He went from sleepy to wide-awake when he saw me.

"What?" He jerked upright. "Ashleigh, what's the matter?"

"Shhhh." I stroked his face, trying to smooth the panic away. This wasn't like the last time when I'd woken him and told him it wasn't our time.

He clasped his hands around my waist and pulled us both back onto the mattress.

"We do need to talk."

"I'm not letting you go, Ashleigh. You're not pushing me away." His words were clipped.

"I don't want to." I swiveled in his arms, and he gave me some room to turn. As I faced him, I brought my fingers to his face, trying to reassure him. "I just think—"

"I don't want to hear any ifs or buts. This is it. We're together now. Nothing else makes sense."

I lifted my chin and pressed my lips to his. "I know."

"You do?" he asked.

I nodded. "I want this to work."

"It is going to work." I could hear the tightness in his throat.

"But—"

"I said no buts."

He was cute when he was argumentative.

"I want this to happen and you have to admit that it is complicated because of our history and what's at stake."

"But nothing we can't handle. We got this. You have to trust me."

I loved hearing his reassurance, his certainty. Everything he was saying made me feel better and better, more and more relaxed. Maybe this would be okay.

"I do trust you. More than anyone. But can I make a suggestion that I think might be good for both of us?"

He let out a short burst of breath like a sulky toddler, and I couldn't help but giggle.

"Just hear me out. I was thinking that maybe we should date."

He didn't respond, instead waiting for me to elaborate.

"What do you think?" I asked.

"I don't understand what you're asking me. What do you mean 'date'?"

"I mean, I think we should go out to dinner and talk, and you can walk me home and maybe kiss me and then we can talk on the phone and flirt and do all those things that people do when they're dating."

"Okay." He eyed me suspiciously.

"So you agree?"

"I guess. Honestly, I think you're trying to say something, and you're handing it to me in a box marked 'let's date.' Can you just spit it out? What are you trying to say?"

Of course he was right, he knew me so well.

"I think that last time we did this thing where we kind of went from naught to sixty in three seconds. I think this time we should give ourselves a bit more time to adjust. I mean, I know we just—"

"Had mind-blowing sex."

I giggled. "Yes, and I'm not trying to put the genie back in the lamp. I'm just saying let's give ourselves some time to get to know each other like this. As a couple." I ran my fingers up his arms, unable to resist. "Maybe we shouldn't spend every second together straight away. I don't want to put more pressure on this situation in the short term, because I want it to work in the long run. Let's take things slow."

"Okay, well thank you for translating Ashleigh language into something I can just about comprehend."

I kicked him in the calf and he grinned.

"So you want to date me?" he asked. He flipped me over onto my back and propped himself up above me before I had the chance to answer.

"Maybe."

"Well, I'm having dinner with my sister and her husband later. Wanna be my date?"

I grinned at him. "Maybe."

He dipped his head and trapped my bottom lip between his teeth and sucked. "I can live with us taking things slow. For now."

"Thank you." I kissed him lightly on his shoulder.

There would never be anyone else for me but Luke.

chapter
TWENTY-THREE

Ashleigh

I stood on the street in front of Haven's building, Luke's arms wrapped around me. It was a cold day, but I couldn't have felt warmer. It had been just eight hours since Luke had shown up on my doorstep, determined to show me that he was over Emma and that he wanted me. We'd spent most of our time since naked. We hadn't discussed anything, hadn't made anything official. Our minds had been taken over by our bodies. It had been beautiful—blissful, even. I didn't have words for what Luke and I were yet, and until I really knew where we stood, I didn't want to expose our new status to any sort of scrutiny.

"You don't think Haven will guess? She knows us both pretty well," Luke said. "We could just be open with her. I don't want to hide anything."

He was right. My best friend knew her brother and me extremely well. One lingering glance and she'd know right away something was up. But despite everything, I wanted to take things slowly. I'd suggested we date. It had taken us this long to start what was between us, so why rush? I wanted to make sure what we had wasn't just physical. I was confident it wasn't for me, but after so many years of my love for Luke being unrequited, I needed time to understand how he felt. Which meant I wasn't ready to tell anyone else.

"Then you're going to have to put your game face on," I said. "I don't want her to guess. It's not that I want to hide anything, but this is so new. We've been . . . dating for less than eight hours. Let's just sit with this for a while."

The first time Luke and I'd kissed, Haven had gone postal, and it had tipped me into a spin. I wanted to make sure I was stronger, more certain of Luke's and my relationship, in case she took things badly again.

"Okay, whatever you need but I'm going to find it hard not to touch you for the next few hours." Luke squeezed me tighter.

"You can do it. I have faith in you." I leaned forward and placed a kiss on his chest. "I need you to take a walk around the block."

"You do?"

"I don't think we should arrive at the same time."

Luke's face dropped, but he nodded. He hugged me closer. "Let's not stay long though, okay?"

I frowned. As far as I was concerned, dating and taking things slow meant that we didn't spend every moment with each other.

"Oh," he said. "You don't want to spend the night together." He removed his hands from my waist and shoved them in his pockets.

"It's not that I don't want to, it's just I thought we agreed we should take things slowly—date, not rush in to anything." Had he misunderstood what I'd suggested?

"Okay, well you're going to have to explain the rules of dating to me so I'm clear."

I tried to keep my wince from showing on my face. "Are you mad?"

"No, not mad. I don't . . . I want to make you happy, but I don't want to waste time, either. I want to speed up, not slow down—make up for all those lost years when we could have been together." He reached and tucked my hair behind my ear. "But if slow is what you need, then that's how we'll go." He smiled softly, but it didn't hide the tinge of disappointment in his voice.

"Thank you."

"Can I at least think about you naked?" he asked.

I grinned. "I would be disappointed if you didn't."

He took a step back, about to make his journey around the block. I reached across and stroked his hard chest.

"See you in a minute." I watched as he headed toward the main road.

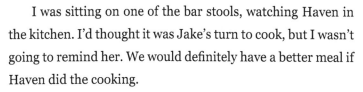

I was sitting on one of the bar stools, watching Haven in the kitchen. I'd thought it was Jake's turn to cook, but I wasn't going to remind her. We would definitely have a better meal if Haven did the cooking.

"I got tickets to The Elephant Man. Jake can't go. Want to come?" she asked as she set wineglasses onto the counter in front of me.

"I've seen it. I told you." I was pretty sure I'd skipped over telling her.

"You did not. When did you see it?"

I shrugged "A couple of weeks ago."

She stopped what she was doing and looked at me.

"With Richard." I checked my phone. Luke had been gone twenty minutes. What was keeping him? I could use a distraction right at that moment. I was about to get the third degree from Haven.

"You're dating again?"

"No, he just had a spare ticket."

She raised her brows and went back to fiddling with the blender. The buzzer went, and Jake raced out of his study. "Is that you?" he bellowed into the intercom.

"What, I'm not good enough for you to come out of your hidey hole for?" I asked.

"You know Haven always sends me away while you talk about penises."

"We weren't talking about penises," I replied.

"You're right. We weren't talking about penises, but we should have been. What's Richard's like?" Haven tilted her head.

The familiar sound of Luke banging about came from behind me, and I had to stop the grin that was trying to break free. Despite seeing him less than half an hour ago, anticipation fluttered in my stomach. "Hey girls," he said. "What's going on?" He strode across to Haven and planted a kiss on her cheek, stealing one of the pastries she was fiddling with as she smacked his hand.

"We're talking about the fact that Ash is secretly dating Richard."

If I didn't know Luke so well, I wouldn't have noticed the almost imperceptible stiffness that ran through him at her words. "We are?" he asked, as he slid his eyes to mine and raised his brows.

I shook my head. "We are not. Haven, stop being a witch." Jesus, I really didn't want Luke getting the wrong idea and thinking that I'd been less than honest with him when he'd asked me if there'd been anyone else. There was enough uncertainty between us; I didn't need to add to it.

"I'm not being witch-like in any way. You just said how you went on a date with Richard."

"I did not." My eyes flitted between Luke and Haven. "I said he had a spare ticket to the theater and that I went with him. As friends. That's it." I wanted to smooth my hands over Luke's jaw, to reassure him that for me Richard could never compare to him. Luke turned to the refrigerator.

"Could friends develop into something more?" Haven asked.

Luke was putting a little too much thought into his choice of beer. I wished he'd come and sit beside me.

"I think he sounds like a good catch. A doctor and stuff. And he's so sweet to you. He treats you really well." Haven glanced across at Luke.

"How can you say that? You of all people?" I replied to Haven. "You didn't settle. You waited for . . ." I circled my hand in Jake's direction. "You know. 'The one.' I don't want to go out with someone because on paper they're a good catch. No, he's firmly in the friend zone."

"I've heard that before," Jake said.

"Jake, don't encourage her," I replied, glancing across at Luke, who was still checking out beer labels. My heart was starting to thump. Was he avoiding me?

"I'm not encouraging her. You're the one who just confessed to going on a date with this Richard guy."

"It wasn't a date." I shook my head.

"Sounds like a date to me," Luke said as he spun to face me, grinning. I let out a breath as I realized he wasn't mad.

"Whatever. Pour me some wine." I pushed my glass across the counter at him.

He smiled as he took my drink, scraping his fingers along mine as he did. I shivered. Why had we come? Why had I suggested that we spend the night apart? Even if he wasn't with me tonight, he would be all I thought about.

Haven shrugged. "I'm just saying, give the guy a break. I want you to be happy, Ash. He must like you if you're still friends after you broke up with him. He might be the one without you even realizing it."

"I think I'll know when I find the one," I mumbled into my glass. How I felt about Luke put any possibility of me ever dating Richard into a box marked never going to happen. He was a nice guy, but he didn't set my skin on fire with a single touch. His smile couldn't heat my cheeks. He just wasn't the one.

"What was that?" Luke asked me.

"What?" I said, pretending not to follow him.

"You said something about the one?" Luke grinned at me, obviously enjoying every moment of my torture.

"What about you, Luke?" Jake interrupted, saving me from further embarrassment. "Have you manned up and asked Fiona out?"

I sucked in a breath. What would he reveal? "Should I take this to the table?" I asked Haven, gesturing at the salad, and trying to cover up the fact that I wanted to hear every last sound that came out of Luke's mouth about Fiona. Haven glanced at me, a sympathetic look on her face, and nodded. She must have thought I didn't want to hear about Luke dating Fiona. I wandered over to the other side of the living space with the bowl.

"Yeah, we went out a couple of times."

"What?" Haven asked. "You've been dating and you've not told me? Do you like her? Are we going to meet her?"

"Yes I like her. She's a nice girl."

Even though I was pretty sure Luke didn't have feelings for Fiona, my stomach twisted. I hated that he'd dated her. It wasn't that he'd done anything wrong—he'd been doing what I'd wanted him to do—but it would have been better if she'd turned out to be a complete crazy person. After all, they still worked in the same office. He saw her regularly. It took every ounce of willpower not to blurt out that Luke and I were together. I wanted to claim him. To stop Haven from talking about other women who would be good for him. I was good for him.

Despite my curiosity, I excused myself to go to the bathroom. I needed to take a beat, get my shit together. Staring into the mirror, I pressed my fingers along my eyebrows, straightening out my frown. I was used to being envious of Emma, but I'd always taken some comfort from the fact that she didn't see the side of Luke that I did. She didn't have the same shared history, couldn't make him laugh the way I could. I didn't know anything about Fiona. She had the triathlon thing in common with Luke, which he seemed to love. And she saw him at work, which I never did. Could she make him laugh? Had I become another Emma to Fiona?

As I wandered back to the living room, everyone had taken their seats around the dining table. I sank into the free seat between Luke and Jake. I tried to convince myself there was an invisible barrier between Luke and me. Touching was an impossibly bad idea if we didn't want Haven and Jake to catch on.

The problem was, my barrier was faulty and acted more like a magnet. Being so close to him made me want to be closer still. I wanted him to hold me. I crossed my arms in front of me, so I didn't lose control and accidently reach for his floppy hair or smooth my hands across his broad back.

I startled when his leg brushed against mine as he reached for the jug of water—was he trying to torture me? I wanted to climb into his lap and feel his arms around me. His hand came to my thigh, and I melted.

He looked at me, and I widened my eyes at him in warning. What was he doing? I was worried Haven would see his hand. He squeezed my leg and removed his hand, leaving my skin buzzing. I glanced across at Haven. Had she seen that?

"So when do you hear about business school, Ash?" Jake asked.

I hesitated as I tried to concentrate on something other

than Luke. "Soon, I think." I'd forgotten that I should have a decision this week.

"How are you going to manage to study and work at the same time?" Haven asked. "Sounds impossible."

"Yeah, I think it will be tough. Richard suggested I go part-time, but there's no way. I mean, no."

"How did he suggest you pay your rent?" Haven asked. "Honestly, men have no common sense."

Jake rolled his eyes, and Luke shook his head at Haven's dismissal of the male species. They both handled her perfectly.

"Oh, he had a solution for that. He said I should move in with him."

Luke had his wineglass to his lips and spluttered into his drink at my revelation. "He said what?" His voice was tight.

I focused on Haven, afraid to meet Luke's eyes. I probably shouldn't have shared that without having mentioned it to Luke first.

"What, he was offering you his spare room?" she asked.

"In return for your vagina?" Jake added.

"It's never okay for you to say vagina," I said, grinning at Jake while Haven playfully smacked him on the arm. Luke didn't join in, but his clenched fists told me he wasn't happy. I desperately wanted to reach across my invisible barrier and drop a small kiss on his shoulder. He had nothing to worry about.

Luke

I believed Ashleigh when she said nothing had happened with Richard, but that didn't stop me from feeling homicidal.

Ashleigh was mine, and everyone needed to know it. I'd been a second away from announcing it to Haven and Jake. The only thing that stopped me was the thought that Ashleigh and I might take two steps back. I didn't have time to do anything but move forward with her. I wanted to start our future together. I just wished she were as eager as I was.

I tried to think of reasons that would persuade her to stay with me tonight. I didn't want to be without her, especially not with conversations of Richard and Fiona on our minds. I didn't want her focused on what might have been. I wanted her focused on us.

"I'm going to head home. I didn't get much sleep last night, and I don't want to start the week tired," Ashleigh said as she closed the dishwasher. She leaned forward to program the machine and gave me an excellent view down her top. Was she wearing a bra? I'd been trying to control my hard-on all night, but my dick was getting sick of holding back. I was close to dragging Ashleigh home to get naked.

"You'll stay for another beer though, right?" Jake asked me.

I wanted to say no, but I glanced at Ashleigh and she gave me a small nod. "Sure," I said. Better to be here with Jake and Haven than at home, on my own, wishing I was with Ashleigh.

I relaxed when Ashleigh left. I'd been on edge all evening, trying to make sure I wasn't giving away how I felt about her. More than once I'd been about to touch her and had to stop myself. It felt so unnatural to be acting as we had for the last two decades.

Things were different now.

"So, you didn't say anything more about Fiona; what's going on there?" Jake asked as we collapsed on the sofas with our beers. Haven followed, bringing her wine.

"There's nothing to say. She's a nice girl, but she's not for me."

"She's not? Does that mean you know who is?" Haven asked.

"Haven, you know that the ball is in Ashleigh's court."

Haven sighed. "I wish you two would just sort it out. Richard clearly isn't any competition. Do what you have to do, Luke. Make her feel special. If she's the one for you, she needs to know that. Take action."

It was good advice. Advice I'd already followed. I just needed Ashleigh to understand we had nothing to hide, that she had nothing to be afraid of. She could trust me.

My phone buzzed.

Ashleigh: Hey.

Me: Hey yourself.

Ashleigh: Did you have a good night?

Me: It would have been better if I'd been able to touch you openly.

Ashleigh: I appreciate your patience.

Me: I'm not sure how long it will last. You're too beautiful to resist and you're mine now. You know you are.

Ashleigh: I am.

Me: Glad you agree.

Ashleigh. I miss you.

Me: Already?

Ashleigh: Already. How about dating starts tomorrow night. Come round when you leave?

I grinned. There was nowhere I'd rather be than with Ashleigh, and she couldn't resist what there was between us anymore than I could. Who was she trying to kid?

chapter
TWENTY-FOUR

Luke

I'd left Haven and Jake's as soon as I'd finished my beer. Maybe it was obvious why I left so soon after Ashleigh, but it was hard to give a shit.

I pressed my forehead to Ashleigh's door, willing myself inside. My heartbeat quickened as I heard her unlock the door.

I'd stopped at a late-night supermarket and picked up chocolate and a small bouquet of flowers. As she opened the door, I held them out to her.

"What's this?" she asked.

"Well, flowers and chocolates are what you bring for dates, aren't they?"

"You are ridiculous." She grinned. "Thank you."

"As long as you're into ridiculous, that's fine by me."

She put her arms around my neck and held my gaze. "I'm very into ridiculous."

It was so good to have her in my arms—evidence that she was mine and not some other man's. My head knew Richard wasn't a threat, but that didn't stop it feeling like a dagger to my stomach every time she talked about him—particularly when she'd said he'd suggested she move in with him. I'd only managed to get my cool back just in time.

I couldn't hold back any longer. I'd waited all night. I crashed my lips into hers, enveloping myself around her. Her moans muffled the sound of flowers and chocolates falling to the floor. She tasted delicious. I just couldn't get enough of her. I wanted to devour her in every way. I couldn't kiss her for long enough.

Everything she had to say was mesmerizing to me—all her little phrases, the way she talked with her fingers . . . Some people talked with their hands, but Ashleigh punctuated almost every sentence with a movement of her fingers. I'd never noticed before.

I started to walk her backward, lost patience and pushed her up against the wall.

"Richard is never touching you again." I circled her waist and pulled her top from her skirt—I needed to feel her skin. "If you're moving in with someone, you're moving in with me." I brushed my hands up her bare back. "Jesus, you were braless all evening. Fuck." I'd suspected as much. My hands roamed to her chest, just to make sure. Double fuck, her nipples tightened under my touch, and she shuddered. I couldn't help but groan against her mouth. Blood rushed to my cock, and I had to get closer, had to see them. I fiddled with the buttons on her shirt, but my fingers weren't working. Something close to panic washed over me. I needed her naked. While I'd been fixating on her chest, Ashleigh had managed to undo my shirt completely. In desperation, I pulled at the fabric of her blouse, then tugged, sending the buttons flying and spilling out her amazing tits.

"These are my reason for living. Right here." My eyes focused on her chest.

Ashleigh messed with my fly. She wanted me naked as much as I wanted her. My dick twitched at the thought. I kicked off my jeans and shrugged off my open shirt.

I took a step back so I could take her in. Naked from the waist up, she looked at me, her hair disheveled, mouth swollen and red from my kisses. She was a goddess. Fuck, I was a lucky guy. How could she not understand that I got how precious she was? She could trust me.

"I'm going to keep you up all night, and you're not even going to remember Richard's name when I'm done." I reached under her skirt and pulled off her underwear in one swift movement. "I have to be inside you right now." I would make it up to her later, but there wasn't time for foreplay—my dick wouldn't allow it. I grabbed her ass, lifting her up against the wall. She wrapped her legs around me.

"Please," she breathed. "Please, I need you."

It was exactly what I needed to hear. I plunged myself into her. It felt perfect. "It feels like forever since I've had you like this," I whispered against her cheek. Even though we'd only been together this morning, it had been too long. She was so wet and ready, and I slid in and out with just the right amount of friction; it was as if I were made for her.

She tilted her head back against the wall, allowing me access to her perfectly smooth neck. I trailed my tongue up the soft column of skin, desperate to taste her. Every part of her was so delicious.

"Luke, it's so deep."

I could do nothing but growl in response as I started to thrust into her. I knew I was being rough, but I couldn't hold back. Seeing her pushed up the wall by my hips, her body yielding to mine, was exactly what I needed. "You're so fucking beautiful, so fucking perfect. I love this feeling of being buried so deep inside you, Ashleigh."

She grasped at my shoulders, then chest. I didn't understand what she wanted until she brought her eyes to mine.

They were wild. For me.

Needy. For me.

Feelings of relief and power swept through me.

This was the Ashleigh who was new to me. Naked Ashleigh. Panting and moaning Ashleigh. She was new but sexy and oh-so-sweet. Delicious. Mine.

I couldn't believe I'd spent two decades fucking around being friends, letting guys like Richard have a shot with her. I could have been making her happy; I could have had hours buried in her. I needed to make up for all that wasted time.

"We're not friends, Ashleigh; do you know that? Not anymore. We're more than that. You're mine. Every part of you. The sooner you get used to that, the better." I sank deeper into her, pulling out and sharply pushing back in.

"Oh God." Her lips parted, and she looked straight at me as she spasmed around me. I watched her orgasm pass through every atom of her. I loved the sounds she made as she came, the heavy breaths, the gasps, the half words. I needed to memorize each one of them. Nothing had ever sounded so sexy.

I wanted to tell her there would never be anyone else. She was my future, my forever. She was exactly what I'd been looking for, but never known I was searching for. But I held back, concerned she would feel it was too soon, that she'd think it was a reaction to my break up with Emma. I knew this had nothing to do with anything other than what I felt for Ashleigh. With Emma, I'd cherished our independence from each other. With Ashleigh, I never wanted to be without her, not for a second. I'd never realized I could feel that way. Ashleigh had awoken it in me.

Love had been hiding in plain sight all along.

Ashleigh

I slumped forward, wrapping my arms around Luke, the afterglow of my orgasm fluttering away down my limbs.

Luke's thrusting became shallower. I could tell he was holding himself back, allowing me to recover before chasing his own release.

"Take me to bed," I whispered into his ear. It was so good to have him here. How had I thought I was going to get through an evening without him?

Still inside me, he walked us into my bedroom as I pressed my lips to his neck, biting across his skin and along his jaw. "You're so sexy." He twitched and I twisted my hips, wanting to feel it again.

He groaned. "Jesus, you're going to kill me." He laid me on my back on the bed, and I pushed his hair away from his face.

"We wouldn't want that. Why don't you let me take some of the burden?"

"Oh, believe me, baby, fucking you will never be anything but my complete pleasure."

I shifted underneath him, and he rolled us over, leaving me on top as I'd wanted. I pushed against his body, savoring the feel of his hard chest beneath my hands. Sitting astride him, I moaned as he plunged deeper into me. I closed my eyes, briefly savoring him so deep. When I opened my eyes, he was staring back at me, watching me enjoy him. No man I'd ever been with had so clearly put my pleasure before his, had been so turned on by what he could do to me. "You feel so, so good," I whispered, gently moving my hips up and then pulling him into me again. "So deep, so hard. I'm so full."

He grunted and thrust his hips off the bed as if he couldn't hold back. We found a rhythm, and my body started to wind and tighten with pleasure.

He reached for my breasts, cupping each one, smoothing his fingers along the underside and brushing his thumbs over my nipples. I took one of his hands and guided him lower.

The scrape of his skin across my clit interrupted my rhythm, and I stopped to bask in the sensation. He withdrew his hand. I twisted my hips in protest and began to rock over him. His hand found my clit again, but I stilled as I let myself savour his skin on mine. As soon as I paused, his fingers did too. It was as if he was rewarding me with his touch. I recommenced my movements, squeezing him as I dragged myself up and off, then plunging back down. It was as if I had to earn his fingers. I was prepared to do whatever it took.

I had to concentrate as his thumb rounded my clit, notching the heat travelling through my body up a level.

"Baby, you're so wet."

"Because of you. It's all for you."

He groaned and removed his hands from where they were eliciting pure sensation from my body. He gripped my waist, pushing his thumbs into the sensitive flesh under my hips, rocking himself up, meeting my movements. I clasped my hands over his as we crashed against each other again and again, each movement bringing my climax closer and closer.

The moonlight flickered through the curtains, catching on the sheen of sweat that had formed a film across Luke's beautiful face.

"When you look at my like that, I can't hold back, baby," he said.

"Don't. Take what you need."

His jaw tightened, and his fingertips pressed harder into my skin as he pushed deeper and faster into me. I gave up control and held myself above him as he pounded into me. It took only a few seconds for another orgasm—just as intense as the last one—to wash over me, pulsing across my skin and surging deep into my very core. My climax allowed Luke to let go, and after three sharp thrusts, he poured himself into me. The muscles in his jaw finally loosened, and I ran my knuckles along the bristles of his five o'clock shadow, just to check.

He pulled me down and trailed his fingers along the side of my body, making me shiver. He kept his legs wrapped around me, and he was still inside me. It was as if he wanted to tell me something, share something important, but couldn't quite form the words.

I loved him. I'd always known I had, but had never allowed myself to give in to it so completely. But with him in my bed, my body so entirely owned by him, I had no defenses left. Now, he was all I felt. He'd cracked me open and my love for him had just poured out. I was coated in it, and I could never be closed back up.

After less than a day of being together, I couldn't bear to give him up, even for one evening.

If he ever left me, I would be broken.

The thought was terrifying. He had the power to destroy me.

We dragged ourselves out of bed the following morning, our fitful sleep punctuated by each other's lips, hands and more than one orgasm. As soon as I hit the cold, crisp air of November in London, I felt anything but heavy. I floated to work, a grin tattooed on my face that I had to concentrate to make smaller so I didn't invite questions.

Halfway through the day, I was called to reception to find an enormous arrangement of peonies and amongst them a handwritten card.

They don't smell as beautiful as you. Luke

I didn't know if the flowers were a conscious sign that he understood I needed his reassurance, but the effect was the same. I didn't want us to fast-forward to complacency. There was a side of me that needed to be wooed by him, needed to be sure that this was about me and not just about having someone.

How was it possible to miss someone you'd known your whole life, and had left just hours earlier? I felt his absence physically, as if a part of me were missing when he wasn't with me.

I texted him. Thank you for the flowers. I'm looking forward to tonight.

I got a reply straight away. I miss you. I can't wait to see you.

My skin hummed and my grin spread.

"Someone's a lucky man." I glanced up to find Richard looking between me and the flowers. My face fell.

"I . . ." How did I respond to that?

He rested his hand on my shoulder. "I mean it. He's a lucky guy. You don't need to explain."

I exhaled. "I'm sorry," I said. I couldn't offer any platitudes. Couldn't say it wasn't serious. I was as serious about Luke as I'd ever been about anything.

"Don't be. You're amazing. Of course you have suitors left and right. I'm surprised I was allowed to be one of them, even if it was for a short time."

My heart ached at his words. He was such a generous man, and in so many ways it would have been so much easier if I could have fallen for him.

"Well, I happen to know that you have them queueing around the block. And rightly so," I said.

He brushed a strand of my hair away from my face and smiled, but didn't reply. My phone buzzing in my pocket interrupted the moment. "I'll see you around," he said, and then he was gone.

"Hi, Haven," I answered. It was unusual for her to call in the middle of the day. My mind flicked to her growing bump. I hoped nothing was wrong.

"I'm sorting out Christmas. We need a plan. You're not going to Hong Kong?"

She was right; I wasn't going to see my parents. There was little chance I'd get enough time off work to fly out there, and anyway, last time I'd been my mother spent the whole time accusing my dad of cheating on her. He'd denied it, but they'd done nothing but row. It had been exhausting and anything but merry. "Nope."

"So I thought it would be easier to eat out rather than do it all ourselves. I found a great place in Mayfair. I've booked us in for dinner tonight to test it out."

"I can't go tonight. Can't you take Jake?"

"No, he has some investor thing, and anyway, I want to go with you."

"Well, I'm busy." I raced through the possible lies I could tell her that might satisfy her that I couldn't cancel when she asked me the inevitable.

"Why can't you come?"

"I have a thing." Could I get away with being vague? I didn't want to lie to her.

"A thing? What sort of thing? What's going on?"

"Nothing, just a business school thing. Like a mixer." I cringed as I spoke.

"Before you've even got in? That's a bit cruel if you don't get accepted, isn't it? They're dangling what might have been in front of you."

My stomach churned, but I just wasn't ready to hear what she had to say about Luke and me. I wanted to be on more solid footing before we told her, before we told anyone. Haven's opinion mattered to both of us, and if she wasn't going to offer her blessing, I needed to feel comfortable enough with Luke and me to give her time to change her mind—to win her over. Of course, what I really wanted to do was separate the part of her that was Luke's sister and tell my best friend that I'd found the love of my life. As much as I was afraid I couldn't handle her disapproval, I still wanted to share my excitement. I knew that the best friend bit of Haven would be nothing but delighted that Luke and I had found a way to be together.

"I don't know. I just have to go."

"Suit yourself. Go meet with new, fun, interesting, childless people. I don't care." Haven's tone was melodramatic, and I couldn't help but laugh.

"I can go tomorrow night. How about that?" As I was saying the words, I realized that it obviously meant that I couldn't see Luke if I was out with Haven, and although I didn't want us to be too much too soon, I wasn't sure how I would handle a whole day without seeing him.

"Okay, I'll rebook. Jake might make tomorrow. Shall I ask Luke and Beth?"

"I don't mind." I tried to sound casual, but I was conflicted. I would get to see Luke, but Beth was one of the most perceptive people I knew. I wasn't sure Luke and I wouldn't give away where we were in our relationship. I was having a hard enough time hiding it at work.

"But you're okay with Luke? It seemed fine yesterday. He was less grumpy than he's been in a while." I could tell she was about to ask for a status update about whether or not I was ready to pursue things with Luke, which I didn't want to get into. Still, I couldn't help but grin at the thought she'd noticed his mood had improved yesterday.

"Yeah, everything's good. Invite him. Seeing him and Beth is always great."

"We haven't talked about it for a while. He seems to be over the Emma thing. You know, what with participating in the triathlon and things. Do you think that maybe you're ready to explore things with him?"

Apparently, Haven wasn't easily dissuaded from asking me difficult questions. I thought I'd gotten away with it. I should have known better. It would have been the perfect moment to tell her that I was more than ready. But my need to be on more solid ground with Luke stopped me. I just didn't want to create expectations in anyone, myself included. I needed time. "Haven."

"Okay, I'll invite them then. Are you expecting to hear about whether or not you got in to business school today? Maybe they'll announce it at the mixer. Oh my God, that's why you're invited. They're going to tell you that you got in. This is so exciting. Tomorrow can be a celebration. Oh, this is amazing—"

"I'm going to have to get back to work, Haven." Her excitement, her every word, increased my guilt. I was lying to my best friend about what I was doing tonight—about Luke and me. I never lied to Haven. She was my family. I just couldn't tell her, not yet.

chapter
TWENTY-FIVE

Luke

I wiped my palms on my trousers. I was actually nervous. Nervous to go to dinner with a woman I'd known my whole life, and had now seen naked on numerous occasions. It was ridiculous. But I wanted tonight to go well. She wanted to date, and I wanted to do whatever made her happy. She needed to be sure of my feelings. I suspected she thought that part of what brought us together was the sex. And she wasn't wrong. She was the best sex I'd ever had. Every curve of her body, flick of her hips, drag of her tongue drove me crazy, and the way her words were a little dirty and her sounds a little filthy made me want to keep her naked for the rest of our lives. But it wasn't just about the physical stuff, and I hoped that dating would help her see that. I wanted Ashleigh Franklin, the whole woman. The woman who made me laugh, who I could talk with for hours, and the woman who made me want to kill any man who had come before me. I even wanted the part of her that cared so much what my sister thought, but wanted me anyway.

I wanted all of her, forever.

One of her neighbors let me into her building. I rapped on the door, clutching flowers in my other hand. She opened the door with a smile, and instantly, I relaxed. That mouth of hers had magical powers in so many ways. Just looking at it soothed me. I had nothing to be nervous about. It was just Ashleigh, the girl I'd grown up with, the woman I couldn't be without.

"Hey, handsome," she said. "You're right on time."

This was our first official date, so there was no way I was going to be late.

"And you look super smart. You said casual, right?" She gestured for me to follow her inside. I did as she asked, handing her the flowers before she turned around. Should I have tried to kiss her? I wasn't sure what the etiquette was tonight.

"These are beautiful. You shouldn't have. I have those gorgeous peonies that you sent earlier, and the flowers from yesterday."

Maybe flowers three times in three days was too much, but I wanted her to know how special she was. I'd never bought things for girls before, so I'd struggled to think what would be appropriate. I'd bought Christmas and birthday gifts for Emma, but she'd always told me what she wanted and I just went and got it. With Ashleigh, I'd bought her flowers because I liked the thought of her smile when she got them. "I wanted to. These don't smell as good as you, either, but they look nice enough. You, on the other hand, look stunning."

"How can you say 'nice enough'? They're beautiful. You really shouldn't have."

I wondered if she couldn't take compliments in general, or whether it was that she just ignored the ones that came from me. She'd have to get used to it.

I followed her into her kitchen, where she unwrapped the lilies and set about cutting off the ends and arranging them in a vase. I stood in the doorway watching her as she decided which flowers to place where in her arrangement. She did a double take when she caught me.

"What?" she asked.

I shrugged. "Nothing. I just like looking at you." Every movement she made was so graceful, so unconsciously sexy.

She smiled shyly and tilted her head to one side. The air crackled around us, and she wet her lips. Jesus, just that simple act had my cock's attention. I wanted to know what that glossy mouth would look like wrapped around my dick. I shifted, trying to get myself under control.

I cleared my throat. "I think we should go."

Ashleigh's smile turned wicked, but she nodded. I moved into the hallway to wait and to tell my cock to stand down. She appeared a minute later, and we headed into the freezing cold, bundling ourselves into a cab as soon as we found one.

"This is a mid-week date, right? So, I've not planned anything fancy. Just dinner."

"I'm not expecting fancy. I just want to spend some time with you fully clothed and in public. I just don't want to skip the good bit and go straight to me moaning about you leaving the toilet seat up, or cleaning the car on a Sunday. Does that make sense?"

I nodded. Any time I got to spend with her, no matter what we were doing, was all good with me. And the sooner we could tell Haven and Jake the better. Then we could be open about being together. Perhaps by the end of the evening I would have convinced her that we were ready to tell the world.

I laced my fingers through hers and squeezed. "It makes perfect sense. We never have to skip to that part, though. I know that's what it was like with Emma and me, but Haven and Jake aren't like that, and we don't have to be either. We can always do the fun stuff. I want to always do the fun stuff with you."

"Okay then. And we're not going to Chiltern Firehouse, are we?"

"We're not. You don't like it there? Just so I know for future fun stuff."

She glanced down at the pavement. "I just . . . I don't like that it's where you took Fiona. I know I told you that you should date and everything, but it doesn't mean that . . ."

Was I an idiot for not going to Ashleigh sooner to tell her I was ready? "I'm sorry. It wasn't serious, and we didn't get naked. I guess I was just—"

"You have nothing to apologize for. Seriously."

"If it makes you feel any better, I'd quite happily murder Richard."

She laughed. It was one of my favorite sounds. Only topped by the breathy noises she made when she had my dick in her or my tongue on her. I swept my thumb across her wrist and caught her shiver in response.

We arrived at the restaurant, an Italian place in Mayfair that had come recommended by a guy at work. I'd visited during my lunch hour just to see if it was a place Ashleigh would like.

"Murano?" Ashleigh asked.

"Yeah, is that okay?"

"It's more than okay. I've always wanted to come here. I thought you said tonight was nothing fancy?"

I grinned. I'd chosen the right place.

"Mr. Daniels, nice to see you again," the host said as we arrived.

I watched as Ashleigh's face dropped. I could tell she thought I'd been here with another woman. I bent and whispered in her ear, "I came earlier today to check it out. I've not been before, and I wanted to make sure it was good enough."

She turned toward me, wrapped her hands around my neck and pressed her mesmerizing lips against mine. "Thank you," she said, pulling away.

"What for?" I wasn't complaining about the kiss, but it had caught me off guard.

"Oh, you know. Just for being wonderful."

My heart swelled at her words. It was incredible to me that this amazing, sexy, caring, funny and gentle woman could think I was wonderful. I wasn't about to question it.

By the end of the evening, I was aching for her. Every minute I spent with her made me realize what a fool I'd been for all these years. She had been right in front of me, wanting me, and I'd never chosen to explore it.

Ashleigh

We stood outside my building, and he brushed my hair from my face. "Ashleigh, thank you for agreeing to come out with me tonight. I've had a great evening, and I'd really like to see you again. Are you free on Saturday, all day?"

Was he calling time on our date already? I wasn't sure I was ready to be apart from him. "Thank you for a wonderful time, and I would love to see you again on Saturday."

He nodded. "May I kiss you?"

My stomach flip-flopped. I slid my hand up his hard chest, taking a half step forward and closing the gap between us. "I would like that, yes."

He cupped my face and dropped a kiss at the corner of my mouth. My lips parted as he traced his tongue across my bottom lip before dipping inside. His hands smoothed down my back, pressing my body against his, making me feel wanted and safe. He gasped as I trailed my fingers along the top of his belt. We'd already slept together, and I really wasn't trying to put the genie back in the lamp. Would he stay if I asked? Before I got a chance to say anything, he broke our kiss and took a step back.

"You're incredible, but I'm having a hard time staying in control." The thought that I could do that to him still took a little getting used to. "I have an early start, so I'm going to go."

I nodded, disappointment flooding my veins. He was set on leaving. He kissed me on the cheek and watched as I made my way into my building.

I felt wooed, cherished. And now I was lying in bed with an ache between my legs that only Luke had a cure for. Should I have invited him in? He hadn't asked, hadn't assumed, and I'd forgotten where we were with things. Did dating for him mean no sex? Now on my own, Luke was all I wanted, and he'd made it more than clear that he wanted me. What was I waiting for? I had a lot to lose, but even more to gain.

I threw on my coat and ran outside. It was late, and I lived some way from a main road where I could catch a passing cab. It took me about twenty minutes before I spotted a taxi with its light on, and when I scrambled in, I realized I didn't know Luke's flat number. I'd been there before, but only once. I spent the journey scrolling my messages, trying to find the text where he'd given me his address. Before I knew it, I was standing on my own outside Luke's building, looking at the dissolving taillights of the cab. Jesus, I was an idiot. What was I doing here? Maybe he hadn't pushed to come in because he didn't want to. Maybe he was feeling unsure about our relationship as well. I started to pace, too panicked to continue my search through old texts. I shouldn't have come. I should have trusted my initial instinct and let us marinate— let us both get used to the idea of being together. What was I thinking, being so presumptuous, assuming I was the only one holding back?

I missed him.

"Ashleigh."

I jumped and spun to find Luke walking toward me.

"What are you doing here?" he asked.

"Uh . . . oh. Um. I don't know." Was he mad? "I'm sorry."

"Don't be sorry. How long have you been here?" He checked his watch then looked at me. He pulled me into his arms. "Are you cold? I'm sorry I wasn't here."

It registered that he'd only just made it home after dropping me off. Where had he been?

"No. I shouldn't have come. I should go. I didn't mean to push." Jesus, I should have just stayed at home. We'd had a wonderful night, and I'd spoiled it by showing up uninvited.

"What do you mean 'push'? Please don't go anywhere," he said into my hair as his arms tightened. "Tell me why you are here."

I took a deep breath. "I missed you." It was so good to be held by him. It felt so safe.

"You did?" He kissed the top of my head. "Let's get you inside. You must be freezing. You shouldn't be out on your own. It's not safe, and I don't want anything to happen to you."

"But if I'm pushing, you have to tell me."

"Pushing me by being here? Ashleigh, I'm ready to run; I'm just waiting for you to catch up, baby."

Everything he said made me feel better. Every moment I spent with him made me feel more certain of our future together.

"Am I crazy?" I asked as we headed inside.

"In general or for some particular reason? Because yes and maybe."

I rolled my eyes and he chuckled.

"For missing you, for turning up here in the middle of the night. I think I'm crazy."

"Well, if that makes you crazy, I like crazy. I thought you didn't want me to stay, and I don't want to push." His brow was furrowed as if he were trying to piece together a puzzle.

"I know what I said, but I've changed my mind." I glanced at the floor. "Dating should include sleepovers. What do you think?"

He stuck his keys in the lock and ushered me inside. "I think that maybe you're beginning to catch up."

He collapsed on the sofa and pulled me onto his lap. "I don't want to waste another moment without you. I feel like a fool for not seeing what was under my nose for so long. Every night should be a sleepover as far as I'm concerned, but I know you have some doubts and you want to protect yourself. I get all that, and I want to go at your pace, but you never need to worry that you're pushing. Everything else I want in life pales in comparison to how much I want you."

My stomach dipped and rolled at his words. Those words had been the stuff of my dreams since I was a teenager. "You're wonderful."

"I'm really not. Ask Emma, or Fiona. Any of my exes. It's different with you. You make me different. Better. I like myself with you more than I do without you."

I wasn't sure that I'd ever been paid such a compliment by anyone. It was close to overwhelming. "Okay, so you're my Mr. Wonderful."

"I can live with that." He linked his fingers through mine and nestled his head against my neck. "Are you feeling better?"

I nodded. It wasn't possible to feel anything other than ecstatic given what he'd just said. "Much."

"We've always been able to talk, Ashleigh, and now that we're together, it doesn't mean that should stop. In fact, in my experience, not talking, not saying how you feel, can only lead to pain."

Now we're together.

The words played on a loop in my head, mixing with his breath on my neck, making my brain fuzzy and my limbs loose. He sounded so sure. So solid. As if it were a done deal, a one-way street.

"Maybe you're right."

"Maybe?" he asked incredulously.

I giggled. "I mean, yes, you're right about the talking, but also when you told me that we had this. Maybe you knew it all along."

"I'm pleased the penny is finally beginning to drop. I have wisdom beyond my years when it comes to how I feel about you, and how things will work out with us. You'll get used to it."

"No one likes a show-off, Luke Daniels."

"Well, you just crossed London for me in the middle of the night. You seem to like me pretty well."

"Again with the showing off," I whispered and dropped a kiss on his jaw. Obviously, I didn't tell him, but he was on to something. We were together now. It made sense to me, and I felt good—no—amazing about that. "I think it's time to tell Haven." I dropped another kiss on his jaw.

"You ready to not care if she's weird about it?"

"You think she'll be weird about it?"

"No, but I want you to be sure of this—of me, of us. I don't want you breaking up with me again if she says something you don't like."

He was right. I'd been all too ready to buy in to Haven's doubts—I'd even enlarged them in my own imagination. "I think she just gave a voice to the feelings I had. Hearing them from her made them bigger than they needed to be. But, you're no longer five seconds out of a long-term relationship, and I believe you when you tell me that I'm not the easy option for you. It's like you've moved out of some rut and are embracing change for the first time ever."

"You're right. I'd tried to make everything around me into some kind of time warp because I thought that was what would make me happy. It's probably been like that since my parents died. I've let go of that need to keep everything the same, and you've helped me with that. You've shown me how good change can be."

He couldn't have said anything that would have made me love him more. "You say the sweetest things."

"I mean every word."

"I'm ready to tell Haven." I reached up and placed a row of kisses down his cheekbone.

"Come on." He lifted me off his lap. "That's reason to do some naked celebrating. Let's get you to bed." His phone began to buzz.

"It's Haven," he said. "It's late; I wonder why she's calling." He silenced the call. By the time we'd made it to the bedroom, my phone was ringing. I knew before checking it would be Haven. It would be too coincidental for our phones to have gone off so close together not to be.

"I have to answer. It could be about the baby, and Jake's out tonight."

"Haven?" I sat on the bed and kicked off my shoes.

"Hi, sorry. Is it too late? I just tried to call Luke but he's not answering, and neither is Jake."

"You okay?"

"Yeah, I just had a weird sensation in my belly, and I got a bit freaked. I spoke to the doctor, and he said it was fine and normal and probably the baby kicking, but I just needed someone I loved to tell me that it's going to be okay."

Luke had stripped down to his boxers and was trying to pull my sweater over my head. He held my phone to my ear to release my arm. Placing my hand back on my phone, he pushed me back onto the bed as Haven continued to chatter.

"It's more than okay. It's so amazing, Haven. You've got a living thing inside you. It's weird, but totally cool."

Luke slid my jeans down my legs, followed by my underwear. I lay naked on the bed.

"So you're okay. Do you want me to come over?" I'd have to have a cold shower before I left, but if she really wanted me to go over, I would. That was the story I was telling myself anyway.

"No, I'm fine. I just needed to hear you tell me that it's okay. I'm just relived, that's all."

Luke began to drop butterfly kisses across my belly. I threaded my free hand through his hair, loving his warmth against my skin.

"How was the mixer? Oh my God? Did you get a place? I'm sorry; I've been whining about me and I forgot to ask. Are you a future MBA graduate?"

My gut sank. Thank God she'd know about us sooner rather than later. I hated lying to her. I twisted away from Luke. He moved to my side and rested his head on his elbow, looking at me. "I didn't hear today. I think it will be this week though."

"But the mixer was good?" she asked.

"Tonight was fine, but I'm really tired. Do you mind if we catch up tomorrow?"

Haven and I exchanged goodbyes, and I hung up and tossed my phone on the nightstand. Luke traced his finger along my jaw. "Is she okay?"

"Yeah, I guess it's first-time jitters."

"Jake will make her feel better. He knows how to handle her."

I nodded. "I can't believe she's going to be a mother. I mean—"

"She's young," he said. It wasn't what I'd been about to say.

"Not really. I meant, it's such a life-changing event, and it wasn't planned. I think she would have liked to have had a bit more time for it to be just her and Jake."

Luke chuckled. "I'm sure Jake feels the same way."

I got the impression from Jake that their pregnancy was exactly what he wanted. He'd been talking about kids for a while. Luke clearly saw things differently, or he was projecting his own feelings about being a father. It was evidence of how new our relationship was that we hadn't discussed a family. Perhaps we didn't need to. He'd been clear about not wanting kids when he was with Emma, and he'd joked with Jake when Haven said she was pregnant that he was glad it wasn't him. I guess I had to accept that if I wanted Luke, a child wouldn't be part of the equation. A hollowness swelled inside me.

"You okay?" he asked, stroking my hair and bringing me back to the present.

"Yeah, just feel terrible about lying to Haven." And about giving up the possibility of being a mother.

"Don't feel bad, beautiful. We'll tell her tomorrow."

Telling Haven would be the next step. I couldn't even manage spending my sleeping hours away from Luke, so she needed to know. Still, my head was full of possibilities of how she would react.

"I need her to be on board, but I'm ready."

"I know. She will be. She was just worried before. She thought I was going to jerk you around, or that it would all go wrong and she'd be left with a broken family. But it's fine. It's different now; she'll see that."

I placed my palm just under his ribcage and watched my hand move up and down with his breathing. "It worries me too," I said in a small voice. "I couldn't handle not having . . ." I had to stop talking because I could feel my voice begin to quiver. The thought of losing him and Haven was too painful.

Luke slid his hand beneath mine. "I'll never let that happen, Ashleigh. We'll always be family to each other. I promise."

I took a deep breath and let myself be comforted by his words.

"How are we going to tell her? This is new and—"

"Ashleigh, this is anything but new. I've known you my whole life. Leave my sister to me. I've got it covered."

chapter
TWENTY-SIX

Luke

Shopping wasn't something I enjoyed, and I certainly would never normally interrupt a day in the office to elbow my way between shoppers, but that was exactly what I was doing. Ashleigh had made it clear that I was going overboard on the flower buying. I just felt such an urge to keep her thinking about me, to make her smile, to do things that I knew would make her happy. So I found myself making some time in the middle of the day to buy her a gift.

I rarely saw her spoil herself. I knew she'd struggled when she bought her flat, and Haven had told me that she hadn't gone to Chicago with them because she couldn't afford it and wouldn't let Jake pay for her flight and hotel room. So if she couldn't spend money on herself, I would make up for it. I had in mind what I wanted to get her. We were going to tell Haven tonight, and I wanted her to feel as good as she looked when we did. I wanted her to be thinking about what I'd do to her later, rather than nervous about dinner. I'd never bought women's underwear before. I really wasn't that kind of man.

Emma had once told me I was the least romantic person she'd ever met, and while we'd been together, she'd been right. Ashleigh had uncovered a new side of me.

"Can I help you, sir?" One of the sales assistants asked as I wandered into the high-end boutique I'd found on Google earlier that morning.

"Yeah, I want to buy a present for . . ." We hadn't dealt with labels yet, I'd been too concerned with letting Ashleigh set the pace. "My girlfriend." Girlfriend sounded good, and I had to consciously stop the corners of my mouth from curling too far up. I didn't want the sales assistant to think I was hitting on her.

"Do you have anything in mind?" she asked.

I glanced around the shop. Ashleigh would look good in any of the things in here. "Any colors you like or don't like?" I shrugged. Perhaps this was too much too soon. I didn't want to push, or make Ashleigh feel that what we had was all about sex. Surely she got that now?

"Any budget you had in mind?"

"I want something nice. That she would choose for herself. I don't want her to think that I'm buying it for me." I wasn't sure that would be much help to the assistant, but she just smiled and led me over to one of the racks.

"What color hair does she have? And skin?"

"Almost black hair and light skin. Quite pale. She says she burns in the sun." It was the reason we used to spend our summers underneath trees as children.

"Red would look beautiful, a deep red, like this." She held up a bra.

I nodded. It would be gorgeous against her skin. I tried not to imagine too vividly exactly what she would look like. That would only lead to trouble.

"So were you thinking bra and panties, or maybe a bustier or garters?"

Holy crap, this was getting complicated. "What would you buy if someone gave you a gift card?"

"I'd skip the garters, buy two pairs of panties and take the bra and bustier."

"Sounds good." I wanted Ashleigh to love her gift, but spoiling my girlfriend was a new experience. An adjustment. Ashleigh was changing me in so many ways.

It took what seemed like an hour and a half to gift wrap the lot, which seemed an overly convoluted process that included wrapping it in white paper, boxing it, tying bows, wrapping it again—this time in black paper—and then placing it in an enormous gift bag. There was a distinct possibility that Ashleigh would think I'd bought her a car rather than just underwear.

As I headed back to work, my phone buzzed in my jacket pocket. "I don't have any pictures of you on my phone." I'd realized as the assistant and I were trying to decide Ashleigh's size that I wanted a photo of her.

"Er, hello. Were you just thinking that as I was calling?"

"It's all I've been thinking about. I want to get you naked and take photos." The thought had my dick stirring in my pants.

"You're a pervert."

"I just love your body." And mind and soul. "You need to learn how to accept compliments."

"It's just weird. I'm used to you teasing me, giving me shit for no reason at all, and then me turning round and giving it to you straight back."

I understood why she thought it was weird, but I didn't feel the same way. For me, the transition she'd made in my head from friend to lover had been effortless. Convincing her she could trust me was more challenging, but my emotions were very clear. "You'll get used to it, baby. Anyway, shouldn't you be saving lives or something? You're not normally able to call in the middle of the day. What's going on?"

"Again, with the palliative care thing. My patients don't get cured."

"Oh, yes, I think I remember you saying that before." I couldn't tame the grin that had taken over my face. I could tell by her voice she was wearing one similar.

"Now, that's better. This Ash and Luke I can do."

"You can do Ashleigh and Luke 2.0 as well. You just need to have a little faith."

"I do. I'm just nervous about tonight. We haven't really discussed what we're going to say or how we're going to say it, and it's just . . . I thought maybe we should have a plan."

"My plan is that you're not allowed to break up with me, no matter what reaction Haven has or doesn't have."

"That's not a plan."

"That's the most important plan. Seriously, Ashleigh, I need to know you're not going to dip straight back into a meltdown." It would quite possibly kill me to lose her now. She felt a part of me.

There was a beat of silence on the other end of the phone, and my heart began to gallop.

"That's not going to happen." Her voice was muffled and small.

I needed her to be more convincing.

"I just don't want to have to choose between pleasing Haven and pleasing you."

"How about you think about what you want? I want you. I hope you want me."

"I do, I just can't . . ."

My heart rate wasn't slowing down. "You can't what, Ashleigh?"

"I can't lose you."

My knees nearly gave way with relief. I shut my eyes so I could concentrate on what she'd just said. "You'll never lose me. Don't worry about tonight. I'll find a way of bringing it up—sooner rather than later so you don't die of a stroke halfway through dinner. It's all going to be fine. I promise."

"Okay, you're right. It's going to be fine. Thank you."

"Good." There wasn't a bigger prize than soothing away Ashleigh's worries. It was as if that were my job now—to take care of her and to make everything better. We were linked. I felt better when Ashleigh felt better. Making her happy made me happy.

"Oh, shit. I forgot to tell you. I called because I got into business school." She elongated the word school in her excitement.

"Are you serious? You're fucking amazing. I had no doubt. We need to celebrate." I was so proud of her, but there was an uneasiness at my edges that I recognized. School would mean change. Her focus would shift. But it could be a positive, right? We couldn't stand still—I'd learned that the hard way. If I could shop for lingerie then all bets were off. If that didn't prove we could adapt then nothing did. Getting through business school would be a breeze. Ashleigh happy was nothing but a good thing.

"We'll celebrate tonight. You'll stay over?"

Her asking made me feel better instantly.

Ashleigh

I arrived home to find a humongous bag from a very expensive lingerie boutique on the mat outside my flat. I smiled, knowing it must be from Luke. I wasn't sure how he'd managed to get in my building, but the fact that Luke had taken time out of what would have been a very busy day to go shopping, then drop it off at my place, was almost as amazing as the gift itself. Almost.

As I dispersed the copious amounts of tissue paper, I pulled out the most beautiful lingerie I'd ever seen in my life. It was a bra, two sets of panties and a bustier, all in gothic, red lace. Quickly, I stripped bare to try it on. It was soft and sexy, the bustier pushing my boobs up and covering my skin just enough so I didn't spill out. I couldn't wait for Luke to see me later that evening. I was pretty sure he'd be happy with his purchase. I wasn't sure the panties would last long under his fingers. I wasn't sure I minded that idea at all.

Amongst the tissue paper was a note.

I want you to feel as amazing as I know you are.

You have nothing to worry about.

We got this. Love, Luke

Being with Luke made me feel like a goddess. I'd never felt so adored. I was beginning to think he was right. Maybe we did have this.

I slipped a black dress over my new underwear and quickly put on some makeup before heading out to meet everyone for dinner.

As I arrived at the restaurant Haven had chosen, my anxiety faded. My focus was on the feel of the lace against my skin and the thought of Luke's face when he saw me later in nothing but what he'd bought me. If distraction had been Luke's intention, then mission accomplished.

"Hey," I said, arriving at our assigned table. I was the last to arrive, which wasn't like me. I clipped people's cheeks with my kisses. Even Beth was here. "This place looks beautiful, Haven."

I took the open slot between Luke and Haven. As I sat down, Luke squeezed my thigh, and my stomach tumbled at his touch. I mouthed the words thank you at him, and he winked at me.

Luke filled my water, and I relaxed back into my chair. What was he going to say? And when? Part of me was nervous, but a bigger part of me was excited. I wanted my family to know that Luke and I were together.

"I hope the food's good," Haven said. "I can't be arsed cooking at Christmas. If I can't drink, there's got to be some upside to the day."

"I've said I don't mind being chef for the day," Beth said.

"No, Haven's right. Going out will be great. It's good to make new traditions," Luke said.

My heart sped up. Was he going to say something now? I wasn't sure I was ready.

"You've totally got to bake something," I said. "That's our new Christmas law. We all have enough baked goods from Beth to incite a diabetic coma." There was a chuckle around the table.

"Well, funny you should say that, that's going to be the tagline to my video clips. Beth's Baked Goods—A Diabetic Coma in the Making."

"Sounds like a winner. How are they going? I saw you had a gazillion hits on the one I looked at over the weekend." I was pretty sure Beth was going to be a YouTube phenomenon sooner rather than later. She looked like a young Elizabeth Taylor and dressed like one, in vintage fifties dresses. She was the kind of girl Haven and I would joke about going gay for.

"You're so sweet to be checking them out. I'm not sure it's quite a gazillion, and I'm positive most of them are just from the people around this table."

"I saw loads of comments. Some pervs, it has to be said. It must be every guy's wet dream to have a woman like you in their kitchen," I said. "Mostly they were from people who loved you and your baking."

Beth blushed. "I just do it for fun, but actually, I got a call yesterday from a guy who wants to talk about me doing a five-minute slot on a Saturday breakfast show in Chicago."

"Are you serious?" Jake asked. "That's amazing. You're going to be a superstar."

Beth pushed Jake off as he tried to grab her for a kiss. "It's only a local TV thing. And it will probably come to nothing, but it's fun. Right?"

"It's bloody fantastic," Luke said. "We're surrounded by incredible women, Jake," he said, shaking his head as if in awe. My need to kiss him was almost too strong to resist.

"I know, right?" Jake replied.

A sommelier busied himself, pouring fizzy courage into flutes. I dreaded to think how much this evening would cost. I'd lined up a second mortgage to pay for the part of my business school fees that the hospital wasn't covering, and I'd applied for several scholarships, but things would be tight for the next few years.

When the waiter had filled all our glasses, Luke pushed back his chair and stood. My heart began to thump so loud I was surprised someone didn't call an ambulance.

"I'd like to say something," he said as everyone stared up at him.

This was it. Excitement built beneath my skin.

"I'm in love with Ashleigh Franklin," he announced.

He looked at me as he spoke, and I couldn't do anything but gaze at him.

He loved me?

Of course he did.

How could I have ever doubted it?

"I'm obsessed to the point of madness. Devoted, besotted, totally and completely in love with her. I hope she feels for me just a tiny fraction of what I feel for her. I intend to spend the rest of my life trying to earn her love and respect. That is all."

In all my years of loving him, I'd never felt more for him than as I did in that moment. He was describing how I felt about him. Our feelings were mutual. I never thought that could be possible.

He scraped my cheekbone with his thumb and placed a soft kiss on my lips. "Breathe," he whispered.

"I'm good. We got this," I replied.

I finally pulled my gaze away from him and scanned the three faces staring at me, focusing on Haven. She grinned like a Cheshire cat and rolled her eyes at me. Jake raised his glass, and Beth had her hands clasped in front of her, a smile on her face.

I turned back to Luke. "I love you too. You know that, right?" I'd known in my heart for so long that I loved him, that I sort of assumed that he knew, but saying it out loud felt . . . right.

"I can only hope that you do."

"You have nothing to hope for. You have my love. All of it. Forever." I drew my eyebrows together, trying to convey how serious I was. He needed to understand that I was only ever going to love him.

"I'm never going to get tired of you telling me."

"I love you," I repeated. I'd loved him for as long as I could remember, but it felt different now. It was deeper, more substantial, almost as if I could reach out and touch whatever it was that was between us.

Luke grinned and squeezed my hand. "I love you."

"Okay, you two. You can stop before I start gagging," Haven said.

"You're okay with this? I need you to be good with this. I won't lose either of you." I hoped her smile was an indication that she had come round to the idea.

"Well, not the PDA, obviously. But I can't think of anything better than you two being together."

I didn't understand. What had changed for her? "But—"

"There's no but," she interrupted. "However, if you fuck this up, I'm going to kill you both. I'm not having my family break apart."

"I can live with that. We're not going to fuck this up," Luke replied.

"So how long have you known, been together?" Beth asked, looking between Luke and me. "You look really together."

My skin heated. We looked like a couple? I glanced over at Haven. Shit, I hope she wasn't mad that she didn't know straight away.

"Just a few days, I guess, but it's been a long time coming," Luke replied. "I knew since I split with Emma. I just needed to grow up a little, and then convince this one." He tilted his head in my direction and slid his arm around the back of my chair, leaning into me.

"And you're convinced?" Haven asked me.

"I am. Are you?"

"She's worried that you won't approve," Luke interjected. I placed my hand on his thigh. Not being with Luke wasn't an option.

"You don't need my approval, and anyway, whatever you do, you'll always have it. I just wanted to make sure you were all clear about the consequences. No matter what, we have a family to hold together. I didn't want you two putting that on the line just to get your rocks off."

I exhaled, relieved that Haven wasn't mad. Not even remotely. I wouldn't have to talk her round, convince her that she wasn't going to lose either of us. She was cheering for us; I could see it in her smile. By raising concerns, she had only ever been trying to protect us both. I grinned as she pulled me toward her and kissed my cheek.

The love surrounding me was overwhelming.

"We know that," Luke said, but I couldn't concentrate on the rest of his sentence. I was replaying the word we in my head again and again. It fit. The heat of his body brought me back into the moment. The skate of his fingers across my back every now and then made me feel safe.

We were a we.

And we were a family.

"We have plenty to celebrate," Jake said.

"Oh, and I got into business school," I added. On an ordinary day, it would have been a huge deal. Today it just felt like the cherry on the top of a huge cake.

The table erupted with congratulations and hugs.

Life was unfolding in the best possible way.

chapter
TWENTY-SEVEN

Luke

"So, was I right?" Jake asked as we recovered from our run. The sun was starting to break through the hostile air, thawing the ice that had collected on the edges of buildings and bus stops, but it was still cold, and we needed to keep moving toward the tube station.

My training had dropped off since Ashleigh and I had become a couple. Understandably, Fiona was no longer so enthusiastic about my participation in the triathlon, but I'd enjoyed the endorphins that almost daily cardio gave me. I also had to make sure I could keep giving Ashleigh what she needed in bed. Sex had been incredible from the beginning, and it kept getting better, and no less frequent.

"Right about what?"

"About Emma. And how it was obvious she wasn't right for you because you didn't want to marry her."

"Oh, about that." Jake had been convinced that when I found the right woman, my thoughts about marriage would change. I grinned. "Yeah, I'll give you that. You were right."

"So, you bought a ring yet?" We turned left; the tube was up ahead. I could probably walk home from where we were just as quickly.

"Mate, I'm going to scare her off if I start talking about marriage. She's still a little wary of my change of heart. I think she saw it as something that should have been a gradual process. I guess that's how it was for her. But for me? I just suddenly woke up and bam, I'm in love with her. I want to have nineteen kids with her, like yesterday. I'd marry her tomorrow if it were up to me. I just don't want to freak her out. She keeps telling me that it's only been a few weeks. It just doesn't feel like that for me. So I'm trying to be patient"

Jake was grinning at me. "Yup. You got it bad. It was exactly like that for me."

"I just don't know how long I can hold myself back from talking about our future. We've lost so much time already—I want to get on with things. She seems happy to stay where we are for now." We'd exchanged I love yous, so we weren't standing still, yet I felt way out ahead in terms of where we were in our relationship. I was constantly checking over my shoulder to make sure she was behind me. I wanted her to let go and just roll with it. Get caught up in it as I had.

"Have you spoken to her about it?"

"No. Telling Haven was a huge deal for her. She's happier now that's done, and so part of me doesn't want to push. But I'm ready for what's next. I guess I'll just have to learn some patience."

"And what is next?" Jake asked.

It was as if I were on an obstacle course, and I'd just

successfully conquered telling our family and saying I love you, and now I'd rounded a corner to find moving in together.

"I want her to live with me. Of course I want her to marry me, but I appreciate that might be too much of a jump."

Jake chuckled. "Maybe living together would be a good interim step. She might be more enthusiastic than you think. When Haven finally understood that we were both in it together forever, she didn't resist at all."

Perhaps Ashleigh was ready. I could start dropping hints about moving in now Haven was on board. Ashleigh could rent her place out, which would help her financially. We were spending every night together anyway. It was nearly Christmas, and we could use the time over the holidays to move her stuff in before she got down to her studies in the New Year. The timing was good. It all made sense. If I convinced her of the practicality of the move, perhaps she'd be distracted from what it meant for our relationship.

I hesitated at the entrance to the tube. "You not going home?" Jake asked.

"I think I'm going to walk, actually." I wanted to think things through, formulate my approach.

He nodded and headed back to Haven. Jake was a good guy. I'd always thought he was a little weak for marrying my sister so quickly after they'd met. I'd felt sorry for him. Before Ashleigh, I'd presumed he'd done it to comfort Haven, to keep her happy. Now I understood that if he felt for Haven half of what I felt for Ashleigh, there just wasn't an alternative if he wanted to be happy. I wanted to bind myself to Ashleigh in every way that I could.

I began to jog home, running through the counter arguments Ashleigh might make if I suggested we live together. It was what I did at the beginning of every new case I worked on. I found myself at the edge of the city, not too far away from home. Taking a shortcut, I made a left onto Hatton Garden, and into the heart of London's jewelry district. Stores lined both sides of the road, their windows full of engagement rings. Burly security guards broke up the throng of couples peering into windows. I was about halfway up before a ring caught my eye, and I dared to stop to take a proper look through the glass. I wasn't sure I'd really noticed an engagement ring until Haven's. She'd been ecstatically happy with hers, and had thrust it in my face several times. The ring I'd spotted wasn't small, but it wasn't huge—certainly not in the same league as Haven's. It was blue—a sapphire, probably. It wasn't a traditional engagement ring, but ours wasn't a traditional love. It looked beautiful without being showy. Like Ashleigh. It had an antique feel to it with a large central square stone surrounded by a ring of tiny diamonds. I grinned. I could imagine it on her finger, both now and in thirty years as she held our grandchildren. It was timeless. I was sure Ashleigh would love it if she ever got to the point where she would consider marrying me.

"It's a beautiful piece, isn't it?" said an elderly woman. She was carrying flowers and making her way into the store.

"It really is."

"Made for a beautiful woman. It's a platinum setting with an untreated medium-dark stone that's just under five carats. It's one of my favorites. It won't be around long. We only get that design once every few years, and it always sells out within days. Getting a stone like that isn't easy."

"It's expensive." I sucked in a slice of air as my eyes focused on the price tag. It wasn't a spur of the moment purchase. This wasn't just underwear.

"It is. Is she worth it?"

I peeled my gaze away from the ring and looked at the woman. "She really is. I need to . . . think."

The woman smiled at me. "Don't leave it long."

When I got home, I found Ashleigh at the breakfast bar in just her underwear and a camisole, poring over her laptop. I'd left her asleep to join Jake on our run.

"You look good enough to eat," I said as she swiveled on the stool to face me.

She uncrossed her legs and parted her thighs, skimming her hands down her milky white skin.

"Yeah?" She tilted her head and took in a breath. Fuck, she was amazing. I couldn't resist what was between those perfect legs.

I moved toward her and skimmed my fingers up her arms. "Yeah," I whispered into her neck.

"How was your run? How was Jake?"

"Good. Interesting." I'd found the ring I wanted to propose with. I just needed to figure out next steps—a strategy to get it on her finger.

"Interesting?"

"Yeah. We were talking about our girls."

"You were? That's cute. What was interesting about it?" She sounded intrigued.

"Well, I was telling him how I wanted us to move in together."

The corners of her mouth turned up, and her eyebrows lifted. I saw surprise, but not horror. "You were? What did Jake say?"

"That when all the pieces are there, it doesn't take long to fit them together." I loved how she looked at me—open and trusting. "Tell me what you're thinking." I traced her collarbone with my fingers, enjoying her shivers as I did so.

"You know what I'm thinking."

She was right. "That it's too soon? That I'll change my mind?"

"It's fast, Luke." Her words were light and soft as if she were easily persuadable.

"It's not that fast. And we're spending most nights together anyway. You could rent your place out. Paying for business school would be easier."

"It feels fast," she whispered.

Slowly, I backed away. "Take your underwear off." I fixated on my prize, staring at the juncture between her thighs. She hesitated, then hooked her thumbs into her panties and peeled the fabric from her skin. Instinctively, her legs closed, and I looked up at her face. "Show me," I said.

"Luke . . ."

"Show me."

She parted her thighs, revealing her sweet pussy. I knelt down in front of her and pushed her knees wider. She leaned back, her elbows against the breakfast bar. She was already wet enough that I could see the moisture glistening around her slit. Had she been sitting here thinking about me? Waiting for me to come back and do this to her? The thought made me groan.

I dragged my thumbs along the juncture of her thighs, holding off delving my tongue right into the core of her. I hadn't recovered fully from my sprint home, and I wasn't sure I'd be able to catch my breath while Ashleigh was naked. She was everything I'd never realized I needed.

She took my breath away.

I blew across her folds.

"Luke." She grabbed my head with one hand. "Please."

"Please what?" I loved hearing her dirty words. They were more evidence that the Ashleigh spread out in front of me was not the Ash that I'd know my whole life.

"Please. Lick me, suck me, fuck me. I need it."

Her words had the effect they always did, and I got a little dizzy as blood rushed to my cock. I grunted and pushed her legs wider.

"Move in with me." It was an unfair question—I was holding her to ransom, but I didn't care how I got my way, just that I did. I grazed my teeth up her inner thigh, torturing her, needing to get her to the point where she was so desperate for my tongue, my cock, my fingers that she'd agree to anything.

"What?"

"You heard me. Move in with me."

"Luke." She shifted on the stool, pushing her hips forward. I pulled back, withholding what she needed.

"Say you'll move in."

"Jesus, this isn't fair. I want to feel you." Her voice was breathy and desperate.

"I want to taste you," I replied, my words humming against her skin.

"Yes, please, Luke, yes. I'll move in. Just please . . ." Her words were sharp and desperate, and the sounds caused a surge of blood to my dick. I couldn't hold back any longer.

Ashleigh

I was a slave to Luke's touch. The things I would do for it. I was going to have to find a way of backtracking. We couldn't move too fast, couldn't move in together. With my arms wrapped around his back and my body still limp with the aftershocks of my orgasm, Luke carried me into the bedroom.

"I need to shower," I said.

"Afterward. I have to get you dirtier first. I need to be inside you without any distractions."

He let go of me, and I slid down his body, backing up onto the bed. "Turn over. On all fours. I just . . . I'll try to . . . Jesus, I'm going to lose it."

I loved that he wanted me so much he couldn't control himself. "Don't try to do anything. Just have me as you want me."

"I don't want—"

"You're not going to hurt me. I want you to show me how much you need me." I turned around, positioned myself on all fours and looked back at him. I was desperate to be fucked by him, to feel the length of him inside me, thickening, hardening. It was a powerful feeling that created a weakness in me at the same time.

"Fuck." He grabbed my hips, pushed into me immediately

and stopped. I gasped at the feel of him. Each time it was unexpected how he filled me, as if I were made only for him.

His breath was hot on my skin as he ran his nose along my spine, gathering his strength and sliding his hands from my waist to my shoulders.

"I'm addicted to how you smell. It reminds me of . . . home." He bit down on my shoulder and sucked until it hurt and I was begging him to fuck me. "And I love to taste you."

I was sure he'd left a mark. I shuddered at having a semi-permanent reminder of him on my skin.

"Please. I want it."

"Tell me," he whispered in my ear. He liked me to talk to him, said he wanted to hear my dirty words. I couldn't stop them from falling from my mouth even if I'd wanted to.

"I want you to fuck me so hard I can't walk for the rest of the day."

He groaned, and I pushed back, urging him to begin his rhythm.

"What else?" he asked.

"I want you to slide inside me and feel how wet you make me. How desperate I am for your cock. How I'd do anything just to have you fuck me—" He extracted truths when he fucked me. I couldn't hide anything when we were together like this.

My words had the desired effect, and he started to pump in and out. I arched my back in relief as he pulled his tacky fingers down my spine, tracing his thumb lower and brushing over the puckered flesh of my anus. I wanted it all; I wanted to feel him in every possible way.

He reached around over my hips, down to my clit and circled the bundle of nerves. My words came more rapidly. "Yes. More. Harder. Just. Like. That."

The skin across my body buzzed and seemed to weaken me. My arms collapsed, and I fell forward, changing the angle of his penetration. I gasped and clenched, eliciting groans from Luke that became louder and louder. He betrayed his desperation, interrupting his rhythm as he tried to get deeper and deeper, grasping my hips, and then at my shoulders, pulling me toward him. I let him take over my body, offering no resistance as he pushed and pulled as he needed. It was too much, too good, too perfect.

His hands were all over me, alternating between rounding my clit, pulling at my painfully hard nipples and grazing my ass. "Yes," I gasped finally as I felt his slick-coated thumb begin to press. He didn't need to hold back. "More."

"Jesus, you're so fucking perfect," he groaned, maintaining his rhythm perfectly as his thumb pushed inside, past the bunched ring of muscles. The sensation was too much. My blood drummed in my ears, and I closed my eyes as my orgasm caught up with me, as if it were breaking out of my core and running along my limbs.

Luke let out an unintelligible cry from behind me, and the pads of his fingers pressed so deep I thought he was climbing inside me. My legs buckled under the force of his thrusts, and I lay flat on the bed as he chased his orgasm. Seconds later, he released himself into me.

He collapsed on top of me then rolled to my side. "What are you doing to me?" His voice was thick with exertion as he pulled my limp body so I was strewn across him. "You're amazing. I love you."

"You're amazing, and I love you."

"Then there will be plenty of amazing to go around in this flat when you move in."

"There's no way you can hold me to that. You were torturing me. You're the lawyer; you should know that evidence obtained as a result of duress doesn't hold up in court."

Luke pushed himself up on his elbows, and I looked at him from my position on his chest. "You're moving in with me, Ashleigh. You agreed and I'm holding you—"

"You don't think it's too fast?" Normal couples didn't live together weeks after getting together. I hated to ruin what we had by moving too quickly.

"We've been waiting our whole lives. We know each other better than almost anyone else in the entire world. Let's not waste any more time." His tone was equally pleading and determined, and I found that I wasn't as panicked as perhaps I should be. Maybe we were special.

I got butterflies at the thought that we might actually be doing this. "I insist on paying you rent."

"You're my lover, not my roommate." He linked his fingers through mine. "We'll be paying a mortgage, and I'll cover it while you're in school."

I pressed my lips to his chest. It was time to believe in the fairytale and take a leap of faith.

"Okay," I mumbled.

"What was that?"

I looked up, and he was grinning at me.

"Okay," I repeated.

"Okay? Okay what?"

Apparently, Luke's desire to torture me hadn't dimmed.

"Okay, I'll move in with you. As long as you promise me orgasms on demand."

"So, you want me to be your Orgasm Netflix?"

I nodded. "Yes, that's exactly what I want."

Luke rolled me over and propped himself up next to me. "Are you just using me for sex?"

I grinned. "Ummm, yes. I thought we were clear about that?"

"Right," he replied, jumping off the bed. I wondered if he was mad until he grabbed me by my feet, pulled me to the edge of the bed and hoisted me over his shoulder.

"If you want orgasms, you're going to have to shower regularly."

I squealed as he slapped my ass and stalked into the bathroom.

chapter
TWENTY-EIGHT

Luke

I slumped on the sofa in Ashleigh's flat.

"You're bored."

Ashleigh was right, but I wasn't exactly trying to hide it.

"I said for you to go for a run while I do this."

We were meant to be packing her flat up, readying for the movers coming tomorrow. But she had so much crap, it didn't seem like we were making much progress. All morning she had been giving me reasons why living together wasn't going to work out, and it was fucking me off.

"I know, but I want to be with you. It's just, you know, this stuff is boring. I want to skip to the bit where we're waking up naked on Sunday morning together."

"Life is boring. We can't spend all our time in bed. If I'm living with you, you're going to be bored more and more often."

I sighed. "You're pissing me off now. It's as if you're looking for an argument, and I'm just not going to give you one. You're not sabotaging this."

"Me?" she yelled. "You're the one that wanted us to move in together. It's your fault."

"Yeah, I guess I'm a terrible person. I just want us to be happy. Go ahead and shoot me."

When Ashleigh didn't reply, I turned. Her mouth was scrunched up. She was clearly thinking about how she was going to respond.

"I'm sorry," she said in a small voice. She moved toward the sofa where I was sitting and stood in front of me. "I'm just nervous. I want everything to be perfect and all my shit is everywhere and there's more than I thought and I don't see how it's all going to fit—"

"Ashleigh, take a breath, or you're going to pass out and that's really going to piss me off." I grabbed her hand and pulled her onto my lap. "We're going to have bumps along the way and nothing's going to be perfect, but that's okay as long as we're both heading in the same direction. You've got to understand that our future is together, and nothing is going to change that."

She pushed her bottom lip out like a toddler. "I love you, and I want to live with you. It's just . . . it's stressful."

I pulled her close and snaked my arms around her waist. "I know it is. But there's nothing to be nervous about. I've seen you hung over with panda eyes. I've seen you ugly cry. I've put up with your crazy when your hormonal hurricane hits. And I don't love you in spite of all that—I love you because of all that stuff. We know each other, Ashleigh."

She smoothed her hands over my chest and rested her cheek against my shirt. "This romantic, grown-up, protective side of you is, well, not new, but more concentrated than before. Does that make sense?"

She was right. I was a little different with her now. I'd always been protective of her, but now I'd kill for her. "I told you. You bring all that stuff, all that good, out in me." I was a better man with her.

"Okay, they're calm," she said, gazing at me.

"Who are?"

"The leprechauns who've been running about in my stomach all morning. They've all had a dose of the Luke Daniels' sedative."

"Now you've got me worried. If you have leprechauns living inside you, then maybe it's not such a good idea to be moving in together. Maybe you're better off in a mental health facility." I chuckled as she rolled her eyes at me as if I were the one who had said something ridiculous. "Actually, speaking of leprechauns, I have a wives and girlfriends thing at work next weekend. I keep meaning to tell you. Can you come?"

"And it involves leprechauns? Well then, yes of course. I love leprechauns."

Now it was my turn to roll my eyes. "I'm serious. It's a client thing. A rugby match—England's playing Ireland on Saturday."

"Sure." She shrugged.

"Sure?" Was it really going to be that easy? Emma had never wanted to come to my work events.

"Yeah, it'll be fun."

And just like that, she was trying to make me happy, wanting to spend time with me, wherever we were. It had never been like that with Emma.

"I'll have to teach you the rules. I don't want you to be like the other WAGs there."

"I've known you for more than twenty years. You think I've not picked up on how Rugby Union is played?"

I bent my head and dropped a kiss on the corner of her mouth, trying to distract myself from the swell of pride in my chest. I loved that my girl knew rugby, that she knew me so well. "You smell good."

"You always say that."

"That's because it's always true."

She pulled away from me. "Okay, let's kick ass with this packing and then go back to yours and get naked."

"Now, there's an incentive. I'll start on the kitchen."

"I'm putting on some motivating music." Ashleigh moved toward her speaker system.

"Okay, but, please God, lay off the P!nk." I found an empty packing box and took it into the kitchen. "Jesus," I whispered to myself as the strains of Taylor Swift filtered in from the living room.

"Sorry," Ashleigh shouted and Miss Swift gave way to Otis Redding. A perfect compromise.

I grinned and started to pull out saucepans from the cupboard nearest the door. We were doing this. We were really doing this. I'd lived with Emma, but for me that had been about pooling resources. With Ashleigh, it was about starting a future together. Emma had told me that moving in, for her, had been the first step toward marriage and kids. I'd never seen it like that. But of course, that was exactly what it should have been. I'd been naïve and unwittingly cruel. A slice of guilt cut through me as I thought about it.

I just hadn't realized how love should be.

I finished the kitchen off quickly and went to see what progress Ashleigh had made. Otis Redding had since melted into Stevie Wonder. I found her in her bedroom, her back toward me and her hands on her hips, looking around for her next task. I knew what Stevie meant—Ashleigh knocked me off my feet.

"I think I'm done," she said as she caught me gazing at her. "How are you getting on?"

I stuffed my hands in my pockets to stop myself from pushing her up against the wall and ripping her underwear off. "Kitchen's all packed up."

"Well then, that's it. I don't need to pack my clothes. The movers said they'd do that. Jesus, how are we going to fit all this stuff in your place?"

"Our place."

Ashleigh smiled. "Yes, I suppose it will be."

"We can move if the space isn't right. I'm only renting month to month. We really should find somewhere to buy together." As usual, my mind was racing forward to the next phase of our lives while Ashleigh was still getting used to moving in together.

"Are you trying to give me a coronary? Let me get used to this first. One step at a time."

And there was the answer to the question of whether or not she was ready for me to propose. My heart sank a little. I'd passed by the jewelers in Hatton Garden twice since I'd first seen the ring I had in mind for her. It was still in the window, but I didn't know how long that would last. I really wanted to show it to her, to ask her. She clearly wasn't ready. Perhaps I could get it now and just hold on to it until the time was right? I was pretty sure I could get Ashleigh to a place where she wanted to be my wife. I just wasn't sure how long it would take.

"Okay, so let's get back for NCN."

"Should I ask what NCN is? Promise me it's not sports." She clasped her hands together in front of herself in a mock prayer.

"Naked Chinese Night, obviously. It can be our first new tradition."

"You're crazy." She pushed at my chest.

"But you love me anyway."

"I love you because you're crazy, not in spite of it." She lifted up on her toes and grazed her lips over my jaw. There was no better feeling. Now I just had to get her to marry me, and life would be perfect.

Ashleigh

"We're going to need a bigger place." Wherever I looked there was a half-unpacked cardboard box. How was it possible to have accumulated so much stuff in less than thirty years on this planet—and on a nurse's salary? With two pairs of evening shoes, I wasn't a girl who thought of herself as having a lot of things. Apparently, I was wrong.

Luke chuckled. "You think? I don't want to say I told you so—hell, what am I saying? I don't mind saying it at all. I told you so."

"Whatever. You were right."

"So, we'll look at places to buy?"

I shrugged. Now I was here with all my things, it felt less strange than I'd expected it to. Luke was right. It was inevitable that we were going to be together, so it was easier to accept that and move forward rather than constantly put the brakes on. "Fine, but can you at least wait until tomorrow to start Googling? We have guests due any minute. Whose idea was it to do Sunday dinner here anyway?" I narrowed my eyes accusingly at Luke.

"Erm, that would be you."

"It can't have been me because, as you know, I'm perfect, and Beth, Jake and Haven arriving in less than thirty minutes is far from perfect. I'm blaming Jake."

"Okay, that works. He'll be fine with that."

The chicken was in the oven, the bathroom clean. I just needed to clear out some of the boxes, and we'd be halfway to making the place look cramped and uncared for, which would be a distinct improvement. I'd wanted to welcome my family into our home, and for everything to be shiny and beautiful. That wasn't going to happen, and I had to accept that.

"What's that smell?" I jerked my head toward the kitchen. Luke bolted for the oven, bringing the glass door down with a thump.

"Crispy chicken is always better than soggy chicken," Luke said as he stared into the cooker. He was authoritative but unconvincing.

My shoulders sagged. "Let's take a look." I peered into the oven to see what looked like a large lump of coal. "Well, at least we can be sure it's dead."

Luke chuckled. "Yes, that's for certain. It doesn't matter. I could do a chili, or what about enchiladas?"

I looked at my watch. "Make out with me?"

"What did you say?"

"I don't care about the chicken or what's going to replace it. I don't care that the place is a mess or that I need to brush my hair. We have twenty-five minutes. It's not long enough to get naked. So let's make out. We can worry about what we're going to eat when people arrive." Having all my stuff unpacked and being able to produce Sunday dinner no longer seemed so important. Luke was what I wanted, and I needed to make sure I didn't lose sight of that. I lifted myself up onto the kitchen counter and grabbed at his shirt, pulling him over to me so he was standing between my legs. "De-stress me."

He smoothed his hands over my hips and kissed my forehead. I sank into his touch, the anxiety seeping away. He was all I needed.

The intercom buzzed, and we pulled away from each other, exchanging confused glances. We should have had twenty-five minutes of delicious kissing before we were interrupted.

"Stay there; maybe it's someone who has the wrong flat." Luke went to investigate. Before he'd reached the intercom, someone was banging on the front door. I slid off the counter. Our make-out session was clearly on hiatus.

I heard Haven scream, and I padded toward the ruckus in time to see her push past Luke and bolt into the guest bathroom.

"Sorry, mate, she's been like that all week," Jake explained as he handed Luke a bottle of wine.

"Irritable and pushy? She's been like that her whole life," Luke responded.

"It's morning sickness," Jake said.

Haven hadn't mentioned being sick when I'd spoken to her earlier in the week.

"Hey there, how are the internet videos going? The feedback on that one with the honey was amazing," I told Beth, who was hiding behind Jake.

"Please don't make my sister sound like a porn star," Jake said on a sigh.

Leaving Haven in the bathroom, the rest of us shuffled into the living room. Jake started to laugh. "Were you not expecting us?"

It really was a total disaster zone. "We were too busy shagging to worry about the state of the place. So distracted in fact that we burnt the chicken—"

"We're going to take you out, if that's okay," Luke interrupted. I was so grateful to him for suggesting that. At least if I wasn't in this place, I wouldn't have to think about the mess it was in. "We'll just wait for Haven to finish vomiting."

Beth started to giggle.

"Sorry," I mumbled.

"Don't be," Beth replied. "It's good to know that you're not perfect. You always seem so together."

Luke burst out laughing, and I playfully smacked him on the arm. "Thank you, but it if seems like that then I need to diagnose you with a serious disease. I mean this with love: you have a severe case of shit in your eyes."

The following day I'd booked off work, so I spent the day getting our place straightened out. It was beginning to look like home, with things of mine nestled against things of his. His books mixed with mine in the study and my toothbrush next to his in the bathroom.

I'd even bought some plant food from the flower shop on the corner for the magnolia tree I'd given Luke. They had some magnolia blooms that I also purchased and arranged in a vase on the table in a bid to show Luke that the collection of sticks poking out of the ground would become something beautiful if we took care of them.

By the time Luke arrived home from work, the place was looking fantastic, and so was I. I'd slipped into the gothic red underwear he'd bought me just a few weeks ago, which were still my favorite despite him giving me several sets since. As I heard his key in the lock, I put on my highest heels and grabbed a cold beer from the fridge.

"Hey, honey, I'm home," he called from the hallway. "Wow, this place is looking great," he said, scanning the living area before he settled his eyes on me. "But not as good as you, apparently."

I took a swig out of the bottle and held it out for him. He moved toward me, took the beer and put it straight on the counter behind me. "I'm not thirsty." His voice had that gravelly edge to it that I was only just getting used to. Lust lapped at my edges, and my eyes flitted to his crotch, then back up to his face.

He raised his eyebrows. "Like what you see?"

"I bought flowers," I stuttered, moving across to the sofa where the magnolia blooms were in a vase on a side table. Luke came up behind me and kissed my neck.

"I can't focus on anything when you're dressed like that. You've got me so hard." He fumbled with his zipper and pushed me gently over the back of the sofa. "Jesus, you're perfect." His fingers slipped inside my underwear, and he groaned. "So wet."

His cock grazed the cleft of my ass, then pushed lower and right up to the hilt. He'd been in the door for under a minute, and he was already fucking me. He knew just what I needed.

His hands scorched my skin as his palms folded over my shoulders and pulled me onto his cock. He thrust forward so our bodies slammed together, hard and fast. Would I ever get enough of him surrounding me like this? Sometimes he'd torture me for what seemed like days before he slid into me. He'd make me come with his fingers and his mouth before I'd finally get his cock. Other times, like this one, it was as if he had no choice but to get inside me and take his own pleasure, as if doing anything else would make him insane.

"I need you so much," he whispered, his softly spoken words in juxtaposition with the hard, sharp movements of his hips and the press of his fingers.

chapter
TWENTY-NINE

Luke

I passed the jewelry store again on my Saturday morning run. Pausing a couple of stores down, I braced my hands on my knees and drew in a few long breaths that filled my lungs and had a near instant effect on my pulse. I'd not found myself in this part of the city by fluke; I'd planned my route deliberately. When I went anywhere close to this street, that ring was all I could think about. Was it still there? Would Ashleigh like it? How would she react when I showed it to her? I'd done a bit of research, and what the jeweler had said about its value and rarity seemed to stack up. Another reason not to buy it disappeared.

Living together, waking up every morning in each other's arms, was just as great as I'd known it would be, and I was becoming impatient again. She seemed to have settled more quickly than I'd expected. I didn't want to miss out on buying her the perfect ring for when the time was right to propose.

Before this visit, I'd transferred some of my savings, so I was prepared just in case.

I stood and looked toward the store. I couldn't make out the individual items in the window, but I knew where Ashleigh's ring should be. I took small steps toward my prize, not taking my eyes from the spot where I expected to find it. My heart thundered in my chest as the gems came into focus. Her ring wasn't where I was used to seeing it. There wasn't even a space for it. Shit, had I left it too long? That ring had been perfect—as if it were made for Ashleigh. It couldn't belong to anyone else. I needed it for her. I scanned the rest of the section, hoping to see it, but nothing. I rubbed my sweaty palms down my shorts and pressed my hands against the glass, trying to find what I was looking for. The elderly owner appeared beside me again as if from nowhere.

"Hello, son, good to see you again," she said, forcing me to look away from the window. My chest squeezed at her term of endearment. It was almost certainly a meaningless phrase for her, but to me it was a reminder of how no one referred to me as their son anymore. I wished my parents were here to see me about to buy a ring for the love of my life, for the woman I hoped would one day have our children. It gave me some comfort that they'd known her and loved her.

"Are you looking for your ring?" she asked, patting my arm. "Follow me. It's inside."

Had I heard her correctly? Did she say she still had it? My body tensed in anticipation.

I focused on the tinkling of the bell over the door as I followed her into the shop. "You have it?"

"Yes, I kept it back here for you. Figured you'd be back again. I've seen that look before. It's the same one my husband had for me. He wanted to give me the world from the moment he met me. And he succeeded. If that's how you feel about your girl, then you should have this ring."

My muscles loosened. I was going home with the ring in my pocket.

"You want to give her the world?" the woman asked.

I nodded. "She always seems to give me more than I could ever give her."

"I bet she says the same about you. That's when you know it's right. When it feels like a privilege to know them."

Ashleigh made me feel like I'd been let into a secret club. A love club. It wasn't that I hadn't been in love before—at least, I thought I had. It was just that it hadn't been close to what I felt for Ashleigh. With her, it felt permanent, fundamental to who I was. With Emma, I hadn't envisioned things changing. With Ashleigh, I knew it was forever.

***

I ran home with the ring in my pocket, reaching for it every block or so, just to check it was there. Like everything good in my life, I wanted to share it with Ashleigh immediately. But I knew I had to be patient. I had to convince her how I felt wasn't going to change. The switch that had awakened my feelings for Ashleigh was strictly one-way. There was no going back, but she wasn't convinced, not yet.

"Hey, I'm back," I shouted.

"I'm in here," Ashleigh called from the bedroom.

Where was I going to hide the ring? I couldn't risk her finding it and bolting. "I'm going for a shower." I hadn't expected her to be still in bed when I got home. I'd thought

I'd stash the ring in the bedroom. "Are you okay?" I asked as I entered the bedroom.

"Just sleepy. I feel like I could sleep for days." The urge to kneel beside her and ask her to marry me right then was huge. She filled up my heart. She looked so relaxed and sexy, lying there with her hair fanned across the pillow in the bed that we now shared, her eyes still heavy with sleep. I took a breath, trying to reason with myself. I couldn't, not yet. I needed to give her a little more time. Convincing her to move in with me was one thing, but I wanted her to say yes without hesitation when I asked her to be my wife.

"How come you're so sleepy? You pregnant?" I laughed, and Ashleigh rolled her eyes.

"Don't be crazy. You kept me up most of the night, if you remember."

I did remember. The sex had been unforgettable.

I sidled into the bathroom, trying to look as if I wasn't concealing where the ring was stashed. When Ashleigh wasn't around, I could carry the ring on me. It wasn't the most security conscious of ideas but better that than her finding it and going into meltdown. When we were together, I needed to stash it somewhere.

I turned on the shower and stripped off my clothes, holding the box in my hand while looking around the bathroom for a hiding place. The door handle jangled. "Luke?"

Shit, I'd locked the door so she didn't walk in on me while I was holding the ring. "Hang on." I dove into the cupboard that held all the clean laundry and buried the box at the bottom of a pile of towels. I'd have to think of a better spot later. I quickly shut the cupboard, spun round and unlocked the door. "Hi."

Ashleigh knitted her eyebrows together. "Er, hi. I was just wondering if you wanted company, but if you'd rather—"

"Of course I want company." I pulled her inside, closed the door and started to undress her.

"You locked the door," she said as she held her hands above her head as I stripped off her tee.

"Force of habit." I buried my head in her neck and pushed her against the wall. It was part desire to distract her and part my reaction to her naked body.

"You're sweaty," she said.

"Hence the shower." I pulled away from her and led her into the shower.

"I like it."

"You do?"

She nodded.

"But you always smell so . . . like summer or home or—"

"You smell like you're mine."

"Well, that's good, because I am."

She wrapped her legs around me as I lifted her and walked under the spray.

Ashleigh

"That one, you can tell by the way he walks," Haven said, gesturing at a guy on the other side of the Mexican restaurant. It was dark and loud, but not so much so that the people at the tables surrounding us hadn't noticed Haven pointing.

"You can't talk about another man's cock when you're carrying your husband's baby."

"Well, apparently I can because I just did. I'm just saying, you can tell. Everything about a man starts with the size of his penis. I'm thinking of writing an article about it."

Part of me was pleased to be out with Haven, but the other part, the part I had a hard time allowing to come to the surface, wanted to spend all my time with Luke. But he was working late tonight, so I wasn't technically giving up time with him. Jesus, when had I become that girl? "I'm going to the loo."

"Again? You just went. I have penises to discuss with you."

"What are you, the toilet police? And if you insist on talking about penises, I'm going to start telling you about your brother's." I gave her a stern look as I headed off to the bathroom, pulling out my phone to see if Luke had messaged me. I grinned as I saw the symbol at the top of the screen confirming he had.

Luke: I'll be home by ten. Hope you're having fun.

Ashleigh: I won't be long after you. The hormones are making Haven crazy.

As soon as I came out of the stall, my phone pinged again.

Luke: It's nothing to do with the hormones. I miss you.

Living together these past few weeks had been going better than I'd expected. I didn't feel the pressure for everything to be perfect the way that I'd thought I would. Everything felt so natural between us, as if we'd been a couple forever.

I went back to the table with more enthusiasm than I'd had when I left. I hoped Haven was done talking about cock.

"Those bathrooms smell of some disgusting air freshener. I hope what they serve up smells better," I said, wrinkling my nose.

"The food is always good here." Haven waved her hand toward the kitchen. "So how's it going with Luke? Are you having the battle of the toilet seat?"

I grinned. "Nope. He's good with putting the lid down."

"He is?"

"It's going well, actually. It doesn't feel like the big adjustment I expected it to be."

"Yeah, it wasn't with Jake either. I guess when it's right, it's not hard work."

"Maybe that's it." It felt right—as if we'd always lived together.

"You'll be getting married next," she said.

"As if. Luke isn't the marrying kind. He's already told me that." I wasn't exactly upset that Luke and I would never get married. More, I'd always seen marriage as part of my future—I'd just have to adjust my happy ever after. It was Luke I wanted. Not simply a husband.

"So you've talked about it?"

"Nope. He told me when he was talking about Emma wanting the big white dress."

"Guys change their minds," she offered.

"He was pretty clear. It broke him and Emma up, if you remember, and I wouldn't place marriage over Luke. It's a small compromise. I know he loves me."

"It's good to see you so happy. You have a little love glow about you."

I grinned. I could barely stop smiling these days.

The waiter brought our food, and we clinked water glasses.

"Will you be my birthing partner?" She munched on a pepper. My stomach churned. The food wasn't as good as it normally was. I couldn't bring myself to eat much of anything. Haven wasn't having the same problem.

"Jake will be your birthing partner, you crazy."

"You know the best thing about being pregnant?"

Apart from the inability to keep on one subject for more than five seconds?

"No periods. The rest of it is terrible and terrifying. But at least I don't have periods."

I grinned then released the muscles in my cheeks as I checked the date on my phone. I couldn't remember the last time I'd had a period. I must have mixed up my dates or my pills or something. I'd have to check when I got home. "What do you find terrifying? Having to give up your freedom?"

"Actually, not so much. More the responsibility. I want my kid to be a good person, but what happens if I fuck it up? Create a monster, or a serial killer? He or she might turn out to be a murderer."

"It worries me that worries you." I shook my head.

"You don't think about it?"

"That I'm going to give birth to a serial killer? Not today or even this week, no. But then again, I'm not pregnant." As I said the words, I started to fit together pieces of the last few weeks. The lethargy, the heightened sense of smell, the fact that food I normally loved wasn't tasting so great—not to mention the distinct lack of my period. I couldn't be, could I? I was on the pill and . . . I must be just sharing symptoms with Haven. I'd read that sometimes happened to close friends. At least, I thought I'd read it. I was probably coming down with something I'd picked up at the hospital. All this talk of Haven's pregnancy was making me paranoid.

"I can't wait for you and Luke to have kids. Say you won't leave it too long. I want ours to be best friends. They can grow up together like we did."

My heart swelled at the thought, but then I caught myself. "We've been living together for five seconds. We're not about to get pregnant. And I'm not sure Luke wants kids. He keeps saying how sorry he feels for Jake being a father so quickly."

"Typical that he doesn't feel sorry for me. You've not talked about kids with him?" Haven asked.

I shrugged. I did want children and not having them would be a far bigger compromise for me than not getting married. I shivered as, for a fleeting second, I considered the possibility of life without Luke. I was pretty sure that if Luke wanted kids, he would have said something by now.

And that's why there was no way I could be pregnant. A pregnancy would destroy Luke and me, and force me to make a choice that I wasn't willing to make.

"What do you mean? You don't want to have my brother's kids?"

"I don't think he wants kids, so we're not getting pregnant." I'd not had time to think about this seriously since we'd been together. I loved him so much that what was important was being together. I'd never let my mind wander past that point.

"Has he actually said that he doesn't want kids with you?"

"We've not discussed it. Are you crazy? Why would we be discussing things like that? I'm not ready to even think about it. And it's pretty clear how Luke feels."

Of course, I'd thought about it in the abstract. I knew I wanted to be a mother at some point. I also knew I wanted to be with Luke, and he had no interest in having children. I guess after being in love with a guy my whole life, somehow I'd not found time to think through the practicalities of actually being with him. Was it possible that he wasn't going to be able to give me the life that I wanted? My stomach flipped as I realized that at some point I'd have to choose—become a mother or be with Luke. Although I hoped I had just gotten my dates mixed up, there was a possibility that I might have to choose sooner rather than later.

"How do you know if he's never told you?"

"You know how he was with Emma. He doesn't do the change thing very well. He wouldn't even marry Emma, let alone have . . ."

"But we're not talking about Luke and Emma. We're talking Luke and you. I'm sure if you want kids, Luke will come round to the idea."

My stomach rolled at the thought of having to convince Luke about what our future together would look like.

"I'm excited to be an unofficial aunt, though," I said, trying to change the subject.

"Jake told me that he'll be on baby duty as often as I want him to. So you and I can still go out like we did before. And I'm going to get a nanny so I can keep working." Jake was a smart guy. He knew as well as I did that as soon as their baby arrived, Haven's huge heart would explode, and she wouldn't let her baby out of her sight. He just was clever enough not to try to tell her before she was ready to hear it.

"You don't need to worry—you'll be a wonderful mother."

"You think?"

She'd be a great mom. "I know." I hoped she'd have the opportunity to say those words back to me someday.

I stuffed the two pregnancy tests back into their box, put the box inside a grocery bag and put the bag into the metal container marked hazardous waste. I was in one of the disabled bathrooms on the ward, and I wasn't sure I was ever going to be able to leave.

My training as a nurse told me that a false positive was much less likely than a false negative, which in itself wasn't very likely. I was pregnant. It had taken me the whole day to work up the courage to take a test, but I'd thrown up this morning so there'd been no more putting it off.

I began to pace. I couldn't have an abortion, I knew that much. But I'd seen Luke's reaction when his sister had announced she was pregnant—he had been happy for her . . . and relieved it wasn't him. He didn't want this baby. For me, it was more complicated. It was a shock, but I also wanted to be a mother.

I ran through my options. I could tell Luke that I was pregnant and that I wanted to keep it and I didn't want to lose him, which was the truth. He'd no doubt accept it on the surface, and we'd raise the child together, but he'd spend the rest of our lives resenting me. I loved him, and I didn't want him unhappy. I couldn't bear the thought that he might hate me or our life together. The alternative was to keep the pregnancy to myself for now, end things between us for some spurious reason and then, when a little time had passed and he had accepted that we were over, I could tell him about the baby and explain that I was going to bring the child up on my own. The latter option might just kill me, but it would protect Luke from the life that he'd never wanted with Emma. I couldn't force that on him. Or my child.

I loved him too much to deny him the future he wanted.

chapter THIRTY

Luke

"I need to talk to you," Ashleigh said, hovering at the door to the living area.

Why did women always want to have a conversation when rugby was on? I reached for her to pull her onto my knee.

"I'm serious. Can we talk?" Her voice was wobbly. I glanced at her face to see if I could read what was going through her head.

"Can I just watch this conversion?" We were neck and neck with the All Blacks.

Ashleigh forced a smile, pushed off my lap and headed back into the bedroom, where she'd been most of the morning. Shit. I muted the TV and followed her. I found her sitting on the bed, her knees pulled to her chest, her eyes fixed to the floor. "I don't think we're going to work out."

I laughed. "Is my rugby watching too much to bear?" I sat down next to her. She moved away from me.

"I'm serious. I think I'm going to move out. The tenant hasn't moved into my place yet. I don't think we're going to work." She stood.

Blood crashed against my ears. Was I hearing things? Was she trying to end things? "What the fuck? Are you serious? What happened?" I stood up and tried to get her to look at me, but she kept moving out of the way.

"Nothing happened. I think this is best."

A suitcase was open on the bed, and she'd started to put clothes in it. What the fuck was going on? She'd been asleep last night when I got in, and she'd been a bit quiet today. What could have happened? My heart was beating so hard my entire body pulsed. The thought of being without her, even for a night, was too much.

"Are you mad I had to work late? Or that I'm watching rugby?"

She shook her head. "No, of course not."

"But you love me. Why do you want to go? Ashleigh, please talk to me."

"I just need to give us both some time."

What the fuck did that mean? How could she possibly be changing her mind, now? Fury ran up my spine. I grabbed the suitcase off the bed and emptied her clothes onto the floor.

"Luke!"

"No, Ashleigh. You're not going anywhere. That's the deal. You and me, we're together. We don't leave each other. I don't need time, but if you do, then you need to tell me why. I deserve that much." My frustration made my voice louder than it should have been. I never wanted to shout at her, but she wasn't talking to me.

She collapsed back on the bed, hands covering her face.

I took a deep breath. "Have you changed your mind about

us?" I asked, lying beside her on the bed, trying to pry her hands away so she'd look at me. Maybe that way I'd be able to tell what the matter was. This had come so out of left field.

"I don't know."

A sharp stabbing pushed into my gut. She'd changed her mind about us? How was that possible?

"I think maybe we want different things."

I stopped trying to move her hands and rolled to my back next to her. I'd been pushing too hard. Even though I'd not proposed, she must have felt pressured. I should have been more patient. Let her take the lead more. But I'd awakened from an Ashleigh coma. I wanted to get on with things. I'd been a fool to think I could hide it.

"I'm sorry if I've been too much. I just love you a crazy amount, and I don't know how to cover it up."

"What?" she asked.

"I should have tried to hold back more—and I shouldn't have pressured you to move in."

"That's not what I meant," she replied.

"Then what? Is it my job?" I didn't understand what was happening. "Are you worried about what my becoming partner will do to us?"

She sat bolt upright. Was that it? She thought I'd spend too much time at work and wouldn't have enough time for her? She clasped her hands over her mouth and fled into the bathroom. I hated seeing her so upset. I wanted to comfort her, reassure her that if that was the problem, I would make time for her. I found her hunched over the toilet.

"Jesus, are you okay? Are you sick?"

On cue, she began to retch. Fuck. I stood beside her and gathered her hair out of her way as she clung to the porcelain and her whole body heaved.

"What have you eaten? I feel fine after that omelet." Of course, she couldn't speak—she was too busy throwing up. I began to rub her back. Maybe she was sick, like terminally ill or something, and was running away so I didn't have to take care of her. She was so selfless; it was the kind of thing she'd do.

"Ashleigh. Are you sick? Is there something wrong? Like seriously wrong? Is that why you want to leave?"

She reached for some toilet paper and wiped her mouth.

"Ashleigh, you're scaring me."

"No, Luke, it's nothing like that . . ." She began to retch again.

Given that she was vomiting like the exorcist, she seemed remarkably calm.

"You're not . . ." I didn't finish my sentence. The words hung in the air between us. She wasn't saying anything, and neither was I.

Jesus, she was pregnant? Was I going to be a father? How fucking terrifying. And how amazingly wonderful. I tried not to grin as Ashleigh continued retching, her breathing labored.

But then why did she want to leave me? Did she not want it? Was it all too much too soon for her? I wanted this baby—a family—with her. Surely I could convince her it would all be okay.

I grabbed a clip from the sink and piled her hair into it as best I could. I knelt down beside her and continued to rub her back.

I was going to be a father. We were going to be parents. This was perfect. Our kids would be the same age as Haven and Jake's. There was nothing to be upset about.

I wanted to ask her a million questions, but she wasn't in a position to answer any of them.

Eventually the heaving slowed, and one-handed, so my hand didn't leave her back, I managed to fill a glass with water.

"Here, drink this," I said softly, sitting back down. "Small sips."

She took the glass from me. "I feel disgusting."

Silently, she stood and washed her face and cleaned her teeth. My eyes didn't leave her for a second.

"Well, you look beautiful." I looked at her. I wanted her to understand that I knew without actually saying so. "You're glowing."

"I'm sorry. It wasn't deliberate, and I know you don't want—you don't have to be involved."

I pulled her onto my lap. "What on earth do you have to be sorry for?"

"I must have messed up my pills or something. I just . . ."

"You're unhappy?" The thought that she didn't want this baby, our baby, made my heart twist. She would make an awesome mother.

"I . . . I . . . I'm sorry, but no, I'm not."

"Why do you keep apologizing? Ashleigh, if—"

"I can do this on my own though, Luke. I don't expect you to—" She started to cry. I hated to see her so upset.

"Why on earth . . . Don't you love me? I don't understand. You're pregnant; we're pregnant."

"I know that it's not what you want. I didn't try and trap you, I can't have you think that, but I can't get rid of this baby."

"Get rid? What the—" I got to my feet, pulled Ashleigh into my arms and carried her back into our bedroom. "You're making no sense. Why would I think you tried to trap me?"

"Because you don't want to get married and—"

Things were starting to come into focus. She thought because I hadn't wanted to marry Emma that I didn't want to get married at all.

"I didn't want to marry Emma."

"I know. And I respect that. It's always been clear—you've not been ambiguous about anything."

She watched me as I went back into the bathroom, opened the cupboard and reached between the towels to find her ring. Maybe taking positive action would help clarify my feelings.

"I don't expect anything from you. I can do this on my own. You don't even need to pay—"

"Stop," I said as I lay down beside her, placing the blue velvet box between us. She followed my gaze until her eyes found the box.

She glanced at my face, then down again.

"What? How did you know? I've not even told Haven—"

"Do you want to see?"

She took a sharp breath. "I don't understand; if you just found—"

I snapped the box open.

Her eyes widened. "It's beautiful."

"Not as beautiful as you, but yes, it is. Ashleigh Franklin, will you marry me?"

She began to smile but then something shifted and tears started to fall, and she covered her face with her hands.

"Are you proposing to make me happy and because I'm pregnant? Because, if you are, one day you'll hate me if I say yes to you now."

She thought I didn't want a life with her and our kids? Those hormones were raging already.

"I found out that you were pregnant about twenty minutes ago when you started vomiting. We'll talk about that another time. I don't like us to have secrets from each other. I don't want to marry you just because you're pregnant. I just want to marry you. I've wanted you to be my wife since I kissed you, maybe even before then." I tucked a strand of hair behind her ear and trailed my thumb across her lips. I couldn't stop touching her, not for a second. "I've been terrified to propose because you're so concerned that we're moving too fast. I'm not. I'd marry you tomorrow if it was up to me. Don't you get it? I don't want to waste a second now we're together. I want to have enough kids with you that we can have our own family rugby team." I couldn't believe I was going to be a father. We were going to be awesome parents. "I want the whole thing with you. I told you—you've changed who I am for the better. I want forever with you. You don't get to leave me. Not now, not ever."

She blinked, long, slow blinks, a question forming. "But . . . you never wanted—"

"I've never wanted to get married before you, you're right. You just don't get how you make it all different for me, do you? I've never wanted it before because it wasn't with you. You're the person that makes me want all this stuff."

She reached up and pressed her palm against my cheek.

"When did you buy it?"

"I don't know. A few weeks ago."

"And you've not asked me yet because . . ."

"Because I knew how freaked out you were about me wanting to move in together so quickly. I thought if I asked you to be my wife, you might have a stroke. I wanted to go at your pace. I was trying to be patient."

"I see."

"What do you see?" She shrugged. "You're going to leave me hanging?" I asked.

The corners of her mouth twitched. "I've messed everything up, haven't I?" And then she frowned.

"Never." This wasn't what I'd planned; I'd wanted this to be a big moment. But I guess it was in other ways.

"Ashleigh Franklin, will you be my wife?" I pulled the ring out of the box and took her hand.

"It's too beautiful."

"Do you like it? I saw it and then couldn't imagine you in anything else."

"I love it. It's more me than I could ever have imagined."

"That's because you just don't know how beautiful you are."

Ashleigh

I wasn't sure if it was the hormones making my head fuzzy, or the gigantic sapphire Luke slipped onto my left ring finger. It fit perfectly. Not thirty minutes ago, I'd been about to move back to my flat, prepared to be a single mother. Now the love of my life had proposed. My heart was too big for my chest. Was it possible to be this happy?

Things had changed, but I had failed to realize the extent of the shift. He had bought a ring for me—wanted to be my husband—and had barely missed a beat when he'd realized I was pregnant. In fact, he was more excited than I was. He was a different Luke in those moments. As much as I thought I'd got to a place where I could trust his feelings for me, I'd never really understood how deep they went . . . until now.

"Hey," he said, tipping my chin up toward him.

"Yes, I'll marry you, Luke."

"I'm very pleased to hear it."

He pressed his lips against mine, and I threaded my hands into his hair. We were going to be together as I'd always wanted. He pulled back and looked down between us. "How long have you known?" He pushed up my top, and his fingers fumbled at the zip on my jeans. I lay on my back as he exposed my belly and stared at it as if he was imagining what grew inside.

"I found out yesterday. I realized something was off during dinner the night before, but I took the test at work. I know the timing isn't ideal, but—"

"The timing is perfect. I know you have business school starting, but you'll be through the first year before you have the baby."

I started to giggle. "I may have to defer."

"No, we'll make it work. I think it would be good to be pregnant in all those lectures. They say you should play Mozart to babies in the womb to make kids more intelligent.

Imagine what lectures on game theory might do. We're going to raise a superhero."

I started to laugh. "Well, as long as we're not creating impossibly high expectations for the kid."

He kissed my belly. "I'm so excited. The baby, you marrying me, it's all so perfect." He looked at me. "But we're going to have to move. And I'll need to get a car. Shall we find a place in the country?"

Apparently, Luke had gone from being scared of change to welcoming it. "Let's just take one step at a time, hey?"

He slouched back on the bed.

"Hey," I said. "Are you okay?"

I propped myself up on my elbow and stroked his chest.

"If you ever left me, it would break me." He stared up at the ceiling as he spoke.

I reached across and dropped a kiss on his jaw. "I'm not going anywhere. I said yes when you proposed, silly." What had gotten in his head?

"You were going to go. Before. You were just going to disappear without any explanation. I can't ask you to marry me again if we're already married when you next freak out. What happens if you try to leave again?"

My earlier nausea returned, but I doubted it had anything to do with the pregnancy this time. "I thought that was what you wanted. Or what you would want when you found out about the baby. I didn't want to guilt you into sticking by me. I didn't want you to think you were trapped."

"Why would being with you ever be a trap? I love you, Ashleigh, and I have to know that you're never going to leave me. That you're never going to try and do what's best for me without asking me."

"Never? Like, not pick up your favorite beer or coconut water while I'm shopping? Or start giving you a blow job while you're sleeping?" I grinned at him and let my hand drift down his chest and circle his cock.

"I'm serious, Ashleigh. You have to promise to talk to me, or I'm going to drive myself crazy waiting for you to leave me again."

"I'm sorry," I said, my heart aching at his hurt.

"Don't do it again."

"I promise."

I trailed my fingers over his chest, then lower and began to unzip his jeans. I wanted him to feel the promise in my touch. He expanded beneath my hand. "I want you so much it scares me," I whispered.

"Do you get that I feel it just as much as you?" he asked. The effort he put into keeping his voice steady showed in his tight jaw.

"I think I do. Now."

He snapped his eyes shut and groaned, pulsing his hips toward my fist.

I'd been too busy with my own feelings to understand what Luke loving me meant. I wanted to make him feel good, safe—like I would never leave. But he was right; I'd assumed the worst—that he wouldn't need me as much as I needed him. I'd skipped past the bit where we told each other how we were feeling. I hadn't trusted him that things were different between us now, that this wasn't an unrequited love affair anymore.

"I'm sorry," I said. "I should never have seen leaving as an option."

He sat up, took off my jeans with lightning speed and pulled me across him so I sat facing him, straddling his hips, our bodies brushing against each other.

"No, you shouldn't have." He smoothed his hands across my lower back and down over my ass, urging me closer. I slid over his cock, feeling the hardness rub through my underwear against my clit. Nobody could make me feel this way. He cracked me open and seeped inside every part of me.

"I'm learning. This adjustment . . . between us, I had to get used to it too. I guess I'm still adjusting." I dipped my head forward and placed a small kiss on the edge of his mouth.

"Let's learn together, baby. Don't shut me out. Don't be doing pregnancy tests without me. I want to share all that shit with you."

"I promise."

He twisted a strand of my hair and tucked it behind my ear. "Good." His face broke out into his most mischievous grin as he gripped my hips and pressed his thumbs under my hips. "And you're not saying that because you want me to make you come?"

I wrapped my arms around his neck, my nipples grazing his hard chest. "Mostly no."

"Incorrigible." He grunted as he pushed me over his cock. I needed my underwear off in a hurry.

Suddenly, he paused. "Shit, are we okay to have sex?"

I frowned. "You going to go nine months without? Of course we're okay."

"I'll be gentle," he whispered.

"You better not be."

He flipped me to my back and trailed his lips down my body, taking my panties as he went. I stripped off my top and bra.

He grinned against my thigh then pushed his tongue down into my slit. I sank into the mattress, his breath wiping away any last flickers of anxiety. He hummed against my sensitive flesh as his tongue stroked and circled, my skin sending tiny vibrations of pleasure to dance outward along my thighs. My back arched, the intensity taking over my body.

I rocked against his mouth, and he slid two fingers into me as his tongue concentrated on my clit. "You taste like love," he murmured.

"You are so good at this."

"We are so good at this." Did he mean sex, or did he mean us? Both, perhaps.

I needed to touch him, and he knew it. His thumb replaced his mouth, and he crawled up my body, allowing me to reach around him and press my palms against his hard, muscular back.

He watched me as I writhed against his touch, almost studying the reaction I had as he slowed his fingers and then sped up; he rubbed his thumb one way and then the other. "So, good, yes."

"Tell me,"

"Like that," I said. The pressure against my clit was perfect, and his fingers twisted inside me.

"Like this?" He repeated the movement.

"Oh God, Luke, yes." He loved to hear me when he touched me, when he was inside me—as if there could be the slightest doubt of the effect his body had on mine.

Luke

I wasn't sure what it was that was sending jolts of pleasure right to my cock. It was difficult to separate the sensation of Ashleigh's pussy clamped around my dick from the sight of her tits bobbing in front of me, tantalizing, begging to be touched. Perhaps it was her hair wrapped around my hand, as I tipped her head back and licked her neck, eliciting a gasp. It was all of those things, but most of all it was the fact that she finally got how I felt about her. Somehow, that truth had been only half revealed to her . . . until today. Before, she'd never let herself open her eyes to the reality that whatever life had in store for us, we would be together. It had always been good between us, but it was as if a final, unseen veil between us had been lifted, and I felt closer to her than ever.

She sank back down onto me and flicked her hips. Fuck, she could be wicked.

She watched me as she gathered her breasts in her hands, pushing them up and together. Jesus, the sight of her tight pink nipples, and the knowledge of how they felt in my mouth made my spine fizz. I had to get myself together, or she was going to make me come too soon. I clasped my hands across her back and flipped her over so I was over her, still inside her.

"You're driving me crazy."

"Because I love your cock so much?"

I groaned, pulling away from her. There was nothing

better than knowing that your wife-to-be worshipped your cock.

"It loves you back, baby," I said as I stabbed back inside her. She tightened in response.

"Yes," she moaned.

"Tell me."

I focused on her words, the so good, so deep, right there, as the booming of my orgasm echoed in the distance, getting louder and louder.

She pressed her fingers into my shoulders, her nails biting into the skin. How could she know exactly how my body worked? That I needed the sharp to spark the pleasure? I dipped my head and licked sloppily over her lips, desperate for a taste of her. Fuck. Her hips tilted up to meet mine as she whispered, "So deep, I need you, don't be gentle."

I pulled back and lifted her leg over my shoulder, going in deeper as if I were chasing something.

"Fuck, baby."

She reached over her head, grabbing at the pillows as I watched her flat stomach ripple and her mouth form a perfect "O".

There was nothing better than giving your wife-to-be an orgasm that showed across her whole body.

Her pussy undulated around my cock, tearing my climax from me.

She was my world.

epilogue

One Week Later—Luke

"The District Line? I didn't even know it was open at the weekend. We have to be at Sunday dinner by two. This isn't just a ruse so you don't have to tell Haven you're pregnant and engaged, is it?" I squeezed her hand.

"I can't wait to tell Haven. In fact, I want to tell everyone. I can't believe I've kept it a secret for a week," she said.

She'd told me we should be prepared for the cold, so as well as looking like we were wintering in Moscow, Ashleigh had insisted we bring an overnight bag full of blankets. My girl was losing it.

"Isn't the cold bad for the baby?"

"How can I be cold when I have you to keep me warm?"

I shook my head and pulled on the sides of her woolen hat, bringing it down over her eyes.

As the tube came to the next stop, she squeezed my arm and stood. I followed her, picking up our overnight bag. I felt a complete tool. Kew Gardens? This was where she wanted to go?

She insisted on paying our entrance fee and seemed to know where she was going. Hand in hand, we passed the palm house and headed toward some trees. The open, grassy spaces were almost deserted, everyone else sensible enough to stay home on a day like today. But despite the cold, the sun was shining, and the sky was a beautiful, bright blue. After what seemed like forever, she stopped abruptly under a leafless tree and reached for the bag, getting out all the blankets and laying two on the ground before sitting and beckoning me to do the same. I huddled down behind her, pulling her close to me as she pulled the remaining blanket around us. She was bat-shit crazy. What I wouldn't do to make this woman happy.

I rested against the trunk of the tree we were under, and Ashleigh turned her head to look at me. The cold had made her cheeks pink. She looked so young, so fresh.

"Luke, I fell in love with you one summer under a magnolia tree, and I've been in love with you ever since. But despite my heart having been yours for so long, I've given you reason to doubt me. I've pushed you away and not trusted you, not thought it was possible that what you felt for me could be anything close to what I feel for you. Well, I wanted to bring you back to where it all began for me. And say, winter or summer, rain or shine, whether the magnolia trees are in bloom or not, I will love you for the rest of my life. Will you marry me?"

My heart was pounding, and I raised my head to study the branches of the tree we were sitting under.

This was why she'd brought me here?

To propose to me under a magnolia tree?

My throat was tight with a thousand things I wanted to say to her.

She pulled out a green velvet pouch from under the blanket and opened the drawstrings that held it together. She dipped inside and brought out a small circle of wood. "It's magnolia." Her eyes darted to mine, checking for a reaction. "Do you like it?"

"I love it." It was perfect, a symbol of our past that would be with us into our future.

"I measured your finger with cotton while you were asleep. It should fit, but I understand if you don't want to wear it." She was babbling, and it was adorable.

"Of course I want to wear it. And of course I will marry you. I love you so much."

She pushed the ring onto my left ring finger and clasped her hand over mine, her sparkling sapphire nestling against the sturdy wood of the magnolia.

"So my proposal wasn't good enough?" I asked, chuckling.

She laughed. "I just thought you deserved to see how much you mean to me. To know that I realize we're forever."

"You're going to be the most incredible wife and mother." I was so proud of her in that moment, so proud of who she was and the mother I knew she would become.

"You're going to be the most amazing husband and father."

I pulled her closer and buried my head in her neck, breathing in her familiar smell of summer. "This is the perfect engagement story to tell our kids and grandkids."

"You think the story where you pulled out a ring while I stank of vomit isn't romantic enough?" She giggled. "For me it was when we finally made sense. I wouldn't trade that moment for anything."

"I wouldn't trade any moment I have with you." Every second was special when I spent it with Ashleigh.

A Few Months Later—Ashleigh

My husband cooing over our daughter had to be one of the sexiest things I'd ever seen. He was just so gigantic next to her delicate newness.

"Welcome home, Maggie," he whispered as he stepped over the threshold of our new house, clutching her like the precious jewel she was. Even at twenty-three hours old, she had Luke's eyes and golden skin. She was perfect. She'd been as desperate to meet us as we her, and the labor had only lasted two hours. A girl after my own heart, she'd arrived just after six, and just in time for cocktails. The hospital had told us we could go home that evening, but Luke, ever protective, had insisted we all stay the night. Luke and I'd spent the entire time holding hands, just staring at her.

A few months earlier, we'd found a house, a Victorian villa with a garden. When we'd moved in, Haven and Jake put an offer in on a place two streets down. Their home was at least nine times the size of ours, but I couldn't wait to have them round the corner. Ours was a fixer-upper, but when it was done, there would be room for more babies and a garden where they could play. Luke insisted that he wanted at least seven more kids. I'd told him that he would have to pray for a medical miracle that made men carrying children possible. Though now that Maggie had arrived, he could probably convince me that I should be pregnant the rest of my life.

"She smells like you," he said, taking a seat in our living room, his eyes not leaving her for a second. I stood next to them, leaning into him, gazing at my daughter as I threaded my fingers through his hair. How had I gotten this lucky?

I bent down to take in her scent. "She smells of the flower she was named after. How is that possible?"

"She's a miracle."

"We have to try not to break her. She's nonrefundable," I said.

"We got this, Ashleigh."

I nodded. "We really do."

There was some scrabbling at the front door, and then I heard voices. Luke looked up at me, and we grinned. The rest of the family had arrived.

I turned around and found myself enveloped in a Beth-and-Haven hug, which was the best kind.

"A two hour labor? Are you shitting me?" Haven asked.

"Giving birth is her superpower," Luke said proudly.

"And you look so good," Beth added. I felt fantastic, elated—as if I were high on a new kind of drug named baby.

Jake carried a sleeping baby Sophia over to the sofa and set her down next to Luke and Maggie as we all gathered around them.

"She's gorgeous," Haven said, mesmerized by Maggie.

"She really is," I replied. "Maggie, meet your future partner in crime, Sophia. You two are going to break some hearts."

Haven and Beth laughed.

"I really don't need to hear about my daughter and boys

the day she's home from the hospital. Are you trying to give me a heart attack?" Luke asked.

"Don't worry, we have a few years to formulate a plan," I replied.

Haven and I exchanged a look. No plan would ever work. We knew how naughty teenage girls could be.

"Can I hold her?" Beth asked me.

"If you can pry her away from her father, then of course."

Luke shot me a glance. He didn't want to lose a second with his daughter, but he reluctantly handed our tiny bundle to Beth.

"You next then, Beth," I said.

Beth smiled. "I don't think so."

"They all say that," Jake said. "Just before they meet the perfect guy. And he better be perfect." He slung his arm around his sister's shoulder. "But in the meantime, you should have some fun."

"Yeah, surely there's a tall, dark stranger waiting for you on one of your trips to Chicago."

"Yes, mindless sex with a stranger. That's what you need." Haven sounded excited, and I couldn't help but giggle at Jake's face as he watched his wife consider the idea.

Beth rolled her eyes. "Let's just concentrate on baby central over here, shall we? Just because you're all domesticated doesn't mean that's my path."

"It's just a matter of time." I grinned at her.

I wrapped my arms around Luke's waist. "Can you believe this?" He bent down and dropped a soft kiss on my lips.

"We brought food and beer," Haven said. I didn't want

to let my baby out of my sight, so I stood as Haven scurried round, finding plates, glasses and cutlery.

"We've set it all out in the garden," she said a few minutes later.

"Please, may I have my daughter?" I asked Beth. I loved her feeling everyone else's love, but I needed a Maggie top-up, just so I could feel her pressing against my heart, to let her know I was still here, as I always would be.

Beth grinned and handed Maggie to me, and she led the way into the garden.

"I hope you don't mind all these noisy people," I whispered to Maggie. "You'll get used to their strange ways soon enough."

"Is she talking back?" Luke asked as he came up behind us in the doorway.

I turned to face him. "She is. She told me she's pleased to have such a handsome, kind and generous daddy."

"She said that to me too," Luke said.

I giggled.

Luke's face broke into a grin, and then his smile fell, his brows knitting together. "God, you're so beautiful." He sounded so serious, my heart skipped at his words. He pulled us into his arms as we watched the rest of them gather around the table.

The air was warm, still full of summer. "Let's show her the tree," Luke suggested.

Our guests made themselves comfortable, content to let the three of us wander about our little oasis. "Thank God I deferred business school. I would have failed all my exams because I was so totally obsessed with our daughter and our life together. But I still want to do it—go back to school. Does that make me a bad mother?"

Luke chuckled as we crossed the lawn. "Of course not. Maggie told me you're the best mother she could have ever wished for. I feel sort of torn. I can't imagine being away from her for a second, but at the same time, I have a near-Neanderthal desire to go out and make a ton of money and lavish it on you both. If I hadn't made partner before she arrived, I think I'd be going crazy right now."

We stopped in front of our tree. "But you did. We have everything we need right here."

When we moved, we'd brought the small magnolia tree that I'd bought Luke as a housewarming present and planted it at the end of the garden. It had flourished in the months since and its flowers this summer had been so big they were in danger of bowing the branches supporting them.

"I can't believe it's still got some petals. It's as if it's been waiting for her. Look, Magnolia, it's almost as pretty as you." I handed her to Luke. I could tell he was just itching to hold her again. She was going to be horribly spoiled, with both parents fighting for her attention as we were.

Luke slid his free arm around my waist. "It's late blooming, which is kinda perfect," he said.

I looked up at my husband. "The wait makes the flowers all the more beautiful when they arrive."

To read Jake and Haven's story, check out *Parisian Nights*.

To read Beth's story, check out *Indigo Nights*.

playlist

I Can't Make You Love Me – Bonnie Raitt

If You Ever Want To Be In Love – James Bay

Landslide – Dixie Chicks

Say You Love Me – Jessie Ware

To Make Her Love Me – Rascal Flatts

If I Knew Then – Lady Antebellum

You Are Everything – Diana Ross

Let's Wait Awhile – Janet Jackson

Here I Am – Leona Lewis

Knocks Me Off My Feet – Stevie Wonder

Where My Heart Belongs – Gloriana

Come Rain Or Come Shine – Ray Charles

acknowledgments

I'm so thankful to you for reading about Luke and Ashleigh's story. It's difficult to explain what a gorgeous lift to my day it is when I get a message from someone telling me how they enjoyed one of my books. Every single interaction on social media and my website means the world to me.

I still have to pinch myself every now and then that people are actually buying and reading my books. It's a lesson to us all that some of our best dreams are the ones we don't plan. I heard Condoleezza Rice say how important it is in life to leave room for serendipity. I've never been good at doing that but dear readers, I'm learning and you've all proved to me that it's worth it –thank you.

To all the bloggers, supporters, champions and cheerleaders that I'm lucky to have in my world – thank you. I love the way you're all on a crusade of positivity. We need more of it in the world.

In a sense it feels wrong to single people out to thank because the smallest like, share, retweet means so much, but I can't leave the stage without just a few others standing to take a bow.

Elizabeth—I really don't have the words to thank you. You've taught me how to write (and induced various meltdowns about my writing) and I will be *forever* grateful. Thank you for being brutal. Here's to being dangerous.

Karen Booth, I just love you more the more I know you. You are so kind and generous and lovely and I'm lucky to have found you.

Jessica Hawkins, you are a rock star and a dear friend. Thank you for all your support and for lending me the wonderful Elizabeth.

Lauren Blakely—thank you for all your generosity and support. I love your spirit.

Jules Rapley Collins and Megan Fields. What can I say? You pair are the girls that keep my spirits lifted and make me laugh with your outrageous confessions. Thank you for letting me share your worlds. Thank you for ALL your support and encouragement.

Thanks to Jacquie Jax Denison, Lucy May, Lauren Hutton, Kingston Westmoreland, Lauren Luman, Mimi Perez Sanchez, Ashton Williams Shone, Tina Haynes Marshall, Susan Ann Whitaker, Sally-Ann Cole and Vicky Marsh. You are so good to me!

Twirly, thank you brain twin for inspiring the line "I've lost my funny." I hope I find it again at some point. PS Juno's "the business" because she's her mother's daughter.

other books by
LOUISE BAY

THE NIGHTS SERIES

(each book is stand alone, focusing on a different couple)

Parisian Nights

Promised Nights

Indigo Nights

OTHER BOOKS

THE EMPIRE STATE SERIES

Hopeful

Faithful

the nights SERIES

Parisian NIGHTS

The moment I laid eyes on the new photographer at work, I had his number. Cocky, arrogant and super wealthy-women were eating out of his hand as soon as his tight ass crossed the threshold of our office.

When we were forced to go to Paris together for an assignment, I wasn't interested in his seductive smile, his sexy accent or his dirty laugh. I wasn't falling for his charms.

Until I did.

Until Paris.

Until he was kissing me and I was wondering how it happened. Until he was dragging his lips across my skin and I was hoping for more. Paris does funny things to a girl and he might have gotten me naked.

But Paris couldn't last forever.

NIGHTS

**The only thing better than cake is cake
with a side of orgasms.**

Dylan James has no expectations when it comes to relationships. He uses women for sex and they use him for his money and power. It's quid pro quo and he's good with that. It works.

Beth Harrison has been burned. She's tired of the lies and the game playing that men bring and has buried herself in her passion—baking which keeps her out of the reach of heartbreak. As she begins her career as a TV baker, a new world opens up to her.

Dylan and Beth both know that casual sex is all about giving what you need to get what you want.

Except that sometimes you give more than you need to and get everything you ever wanted.

The Empire State Series

A series of three novellas
Part One: *A Week in New York*
Part Two: *Autumn in London*
Part Three: *New Year in Manhattan*

Anna Kirby is sick of dating. She's tired of heartbreak. Despite being smart, sexy, and funny, she's a magnet for men who don't deserve her.

A week's vacation in New York is the ultimate distraction from her most recent break-up, as well as a great place to meet a stranger and have some summer fun. But to protect her still-bruised heart, fun comes with rules. There will be no sharing stories, no swapping numbers, and no real names. Just one night of uncomplicated fun.

Super-successful serial seducer Ethan Scott has some rules of his own. He doesn't date, he doesn't stay the night, and he doesn't make any promises.

It should be a match made in heaven. But rules are made to be broken.

HOPEFUL

Guys like Joel Wentworth weren›t supposed to fall in love with girls like me. He could have had his pick of the girls on campus, but somehow the laws of nature were defied and we fell crazy in love.

After graduation, Joel left for New York. And, despite him wanting me to go with him, I'd refused, unwilling to disappoint my parents and risk the judgment of my friends. I hadn't seen him again. Never even spoke to him.

I've spent the last eight years working hard to put my career front and center in my life, dodging any personal complications. I have a strict no-dating policy. I've managed to piece together a reality that works for me.

Until now.

Now, Joel's coming back to London.

And I need to get over him before he gets over here.

Hopeful is a stand-alone novel.

FAITHFUL

Leah Thompson's life in London is everything she›s supposed to want: a successful career, the best girlfriends a bottle of sauvignon blanc can buy, and a wealthy boyfriend who has just proposed. But something doesn›t feel right. Is it simply a case of 'be careful what you wish for'?

Uncertain about her future, Leah looks to her past, where she finds her high school crush, Daniel Armitage, online. Daniel is one of London's most eligible bachelors. He knows what and who he wants, and he wants Leah. Leah resists Daniel's advances as she concentrates on being the perfect fiancé.

She soon finds that she should have trusted her instincts when she realises she's been betrayed by the men and women in her life.

Leah's heart has been crushed. Will ever be able to trust again? And will Daniel be there when she is?

Faithful is a stand-alone novel.

let's CONNECT

If you enjoyed Parisian Nights, please leave a review. Good reviews really help indie authors!

I love hearing from readers – get in touch!

Instagram me

@louiseSbay

Tweet me

twitter.com/louisesbay (@louisesbay)

Friend me

www.facebook.com/louisesbay

Like me

www.facebook.com/authorlouisebay

Pin me

www.pinterest.com/LouiseBay

Friend me

www.goodreads.com/author/show/8056592.Louise_Bay

Circle me

https://plus.google.com/u/0/+LouiseBayauthor

Find me at home

www.louisebay.com

Made in the USA
Middletown, DE
14 July 2019